image comics presents

THE WALKING DEAD ™

ROBERT KIRKMAN
CREATOR, WRITER

CHARLIE ADLARD
PENCILER, INKER

CLIFF RATHBURN
GRAY TONES

RUS WOOTON
LETTERER

CHARLIE ADLARD
&
CLIFF RATHBURN
COVER

For SKYBOUND ENTERTAINMENT

Robert Kirkman - CEO
J.J. Didde - President
Sina Grace - Editorial Director
Shawn Kirkham - Director of Business Development
Tim Daniel - Digital Content Manager
Chad Manion - Assistant to Mr. Grace
Sydney Pennington - Assistant to Mr. Kirkham
Feldman Public Relations LA - Public Relations

FOR INTERNATIONAL RIGHTS INQUIRIES,
PLEASE CONTACT FOREIGN@SKYBOUND.COM

WWW.SKYBOUND.COM

IMAGE COMICS, INC.
Robert Kirkman - chief operating officer
Erik Larsen - chief financial officer
Todd McFarlane - president
Marc Silvestri - chief executive officer
Jim Valentino - vice-president

Eric Stephenson - publisher
Todd Martinez - sales & licensing coordinator
Jennifer de Guzman - pr & marketing director
Branwyn Bigglestone - accounts manager
Emily Miller - administrative assistant
Jamie Parreno - marketing assistant
Sarah deLaine - events coordinator
Kevin Yuen - digital rights coordinator
Tyler Shainline - production manager
Drew Gill - art director
Jonathan Chan - design director
Monica Garcia - production artist
Vincent Kukua - production artist
Jana Cook - production artist
www.imagecomics.com

THE WALKING DEAD, VOL. 5: THE BEST DEFENSE. Fifth Printing. Published by Image Comics, Inc. Office of publication: 2134 Allston Way, 2nd Floor, Berkeley, California 94704.

PRINTED IN THE USA

ISBN: 978-1-58240-612-1

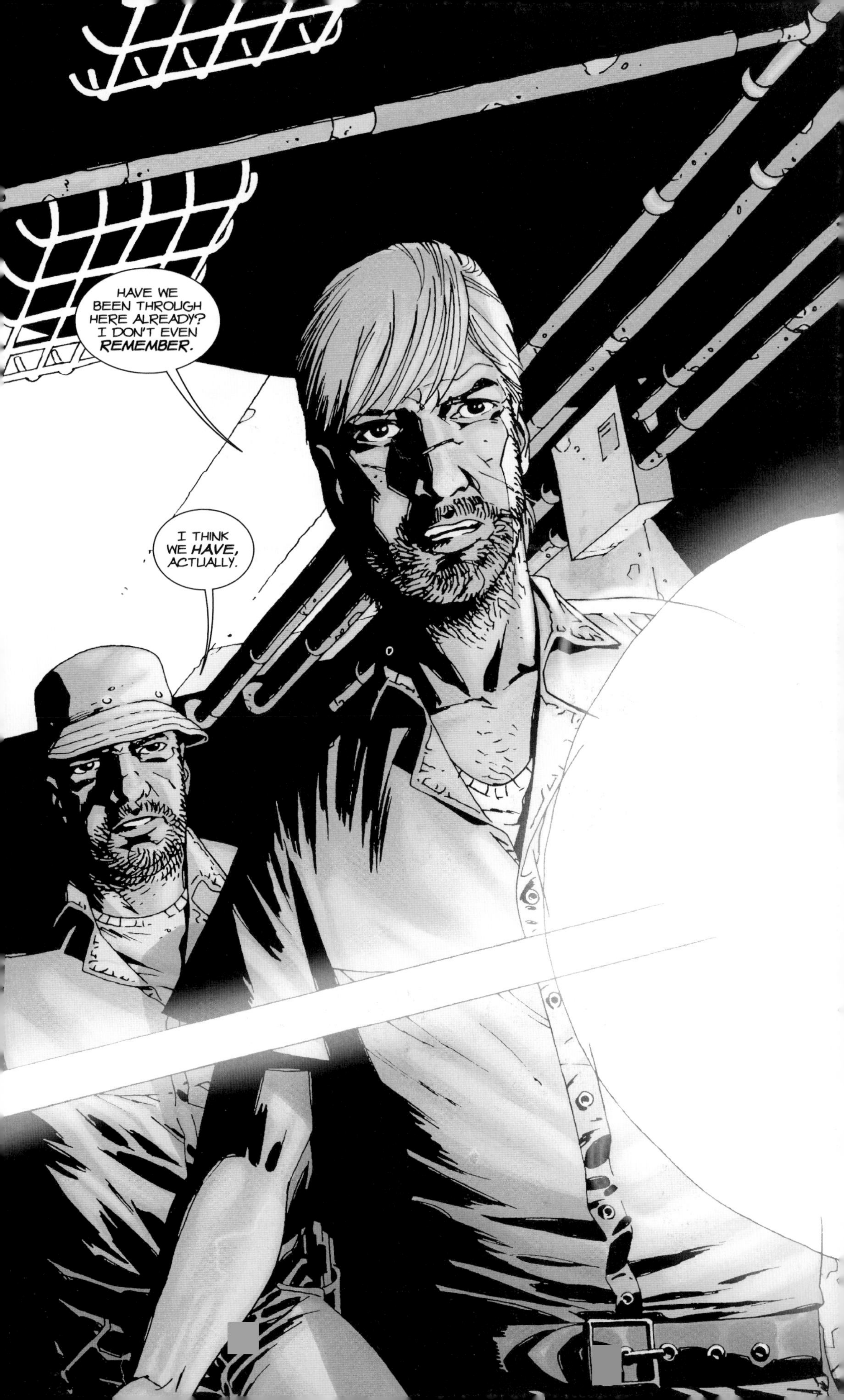
HAVE WE BEEN THROUGH HERE ALREADY? I DON'T EVEN REMEMBER.
I THINK WE HAVE, ACTUALLY.

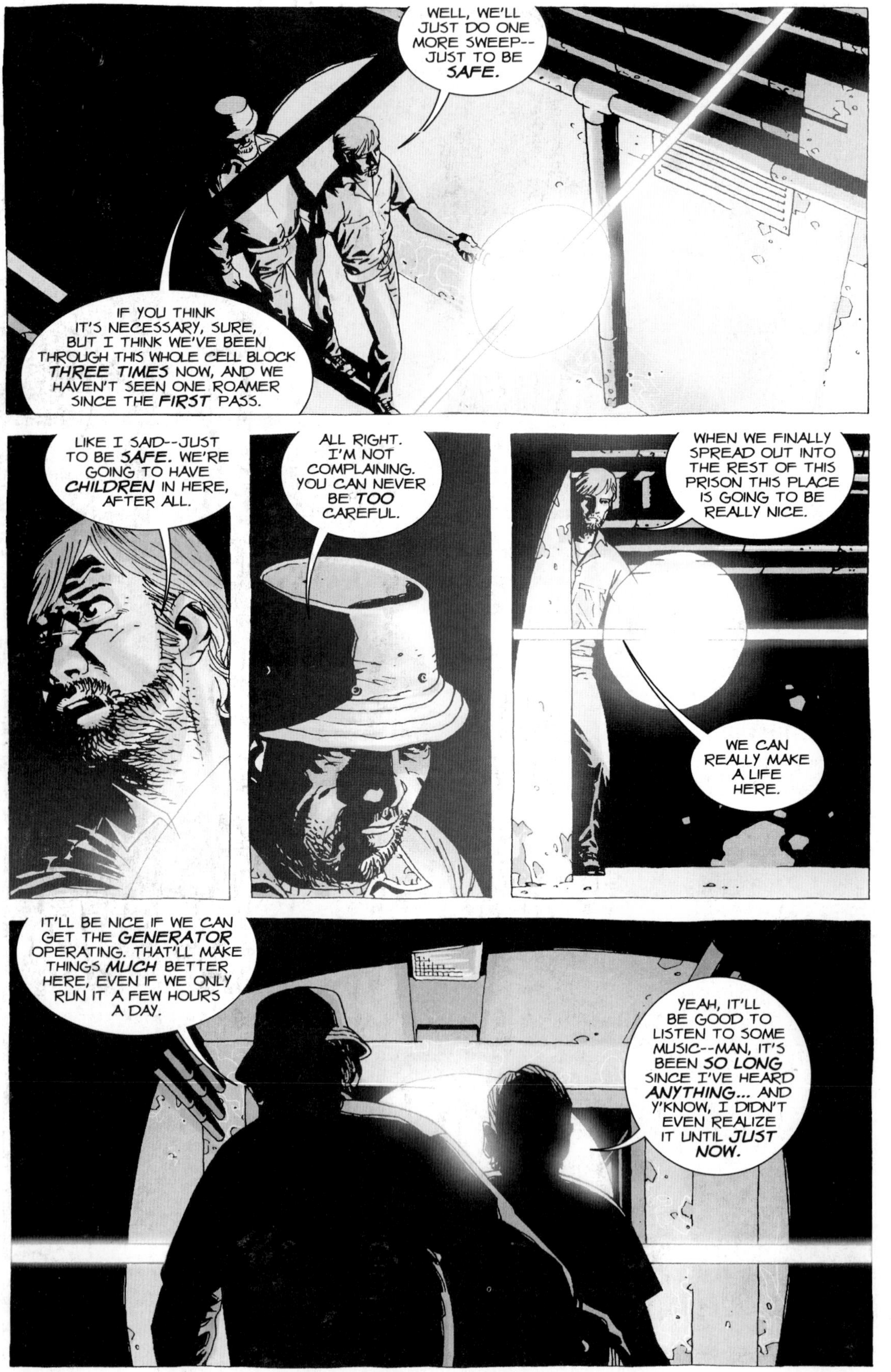
WELL, WE'LL JUST DO ONE MORE SWEEP-- JUST TO BE SAFE.
IF YOU THINK IT'S NECESSARY, SURE, BUT I THINK WE'VE BEEN THROUGH THIS WHOLE CELL BLOCK THREE TIMES NOW, AND WE HAVEN'T SEEN ONE ROAMER SINCE THE FIRST PASS.
LIKE I SAID--JUST TO BE SAFE. WE'RE GOING TO HAVE CHILDREN IN HERE, AFTER ALL.
ALL RIGHT. I'M NOT COMPLAINING. YOU CAN NEVER BE TOO CAREFUL.
WHEN WE FINALLY SPREAD OUT INTO THE REST OF THIS PRISON THIS PLACE IS GOING TO BE REALLY NICE.
WE CAN REALLY MAKE A LIFE HERE.
IT'LL BE NICE IF WE CAN GET THE GENERATOR OPERATING. THAT'LL MAKE THINGS MUCH BETTER HERE, EVEN IF WE ONLY RUN IT A FEW HOURS A DAY.
YEAH, IT'LL BE GOOD TO LISTEN TO SOME MUSIC--MAN, IT'S BEEN SO LONG SINCE I'VE HEARD ANYTHING... AND Y'KNOW, I DIDN'T EVEN REALIZE IT UNTIL JUST NOW.

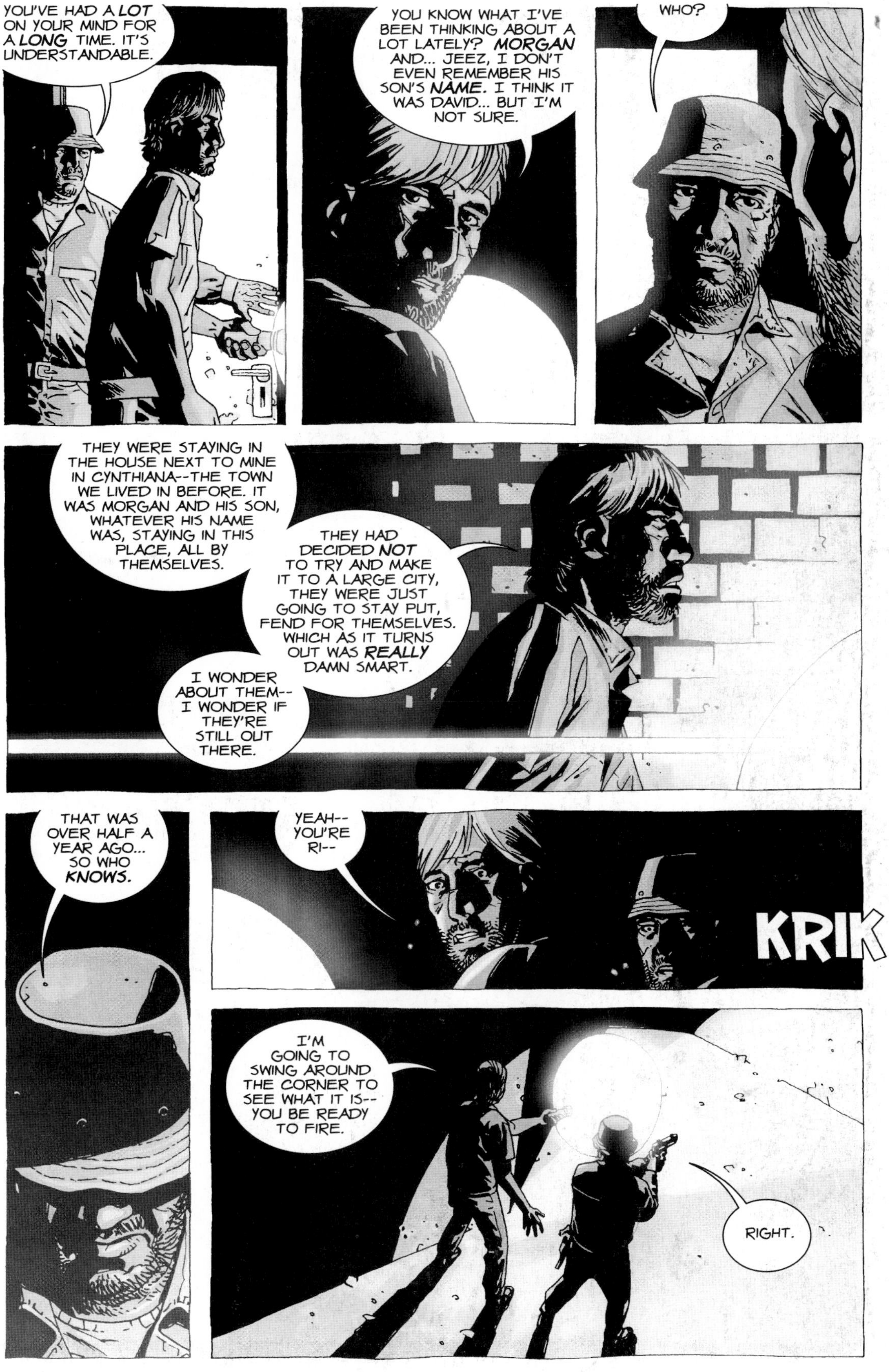
YOU'VE HAD A LOT ON YOUR MIND FOR A LONG TIME. IT'S UNDERSTANDABLE.
YOU KNOW WHAT I'VE BEEN THINKING ABOUT A LOT LATELY? MORGAN AND... JEEZ, I DON'T EVEN REMEMBER HIS SON'S NAME. I THINK IT WAS DAVID... BUT I'M NOT SURE.
WHO?
THEY WERE STAYING IN THE HOUSE NEXT TO MINE IN CYNTHIANA--THE TOWN WE LIVED IN BEFORE. IT WAS MORGAN AND HIS SON, WHATEVER HIS NAME WAS, STAYING IN THIS PLACE, ALL BY THEMSELVES.
THEY HAD DECIDED NOT TO TRY AND MAKE IT TO A LARGE CITY, THEY WERE JUST GOING TO STAY PUT, FEND FOR THEMSELVES. WHICH AS IT TURNS OUT WAS REALLY DAMN SMART.
I WONDER ABOUT THEM-- I WONDER IF THEY'RE STILL OUT THERE.
THAT WAS OVER HALF A YEAR AGO... SO WHO KNOWS.
YEAH-- YOU'RE RI--
KRIK
I'M GOING TO SWING AROUND THE CORNER TO SEE WHAT IT IS-- YOU BE READY TO FIRE.
RIGHT.

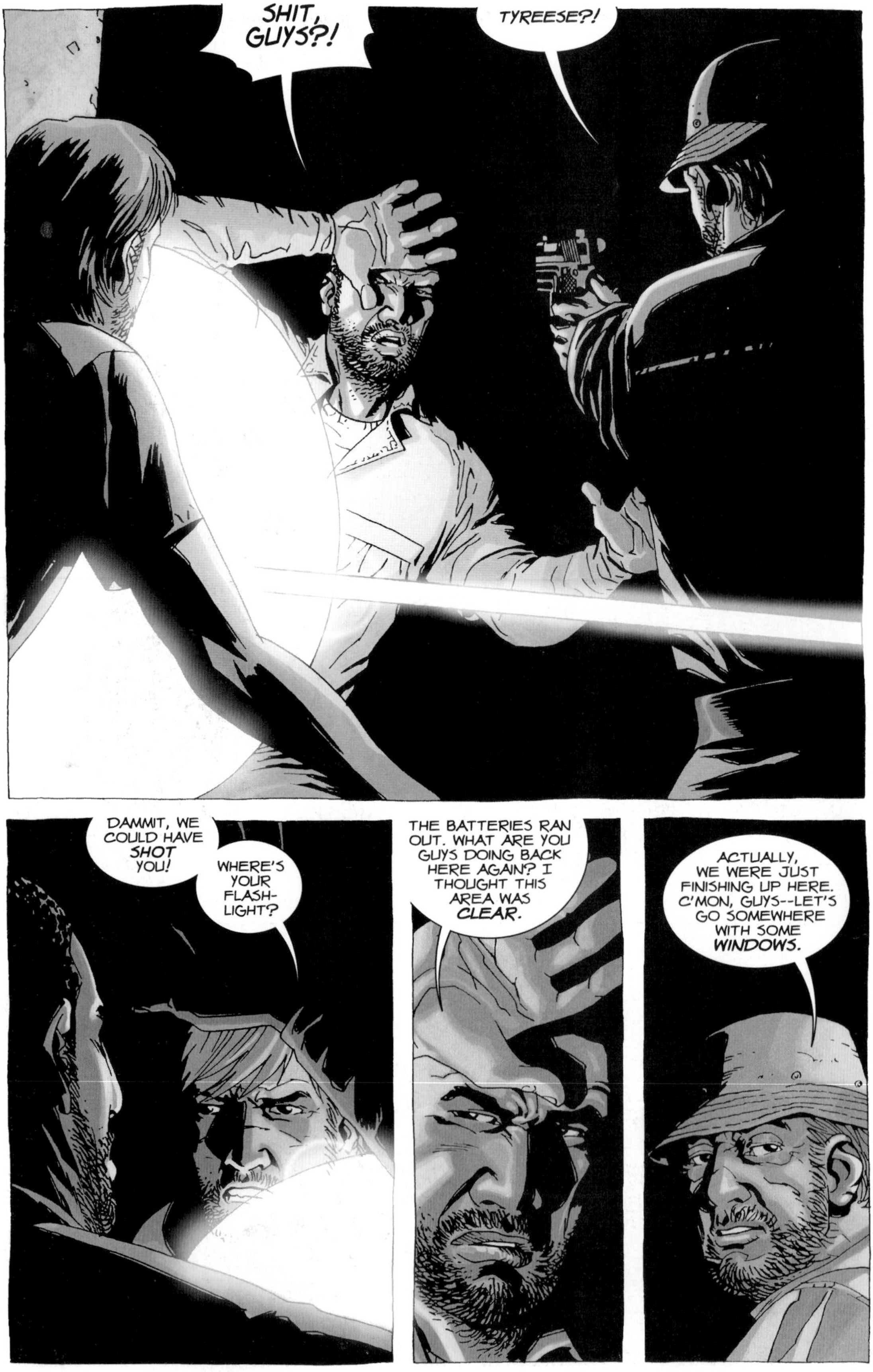
SHIT, GUYS?!
TYREESE?!
DAMMIT, WE COULD HAVE SHOT YOU!
WHERE'S YOUR FLASH-LIGHT?
THE BATTERIES RAN OUT. WHAT ARE YOU GUYS DOING BACK HERE AGAIN? I THOUGHT THIS AREA WAS CLEAR.
ACTUALLY, WE WERE JUST FINISHING UP HERE. C'MON, GUYS--LET'S GO SOMEWHERE WITH SOME WINDOWS.

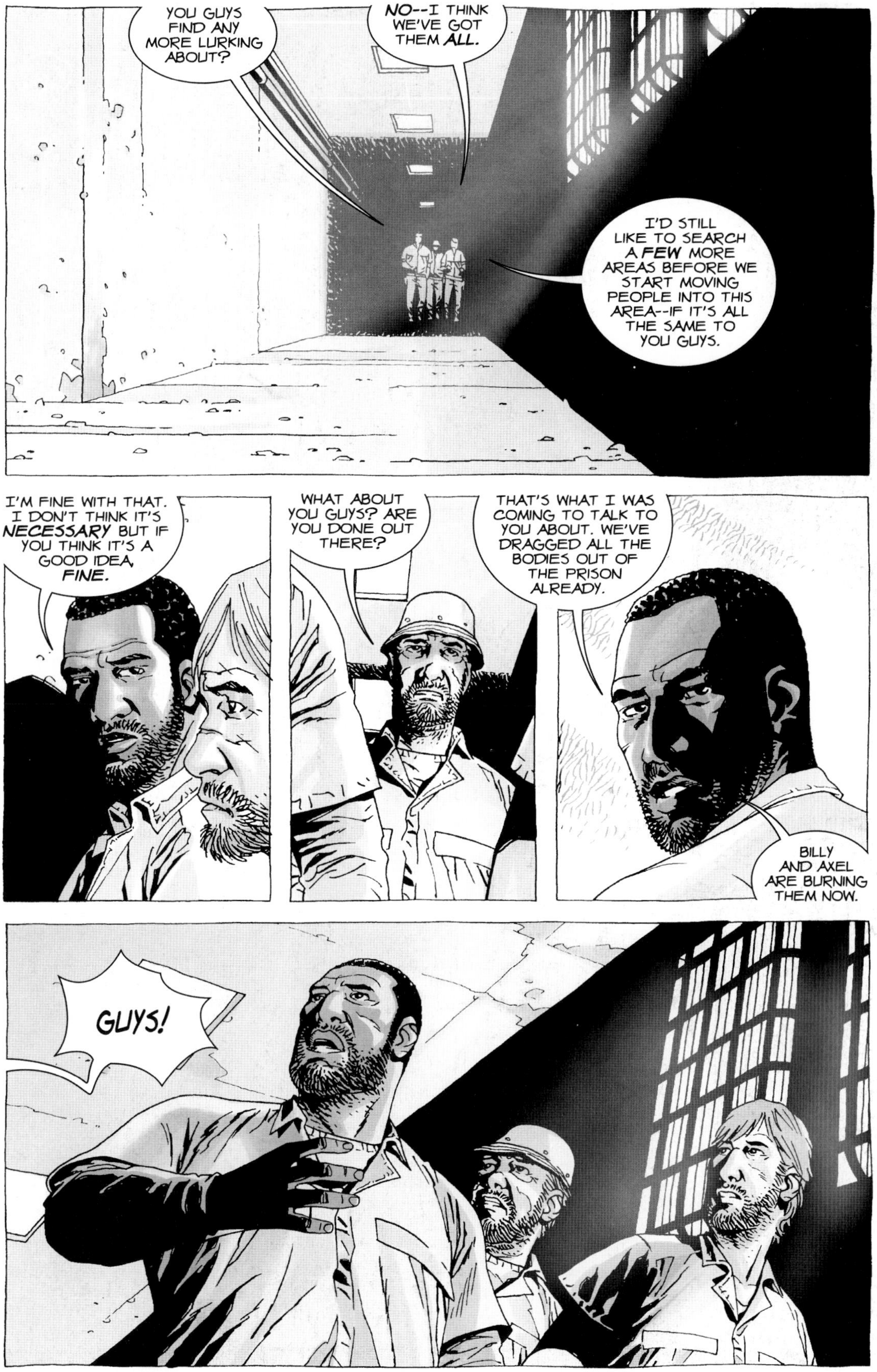
YOU GUYS FIND ANY MORE LURKING ABOUT?
NO--I THINK WE'VE GOT THEM ALL.
I'D STILL LIKE TO SEARCH A FEW MORE AREAS BEFORE WE START MOVING PEOPLE INTO THIS AREA--IF IT'S ALL THE SAME TO YOU GUYS.
I'M FINE WITH THAT. I DON'T THINK IT'S NECESSARY BUT IF YOU THINK IT'S A GOOD IDEA, FINE.
WHAT ABOUT YOU GUYS? ARE YOU DONE OUT THERE?
THAT'S WHAT I WAS COMING TO TALK TO YOU ABOUT. WE'VE DRAGGED ALL THE BODIES OUT OF THE PRISON ALREADY.
BILLY AND AXEL ARE BURNING THEM NOW.
GUYS!

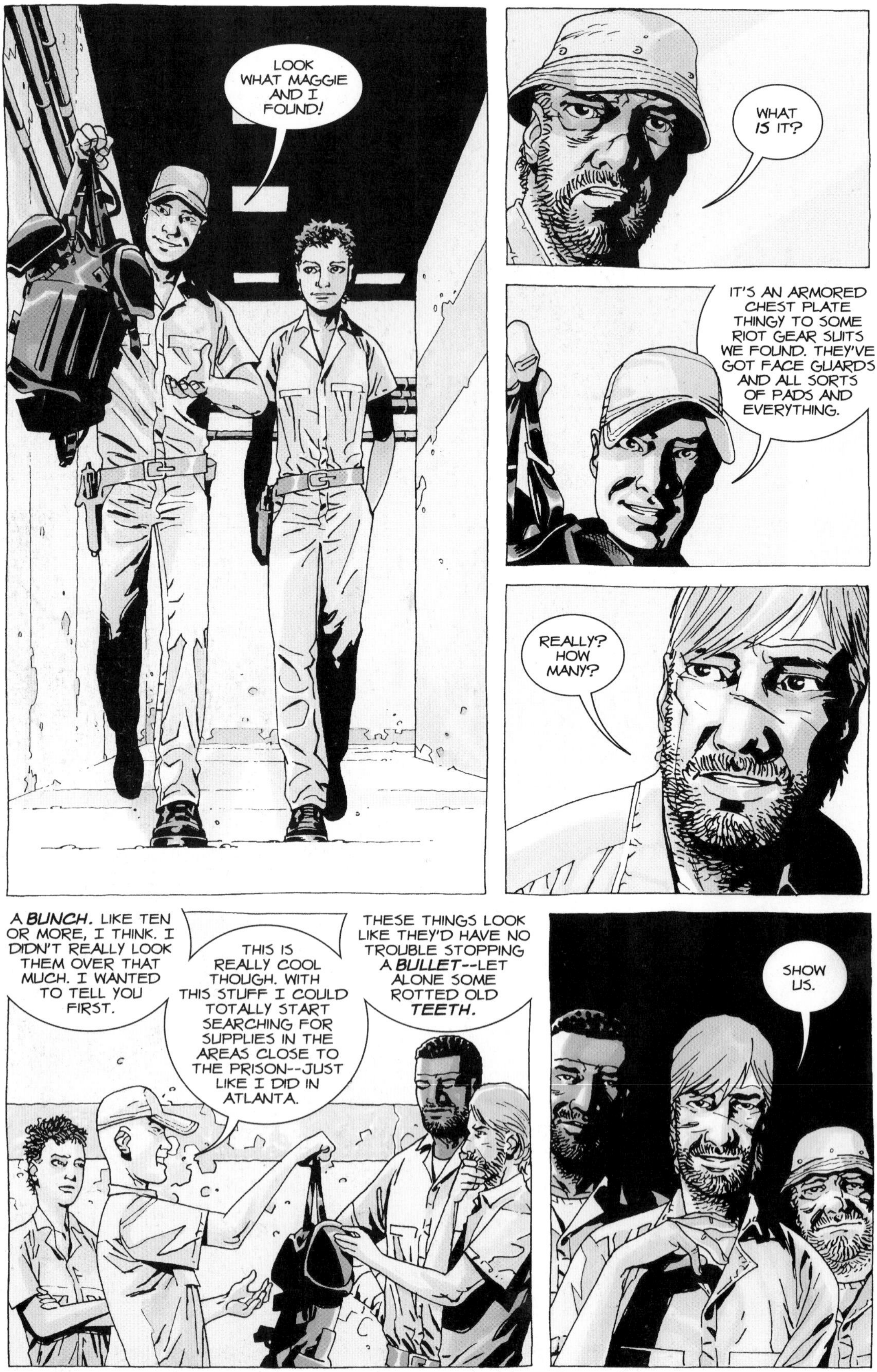
LOOK WHAT MAGGIE AND I FOUND!
WHAT *IS* IT?
IT'S AN ARMORED CHEST PLATE THINGY TO SOME RIOT GEAR SUITS WE FOUND. THEY'VE GOT FACE GUARDS AND ALL SORTS OF PADS AND EVERYTHING.
REALLY? HOW MANY?
A *BUNCH.* LIKE TEN OR MORE, I THINK. I DIDN'T REALLY LOOK THEM OVER THAT MUCH. I WANTED TO TELL YOU FIRST.
THIS IS REALLY COOL THOUGH. WITH THIS STUFF I COULD TOTALLY START SEARCHING FOR SUPPLIES IN THE AREAS CLOSE TO THE PRISON--JUST LIKE I DID IN ATLANTA.
THESE THINGS LOOK LIKE THEY'D HAVE NO TROUBLE STOPPING A *BULLET*--LET ALONE SOME ROTTED OLD *TEETH.*
SHOW US.

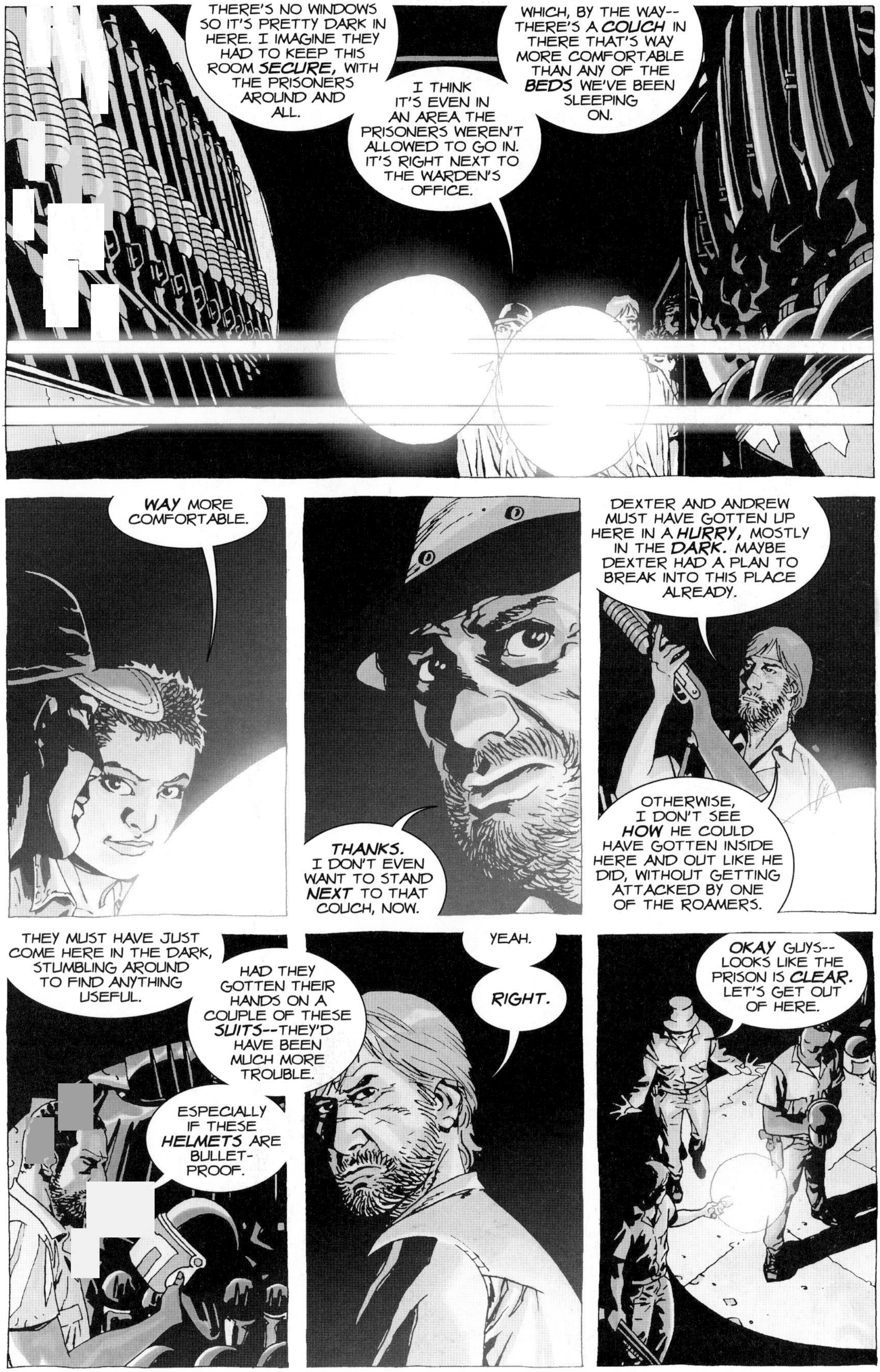
THERE'S NO WINDOWS SO IT'S PRETTY DARK IN HERE. I IMAGINE THEY HAD TO KEEP THIS ROOM SECURE, WITH THE PRISONERS AROUND AND ALL.
I THINK IT'S EVEN IN AN AREA THE PRISONERS WEREN'T ALLOWED TO GO IN. IT'S RIGHT NEXT TO THE WARDEN'S OFFICE.
WHICH, BY THE WAY-- THERE'S A COUCH IN THERE THAT'S WAY MORE COMFORTABLE THAN ANY OF THE BEDS WE'VE BEEN SLEEPING ON.
WAY MORE COMFORTABLE.
THANKS. I DON'T EVEN WANT TO STAND NEXT TO THAT COUCH, NOW.
DEXTER AND ANDREW MUST HAVE GOTTEN UP HERE IN A HURRY, MOSTLY IN THE DARK. MAYBE DEXTER HAD A PLAN TO BREAK INTO THIS PLACE ALREADY.
OTHERWISE, I DON'T SEE HOW HE COULD HAVE GOTTEN INSIDE HERE AND OUT LIKE HE DID, WITHOUT GETTING ATTACKED BY ONE OF THE ROAMERS.
THEY MUST HAVE JUST COME HERE IN THE DARK, STUMBLING AROUND TO FIND ANYTHING USEFUL.
HAD THEY GOTTEN THEIR HANDS ON A COUPLE OF THESE SUITS--THEY'D HAVE BEEN MUCH MORE TROUBLE.
ESPECIALLY IF THESE HELMETS ARE BULLET-PROOF.
YEAH.
RIGHT.
OKAY GUYS-- LOOKS LIKE THE PRISON IS CLEAR. LET'S GET OUT OF HERE.

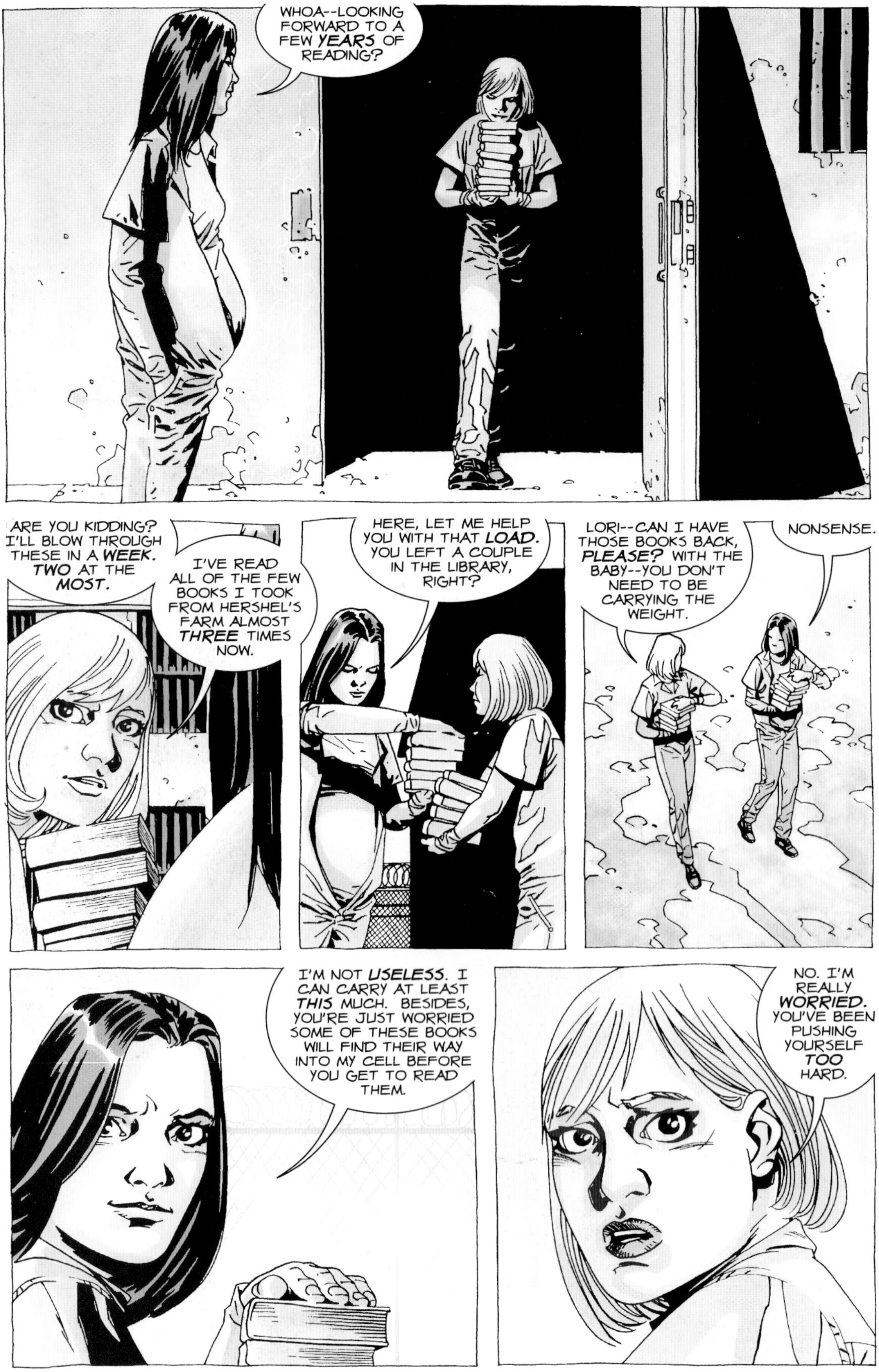
WHOA--LOOKING FORWARD TO A FEW YEARS OF READING?
ARE YOU KIDDING? I'LL BLOW THROUGH THESE IN A WEEK. TWO AT THE MOST.
I'VE READ ALL OF THE FEW BOOKS I TOOK FROM HERSHEL'S FARM ALMOST THREE TIMES NOW.
HERE, LET ME HELP YOU WITH THAT LOAD. YOU LEFT A COUPLE IN THE LIBRARY, RIGHT?
LORI--CAN I HAVE THOSE BOOKS BACK, PLEASE? WITH THE BABY--YOU DON'T NEED TO BE CARRYING THE WEIGHT.
NONSENSE.
I'M NOT USELESS. I CAN CARRY AT LEAST THIS MUCH. BESIDES, YOU'RE JUST WORRIED SOME OF THESE BOOKS WILL FIND THEIR WAY INTO MY CELL BEFORE YOU GET TO READ THEM.
NO. I'M REALLY WORRIED. YOU'VE BEEN PUSHING YOURSELF TOO HARD.

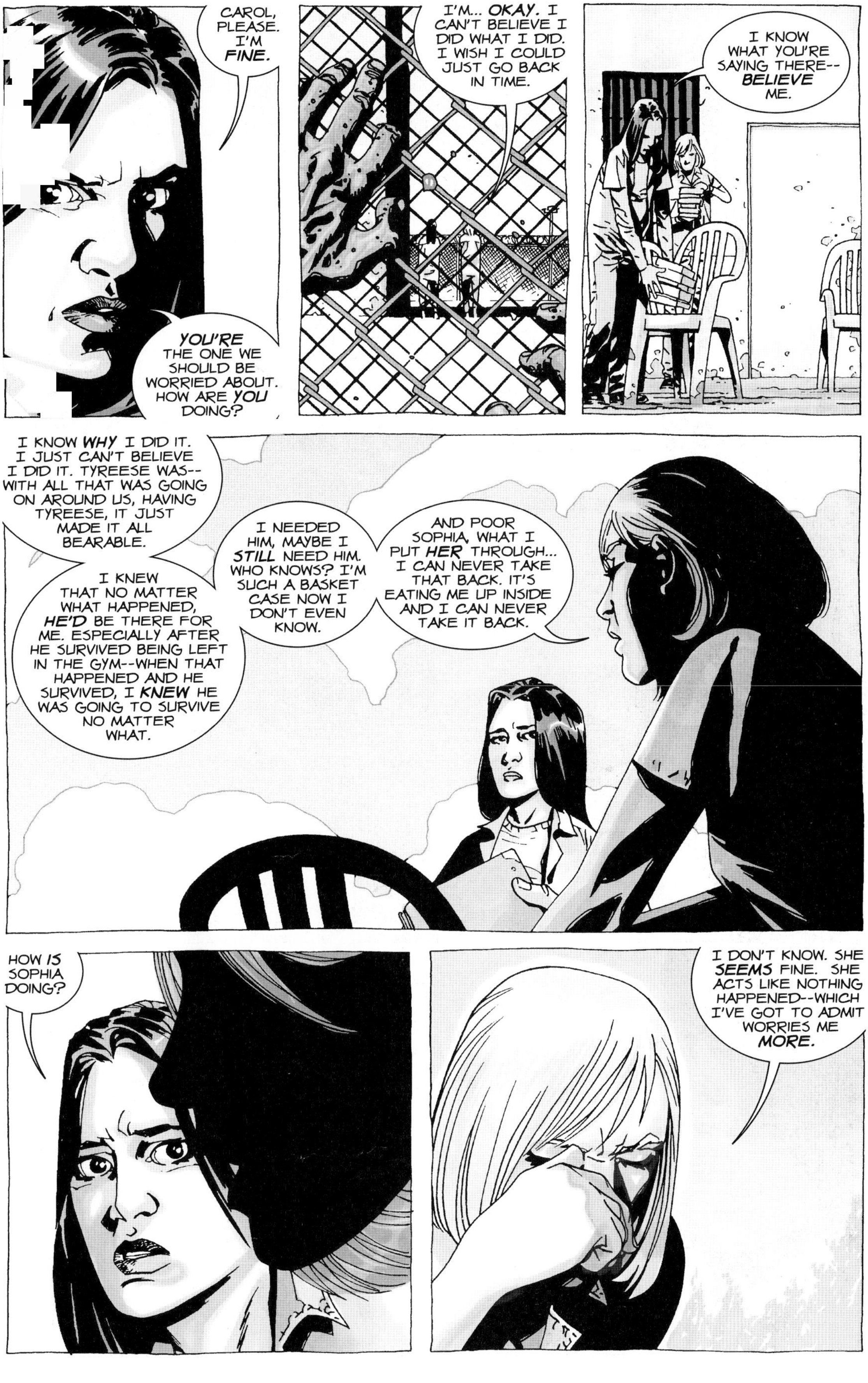

CAROL, PLEASE. I'M FINE.
YOU'RE THE ONE WE SHOULD BE WORRIED ABOUT. HOW ARE YOU DOING?
I'M... OKAY. I CAN'T BELIEVE I DID WHAT I DID. I WISH I COULD JUST GO BACK IN TIME.
I KNOW WHAT YOU'RE SAYING THERE-- BELIEVE ME.
I KNOW WHY I DID IT. I JUST CAN'T BELIEVE I DID IT. TYREESE WAS-- WITH ALL THAT WAS GOING ON AROUND US, HAVING TYREESE, IT JUST MADE IT ALL BEARABLE.
I KNEW THAT NO MATTER WHAT HAPPENED, HE'D BE THERE FOR ME. ESPECIALLY AFTER HE SURVIVED BEING LEFT IN THE GYM--WHEN THAT HAPPENED AND HE SURVIVED, I KNEW HE WAS GOING TO SURVIVE NO MATTER WHAT.
I NEEDED HIM, MAYBE I STILL NEED HIM. WHO KNOWS? I'M SUCH A BASKET CASE NOW I DON'T EVEN KNOW.
AND POOR SOPHIA, WHAT I PUT HER THROUGH... I CAN NEVER TAKE THAT BACK. IT'S EATING ME UP INSIDE AND I CAN NEVER TAKE IT BACK.
HOW IS SOPHIA DOING?
I DON'T KNOW. SHE SEEMS FINE. SHE ACTS LIKE NOTHING HAPPENED--WHICH I'VE GOT TO ADMIT WORRIES ME MORE.

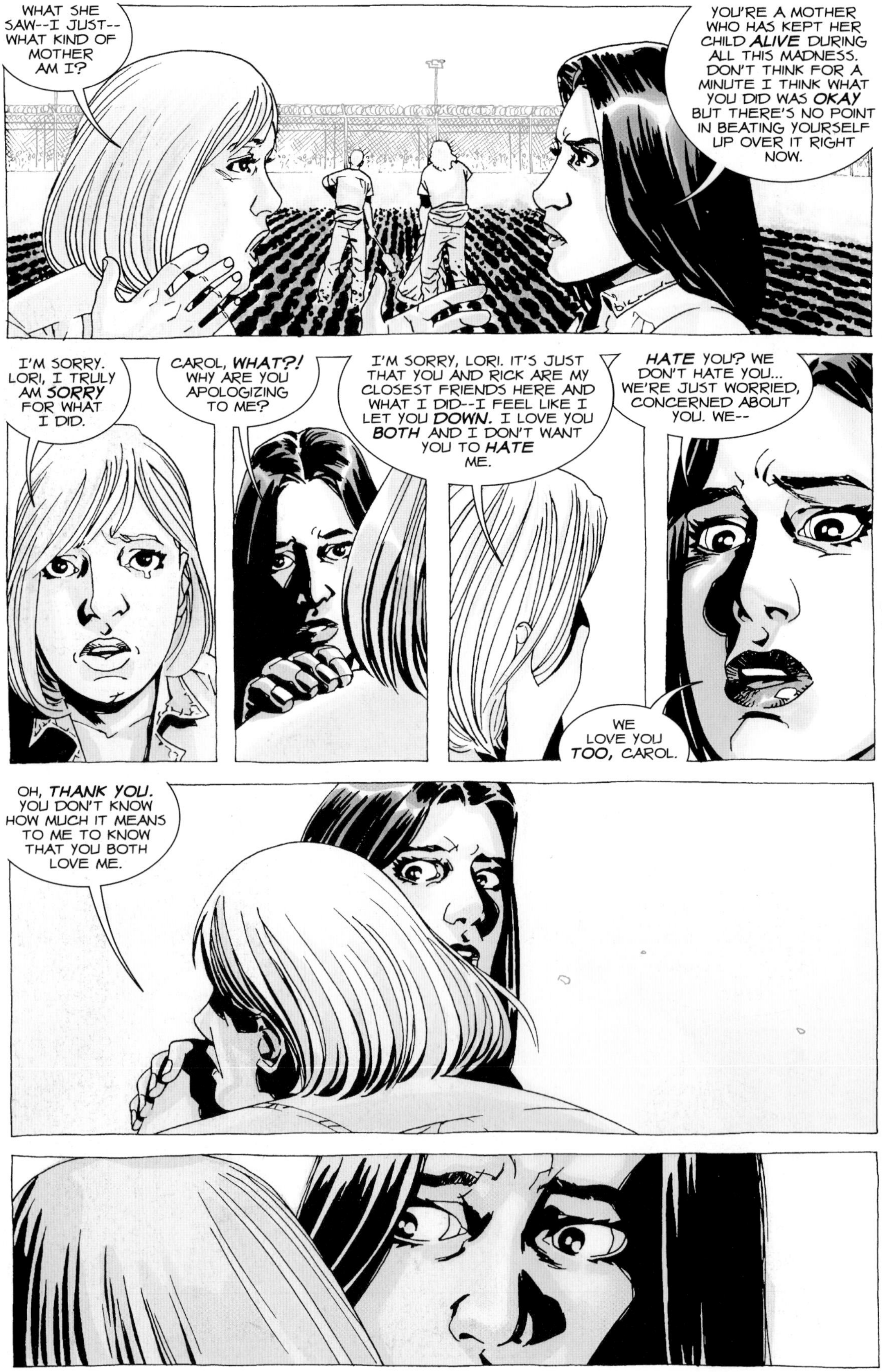
WHAT SHE SAW--I JUST-- WHAT KIND OF MOTHER AM I?
YOU'RE A MOTHER WHO HAS KEPT HER CHILD ALIVE DURING ALL THIS MADNESS. DON'T THINK FOR A MINUTE I THINK WHAT YOU DID WAS OKAY BUT THERE'S NO POINT IN BEATING YOURSELF UP OVER IT RIGHT NOW.
I'M SORRY. LORI, I TRULY AM SORRY FOR WHAT I DID.
CAROL, WHAT?! WHY ARE YOU APOLOGIZING TO ME?
I'M SORRY, LORI. IT'S JUST THAT YOU AND RICK ARE MY CLOSEST FRIENDS HERE AND WHAT I DID--I FEEL LIKE I LET YOU DOWN. I LOVE YOU BOTH AND I DON'T WANT YOU TO HATE ME.
HATE YOU? WE DON'T HATE YOU... WE'RE JUST WORRIED, CONCERNED ABOUT YOU. WE--
WE LOVE YOU TOO, CAROL.
OH, THANK YOU. YOU DON'T KNOW HOW MUCH IT MEANS TO ME TO KNOW THAT YOU BOTH LOVE ME.

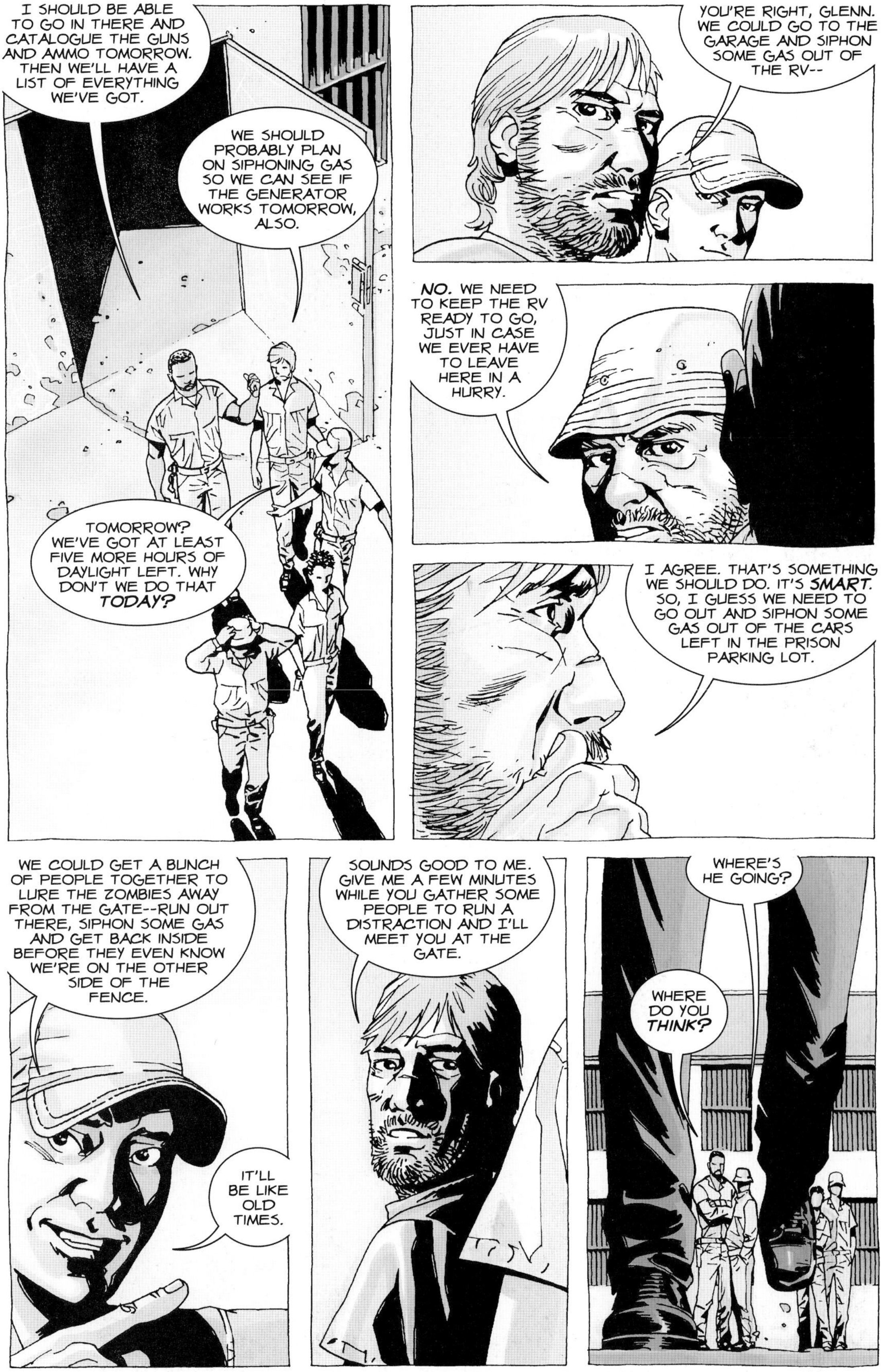

I SHOULD BE ABLE TO GO IN THERE AND CATALOGUE THE GUNS AND AMMO TOMORROW. THEN WE'LL HAVE A LIST OF EVERYTHING WE'VE GOT.
WE SHOULD PROBABLY PLAN ON SIPHONING GAS SO WE CAN SEE IF THE GENERATOR WORKS TOMORROW, ALSO.
TOMORROW? WE'VE GOT AT LEAST FIVE MORE HOURS OF DAYLIGHT LEFT. WHY DON'T WE DO THAT TODAY?
YOU'RE RIGHT, GLENN. WE COULD GO TO THE GARAGE AND SIPHON SOME GAS OUT OF THE RV--
NO. WE NEED TO KEEP THE RV READY TO GO, JUST IN CASE WE EVER HAVE TO LEAVE HERE IN A HURRY.
I AGREE. THAT'S SOMETHING WE SHOULD DO. IT'S SMART. SO, I GUESS WE NEED TO GO OUT AND SIPHON SOME GAS OUT OF THE CARS LEFT IN THE PRISON PARKING LOT.
WE COULD GET A BUNCH OF PEOPLE TOGETHER TO LURE THE ZOMBIES AWAY FROM THE GATE--RUN OUT THERE, SIPHON SOME GAS AND GET BACK INSIDE BEFORE THEY EVEN KNOW WE'RE ON THE OTHER SIDE OF THE FENCE.
IT'LL BE LIKE OLD TIMES.
SOUNDS GOOD TO ME. GIVE ME A FEW MINUTES WHILE YOU GATHER SOME PEOPLE TO RUN A DISTRACTION AND I'LL MEET YOU AT THE GATE.
WHERE'S HE GOING?
WHERE DO YOU THINK?

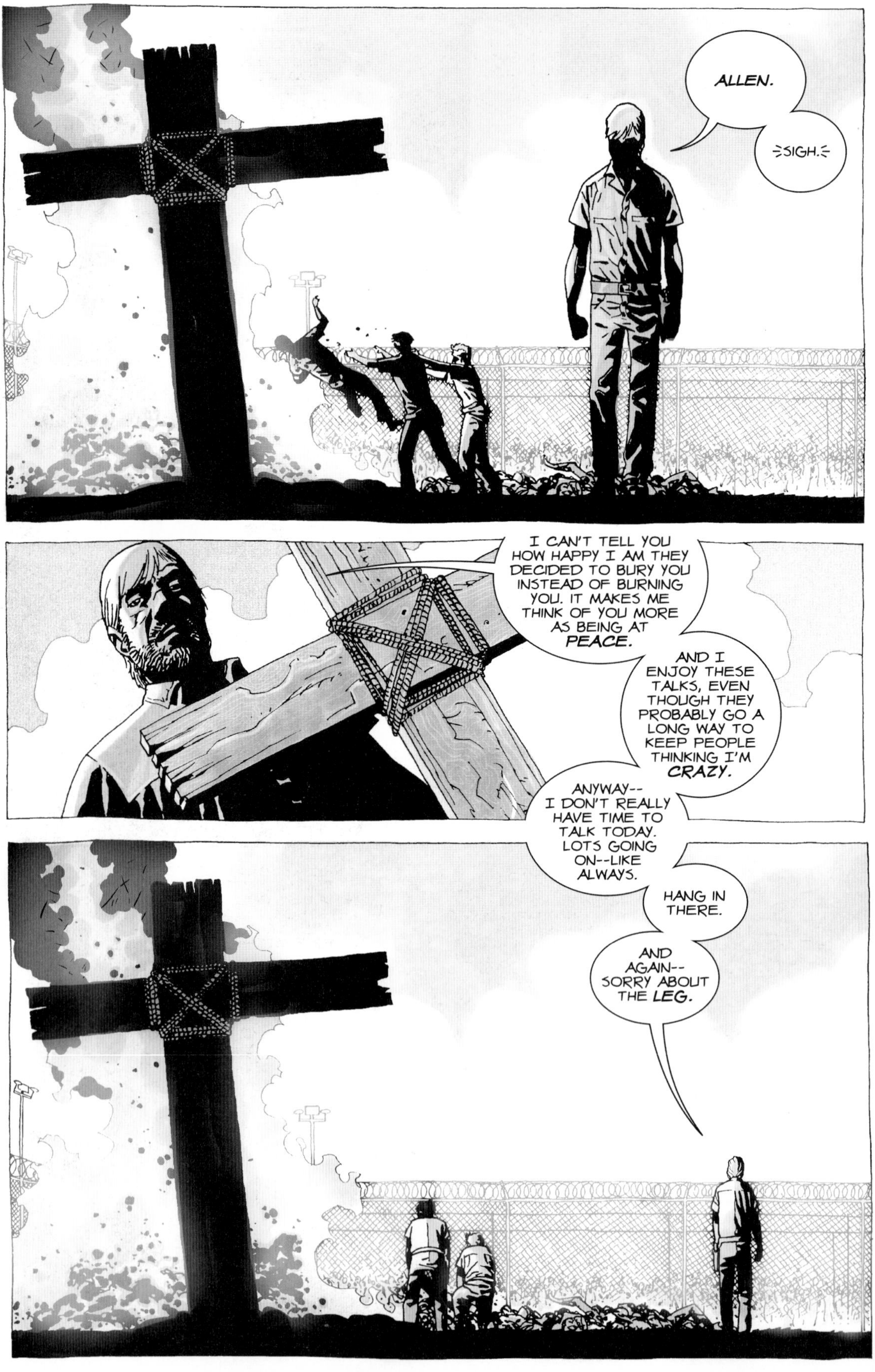
ALLEN.
=SIGH.=
I CAN'T TELL YOU HOW HAPPY I AM THEY DECIDED TO BURY YOU INSTEAD OF BURNING YOU. IT MAKES ME THINK OF YOU MORE AS BEING AT *PEACE.*
AND I ENJOY THESE TALKS, EVEN THOUGH THEY PROBABLY GO A LONG WAY TO KEEP PEOPLE THINKING I'M *CRAZY.*
ANYWAY-- I DON'T REALLY HAVE TIME TO TALK TODAY. LOTS GOING ON--LIKE ALWAYS.
HANG IN THERE.
AND AGAIN-- SORRY ABOUT THE *LEG.*

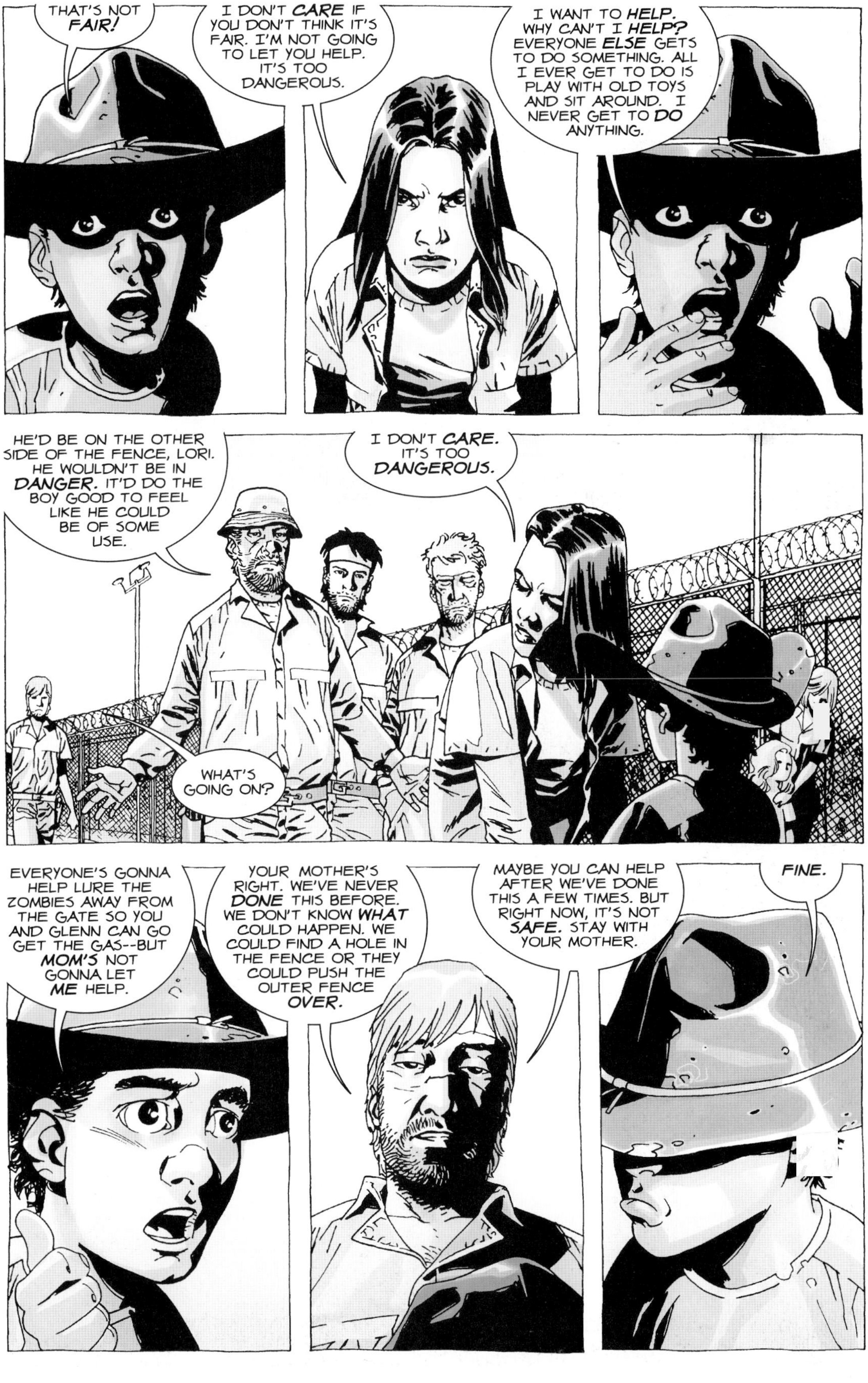
THAT'S NOT FAIR!
I DON'T CARE IF YOU DON'T THINK IT'S FAIR. I'M NOT GOING TO LET YOU HELP. IT'S TOO DANGEROUS.
I WANT TO HELP. WHY CAN'T I HELP? EVERYONE ELSE GETS TO DO SOMETHING. ALL I EVER GET TO DO IS PLAY WITH OLD TOYS AND SIT AROUND. I NEVER GET TO DO ANYTHING.
HE'D BE ON THE OTHER SIDE OF THE FENCE, LORI. HE WOULDN'T BE IN DANGER. IT'D DO THE BOY GOOD TO FEEL LIKE HE COULD BE OF SOME USE.
I DON'T CARE. IT'S TOO DANGEROUS.
WHAT'S GOING ON?
EVERYONE'S GONNA HELP LURE THE ZOMBIES AWAY FROM THE GATE SO YOU AND GLENN CAN GO GET THE GAS--BUT MOM'S NOT GONNA LET ME HELP.
YOUR MOTHER'S RIGHT. WE'VE NEVER DONE THIS BEFORE. WE DON'T KNOW WHAT COULD HAPPEN. WE COULD FIND A HOLE IN THE FENCE OR THEY COULD PUSH THE OUTER FENCE OVER.
MAYBE YOU CAN HELP AFTER WE'VE DONE THIS A FEW TIMES. BUT RIGHT NOW, IT'S NOT SAFE. STAY WITH YOUR MOTHER.
FINE.

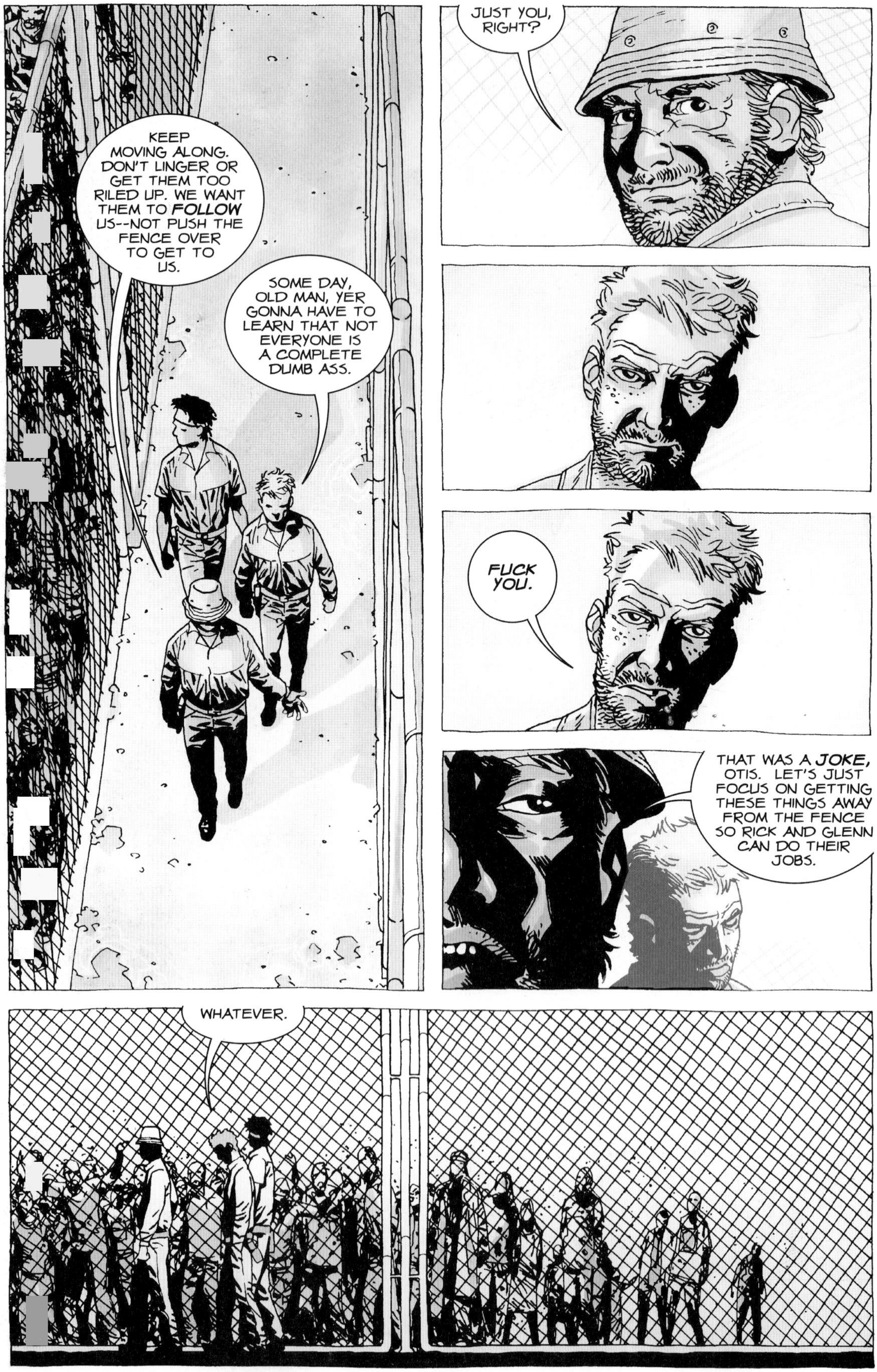
KEEP MOVING ALONG. DON'T LINGER OR GET THEM TOO RILED UP. WE WANT THEM TO FOLLOW US--NOT PUSH THE FENCE OVER TO GET TO US.
SOME DAY, OLD MAN, YER GONNA HAVE TO LEARN THAT NOT EVERYONE IS A COMPLETE DUMB ASS.
JUST YOU, RIGHT?
FUCK YOU.
THAT WAS A JOKE, OTIS. LET'S JUST FOCUS ON GETTING THESE THINGS AWAY FROM THE FENCE SO RICK AND GLENN CAN DO THEIR JOBS.
WHATEVER.

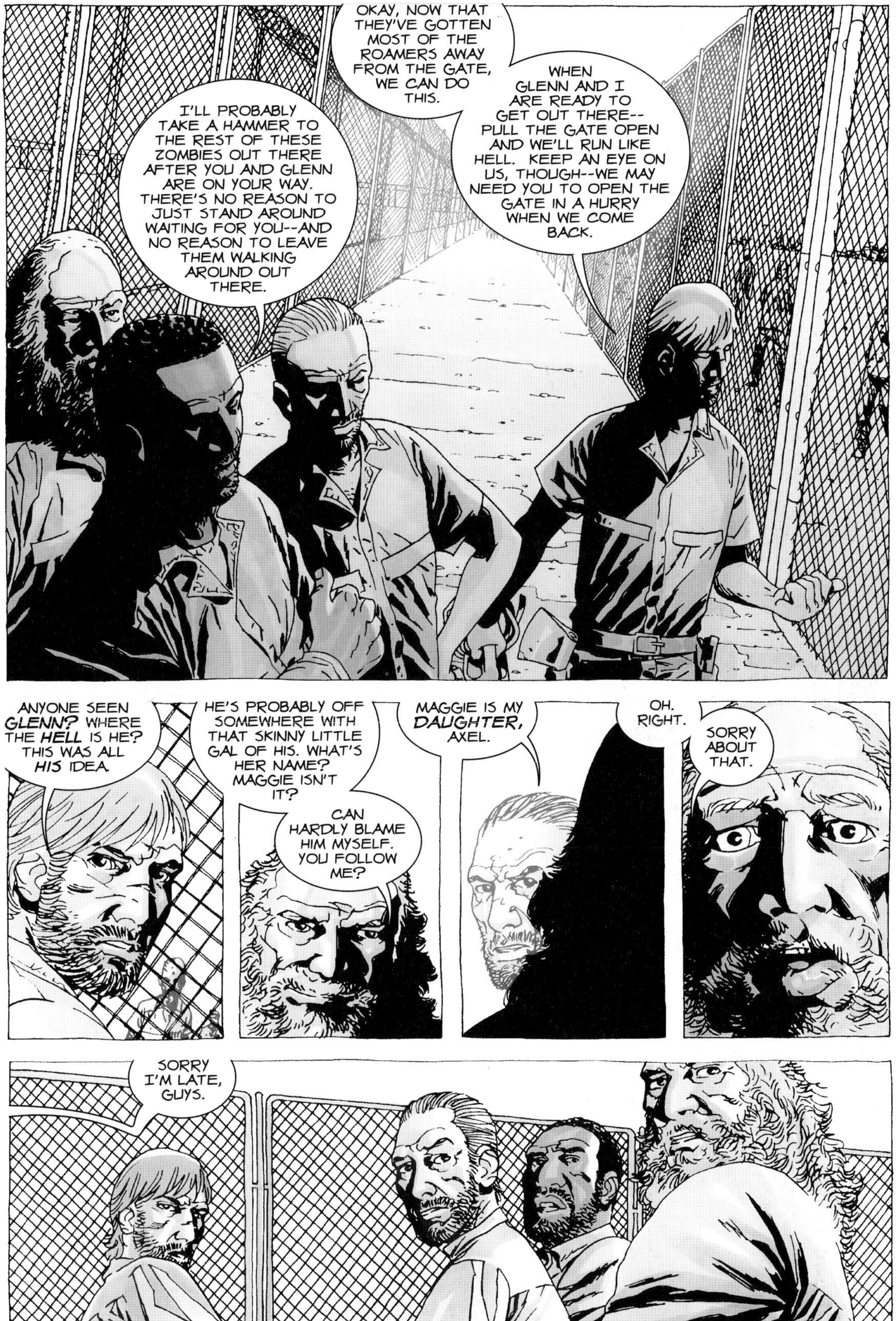
OKAY, NOW THAT THEY'VE GOTTEN MOST OF THE ROAMERS AWAY FROM THE GATE, WE CAN DO THIS.
WHEN GLENN AND I ARE READY TO GET OUT THERE-- PULL THE GATE OPEN AND WE'LL RUN LIKE HELL. KEEP AN EYE ON US, THOUGH--WE MAY NEED YOU TO OPEN THE GATE IN A HURRY WHEN WE COME BACK.
I'LL PROBABLY TAKE A HAMMER TO THE REST OF THESE ZOMBIES OUT THERE AFTER YOU AND GLENN ARE ON YOUR WAY. THERE'S NO REASON TO JUST STAND AROUND WAITING FOR YOU--AND NO REASON TO LEAVE THEM WALKING AROUND OUT THERE.
ANYONE SEEN GLENN? WHERE THE HELL IS HE? THIS WAS ALL HIS IDEA.
HE'S PROBABLY OFF SOMEWHERE WITH THAT SKINNY LITTLE GAL OF HIS. WHAT'S HER NAME? MAGGIE ISN'T IT?
CAN HARDLY BLAME HIM MYSELF. YOU FOLLOW ME?
MAGGIE IS MY DAUGHTER, AXEL.
OH. RIGHT.
SORRY ABOUT THAT.
SORRY I'M LATE, GUYS.

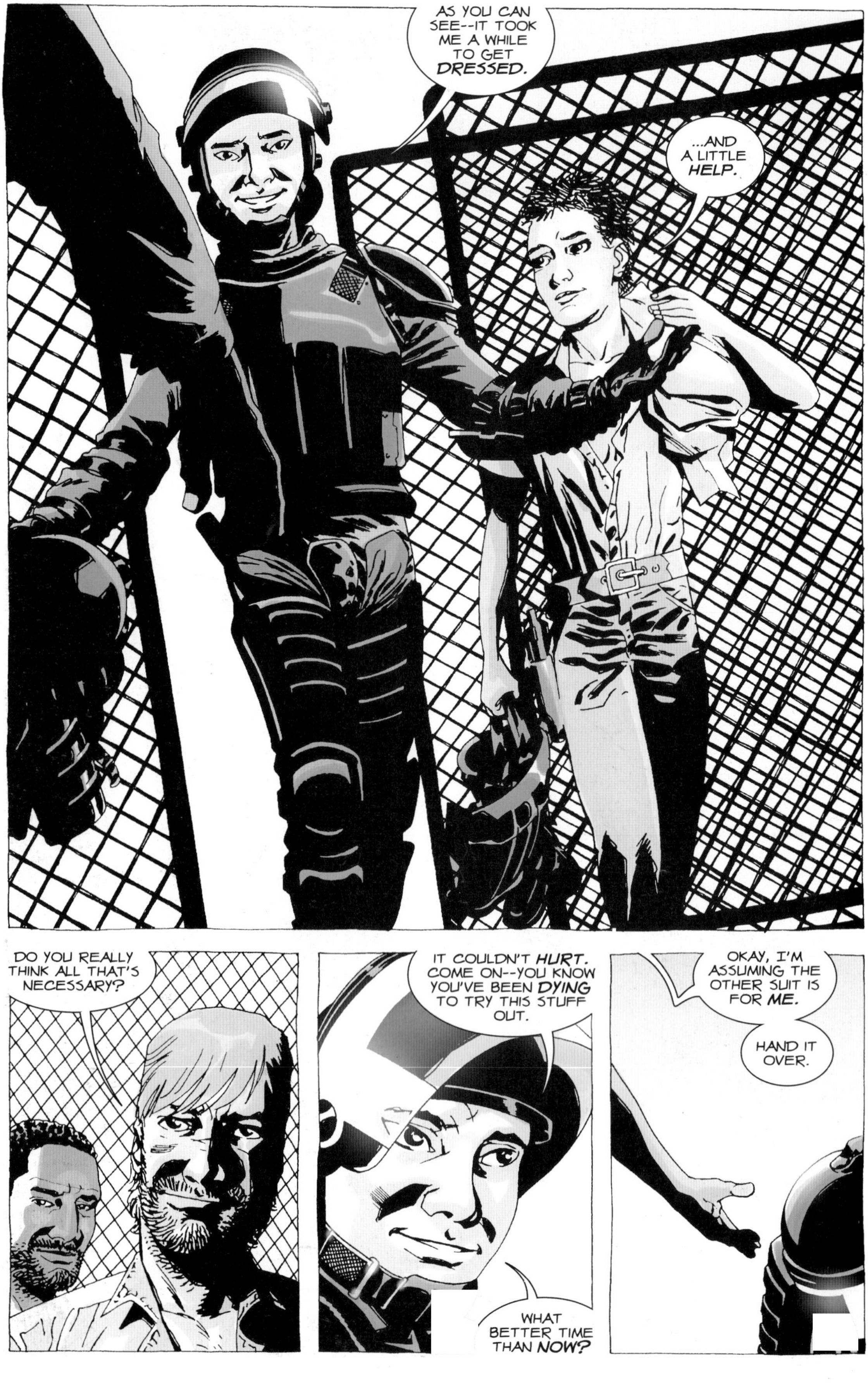
AS YOU CAN SEE--IT TOOK ME A WHILE TO GET DRESSED.
...AND A LITTLE HELP.
DO YOU REALLY THINK ALL THAT'S NECESSARY?
IT COULDN'T HURT. COME ON--YOU KNOW YOU'VE BEEN DYING TO TRY THIS STUFF OUT.
WHAT BETTER TIME THAN NOW?
OKAY, I'M ASSUMING THE OTHER SUIT IS FOR ME.
HAND IT OVER.

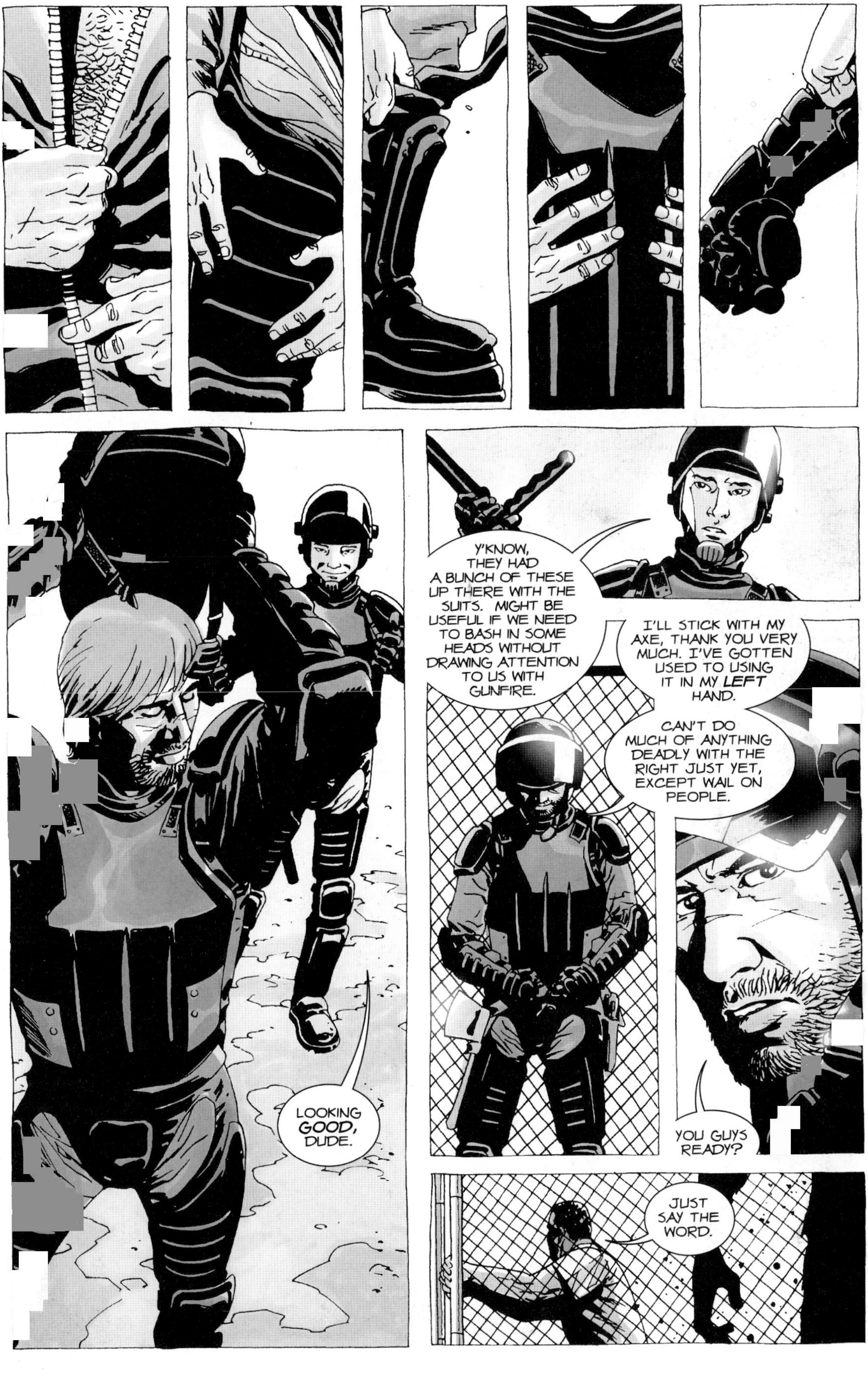
LOOKING GOOD, DUDE.
Y'KNOW, THEY HAD A BUNCH OF THESE UP THERE WITH THE SUITS. MIGHT BE USEFUL IF WE NEED TO BASH IN SOME HEADS WITHOUT DRAWING ATTENTION TO US WITH GUNFIRE.
I'LL STICK WITH MY AXE, THANK YOU VERY MUCH. I'VE GOTTEN USED TO USING IT IN MY LEFT HAND.
CAN'T DO MUCH OF ANYTHING DEADLY WITH THE RIGHT JUST YET, EXCEPT WAIL ON PEOPLE.
YOU GUYS READY?
JUST SAY THE WORD.

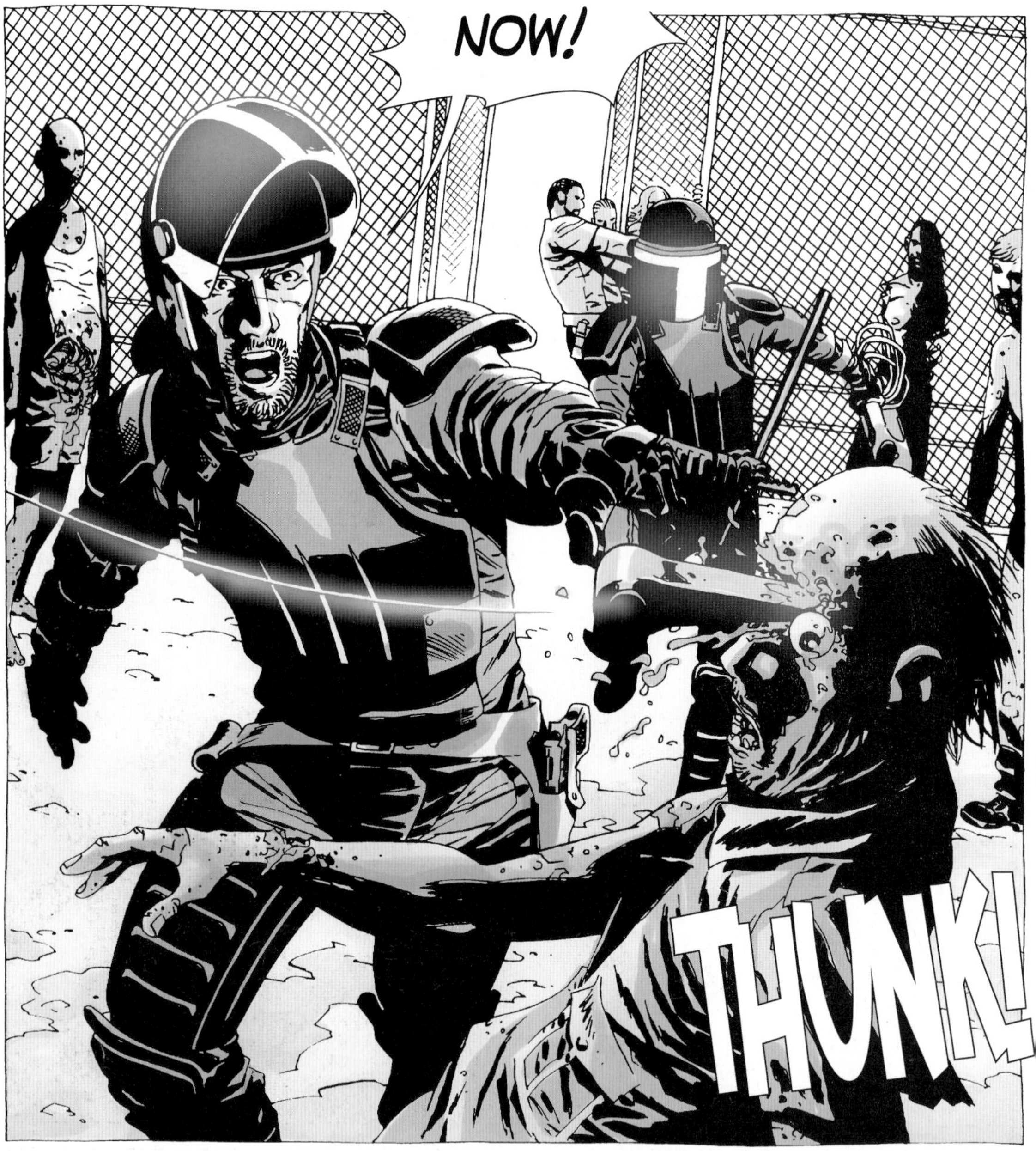
NOW!
THUNK!

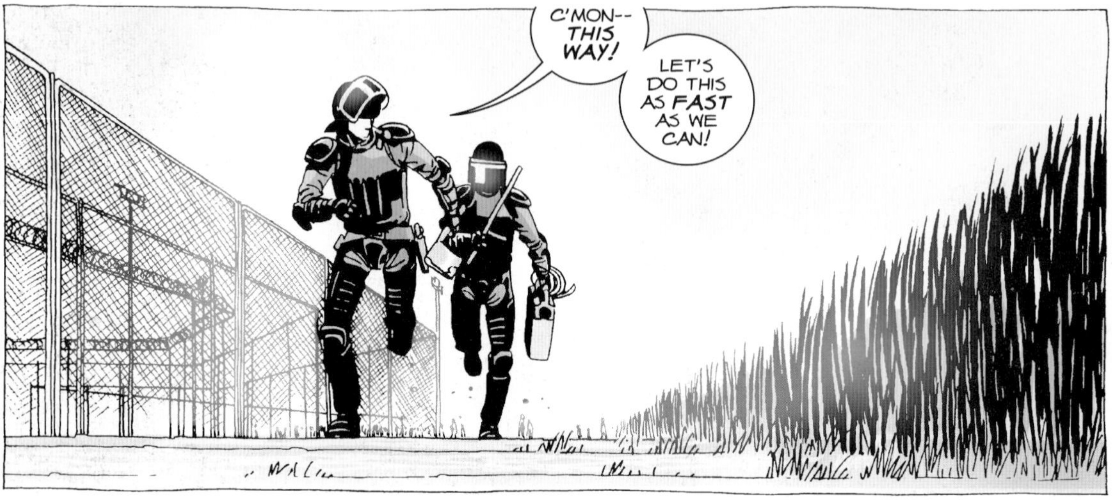
C'MON-- THIS WAY!
LET'S DO THIS AS FAST AS WE CAN!

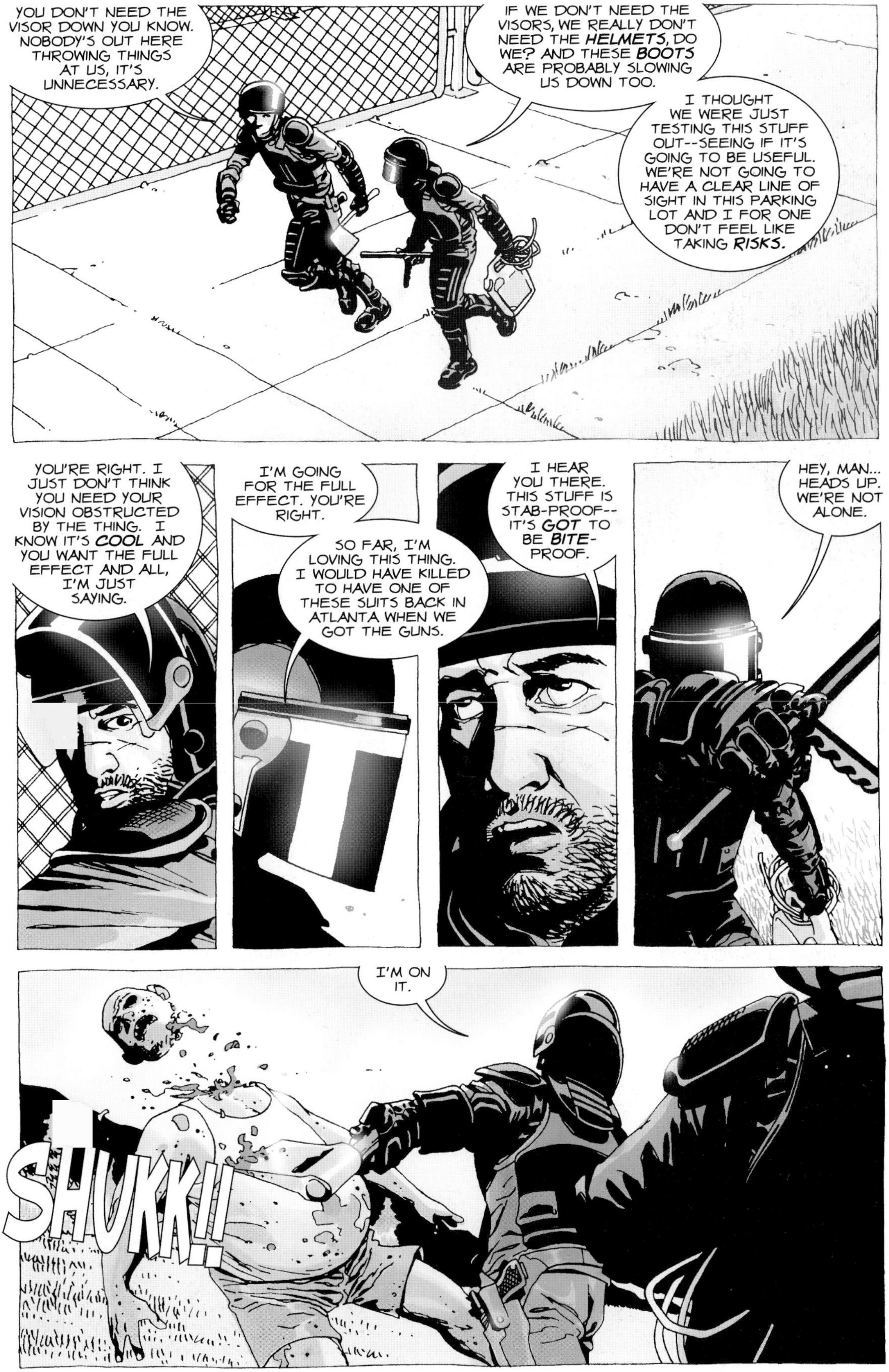
YOU DON'T NEED THE VISOR DOWN YOU KNOW. NOBODY'S OUT HERE THROWING THINGS AT US, IT'S UNNECESSARY.
IF WE DON'T NEED THE VISORS, WE REALLY DON'T NEED THE HELMETS, DO WE? AND THESE BOOTS ARE PROBABLY SLOWING US DOWN TOO.
I THOUGHT WE WERE JUST TESTING THIS STUFF OUT--SEEING IF IT'S GOING TO BE USEFUL. WE'RE NOT GOING TO HAVE A CLEAR LINE OF SIGHT IN THIS PARKING LOT AND I FOR ONE DON'T FEEL LIKE TAKING RISKS.
YOU'RE RIGHT. I JUST DON'T THINK YOU NEED YOUR VISION OBSTRUCTED BY THE THING. I KNOW IT'S COOL AND YOU WANT THE FULL EFFECT AND ALL, I'M JUST SAYING.
I'M GOING FOR THE FULL EFFECT. YOU'RE RIGHT.
SO FAR, I'M LOVING THIS THING. I WOULD HAVE KILLED TO HAVE ONE OF THESE SUITS BACK IN ATLANTA WHEN WE GOT THE GUNS.
I HEAR YOU THERE. THIS STUFF IS STAB-PROOF-- IT'S GOT TO BE BITE-PROOF.
HEY, MAN... HEADS UP. WE'RE NOT ALONE.
I'M ON IT.
SHUKK!!

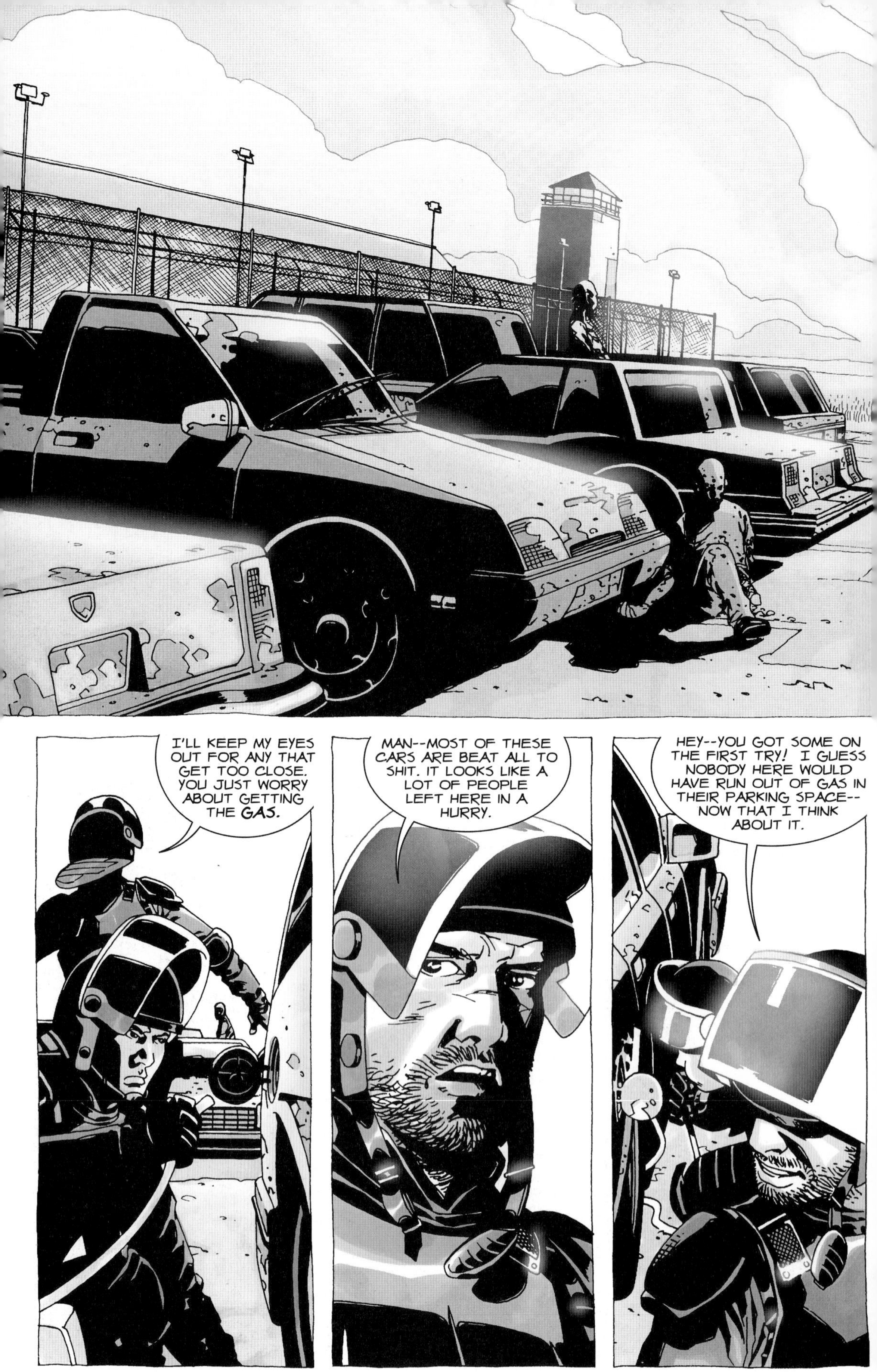
I'LL KEEP MY EYES OUT FOR ANY THAT GET TOO CLOSE. YOU JUST WORRY ABOUT GETTING THE GAS.
MAN--MOST OF THESE CARS ARE BEAT ALL TO SHIT. IT LOOKS LIKE A LOT OF PEOPLE LEFT HERE IN A HURRY.
HEY--YOU GOT SOME ON THE FIRST TRY! I GUESS NOBODY HERE WOULD HAVE RUN OUT OF GAS IN THEIR PARKING SPACE--NOW THAT I THINK ABOUT IT.

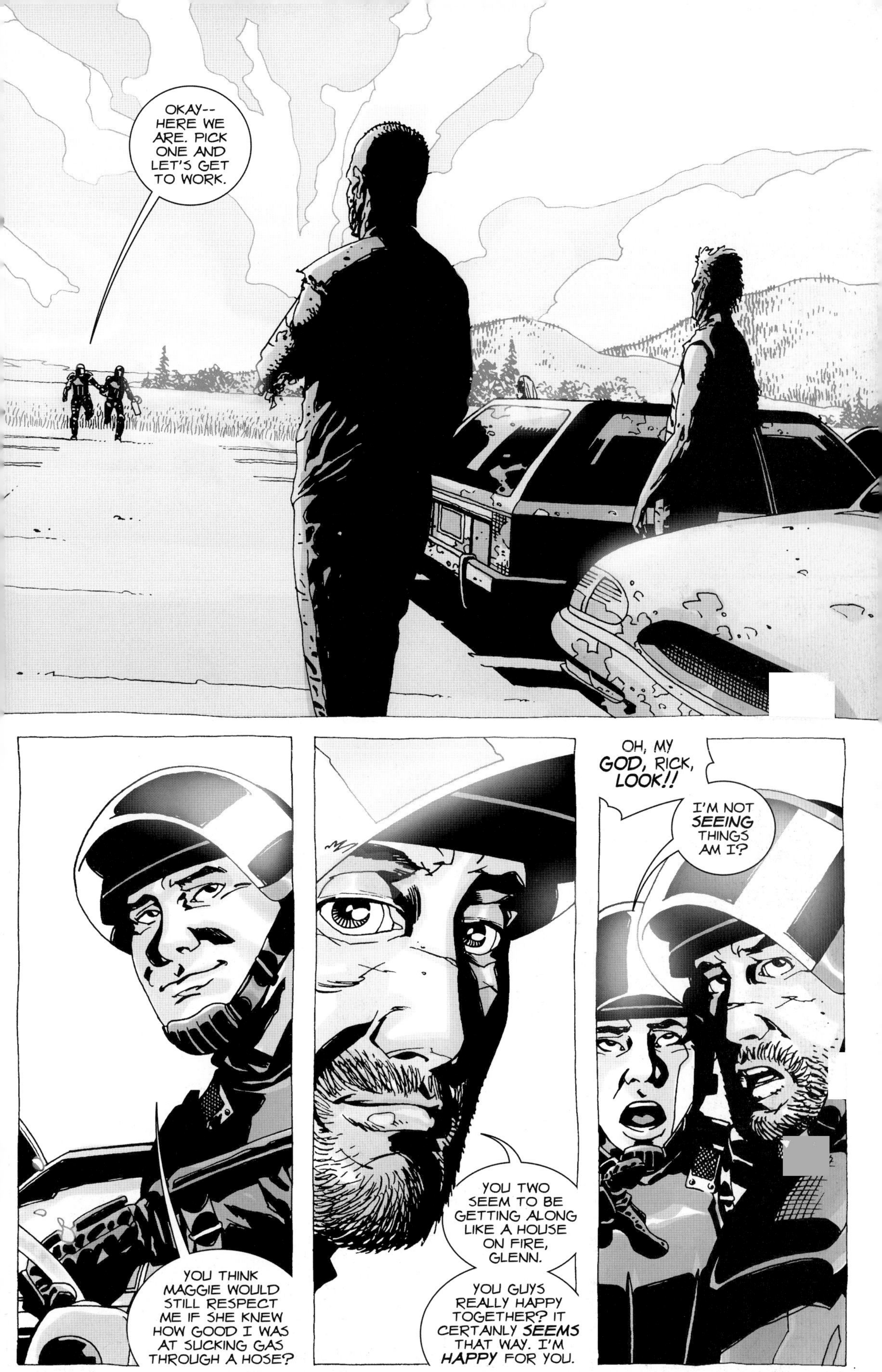
OKAY-- HERE WE ARE. PICK ONE AND LET'S GET TO WORK.
YOU THINK MAGGIE WOULD STILL RESPECT ME IF SHE KNEW HOW GOOD I WAS AT SUCKING GAS THROUGH A HOSE?
YOU TWO SEEM TO BE GETTING ALONG LIKE A HOUSE ON FIRE, GLENN.
YOU GUYS REALLY HAPPY TOGETHER? IT CERTAINLY SEEMS THAT WAY. I'M HAPPY FOR YOU.
OH, MY GOD, RICK, LOOK!!
I'M NOT SEEING THINGS AM I?

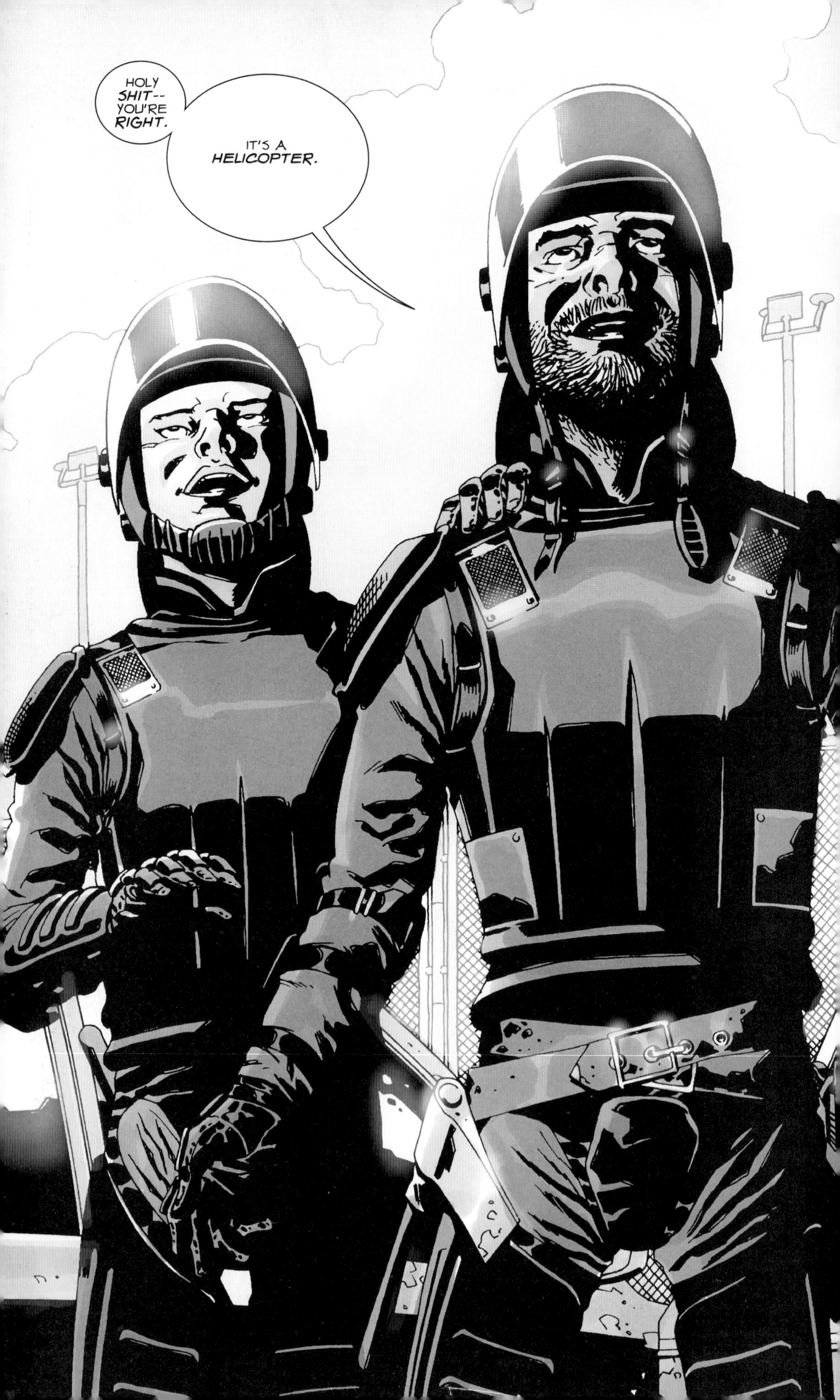

HOLY SHIT-- YOU'RE RIGHT.
IT'S A HELICOPTER.

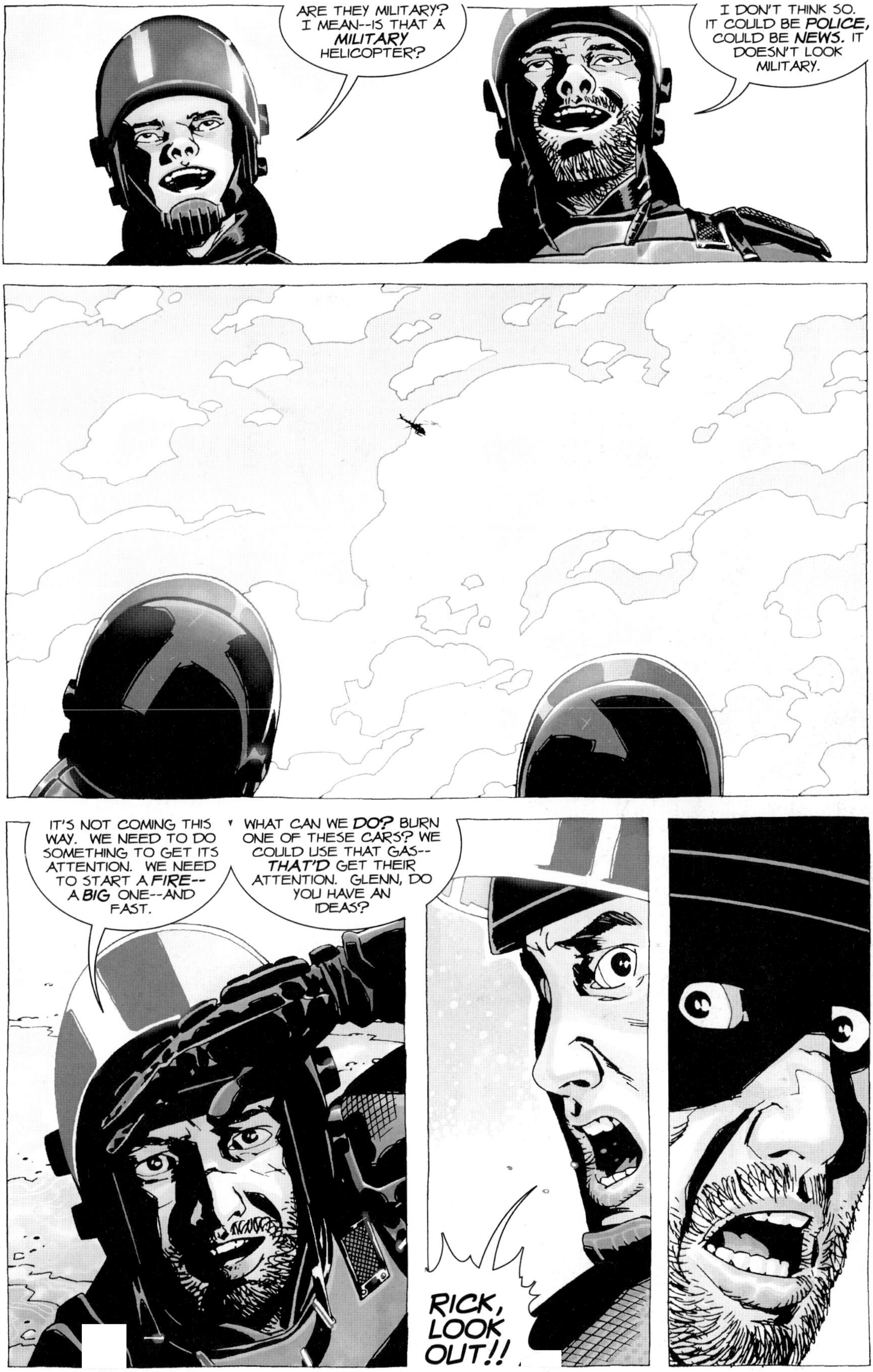
ARE THEY MILITARY? I MEAN--IS THAT A MILITARY HELICOPTER?
I DON'T THINK SO. IT COULD BE POLICE, COULD BE NEWS. IT DOESN'T LOOK MILITARY.
IT'S NOT COMING THIS WAY. WE NEED TO DO SOMETHING TO GET ITS ATTENTION. WE NEED TO START A FIRE-- A BIG ONE--AND FAST.
WHAT CAN WE DO? BURN ONE OF THESE CARS? WE COULD USE THAT GAS-- THAT'D GET THEIR ATTENTION. GLENN, DO YOU HAVE AN IDEAS?
RICK, LOOK OUT!!

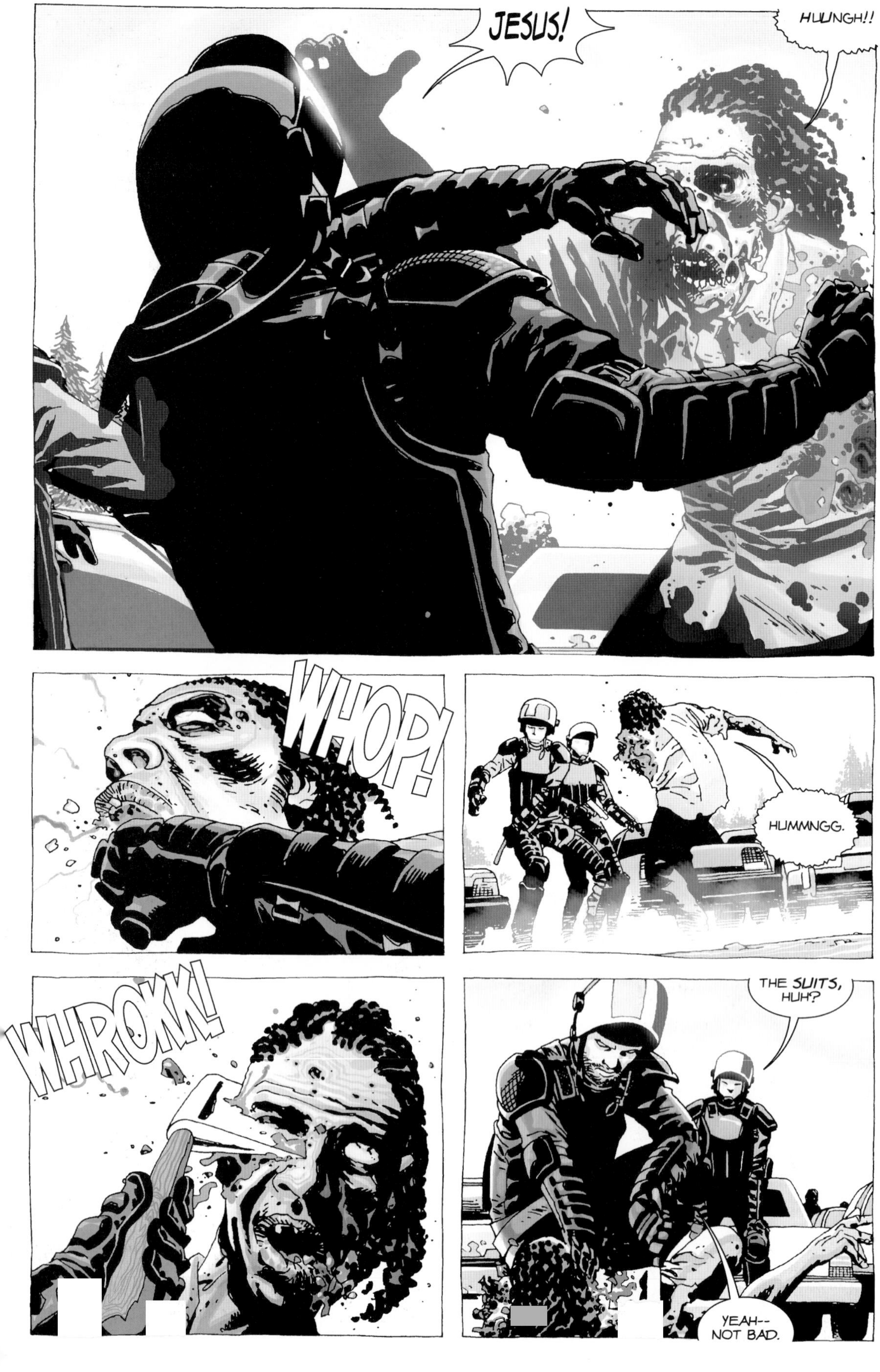
JESUS!
HUUNGH!!
WHOP!
HUMMNGG.
WHROKK!
THE SUITS, HUH?
YEAH-- NOT BAD.

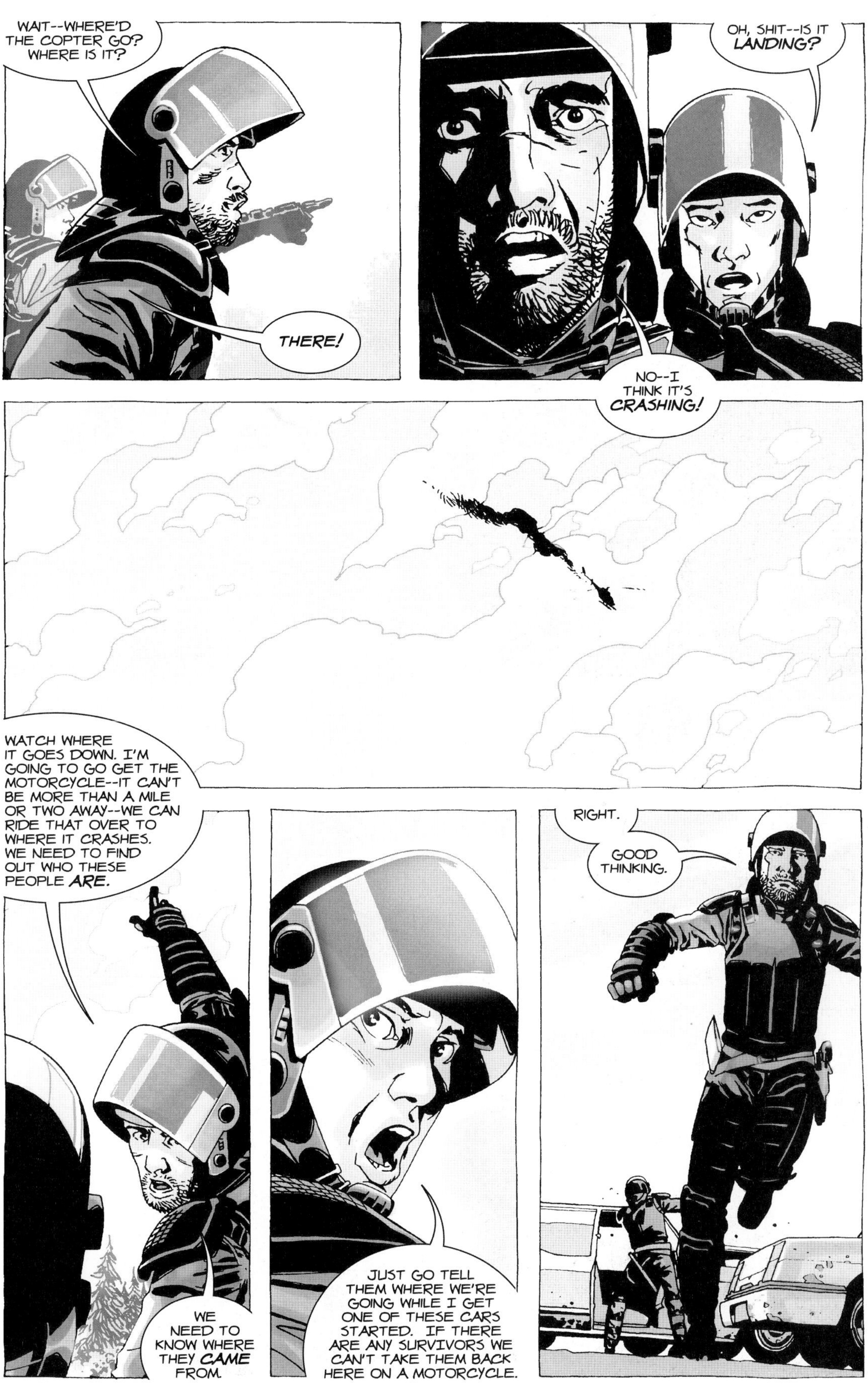
WAIT--WHERE'D THE COPTER GO? WHERE IS IT?
THERE!
OH, SHIT--IS IT LANDING?
NO--I THINK IT'S CRASHING!
WATCH WHERE IT GOES DOWN. I'M GOING TO GO GET THE MOTORCYCLE--IT CAN'T BE MORE THAN A MILE OR TWO AWAY--WE CAN RIDE THAT OVER TO WHERE IT CRASHES. WE NEED TO FIND OUT WHO THESE PEOPLE ARE.
WE NEED TO KNOW WHERE THEY CAME FROM.
JUST GO TELL THEM WHERE WE'RE GOING WHILE I GET ONE OF THESE CARS STARTED. IF THERE ARE ANY SURVIVORS WE CAN'T TAKE THEM BACK HERE ON A MOTORCYCLE.
RIGHT.
GOOD THINKING.

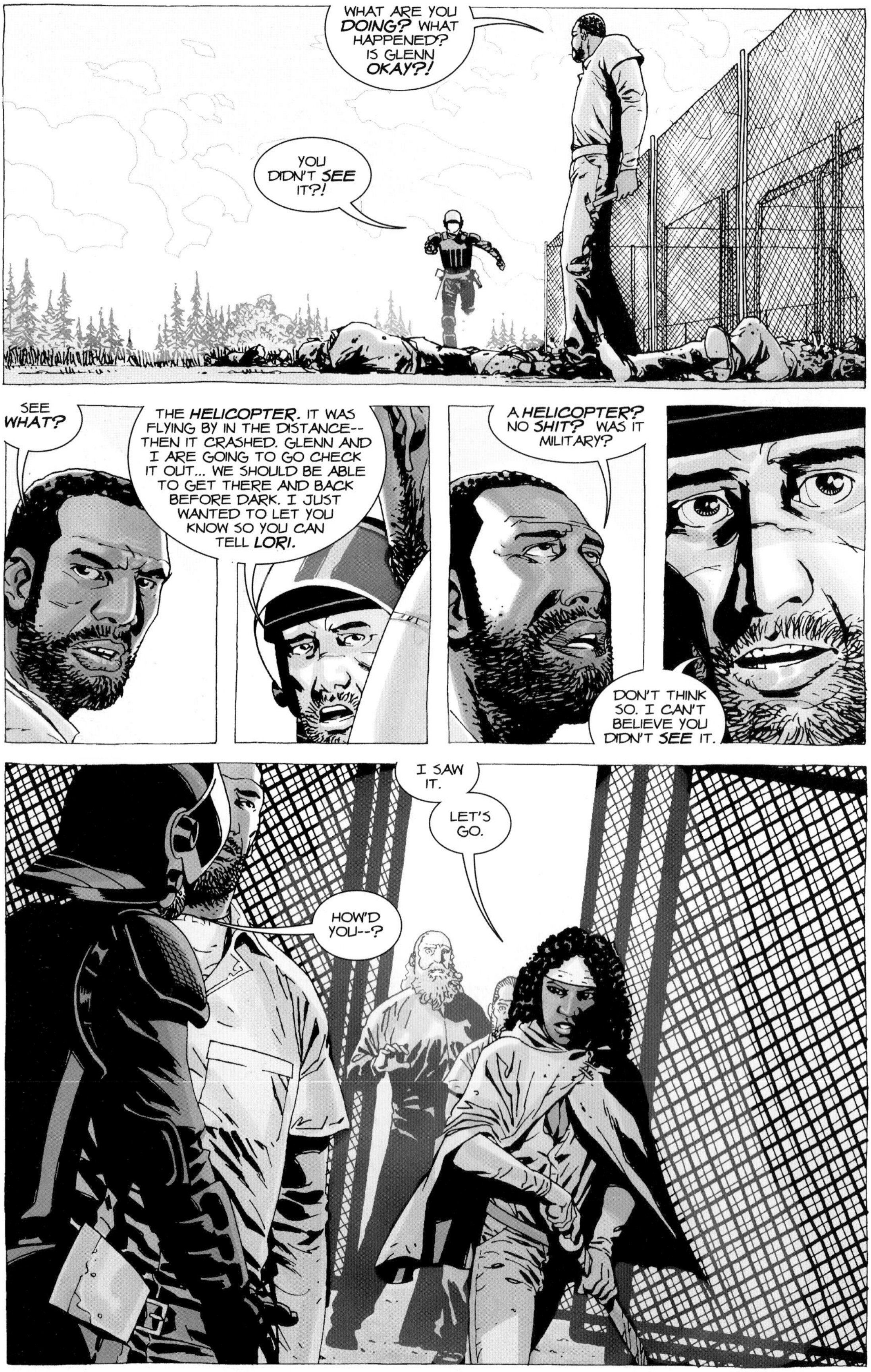
WHAT ARE YOU DOING? WHAT HAPPENED? IS GLENN OKAY?!
YOU DIDN'T SEE IT?!
SEE WHAT?
THE HELICOPTER. IT WAS FLYING BY IN THE DISTANCE-- THEN IT CRASHED. GLENN AND I ARE GOING TO GO CHECK IT OUT... WE SHOULD BE ABLE TO GET THERE AND BACK BEFORE DARK. I JUST WANTED TO LET YOU KNOW SO YOU CAN TELL LORI.
A HELICOPTER? NO SHIT? WAS IT MILITARY?
DON'T THINK SO. I CAN'T BELIEVE YOU DIDN'T SEE IT.
I SAW IT.
LET'S GO.
HOW'D YOU--?

DID YOU THINK I WOULDN'T FIND IT IF YOU HID IT IN DALE'S RV? *PLEASE.*

I'VE HAD THIS SWORD FOR A WEEK. YOU CAN *TRUST* ME.

I'M PRETTY SURE THAT PROVES *OTHERWISE.*

LET'S DEAL WITH THAT *LATER.* WE NEED TO *GO.* I SURVIVED OUT THERE ON MY OWN. I'M YOUR BEST BET AT GETTING THERE AND BACK IN *ONE PIECE.* YOU NEED ME WITH YOU--AND I COULD USE THE *EXERCISE.*

WE'RE NOT GOING TO *RUN* THERE.

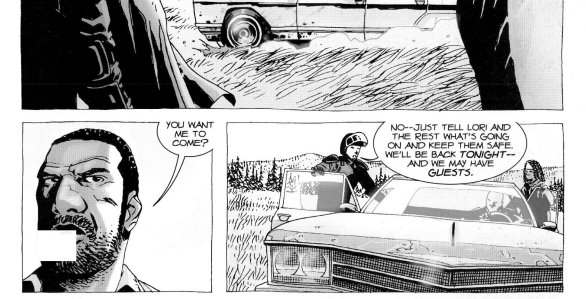

YOU GUYS *READY?*

YOU WANT ME TO COME?

NO--JUST TELL LORI AND THE REST WHAT'S GOING ON AND KEEP THEM SAFE. WE'LL BE BACK *TONIGHT*-- AND WE MAY HAVE *GUESTS.*

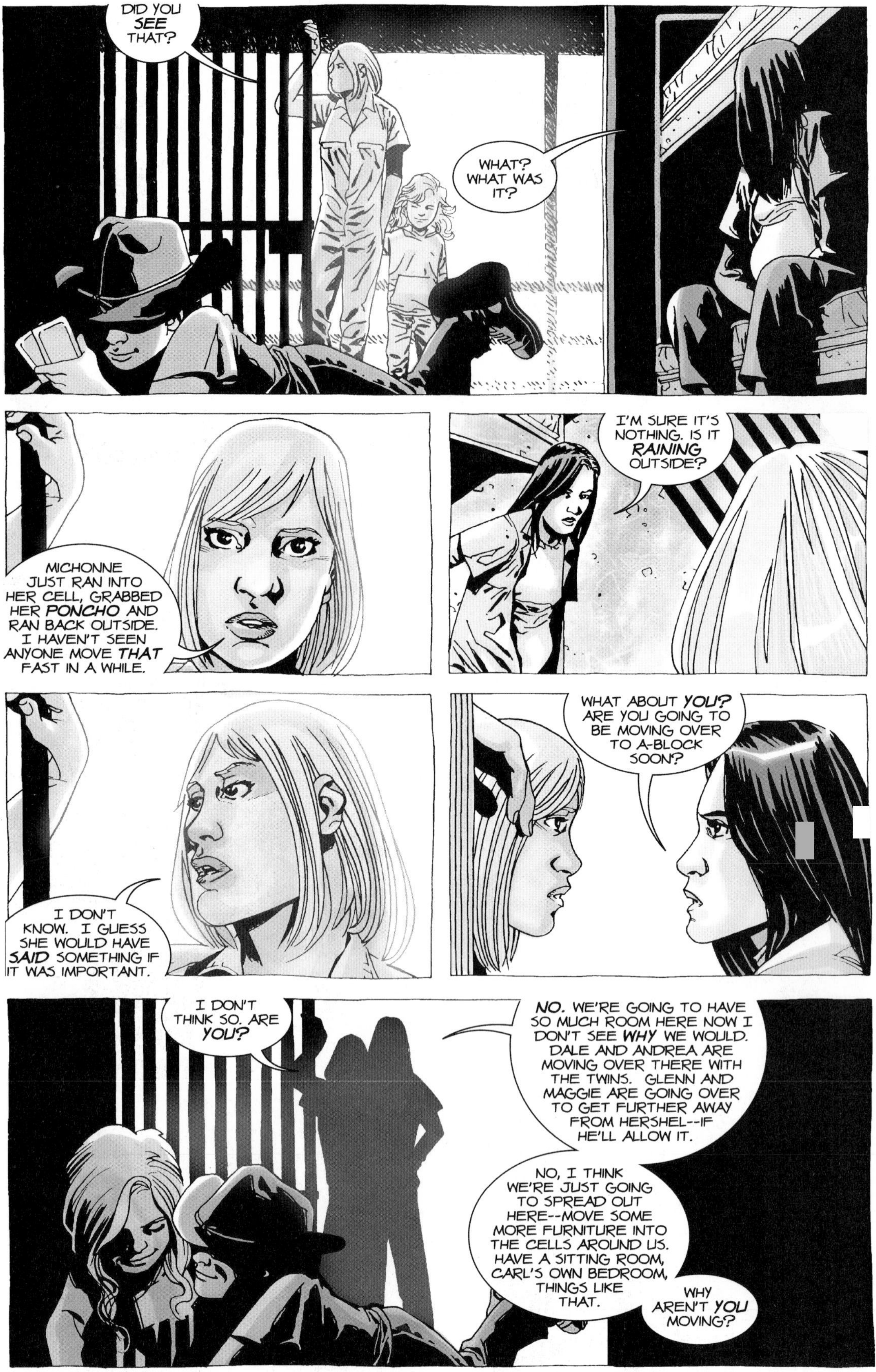
DID YOU SEE THAT?
WHAT? WHAT WAS IT?
MICHONNE JUST RAN INTO HER CELL, GRABBED HER PONCHO AND RAN BACK OUTSIDE. I HAVEN'T SEEN ANYONE MOVE THAT FAST IN A WHILE.
I'M SURE IT'S NOTHING. IS IT RAINING OUTSIDE?
I DON'T KNOW. I GUESS SHE WOULD HAVE SAID SOMETHING IF IT WAS IMPORTANT.
WHAT ABOUT YOU? ARE YOU GOING TO BE MOVING OVER TO A-BLOCK SOON?
I DON'T THINK SO. ARE YOU?
NO. WE'RE GOING TO HAVE SO MUCH ROOM HERE NOW I DON'T SEE WHY WE WOULD. DALE AND ANDREA ARE MOVING OVER THERE WITH THE TWINS. GLENN AND MAGGIE ARE GOING OVER TO GET FURTHER AWAY FROM HERSHEL--IF HE'LL ALLOW IT.
NO, I THINK WE'RE JUST GOING TO SPREAD OUT HERE--MOVE SOME MORE FURNITURE INTO THE CELLS AROUND US. HAVE A SITTING ROOM, CARL'S OWN BEDROOM, THINGS LIKE THAT.
WHY AREN'T YOU MOVING?

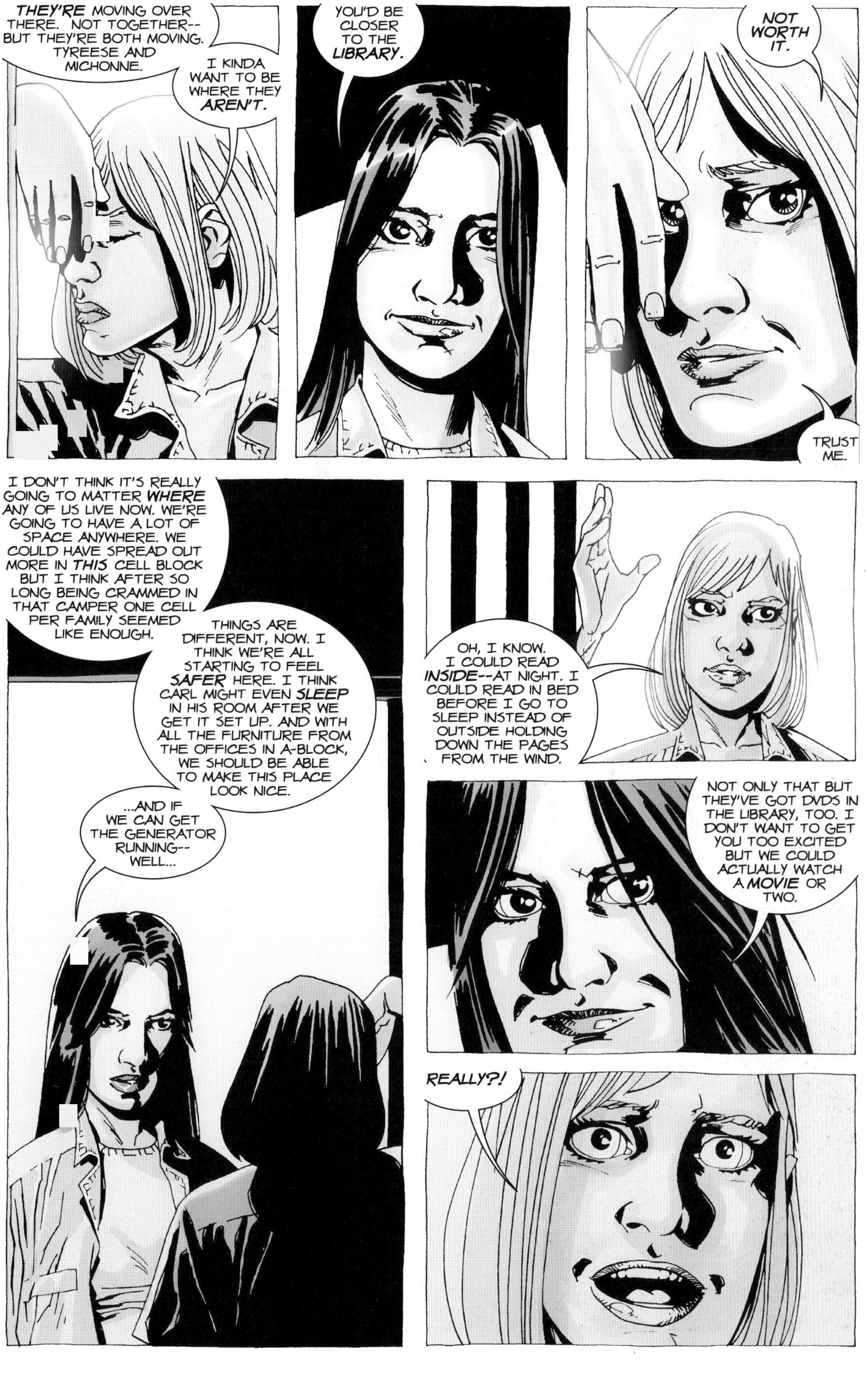
THEY'RE MOVING OVER THERE. NOT TOGETHER-- BUT THEY'RE BOTH MOVING. TYREESE AND MICHONNE.
I KINDA WANT TO BE WHERE THEY AREN'T.
YOU'D BE CLOSER TO THE LIBRARY.
NOT WORTH IT.
TRUST ME.
I DON'T THINK IT'S REALLY GOING TO MATTER WHERE ANY OF US LIVE NOW. WE'RE GOING TO HAVE A LOT OF SPACE ANYWHERE. WE COULD HAVE SPREAD OUT MORE IN THIS CELL BLOCK BUT I THINK AFTER SO LONG BEING CRAMMED IN THAT CAMPER ONE CELL PER FAMILY SEEMED LIKE ENOUGH.
THINGS ARE DIFFERENT, NOW. I THINK WE'RE ALL STARTING TO FEEL SAFER HERE. I THINK CARL MIGHT EVEN SLEEP IN HIS ROOM AFTER WE GET IT SET UP. AND WITH ALL THE FURNITURE FROM THE OFFICES IN A-BLOCK, WE SHOULD BE ABLE TO MAKE THIS PLACE LOOK NICE.
...AND IF WE CAN GET THE GENERATOR RUNNING-- WELL...
OH, I KNOW. I COULD READ INSIDE--AT NIGHT. I COULD READ IN BED BEFORE I GO TO SLEEP INSTEAD OF OUTSIDE HOLDING DOWN THE PAGES FROM THE WIND.
NOT ONLY THAT BUT THEY'VE GOT DVDS IN THE LIBRARY, TOO. I DON'T WANT TO GET YOU TOO EXCITED BUT WE COULD ACTUALLY WATCH A MOVIE OR TWO.
REALLY?!

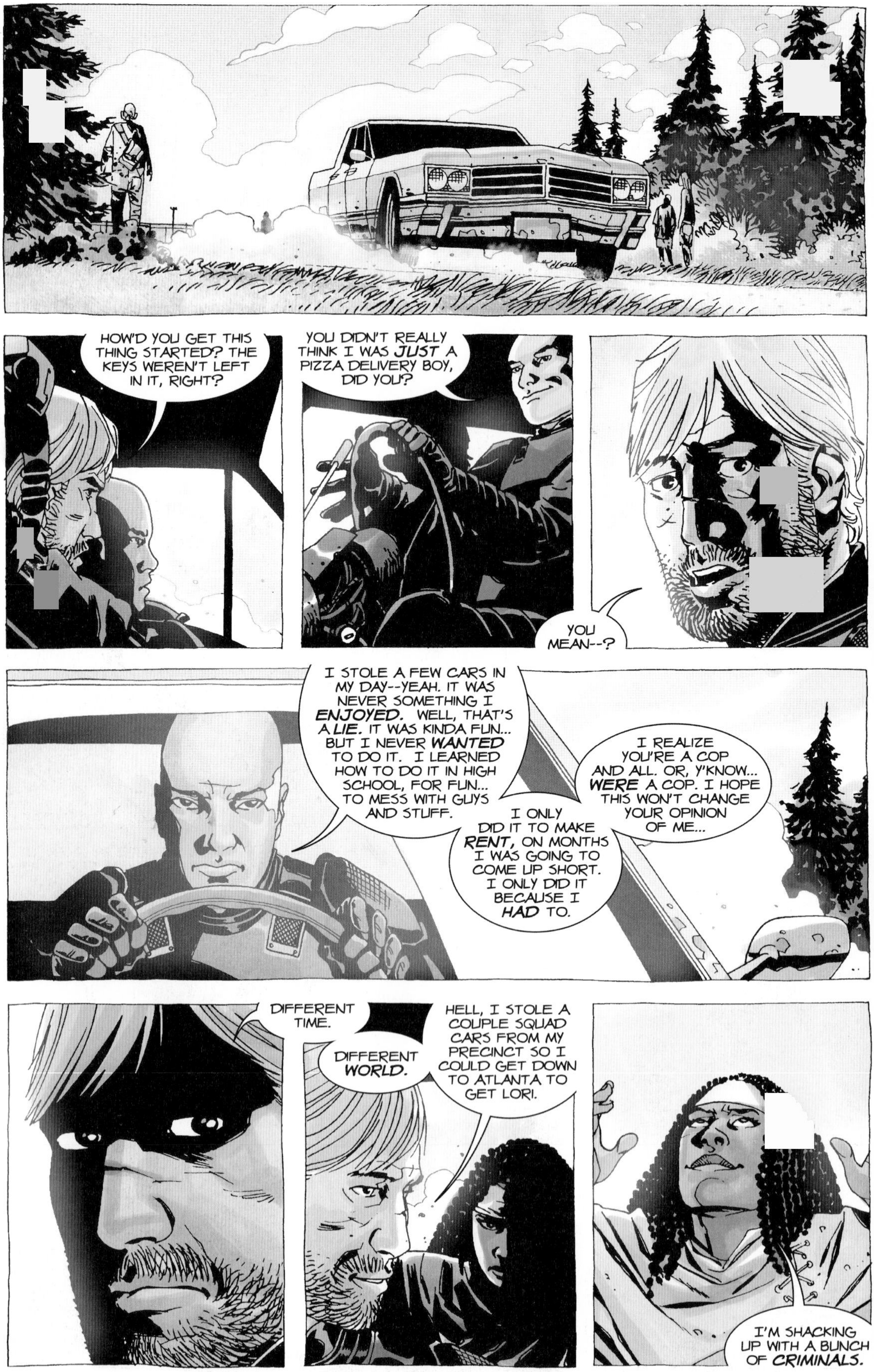
HOW'D YOU GET THIS THING STARTED? THE KEYS WEREN'T LEFT IN IT, RIGHT?
YOU DIDN'T REALLY THINK I WAS JUST A PIZZA DELIVERY BOY, DID YOU?
YOU MEAN--?
I STOLE A FEW CARS IN MY DAY--YEAH. IT WAS NEVER SOMETHING I ENJOYED. WELL, THAT'S A LIE. IT WAS KINDA FUN... BUT I NEVER WANTED TO DO IT. I LEARNED HOW TO DO IT IN HIGH SCHOOL, FOR FUN... TO MESS WITH GUYS AND STUFF.
I ONLY DID IT TO MAKE RENT, ON MONTHS I WAS GOING TO COME UP SHORT. I ONLY DID IT BECAUSE I HAD TO.
I REALIZE YOU'RE A COP AND ALL. OR, Y'KNOW... WERE A COP. I HOPE THIS WON'T CHANGE YOUR OPINION OF ME...
DIFFERENT TIME.
DIFFERENT WORLD.
HELL, I STOLE A COUPLE SQUAD CARS FROM MY PRECINCT SO I COULD GET DOWN TO ATLANTA TO GET LORI.
I'M SHACKING UP WITH A BUNCH OF CRIMINALS.

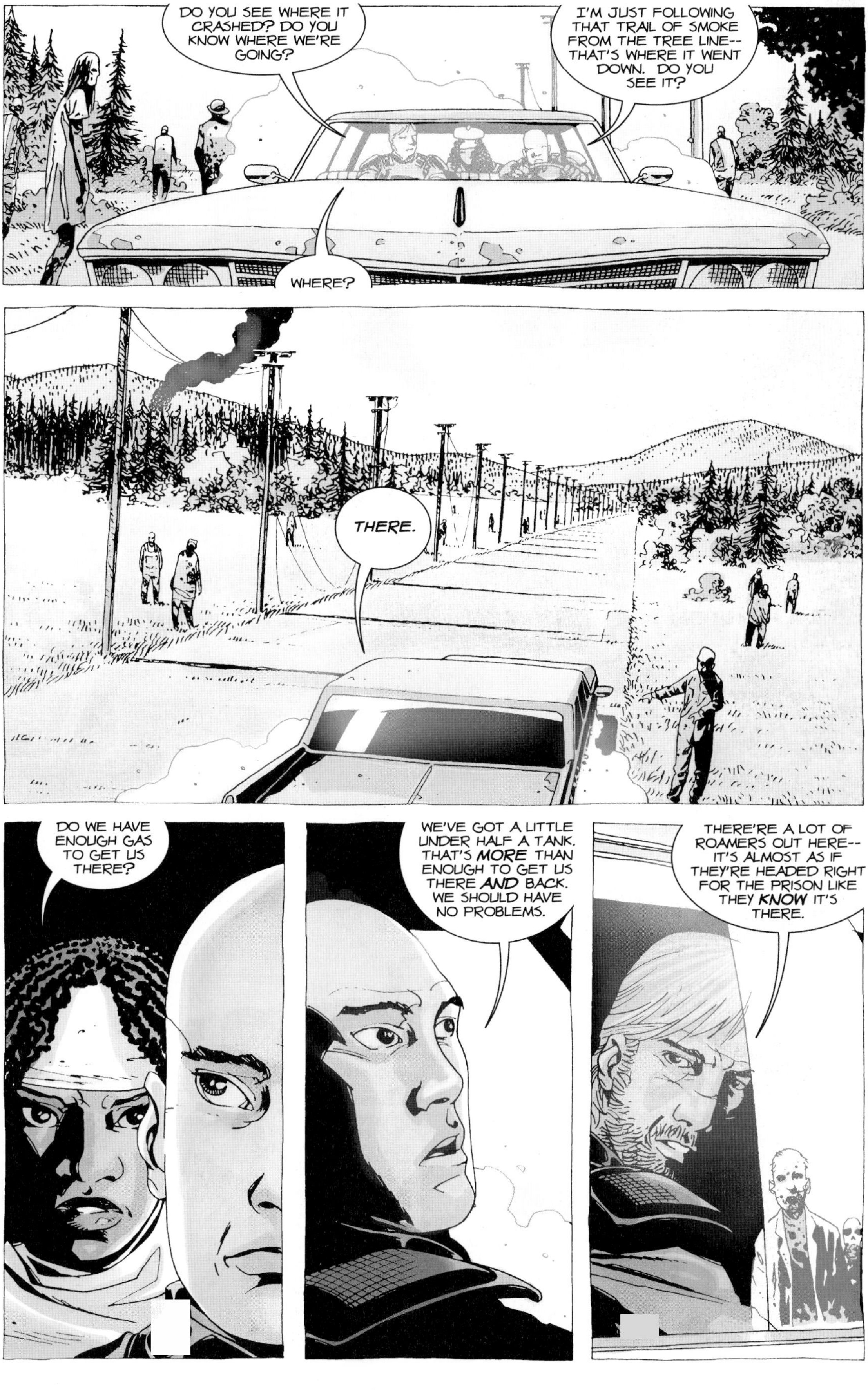
DO YOU SEE WHERE IT CRASHED? DO YOU KNOW WHERE WE'RE GOING?
I'M JUST FOLLOWING THAT TRAIL OF SMOKE FROM THE TREE LINE-- THAT'S WHERE IT WENT DOWN. DO YOU SEE IT?
WHERE?
THERE.
DO WE HAVE ENOUGH GAS TO GET US THERE?
WE'VE GOT A LITTLE UNDER HALF A TANK. THAT'S MORE THAN ENOUGH TO GET US THERE AND BACK. WE SHOULD HAVE NO PROBLEMS.
THERE'RE A LOT OF ROAMERS OUT HERE-- IT'S ALMOST AS IF THEY'RE HEADED RIGHT FOR THE PRISON LIKE THEY KNOW IT'S THERE.

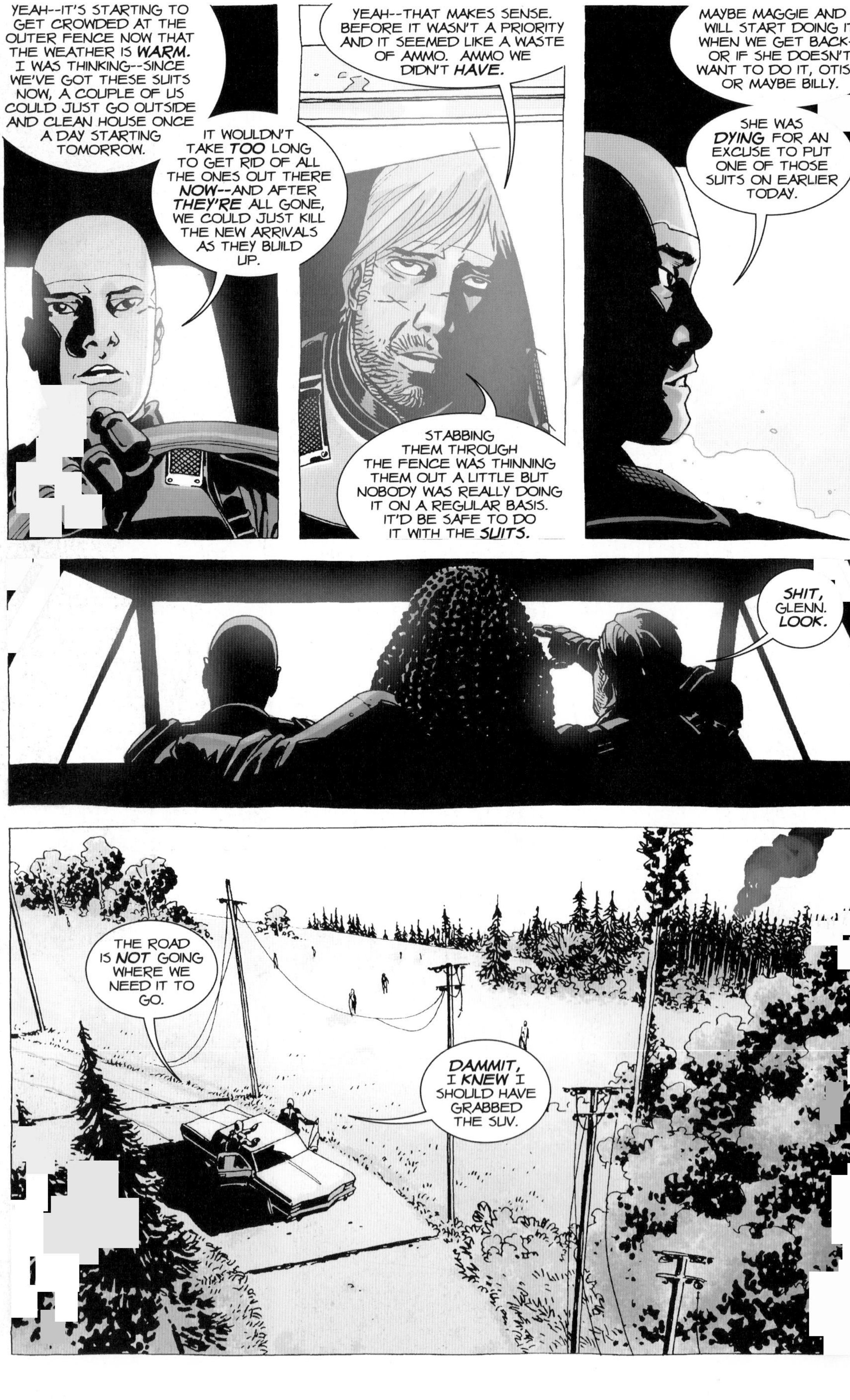

YEAH--IT'S STARTING TO GET CROWDED AT THE OUTER FENCE NOW THAT THE WEATHER IS WARM. I WAS THINKING--SINCE WE'VE GOT THESE SUITS NOW, A COUPLE OF US COULD JUST GO OUTSIDE AND CLEAN HOUSE ONCE A DAY STARTING TOMORROW.
IT WOULDN'T TAKE TOO LONG TO GET RID OF ALL THE ONES OUT THERE NOW--AND AFTER THEY'RE ALL GONE, WE COULD JUST KILL THE NEW ARRIVALS AS THEY BUILD UP.
YEAH--THAT MAKES SENSE. BEFORE IT WASN'T A PRIORITY AND IT SEEMED LIKE A WASTE OF AMMO. AMMO WE DIDN'T HAVE.
STABBING THEM THROUGH THE FENCE WAS THINNING THEM OUT A LITTLE BUT NOBODY WAS REALLY DOING IT ON A REGULAR BASIS. IT'D BE SAFE TO DO IT WITH THE SUITS.
MAYBE MAGGIE AND I WILL START DOING IT WHEN WE GET BACK--OR IF SHE DOESN'T WANT TO DO IT, OTIS--OR MAYBE BILLY.
SHE WAS DYING FOR AN EXCUSE TO PUT ONE OF THOSE SUITS ON EARLIER TODAY.
SHIT, GLENN. LOOK.
THE ROAD IS NOT GOING WHERE WE NEED IT TO GO.
DAMMIT, I KNEW I SHOULD HAVE GRABBED THE SUV.

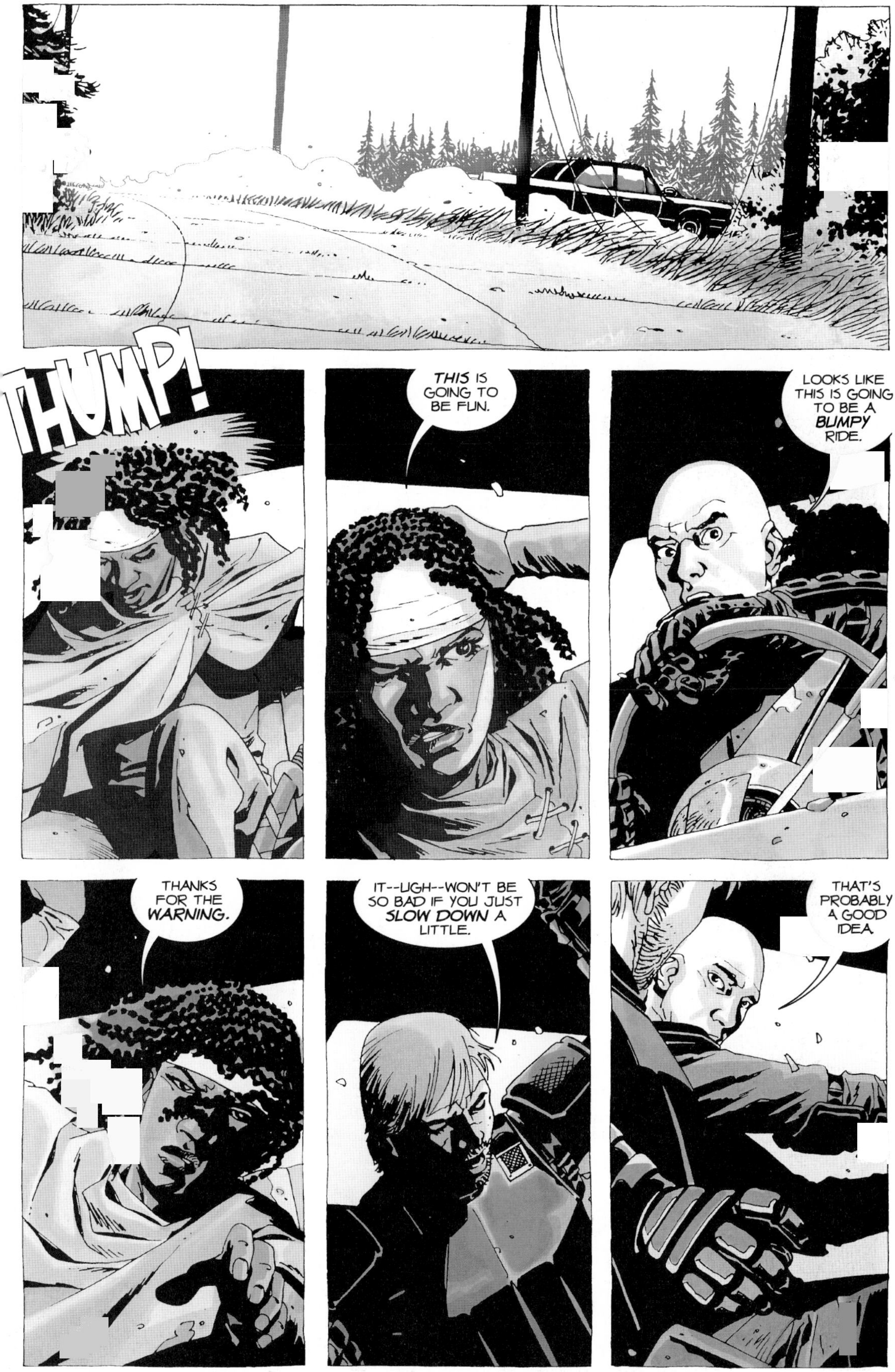
THUMP!
THIS IS GOING TO BE FUN.
LOOKS LIKE THIS IS GOING TO BE A BUMPY RIDE.
THANKS FOR THE WARNING.
IT--UGH--WON'T BE SO BAD IF YOU JUST SLOW DOWN A LITTLE.
THAT'S PROBABLY A GOOD IDEA.

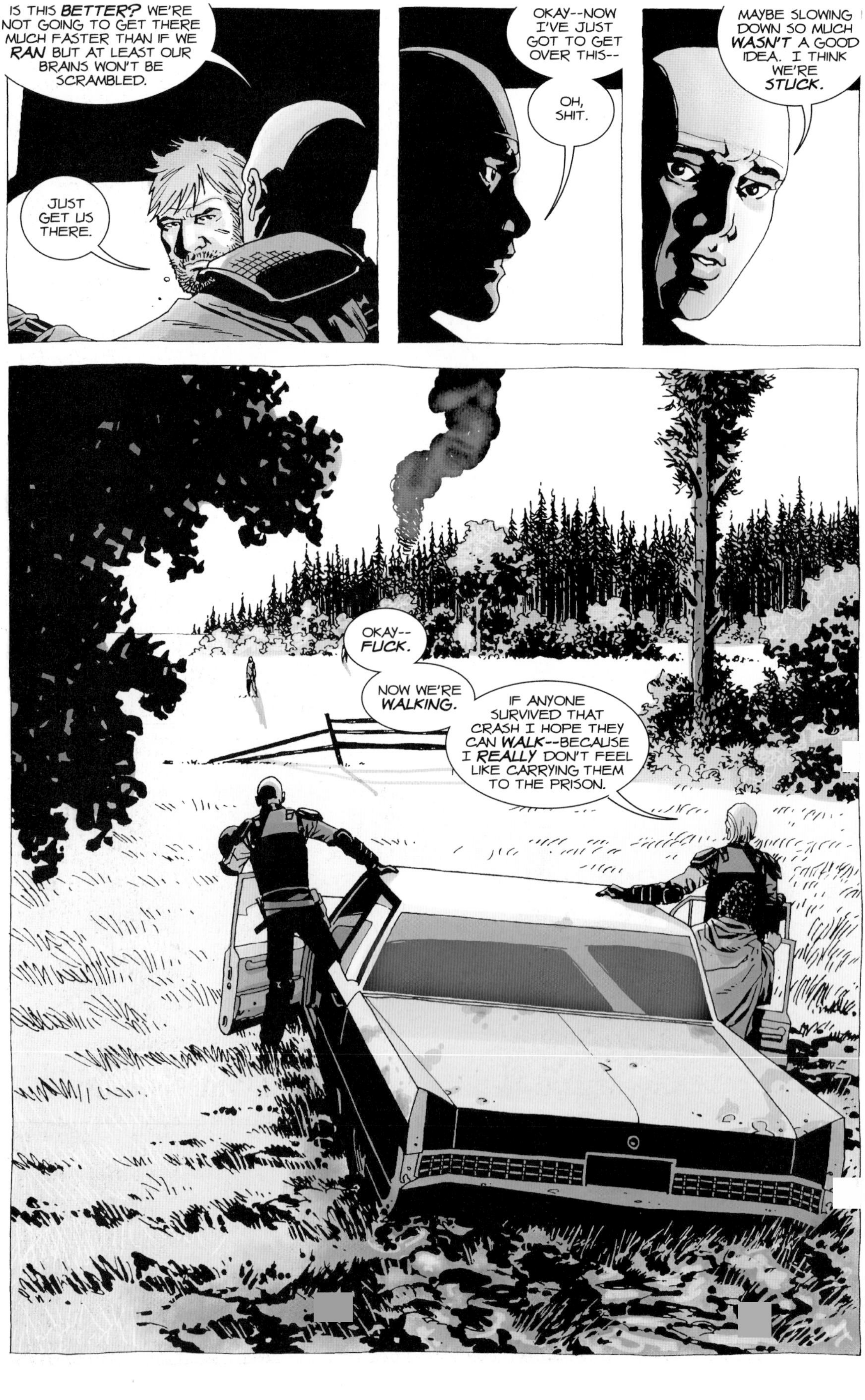
IS THIS BETTER? WE'RE NOT GOING TO GET THERE MUCH FASTER THAN IF WE RAN BUT AT LEAST OUR BRAINS WON'T BE SCRAMBLED.
JUST GET US THERE.
OKAY--NOW I'VE JUST GOT TO GET OVER THIS--
OH, SHIT.
MAYBE SLOWING DOWN SO MUCH WASN'T A GOOD IDEA. I THINK WE'RE STUCK.
OKAY-- FUCK.
NOW WE'RE WALKING.
IF ANYONE SURVIVED THAT CRASH I HOPE THEY CAN WALK--BECAUSE I REALLY DON'T FEEL LIKE CARRYING THEM TO THE PRISON.

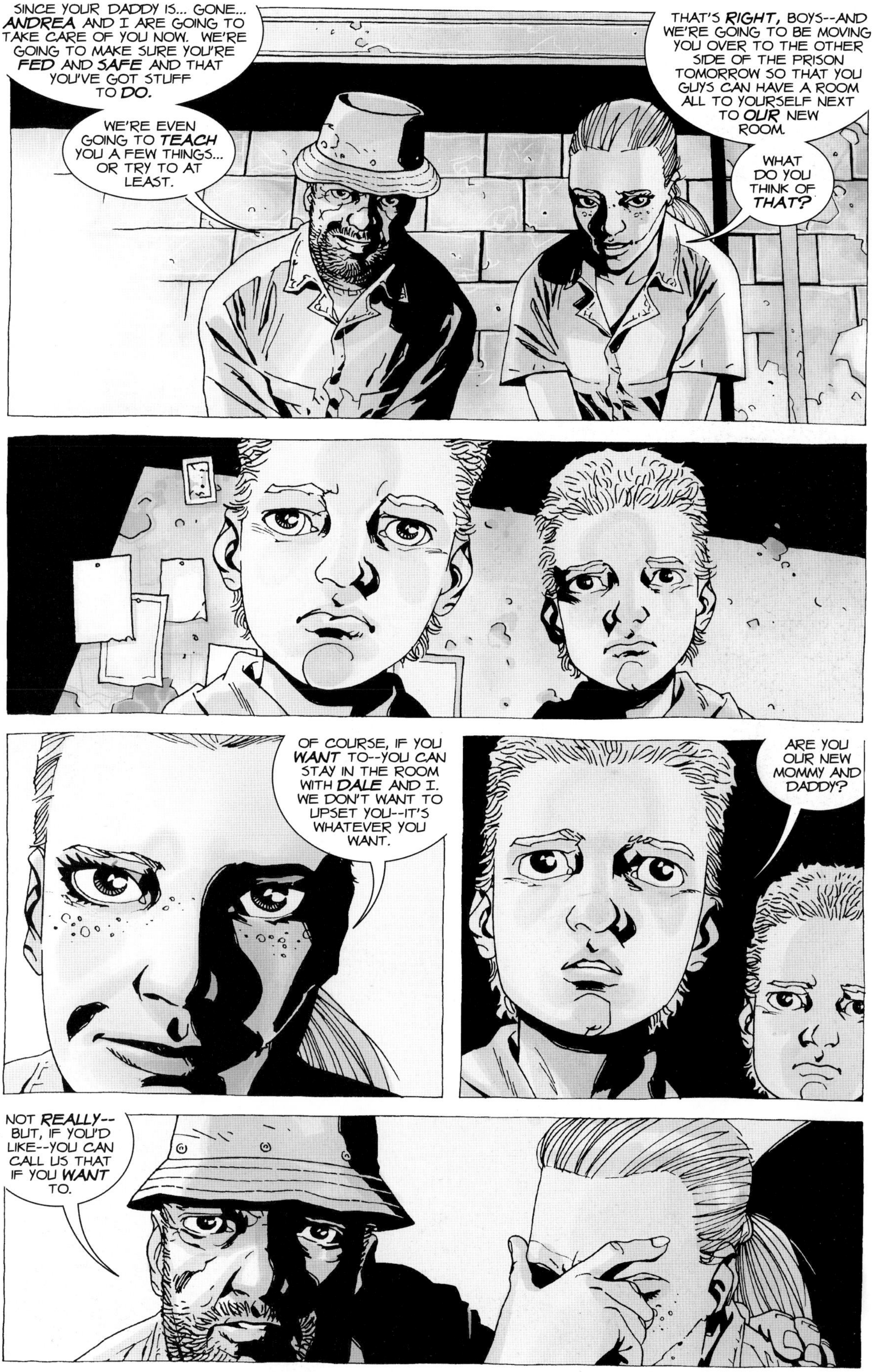
SINCE YOUR DADDY IS... GONE... ANDREA AND I ARE GOING TO TAKE CARE OF YOU NOW. WE'RE GOING TO MAKE SURE YOU'RE FED AND SAFE AND THAT YOU'VE GOT STUFF TO DO.
WE'RE EVEN GOING TO TEACH YOU A FEW THINGS... OR TRY TO AT LEAST.
THAT'S RIGHT, BOYS--AND WE'RE GOING TO BE MOVING YOU OVER TO THE OTHER SIDE OF THE PRISON TOMORROW SO THAT YOU GUYS CAN HAVE A ROOM ALL TO YOURSELF NEXT TO OUR NEW ROOM.
WHAT DO YOU THINK OF THAT?
OF COURSE, IF YOU WANT TO--YOU CAN STAY IN THE ROOM WITH DALE AND I. WE DON'T WANT TO UPSET YOU--IT'S WHATEVER YOU WANT.
ARE YOU OUR NEW MOMMY AND DADDY?
NOT REALLY-- BUT, IF YOU'D LIKE--YOU CAN CALL US THAT IF YOU WANT TO.

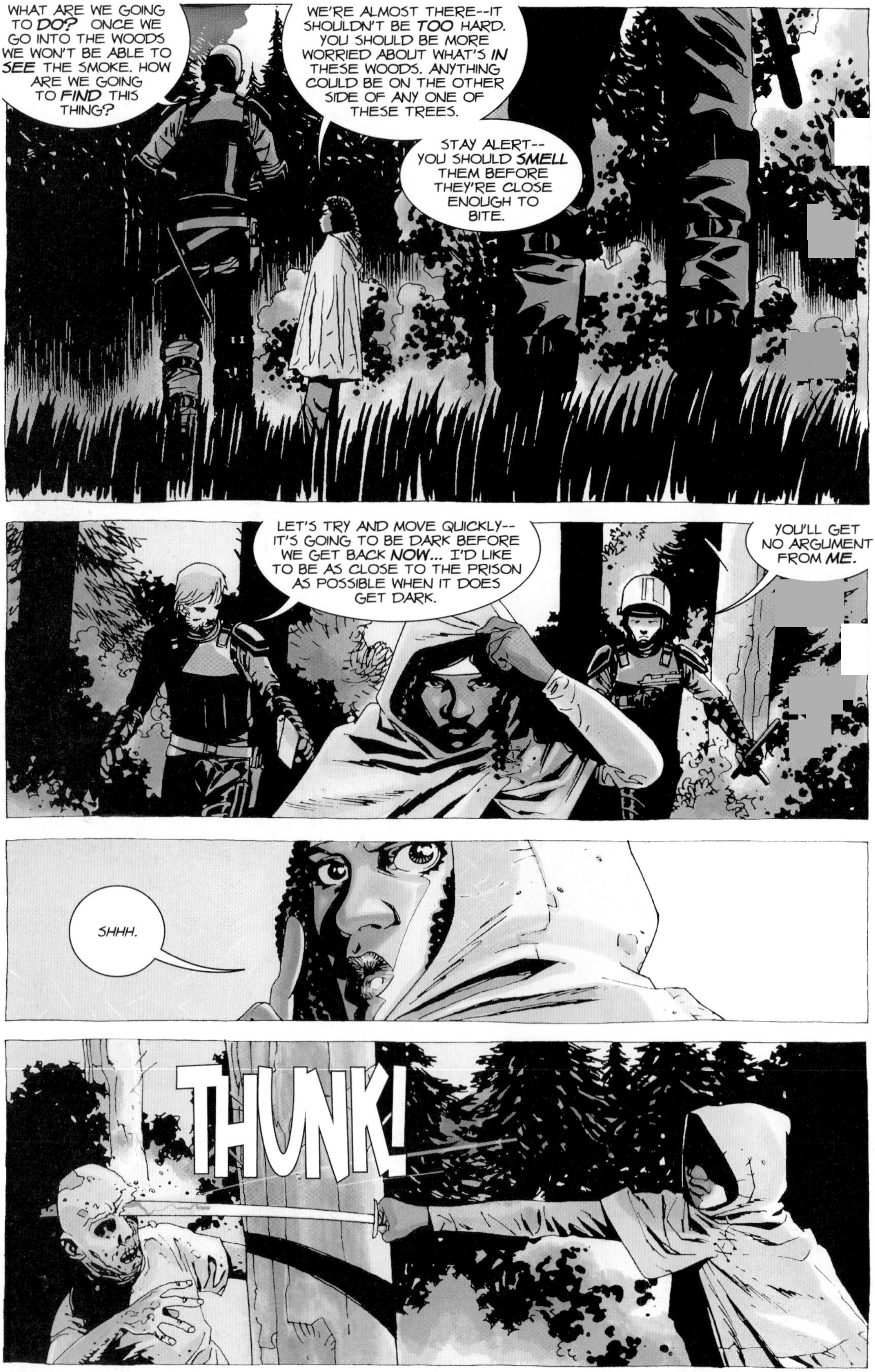
WHAT ARE WE GOING TO DO? ONCE WE GO INTO THE WOODS WE WON'T BE ABLE TO SEE THE SMOKE. HOW ARE WE GOING TO FIND THIS THING?
WE'RE ALMOST THERE--IT SHOULDN'T BE TOO HARD. YOU SHOULD BE MORE WORRIED ABOUT WHAT'S IN THESE WOODS. ANYTHING COULD BE ON THE OTHER SIDE OF ANY ONE OF THESE TREES.
STAY ALERT-- YOU SHOULD SMELL THEM BEFORE THEY'RE CLOSE ENOUGH TO BITE.
LET'S TRY AND MOVE QUICKLY-- IT'S GOING TO BE DARK BEFORE WE GET BACK NOW... I'D LIKE TO BE AS CLOSE TO THE PRISON AS POSSIBLE WHEN IT DOES GET DARK.
YOU'LL GET NO ARGUMENT FROM ME.
SHHH.
THUNK!

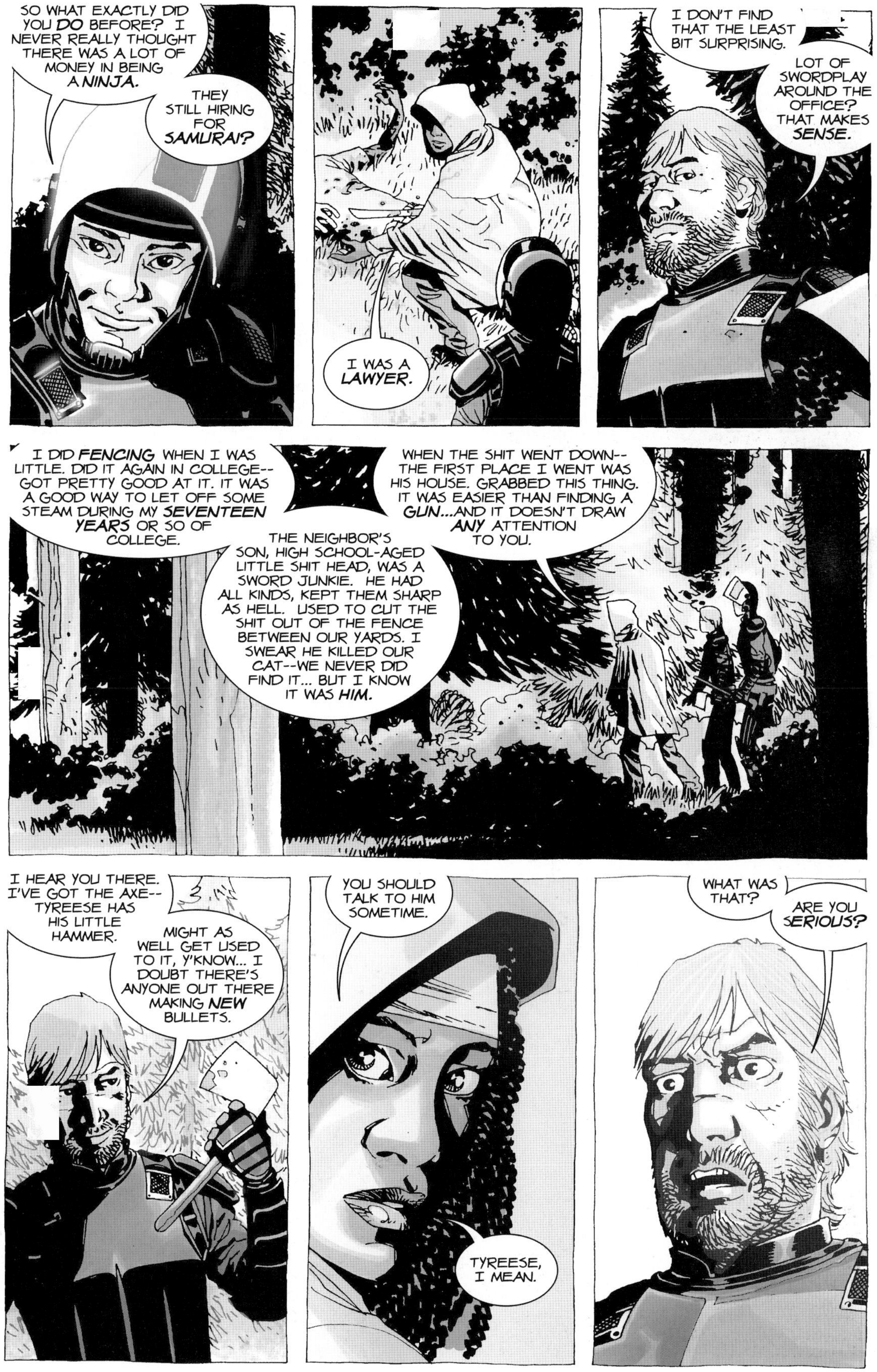

SO WHAT EXACTLY DID YOU DO BEFORE? I NEVER REALLY THOUGHT THERE WAS A LOT OF MONEY IN BEING A NINJA.
THEY STILL HIRING FOR SAMURAI?
I WAS A LAWYER.
I DON'T FIND THAT THE LEAST BIT SURPRISING.
LOT OF SWORDPLAY AROUND THE OFFICE? THAT MAKES SENSE.
I DID FENCING WHEN I WAS LITTLE. DID IT AGAIN IN COLLEGE-- GOT PRETTY GOOD AT IT. IT WAS A GOOD WAY TO LET OFF SOME STEAM DURING MY SEVENTEEN YEARS OR SO OF COLLEGE.
THE NEIGHBOR'S SON, HIGH SCHOOL-AGED LITTLE SHIT HEAD, WAS A SWORD JUNKIE. HE HAD ALL KINDS, KEPT THEM SHARP AS HELL. USED TO CUT THE SHIT OUT OF THE FENCE BETWEEN OUR YARDS. I SWEAR HE KILLED OUR CAT--WE NEVER DID FIND IT... BUT I KNOW IT WAS HIM.
WHEN THE SHIT WENT DOWN-- THE FIRST PLACE I WENT WAS HIS HOUSE. GRABBED THIS THING. IT WAS EASIER THAN FINDING A GUN...AND IT DOESN'T DRAW ANY ATTENTION TO YOU.
I HEAR YOU THERE. I'VE GOT THE AXE-- TYREESE HAS HIS LITTLE HAMMER.
MIGHT AS WELL GET USED TO IT, Y'KNOW... I DOUBT THERE'S ANYONE OUT THERE MAKING NEW BULLETS.
YOU SHOULD TALK TO HIM SOMETIME.
TYREESE, I MEAN.
WHAT WAS THAT?
ARE YOU SERIOUS?

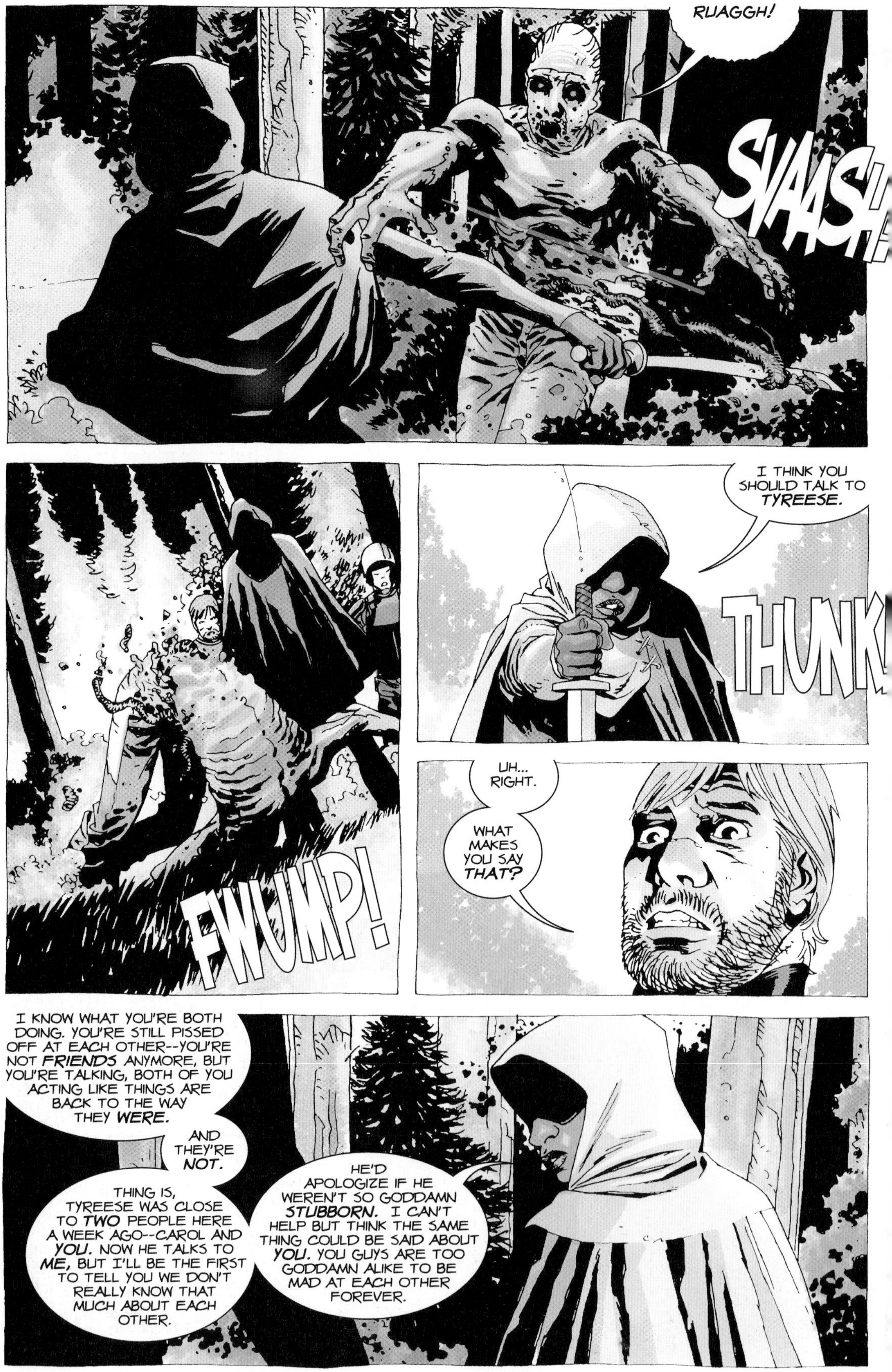
RUAGGH!
SVAASH!
FWUMP!
I THINK YOU SHOULD TALK TO TYREESE.
THUNK!
UH... RIGHT.
WHAT MAKES YOU SAY THAT?
I KNOW WHAT YOU'RE BOTH DOING. YOU'RE STILL PISSED OFF AT EACH OTHER--YOU'RE NOT FRIENDS ANYMORE, BUT YOU'RE TALKING, BOTH OF YOU ACTING LIKE THINGS ARE BACK TO THE WAY THEY WERE.
AND THEY'RE NOT.
THING IS, TYREESE WAS CLOSE TO TWO PEOPLE HERE A WEEK AGO--CAROL AND YOU. NOW HE TALKS TO ME, BUT I'LL BE THE FIRST TO TELL YOU WE DON'T REALLY KNOW THAT MUCH ABOUT EACH OTHER.
HE'D APOLOGIZE IF HE WEREN'T SO GODDAMN STUBBORN. I CAN'T HELP BUT THINK THE SAME THING COULD BE SAID ABOUT YOU. YOU GUYS ARE TOO GODDAMN ALIKE TO BE MAD AT EACH OTHER FOREVER.

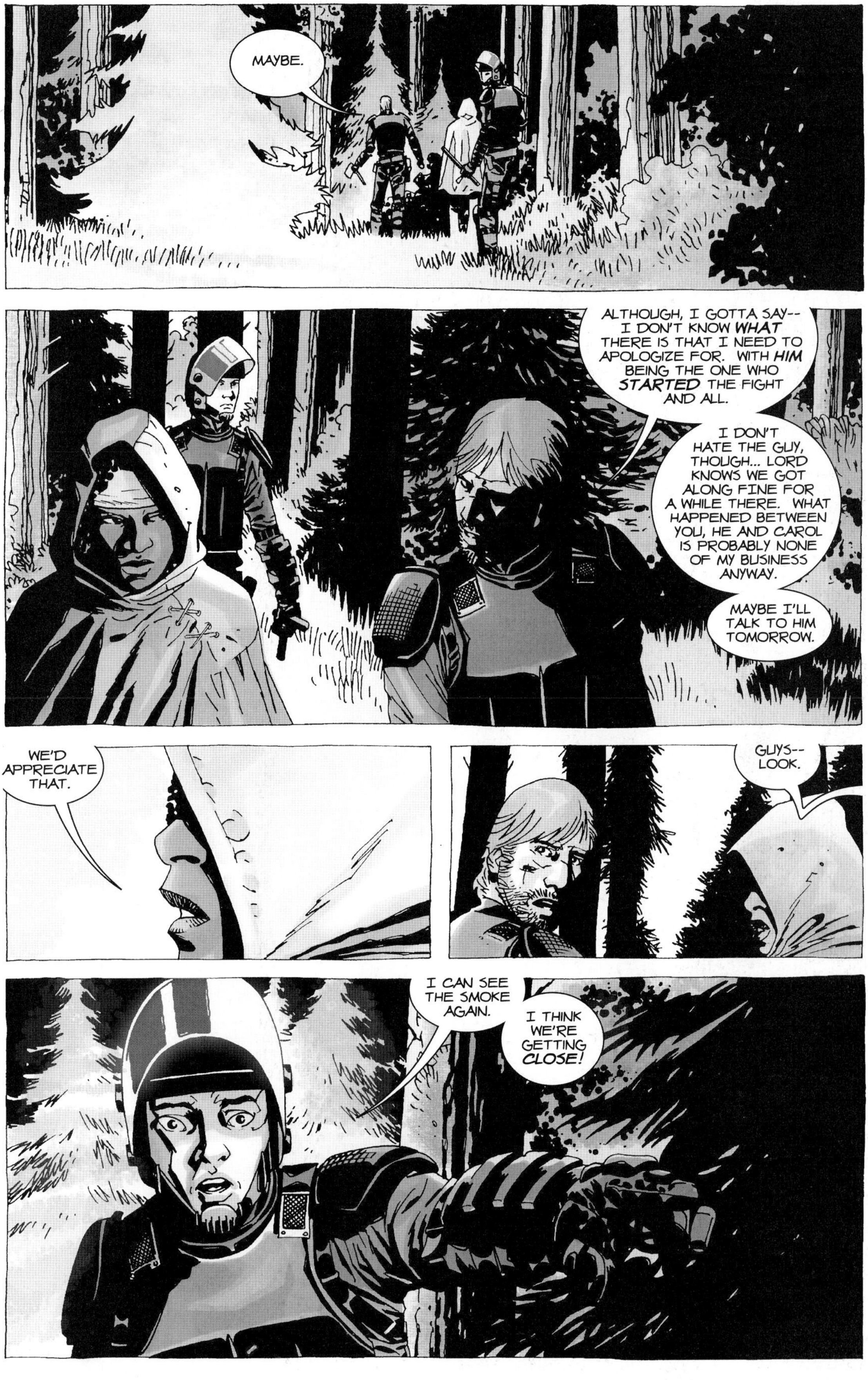
MAYBE.
ALTHOUGH, I GOTTA SAY-- I DON'T KNOW WHAT THERE IS THAT I NEED TO APOLOGIZE FOR. WITH HIM BEING THE ONE WHO STARTED THE FIGHT AND ALL.
I DON'T HATE THE GUY, THOUGH... LORD KNOWS WE GOT ALONG FINE FOR A WHILE THERE. WHAT HAPPENED BETWEEN YOU, HE AND CAROL IS PROBABLY NONE OF MY BUSINESS ANYWAY.
MAYBE I'LL TALK TO HIM TOMORROW.
WE'D APPRECIATE THAT.
GUYS-- LOOK.
I CAN SEE THE SMOKE AGAIN.
I THINK WE'RE GETTING CLOSE!

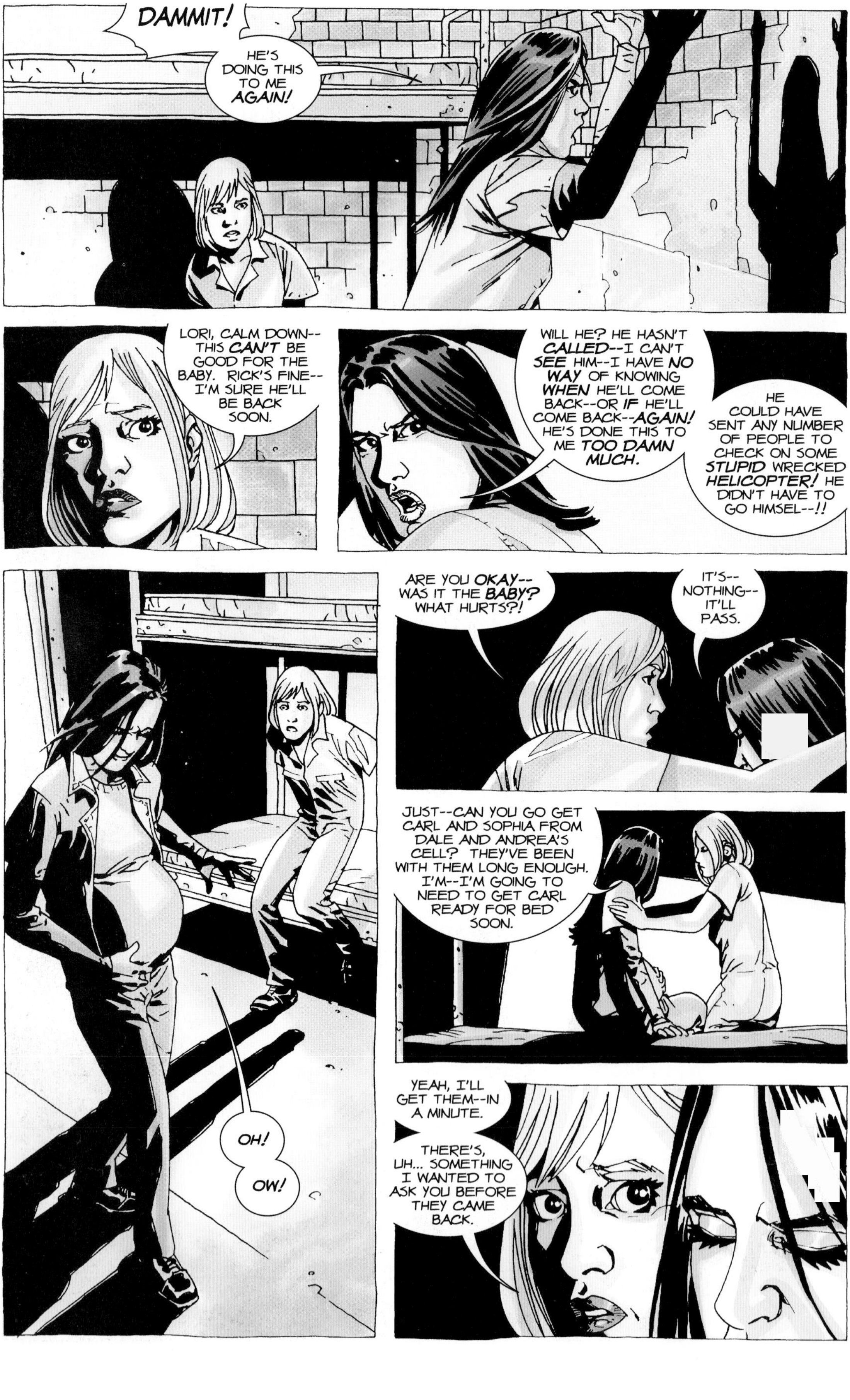
DAMMIT!
HE'S DOING THIS TO ME AGAIN!
LORI, CALM DOWN-- THIS CAN'T BE GOOD FOR THE BABY. RICK'S FINE-- I'M SURE HE'LL BE BACK SOON.
WILL HE? HE HASN'T CALLED--I CAN'T SEE HIM--I HAVE NO WAY OF KNOWING WHEN HE'LL COME BACK--OR IF HE'LL COME BACK--AGAIN! HE'S DONE THIS TO ME TOO DAMN MUCH.
HE COULD HAVE SENT ANY NUMBER OF PEOPLE TO CHECK ON SOME STUPID WRECKED HELICOPTER! HE DIDN'T HAVE TO GO HIMSEL--!!
OH!
OW!
ARE YOU OKAY-- WAS IT THE BABY? WHAT HURTS?!
IT'S-- NOTHING-- IT'LL PASS.
JUST--CAN YOU GO GET CARL AND SOPHIA FROM DALE AND ANDREA'S CELL? THEY'VE BEEN WITH THEM LONG ENOUGH. I'M--I'M GOING TO NEED TO GET CARL READY FOR BED SOON.
YEAH, I'LL GET THEM--IN A MINUTE.
THERE'S, UH... SOMETHING I WANTED TO ASK YOU BEFORE THEY CAME BACK.

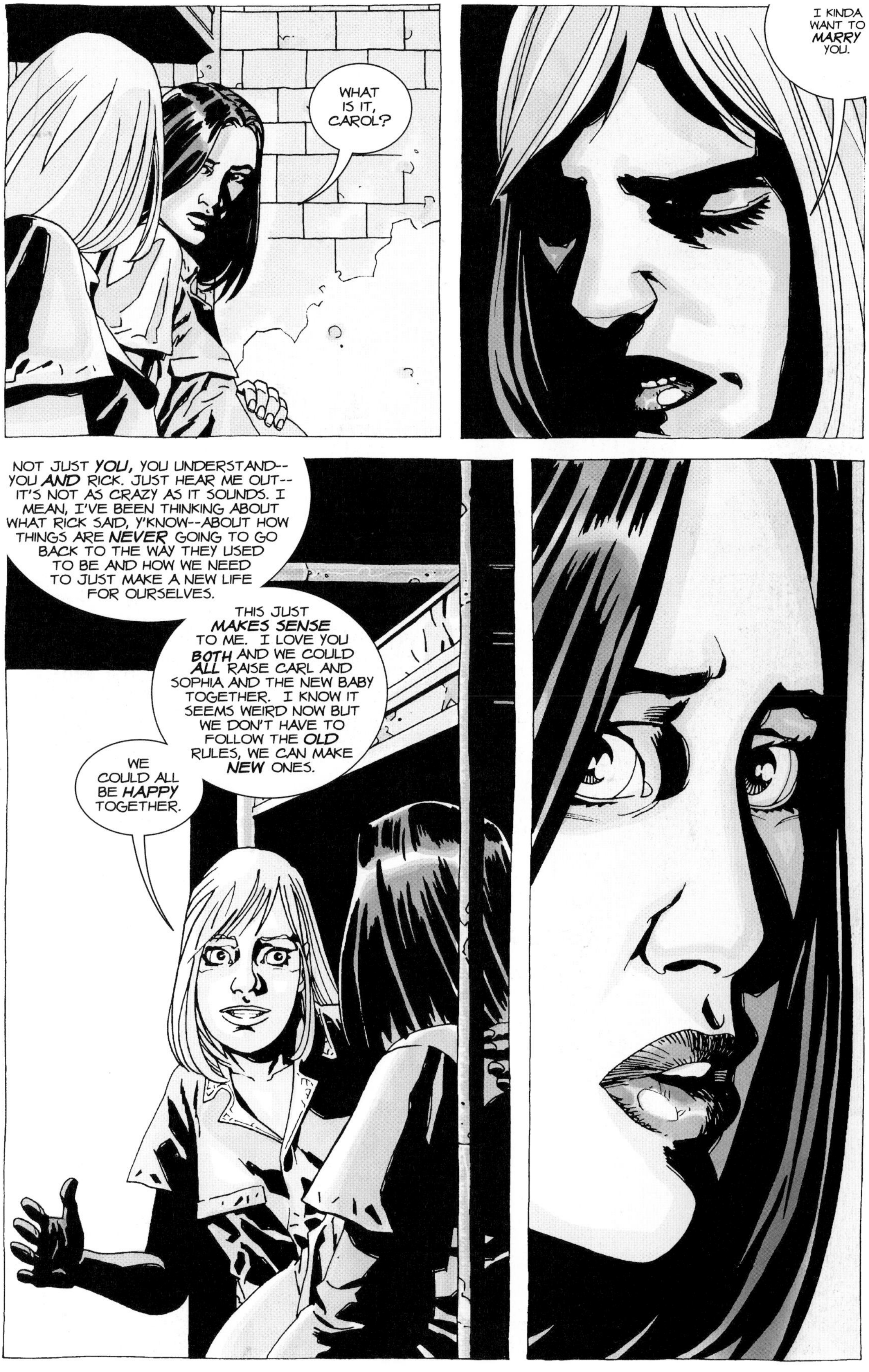
WHAT IS IT, CAROL?
I KINDA WANT TO MARRY YOU.
NOT JUST YOU, YOU UNDERSTAND-- YOU AND RICK. JUST HEAR ME OUT-- IT'S NOT AS CRAZY AS IT SOUNDS. I MEAN, I'VE BEEN THINKING ABOUT WHAT RICK SAID, Y'KNOW--ABOUT HOW THINGS ARE NEVER GOING TO GO BACK TO THE WAY THEY USED TO BE AND HOW WE NEED TO JUST MAKE A NEW LIFE FOR OURSELVES.
THIS JUST MAKES SENSE TO ME. I LOVE YOU BOTH AND WE COULD ALL RAISE CARL AND SOPHIA AND THE NEW BABY TOGETHER. I KNOW IT SEEMS WEIRD NOW BUT WE DON'T HAVE TO FOLLOW THE OLD RULES, WE CAN MAKE NEW ONES.
WE COULD ALL BE HAPPY TOGETHER.

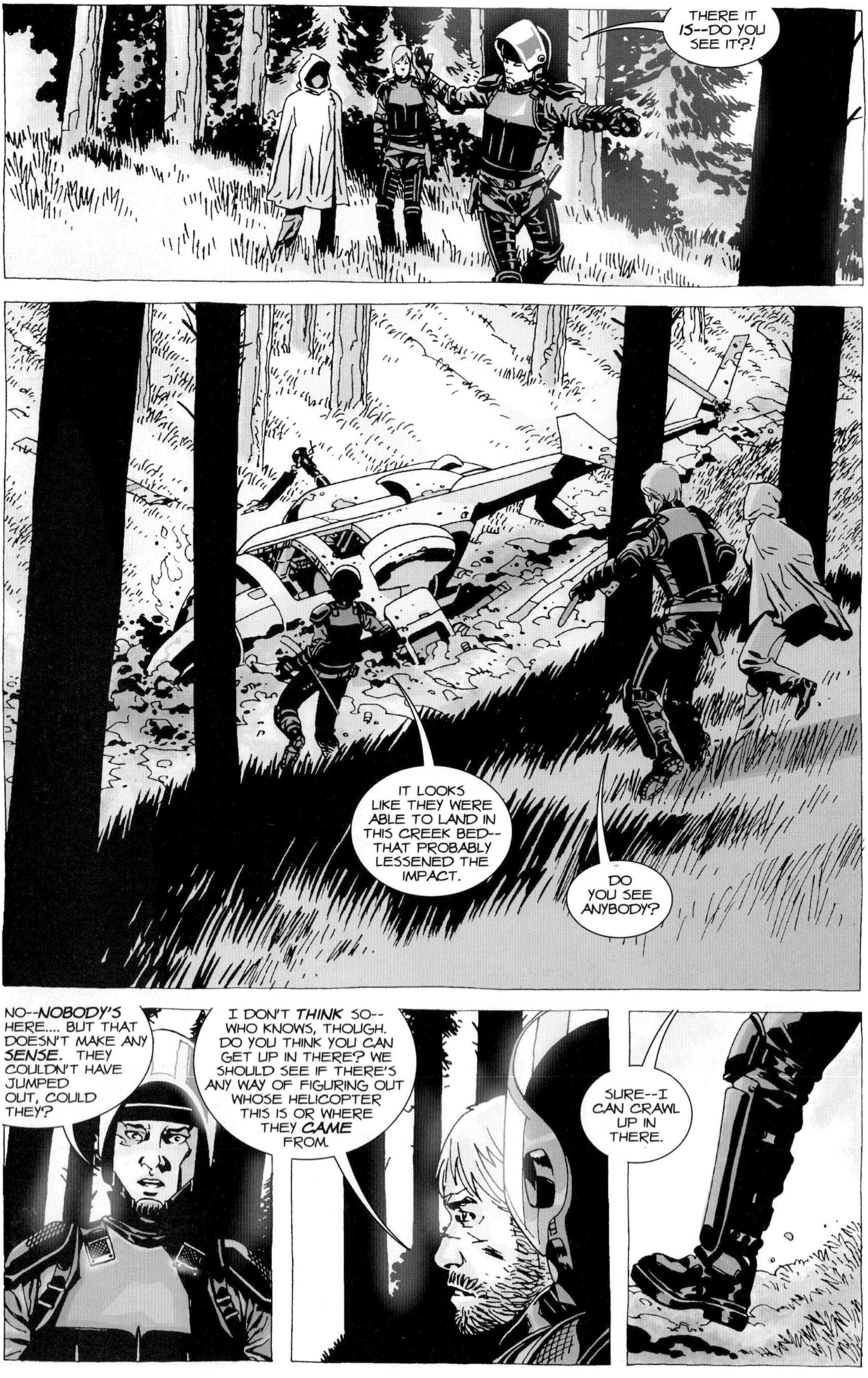
THERE IT IS--DO YOU SEE IT?!
IT LOOKS LIKE THEY WERE ABLE TO LAND IN THIS CREEK BED--THAT PROBABLY LESSENED THE IMPACT.
DO YOU SEE ANYBODY?
NO--NOBODY'S HERE.... BUT THAT DOESN'T MAKE ANY SENSE. THEY COULDN'T HAVE JUMPED OUT, COULD THEY?
I DON'T THINK SO--WHO KNOWS, THOUGH. DO YOU THINK YOU CAN GET UP IN THERE? WE SHOULD SEE IF THERE'S ANY WAY OF FIGURING OUT WHOSE HELICOPTER THIS IS OR WHERE THEY CAME FROM.
SURE--I CAN CRAWL UP IN THERE.

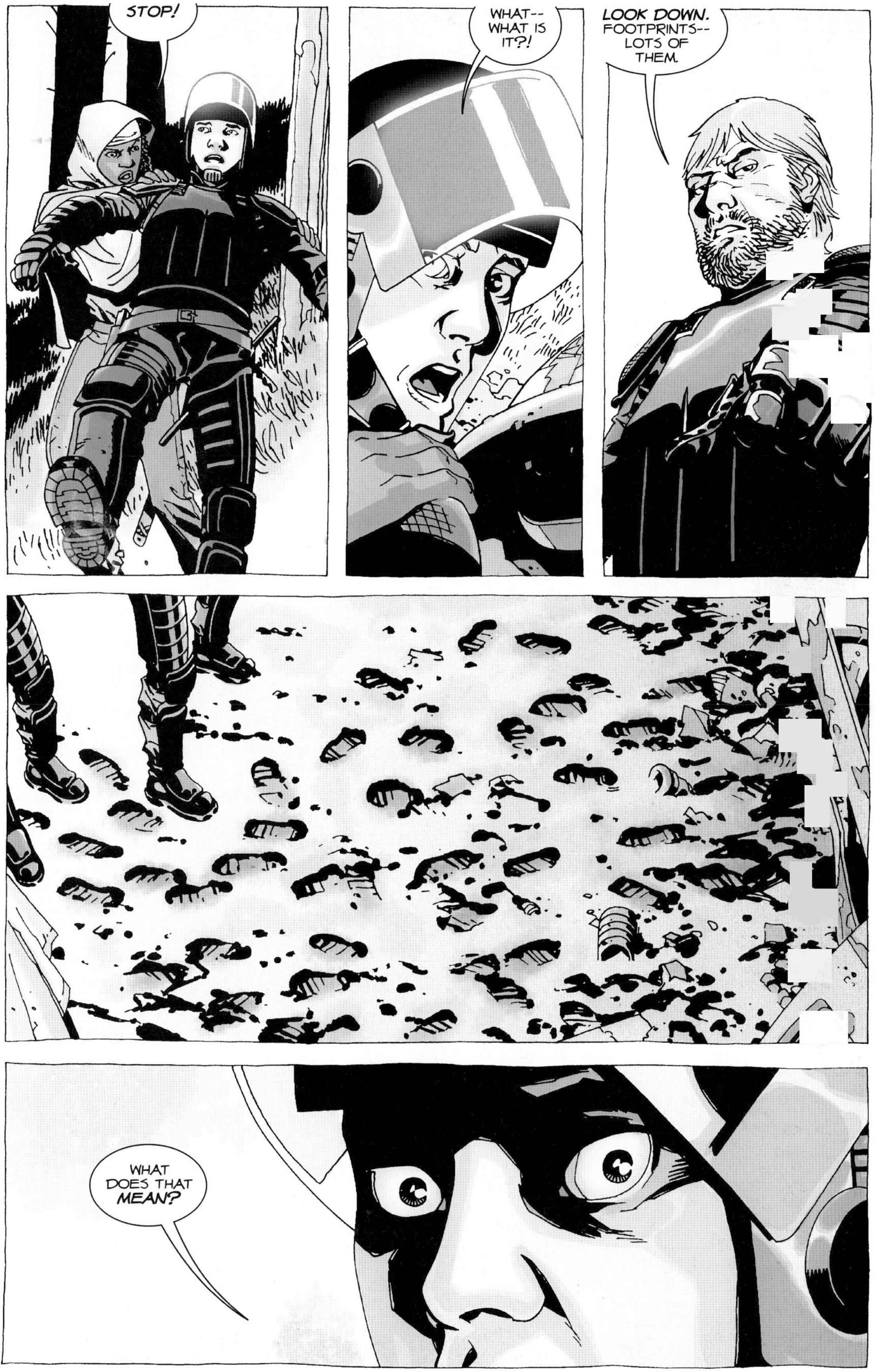
STOP!
WHAT-- WHAT IS IT?!
LOOK DOWN. FOOTPRINTS-- LOTS OF THEM.
WHAT DOES THAT MEAN?

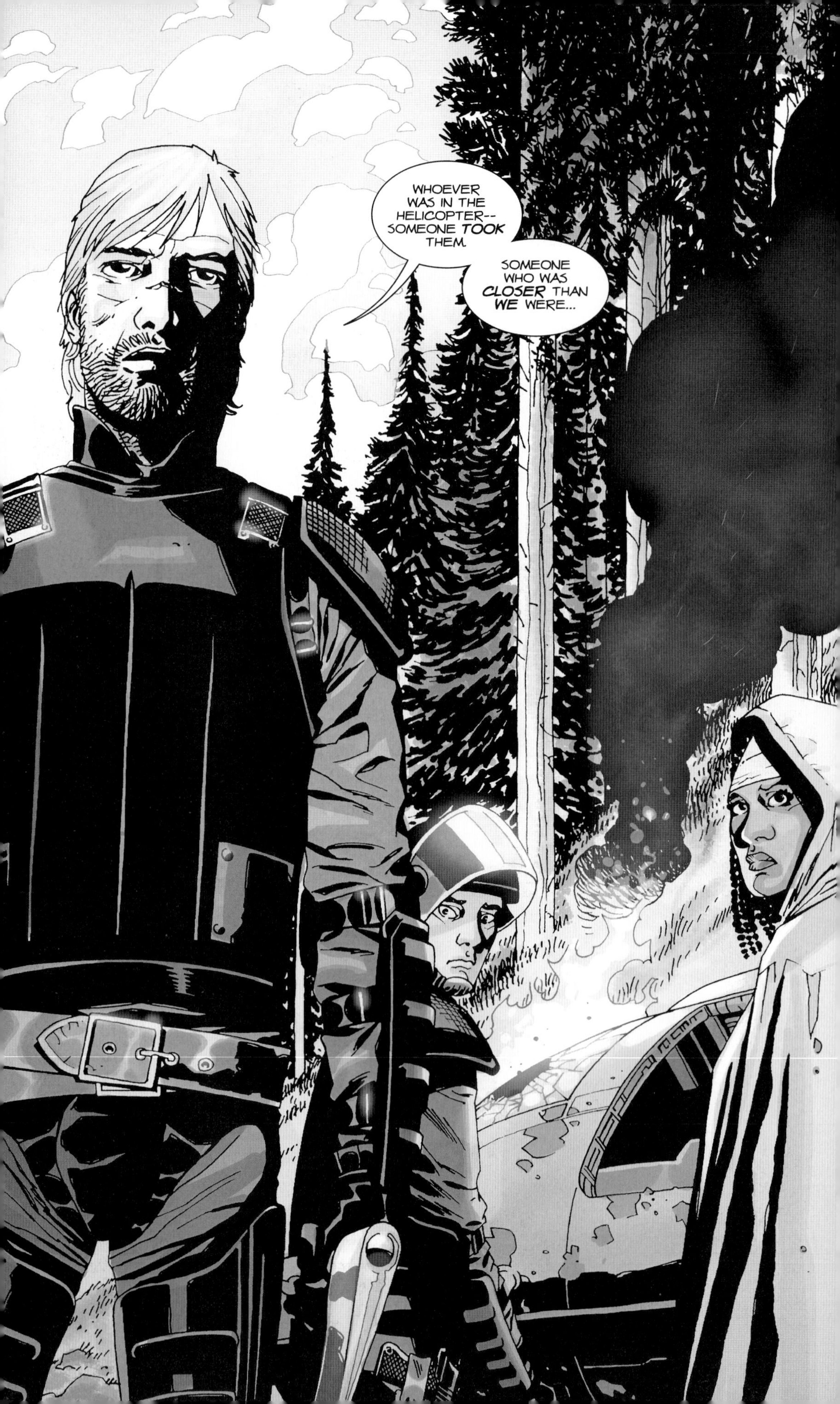
WHOEVER WAS IN THE HELICOPTER-- SOMEONE TOOK THEM.
SOMEONE WHO WAS CLOSER THAN WE WERE...

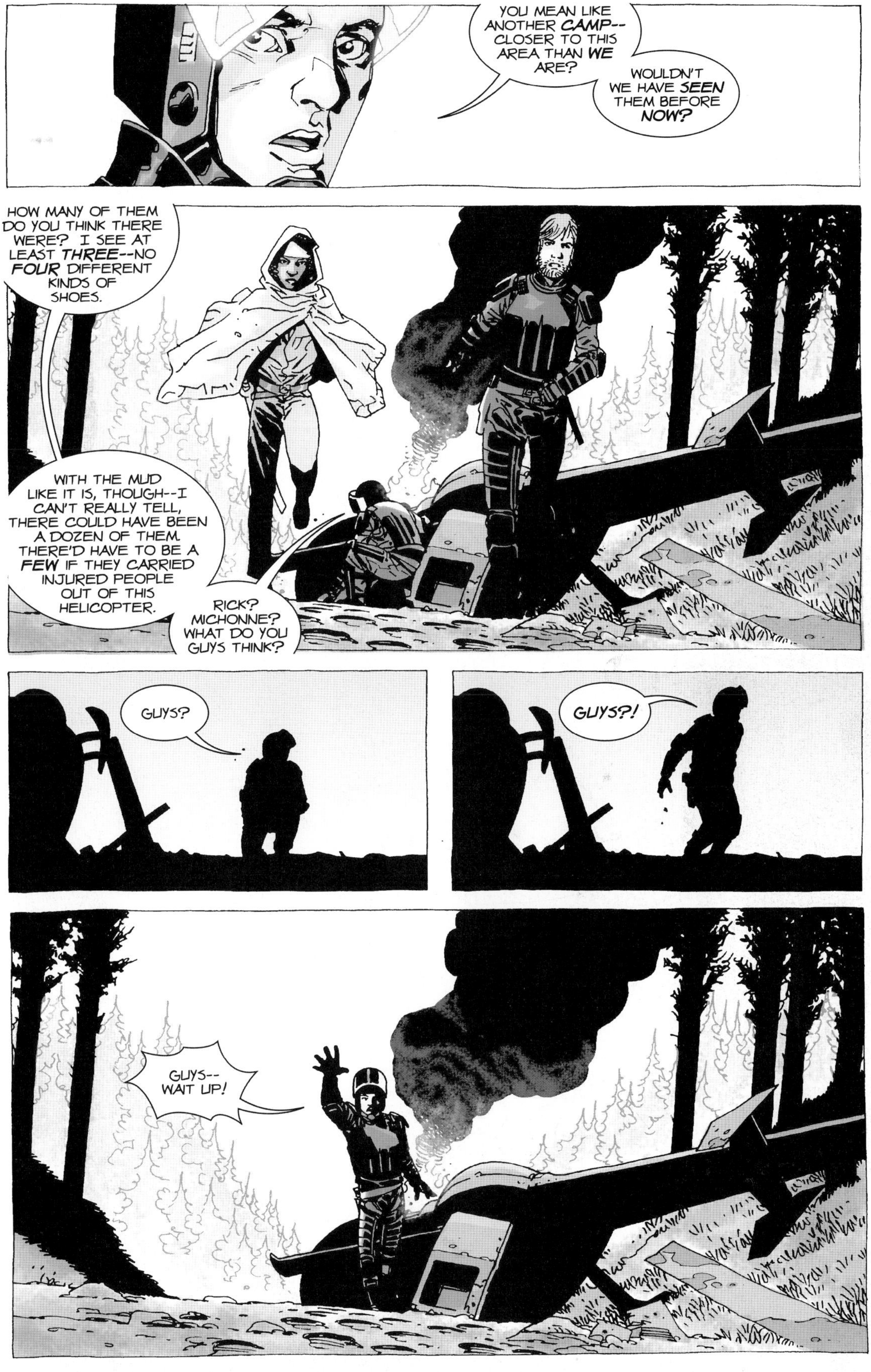

YOU MEAN LIKE ANOTHER CAMP-- CLOSER TO THIS AREA THAN WE ARE?
WOULDN'T WE HAVE SEEN THEM BEFORE NOW?
HOW MANY OF THEM DO YOU THINK THERE WERE? I SEE AT LEAST THREE--NO FOUR DIFFERENT KINDS OF SHOES.
WITH THE MUD LIKE IT IS, THOUGH--I CAN'T REALLY TELL, THERE COULD HAVE BEEN A DOZEN OF THEM. THERE'D HAVE TO BE A FEW IF THEY CARRIED INJURED PEOPLE OUT OF THIS HELICOPTER.
RICK? MICHONNE? WHAT DO YOU GUYS THINK?
GUYS?
GUYS?!
GUYS-- WAIT UP!

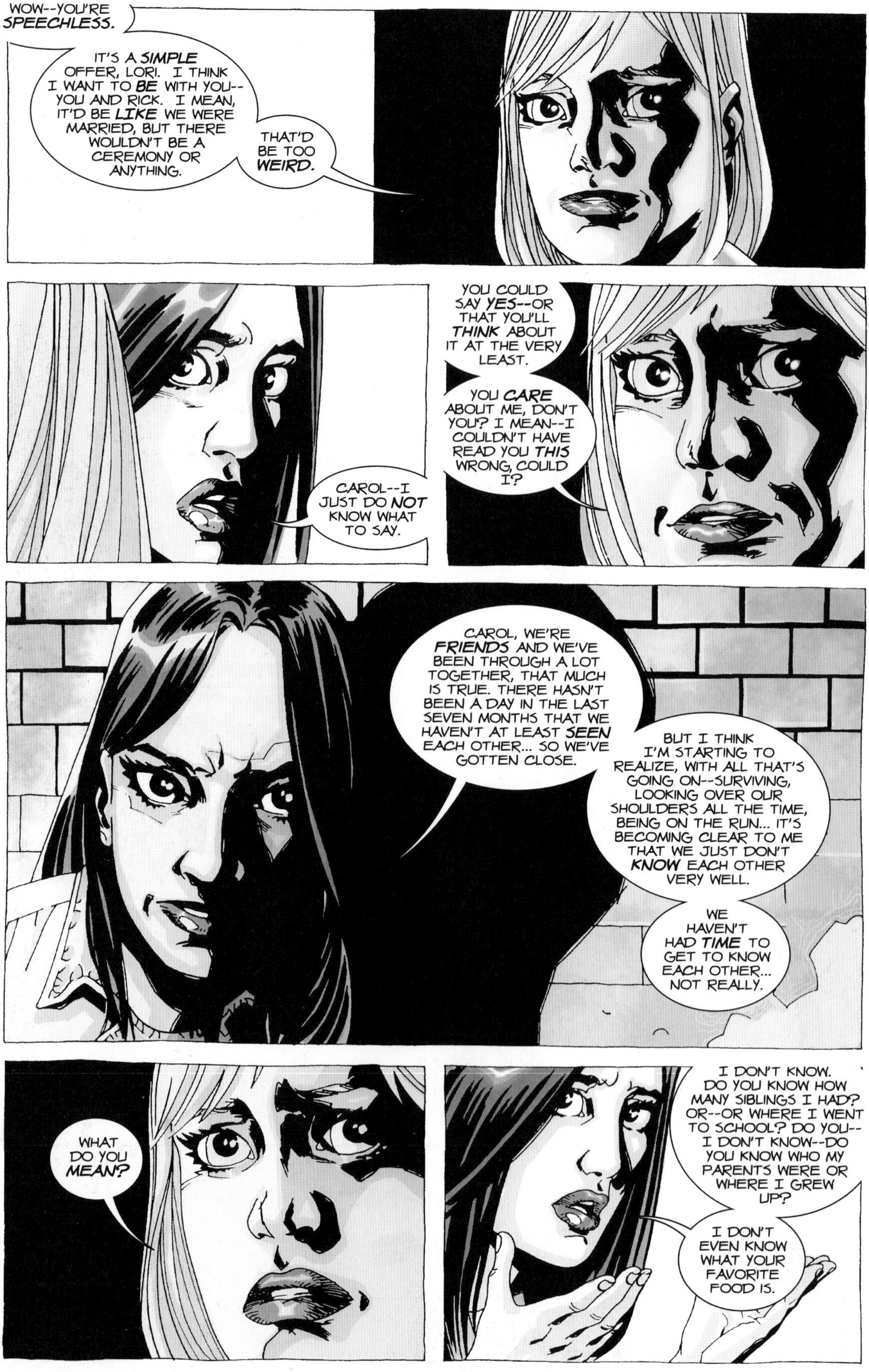
WOW--YOU'RE SPEECHLESS.
IT'S A SIMPLE OFFER, LORI. I THINK I WANT TO BE WITH YOU-- YOU AND RICK. I MEAN, IT'D BE LIKE WE WERE MARRIED, BUT THERE WOULDN'T BE A CEREMONY OR ANYTHING.
THAT'D BE TOO WEIRD.
CAROL--I JUST DO NOT KNOW WHAT TO SAY.
YOU COULD SAY YES--OR THAT YOU'LL THINK ABOUT IT AT THE VERY LEAST.
YOU CARE ABOUT ME, DON'T YOU? I MEAN--I COULDN'T HAVE READ YOU THIS WRONG, COULD I?
CAROL, WE'RE FRIENDS AND WE'VE BEEN THROUGH A LOT TOGETHER, THAT MUCH IS TRUE. THERE HASN'T BEEN A DAY IN THE LAST SEVEN MONTHS THAT WE HAVEN'T AT LEAST SEEN EACH OTHER... SO WE'VE GOTTEN CLOSE.
BUT I THINK I'M STARTING TO REALIZE, WITH ALL THAT'S GOING ON--SURVIVING, LOOKING OVER OUR SHOULDERS ALL THE TIME, BEING ON THE RUN... IT'S BECOMING CLEAR TO ME THAT WE JUST DON'T KNOW EACH OTHER VERY WELL.
WE HAVEN'T HAD TIME TO GET TO KNOW EACH OTHER... NOT REALLY.
WHAT DO YOU MEAN?
I DON'T KNOW. DO YOU KNOW HOW MANY SIBLINGS I HAD? OR--OR WHERE I WENT TO SCHOOL? DO YOU-- I DON'T KNOW--DO YOU KNOW WHO MY PARENTS WERE OR WHERE I GREW UP?
I DON'T EVEN KNOW WHAT YOUR FAVORITE FOOD IS.

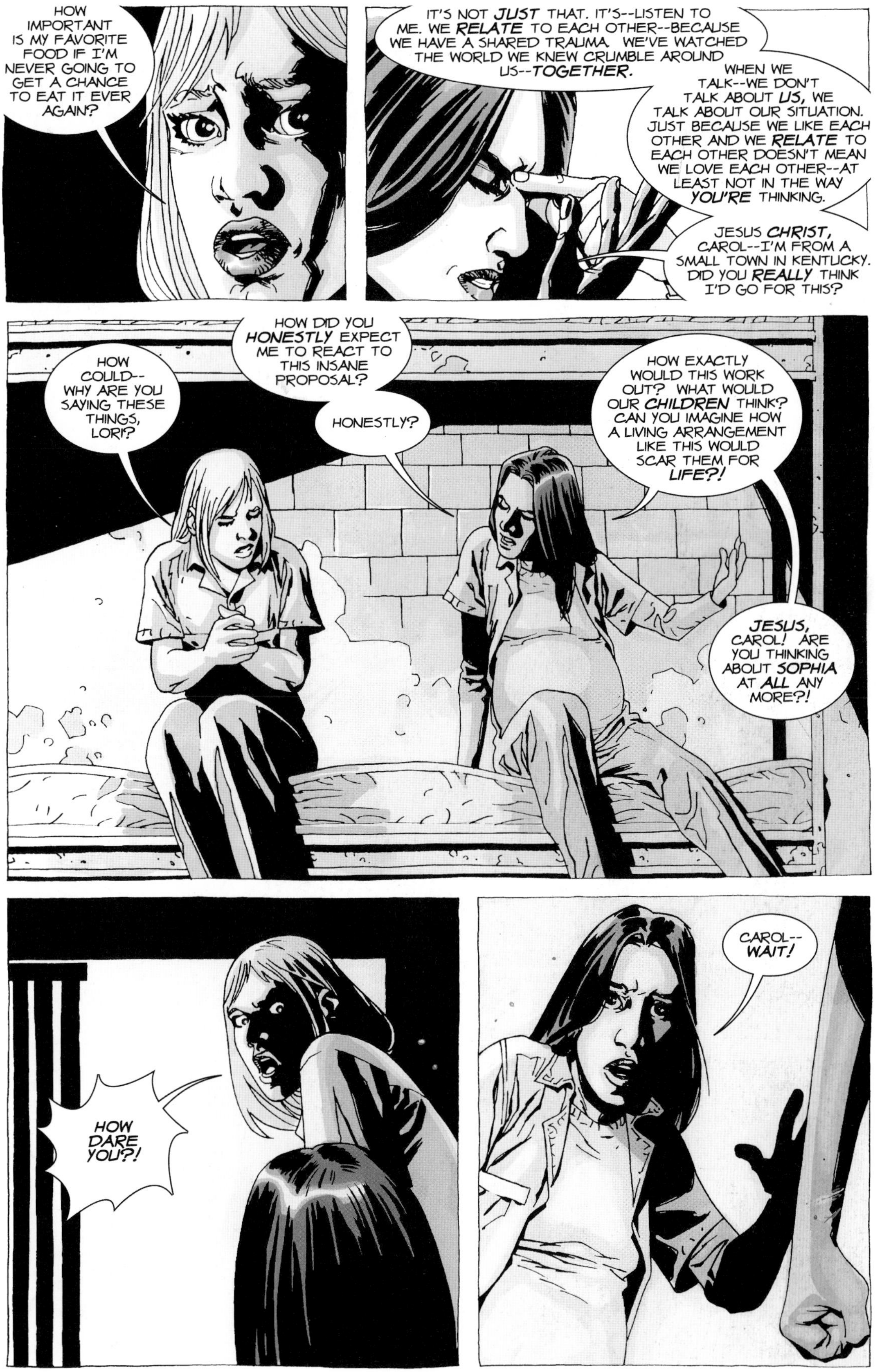
HOW IMPORTANT IS MY FAVORITE FOOD IF I'M NEVER GOING TO GET A CHANCE TO EAT IT EVER AGAIN?
IT'S NOT JUST THAT. IT'S--LISTEN TO ME. WE RELATE TO EACH OTHER--BECAUSE WE HAVE A SHARED TRAUMA. WE'VE WATCHED THE WORLD WE KNEW CRUMBLE AROUND US--TOGETHER.
WHEN WE TALK--WE DON'T TALK ABOUT US, WE TALK ABOUT OUR SITUATION. JUST BECAUSE WE LIKE EACH OTHER AND WE RELATE TO EACH OTHER DOESN'T MEAN WE LOVE EACH OTHER--AT LEAST NOT IN THE WAY YOU'RE THINKING.
JESUS CHRIST, CAROL--I'M FROM A SMALL TOWN IN KENTUCKY. DID YOU REALLY THINK I'D GO FOR THIS?
HOW COULD-- WHY ARE YOU SAYING THESE THINGS, LORI?
HOW DID YOU HONESTLY EXPECT ME TO REACT TO THIS INSANE PROPOSAL?
HONESTLY?
HOW EXACTLY WOULD THIS WORK OUT? WHAT WOULD OUR CHILDREN THINK? CAN YOU IMAGINE HOW A LIVING ARRANGEMENT LIKE THIS WOULD SCAR THEM FOR LIFE?!
JESUS, CAROL! ARE YOU THINKING ABOUT SOPHIA AT ALL ANY MORE?!
HOW DARE YOU?!
CAROL-- WAIT!

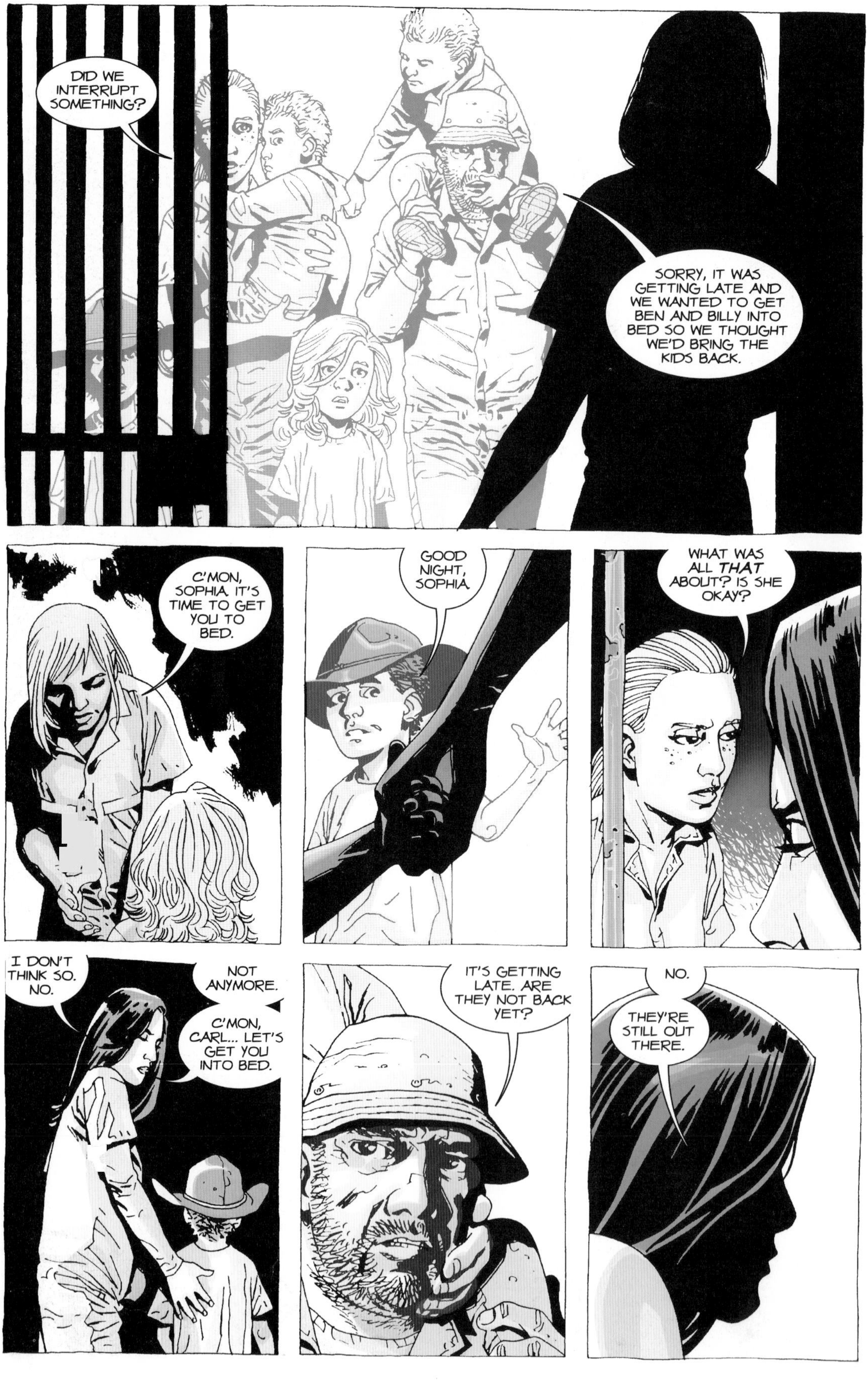
DID WE INTERRUPT SOMETHING?
SORRY, IT WAS GETTING LATE AND WE WANTED TO GET BEN AND BILLY INTO BED SO WE THOUGHT WE'D BRING THE KIDS BACK.
C'MON, SOPHIA. IT'S TIME TO GET YOU TO BED.
GOOD NIGHT, SOPHIA.
WHAT WAS ALL THAT ABOUT? IS SHE OKAY?
I DON'T THINK SO. NO.
NOT ANYMORE.
C'MON, CARL... LET'S GET YOU INTO BED.
IT'S GETTING LATE. ARE THEY NOT BACK YET?
NO.
THEY'RE STILL OUT THERE.

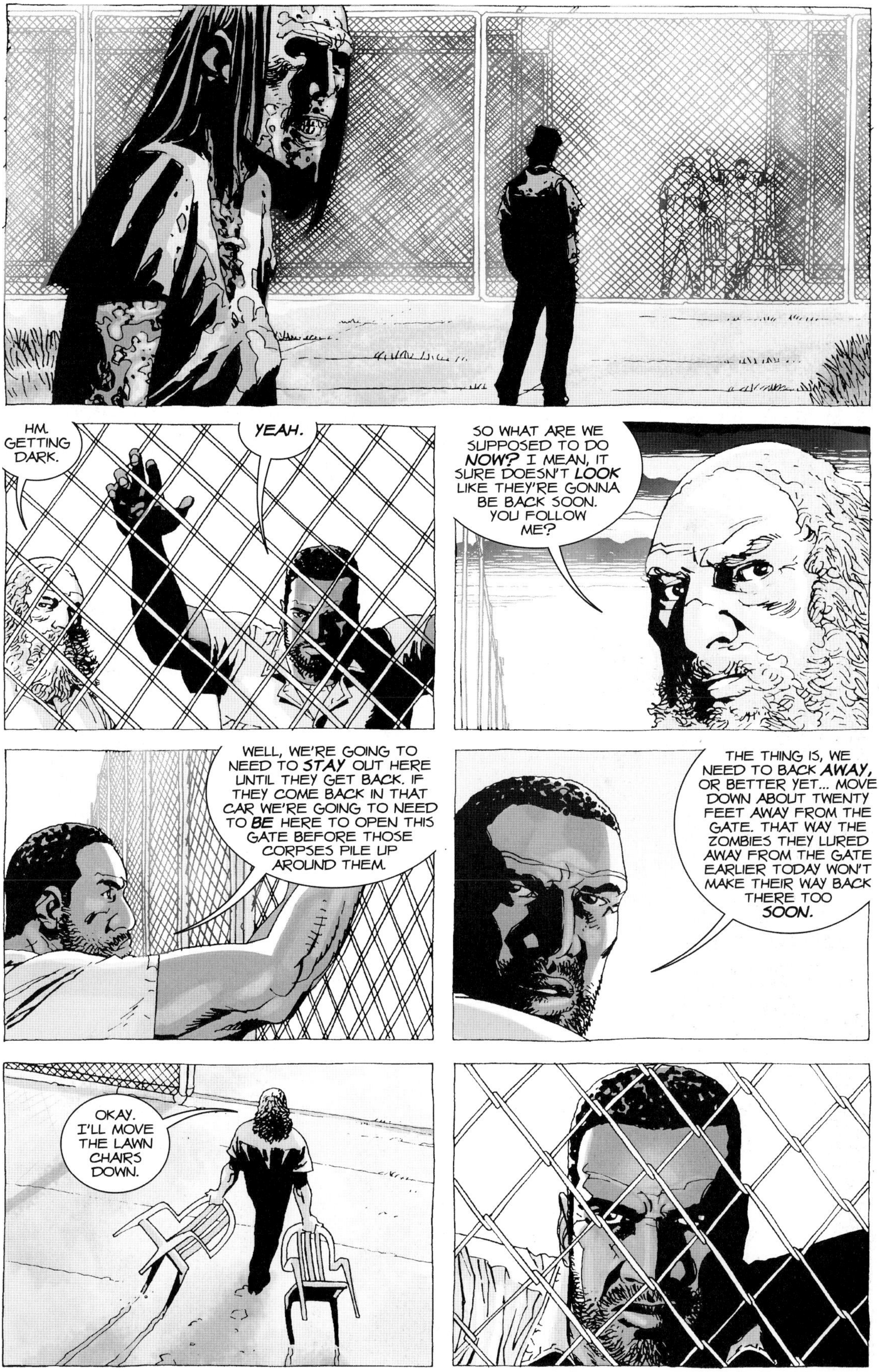
HM. GETTING DARK.
YEAH.
SO WHAT ARE WE SUPPOSED TO DO NOW? I MEAN, IT SURE DOESN'T LOOK LIKE THEY'RE GONNA BE BACK SOON. YOU FOLLOW ME?
WELL, WE'RE GOING TO NEED TO STAY OUT HERE UNTIL THEY GET BACK. IF THEY COME BACK IN THAT CAR WE'RE GOING TO NEED TO BE HERE TO OPEN THIS GATE BEFORE THOSE CORPSES PILE UP AROUND THEM.
THE THING IS, WE NEED TO BACK AWAY, OR BETTER YET... MOVE DOWN ABOUT TWENTY FEET AWAY FROM THE GATE. THAT WAY THE ZOMBIES THEY LURED AWAY FROM THE GATE EARLIER TODAY WON'T MAKE THEIR WAY BACK THERE TOO SOON.
OKAY. I'LL MOVE THE LAWN CHAIRS DOWN.

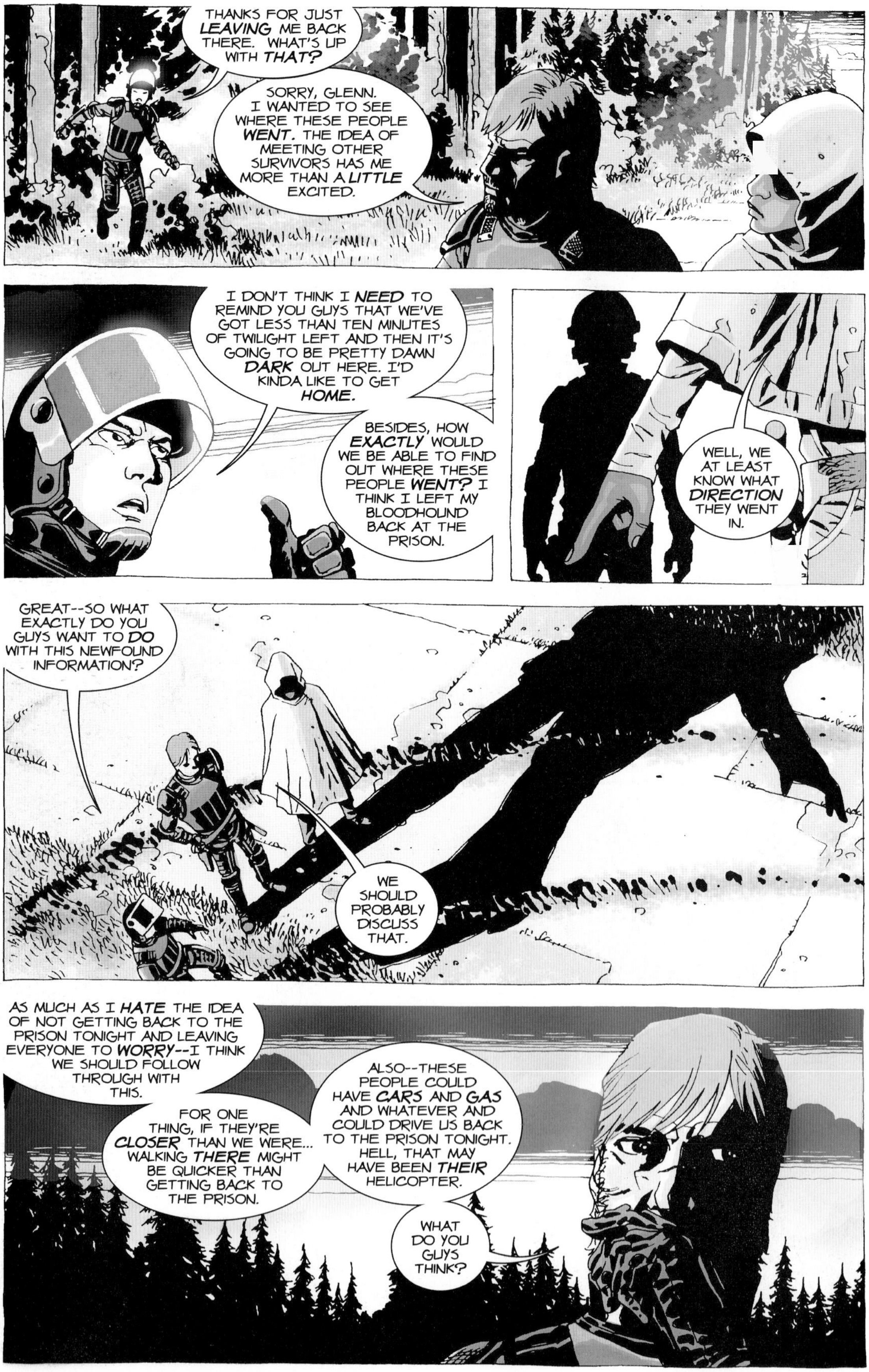
THANKS FOR JUST LEAVING ME BACK THERE. WHAT'S UP WITH THAT?
SORRY, GLENN. I WANTED TO SEE WHERE THESE PEOPLE WENT. THE IDEA OF MEETING OTHER SURVIVORS HAS ME MORE THAN A LITTLE EXCITED.
I DON'T THINK I NEED TO REMIND YOU GUYS THAT WE'VE GOT LESS THAN TEN MINUTES OF TWILIGHT LEFT AND THEN IT'S GOING TO BE PRETTY DAMN DARK OUT HERE. I'D KINDA LIKE TO GET HOME.
BESIDES, HOW EXACTLY WOULD WE BE ABLE TO FIND OUT WHERE THESE PEOPLE WENT? I THINK I LEFT MY BLOODHOUND BACK AT THE PRISON.
WELL, WE AT LEAST KNOW WHAT DIRECTION THEY WENT IN.
GREAT--SO WHAT EXACTLY DO YOU GUYS WANT TO DO WITH THIS NEWFOUND INFORMATION?
WE SHOULD PROBABLY DISCUSS THAT.
AS MUCH AS I HATE THE IDEA OF NOT GETTING BACK TO THE PRISON TONIGHT AND LEAVING EVERYONE TO WORRY--I THINK WE SHOULD FOLLOW THROUGH WITH THIS.
FOR ONE THING, IF THEY'RE CLOSER THAN WE WERE... WALKING THERE MIGHT BE QUICKER THAN GETTING BACK TO THE PRISON.
ALSO--THESE PEOPLE COULD HAVE CARS AND GAS AND WHATEVER AND COULD DRIVE US BACK TO THE PRISON TONIGHT. HELL, THAT MAY HAVE BEEN THEIR HELICOPTER.
WHAT DO YOU GUYS THINK?

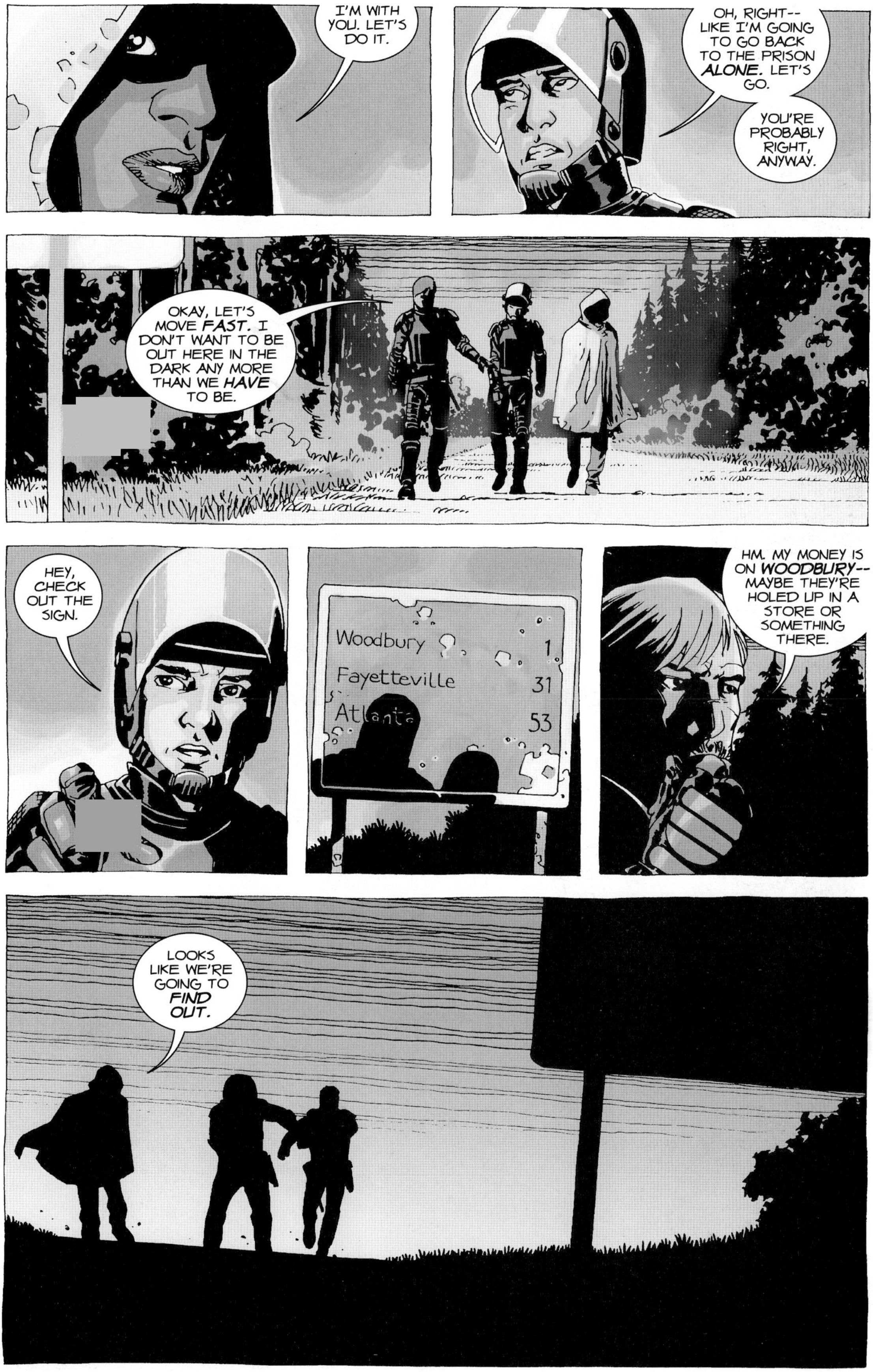

I'M WITH YOU. LET'S DO IT.
OH, RIGHT-- LIKE I'M GOING TO GO BACK TO THE PRISON ALONE. LET'S GO.
YOU'RE PROBABLY RIGHT, ANYWAY.
OKAY, LET'S MOVE FAST. I DON'T WANT TO BE OUT HERE IN THE DARK ANY MORE THAN WE HAVE TO BE.
HEY, CHECK OUT THE SIGN.
Woodbury 1
Fayetteville 31
Atlanta 53
HM. MY MONEY IS ON WOODBURY-- MAYBE THEY'RE HOLED UP IN A STORE OR SOMETHING THERE.
LOOKS LIKE WE'RE GOING TO FIND OUT.

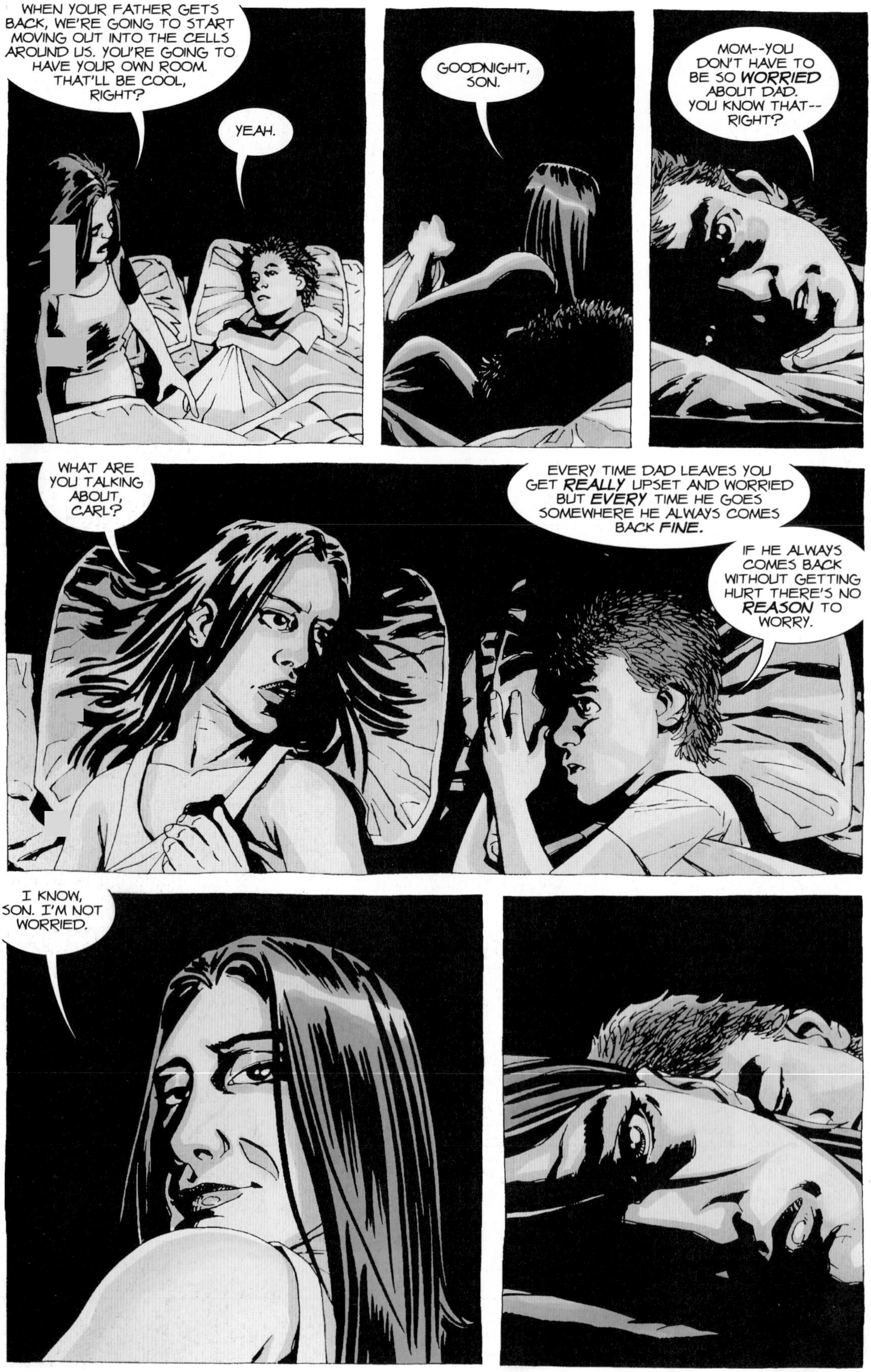
WHEN YOUR FATHER GETS BACK, WE'RE GOING TO START MOVING OUT INTO THE CELLS AROUND US. YOU'RE GOING TO HAVE YOUR OWN ROOM. THAT'LL BE COOL, RIGHT?
YEAH.
GOODNIGHT, SON.
MOM--YOU DON'T HAVE TO BE SO WORRIED ABOUT DAD. YOU KNOW THAT-- RIGHT?
WHAT ARE YOU TALKING ABOUT, CARL?
EVERY TIME DAD LEAVES YOU GET REALLY UPSET AND WORRIED BUT EVERY TIME HE GOES SOMEWHERE HE ALWAYS COMES BACK FINE.
IF HE ALWAYS COMES BACK WITHOUT GETTING HURT THERE'S NO REASON TO WORRY.
I KNOW, SON. I'M NOT WORRIED.

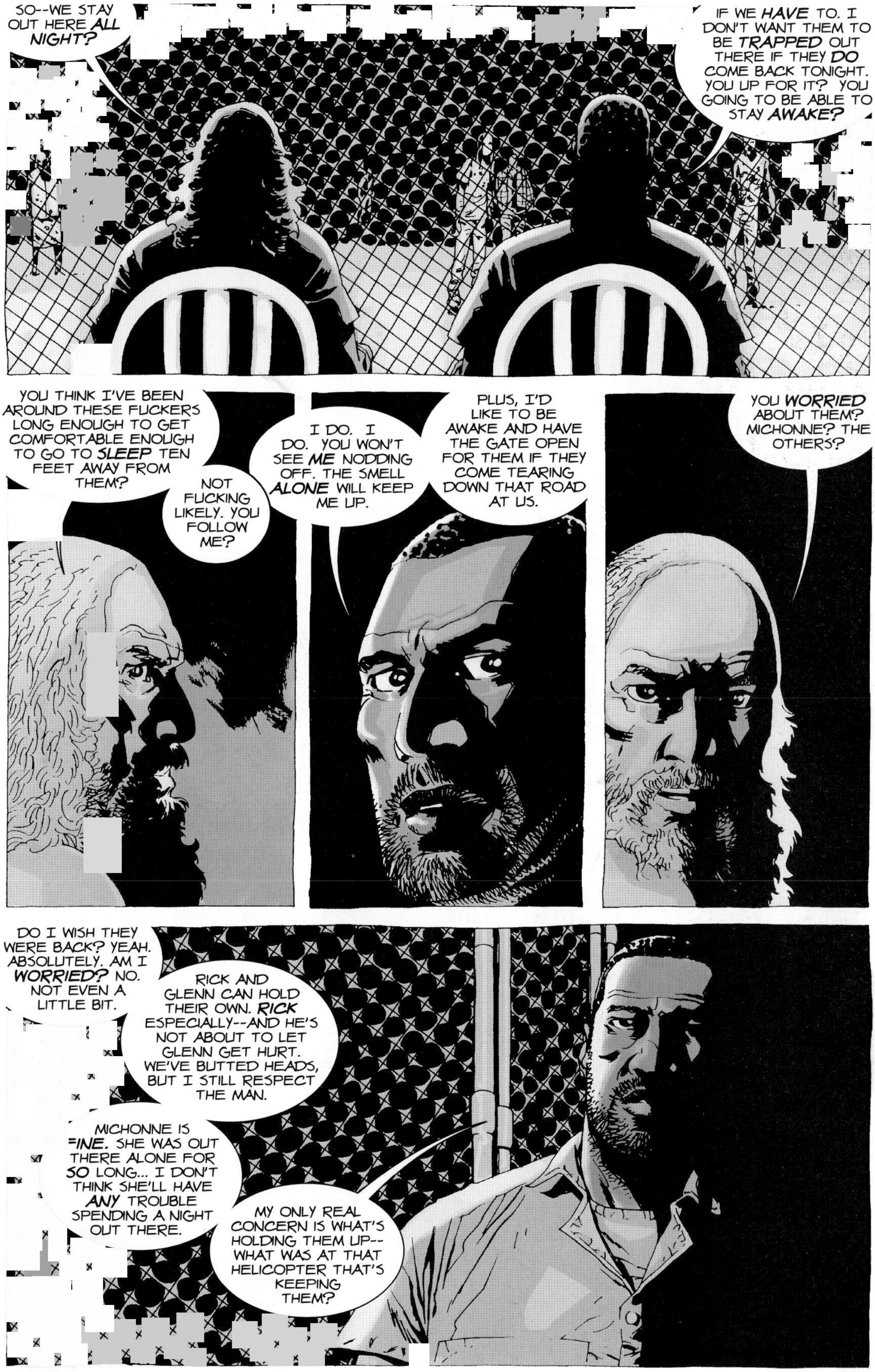

SO--WE STAY OUT HERE ALL NIGHT?
IF WE HAVE TO. I DON'T WANT THEM TO BE TRAPPED OUT THERE IF THEY DO COME BACK TONIGHT. YOU UP FOR IT? YOU GOING TO BE ABLE TO STAY AWAKE?
YOU THINK I'VE BEEN AROUND THESE FUCKERS LONG ENOUGH TO GET COMFORTABLE ENOUGH TO GO TO SLEEP TEN FEET AWAY FROM THEM?
NOT FUCKING LIKELY. YOU FOLLOW ME?
I DO. I DO. YOU WON'T SEE ME NODDING OFF. THE SMELL ALONE WILL KEEP ME UP.
PLUS, I'D LIKE TO BE AWAKE AND HAVE THE GATE OPEN FOR THEM IF THEY COME TEARING DOWN THAT ROAD AT US.
YOU WORRIED ABOUT THEM? MICHONNE? THE OTHERS?
DO I WISH THEY WERE BACK? YEAH. ABSOLUTELY. AM I WORRIED? NO. NOT EVEN A LITTLE BIT.
RICK AND GLENN CAN HOLD THEIR OWN. RICK ESPECIALLY--AND HE'S NOT ABOUT TO LET GLENN GET HURT. WE'VE BUTTED HEADS, BUT I STILL RESPECT THE MAN.
MICHONNE IS FINE. SHE WAS OUT THERE ALONE FOR SO LONG... I DON'T THINK SHE'LL HAVE ANY TROUBLE SPENDING A NIGHT OUT THERE.
MY ONLY REAL CONCERN IS WHAT'S HOLDING THEM UP-- WHAT WAS AT THAT HELICOPTER THAT'S KEEPING THEM?

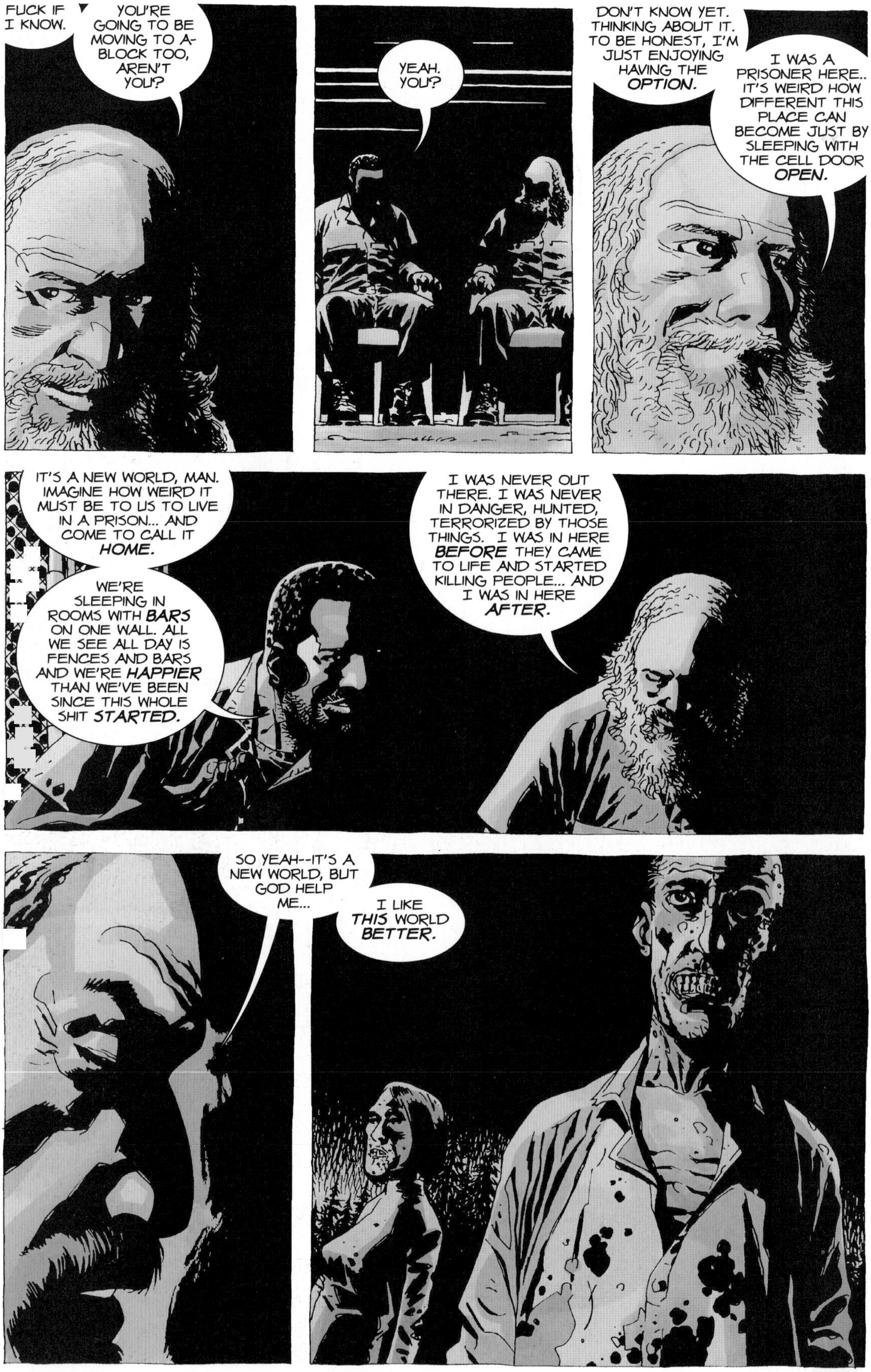

FUCK IF I KNOW.
YOU'RE GOING TO BE MOVING TO A-BLOCK TOO, AREN'T YOU?
YEAH. YOU?
DON'T KNOW YET. THINKING ABOUT IT. TO BE HONEST, I'M JUST ENJOYING HAVING THE OPTION.
I WAS A PRISONER HERE.. IT'S WEIRD HOW DIFFERENT THIS PLACE CAN BECOME JUST BY SLEEPING WITH THE CELL DOOR OPEN.
IT'S A NEW WORLD, MAN. IMAGINE HOW WEIRD IT MUST BE TO US TO LIVE IN A PRISON... AND COME TO CALL IT HOME.
WE'RE SLEEPING IN ROOMS WITH BARS ON ONE WALL. ALL WE SEE ALL DAY IS FENCES AND BARS AND WE'RE HAPPIER THAN WE'VE BEEN SINCE THIS WHOLE SHIT STARTED.
I WAS NEVER OUT THERE. I WAS NEVER IN DANGER, HUNTED, TERRORIZED BY THOSE THINGS. I WAS IN HERE BEFORE THEY CAME TO LIFE AND STARTED KILLING PEOPLE... AND I WAS IN HERE AFTER.
SO YEAH--IT'S A NEW WORLD, BUT GOD HELP ME...
I LIKE THIS WORLD BETTER.

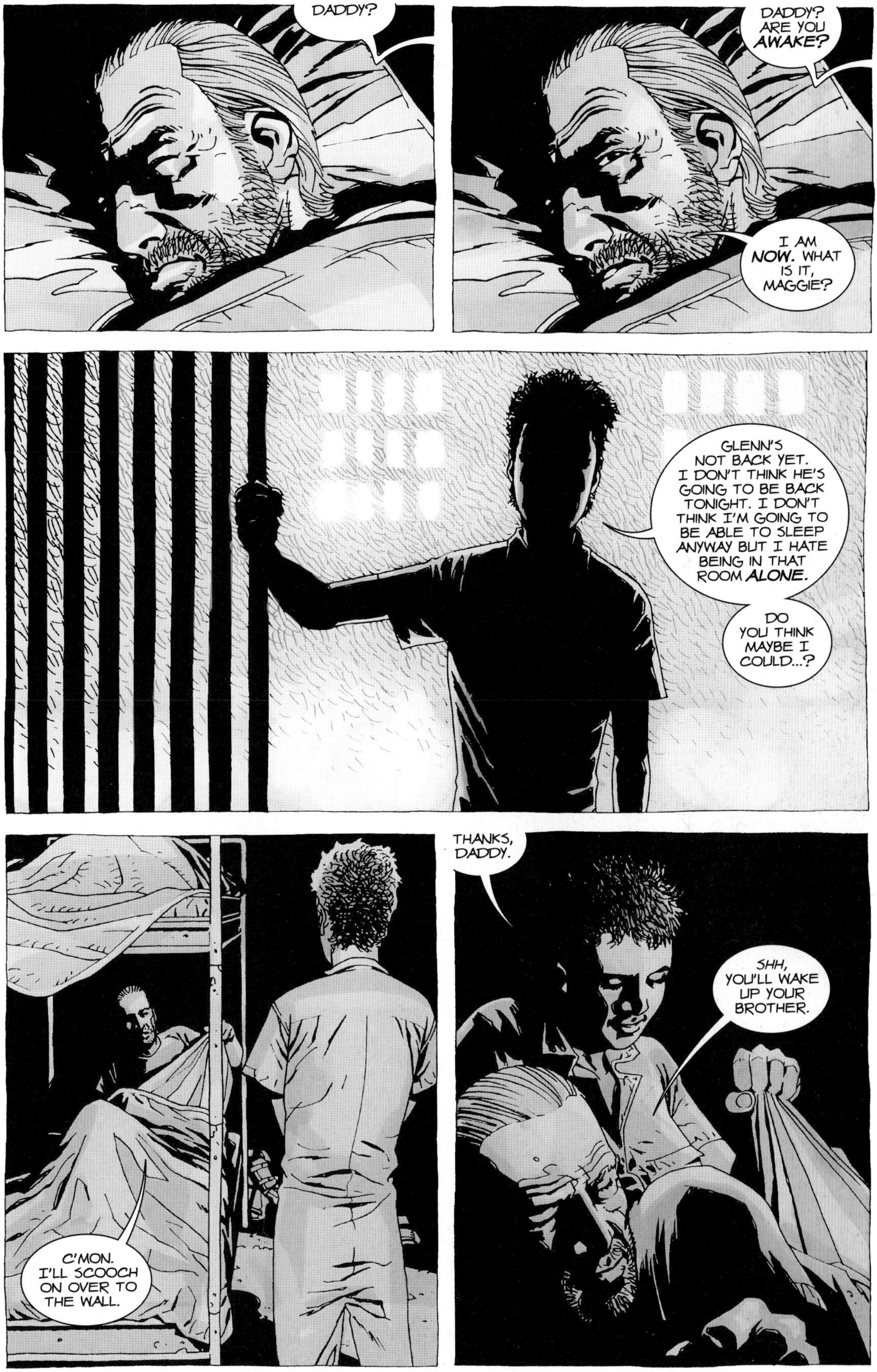
DADDY?
DADDY? ARE YOU *AWAKE?*
I AM *NOW.* WHAT IS IT, MAGGIE?
GLENN'S NOT BACK YET. I DON'T THINK HE'S GOING TO BE BACK TONIGHT. I DON'T THINK I'M GOING TO BE ABLE TO SLEEP ANYWAY BUT I HATE BEING IN THAT ROOM *ALONE.*
DO YOU THINK MAYBE I COULD...?
C'MON. I'LL SCOOCH ON OVER TO THE WALL.
THANKS, DADDY.
SHH, YOU'LL WAKE UP YOUR BROTHER.

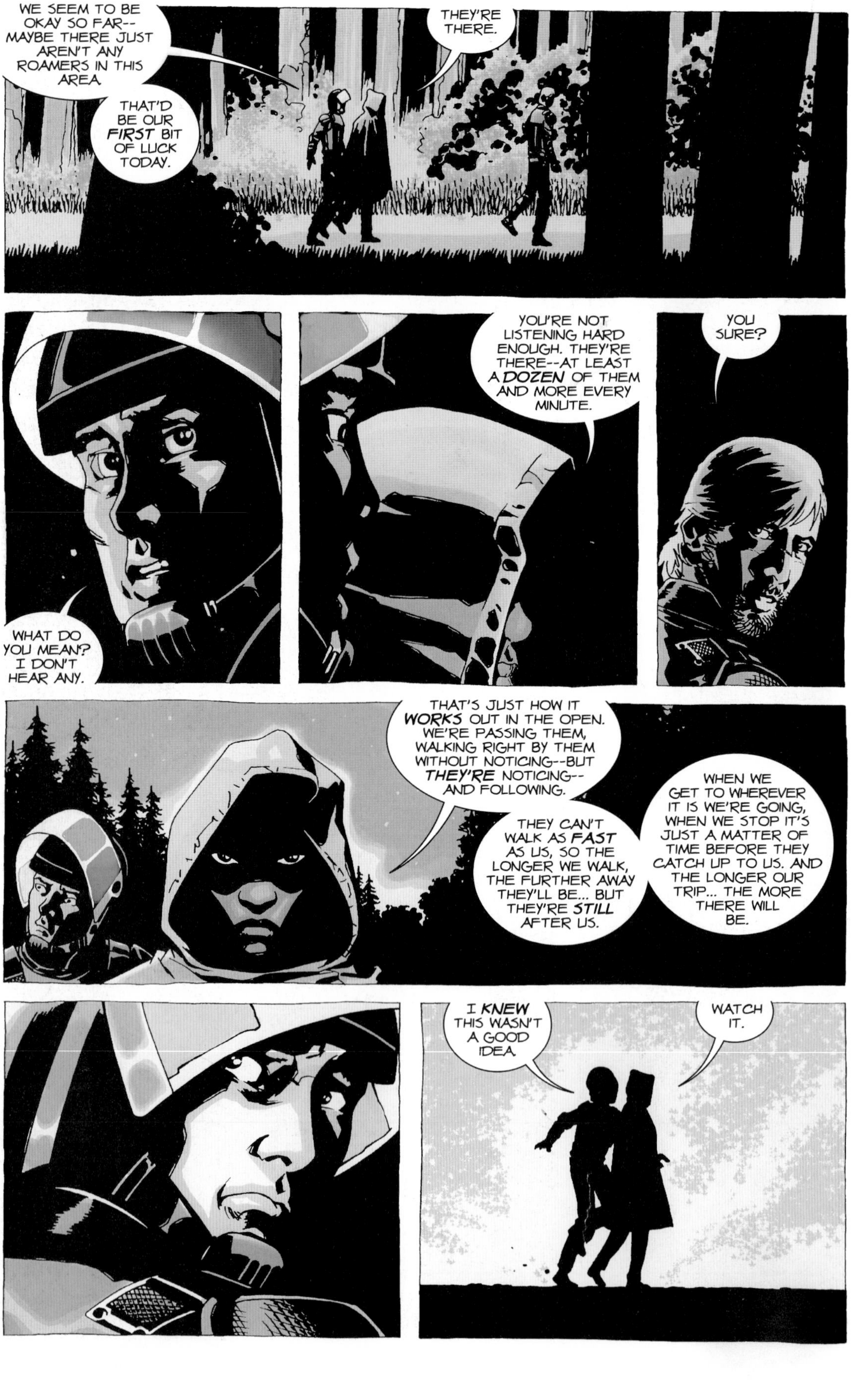
WE SEEM TO BE OKAY SO FAR-- MAYBE THERE JUST AREN'T ANY ROAMERS IN THIS AREA.
THAT'D BE OUR FIRST BIT OF LUCK TODAY.
THEY'RE THERE.
WHAT DO YOU MEAN? I DON'T HEAR ANY.
YOU'RE NOT LISTENING HARD ENOUGH. THEY'RE THERE--AT LEAST A DOZEN OF THEM AND MORE EVERY MINUTE.
YOU SURE?
THAT'S JUST HOW IT WORKS OUT IN THE OPEN. WE'RE PASSING THEM, WALKING RIGHT BY THEM WITHOUT NOTICING--BUT THEY'RE NOTICING-- AND FOLLOWING.
THEY CAN'T WALK AS FAST AS US, SO THE LONGER WE WALK, THE FURTHER AWAY THEY'LL BE... BUT THEY'RE STILL AFTER US.
WHEN WE GET TO WHEREVER IT IS WE'RE GOING, WHEN WE STOP IT'S JUST A MATTER OF TIME BEFORE THEY CATCH UP TO US. AND THE LONGER OUR TRIP... THE MORE THERE WILL BE.
I KNEW THIS WASN'T A GOOD IDEA.
WATCH IT.

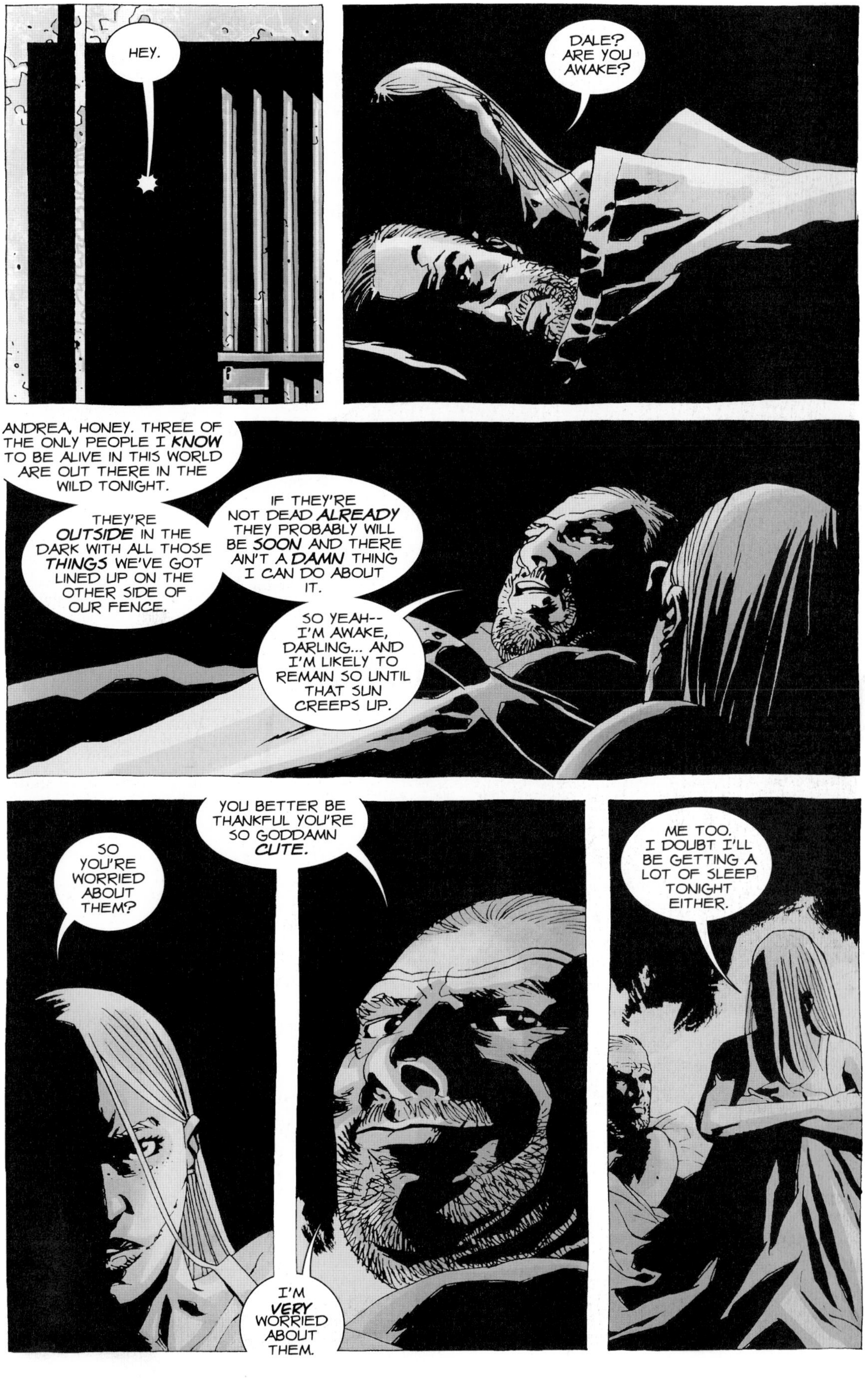
HEY.
DALE? ARE YOU AWAKE?
ANDREA, HONEY. THREE OF THE ONLY PEOPLE I KNOW TO BE ALIVE IN THIS WORLD ARE OUT THERE IN THE WILD TONIGHT.
THEY'RE OUTSIDE IN THE DARK WITH ALL THOSE THINGS WE'VE GOT LINED UP ON THE OTHER SIDE OF OUR FENCE.
IF THEY'RE NOT DEAD ALREADY THEY PROBABLY WILL BE SOON AND THERE AIN'T A DAMN THING I CAN DO ABOUT IT.
SO YEAH-- I'M AWAKE, DARLING... AND I'M LIKELY TO REMAIN SO UNTIL THAT SUN CREEPS UP.
SO YOU'RE WORRIED ABOUT THEM?
YOU BETTER BE THANKFUL YOU'RE SO GODDAMN CUTE.
I'M VERY WORRIED ABOUT THEM.
ME TOO. I DOUBT I'LL BE GETTING A LOT OF SLEEP TONIGHT EITHER.

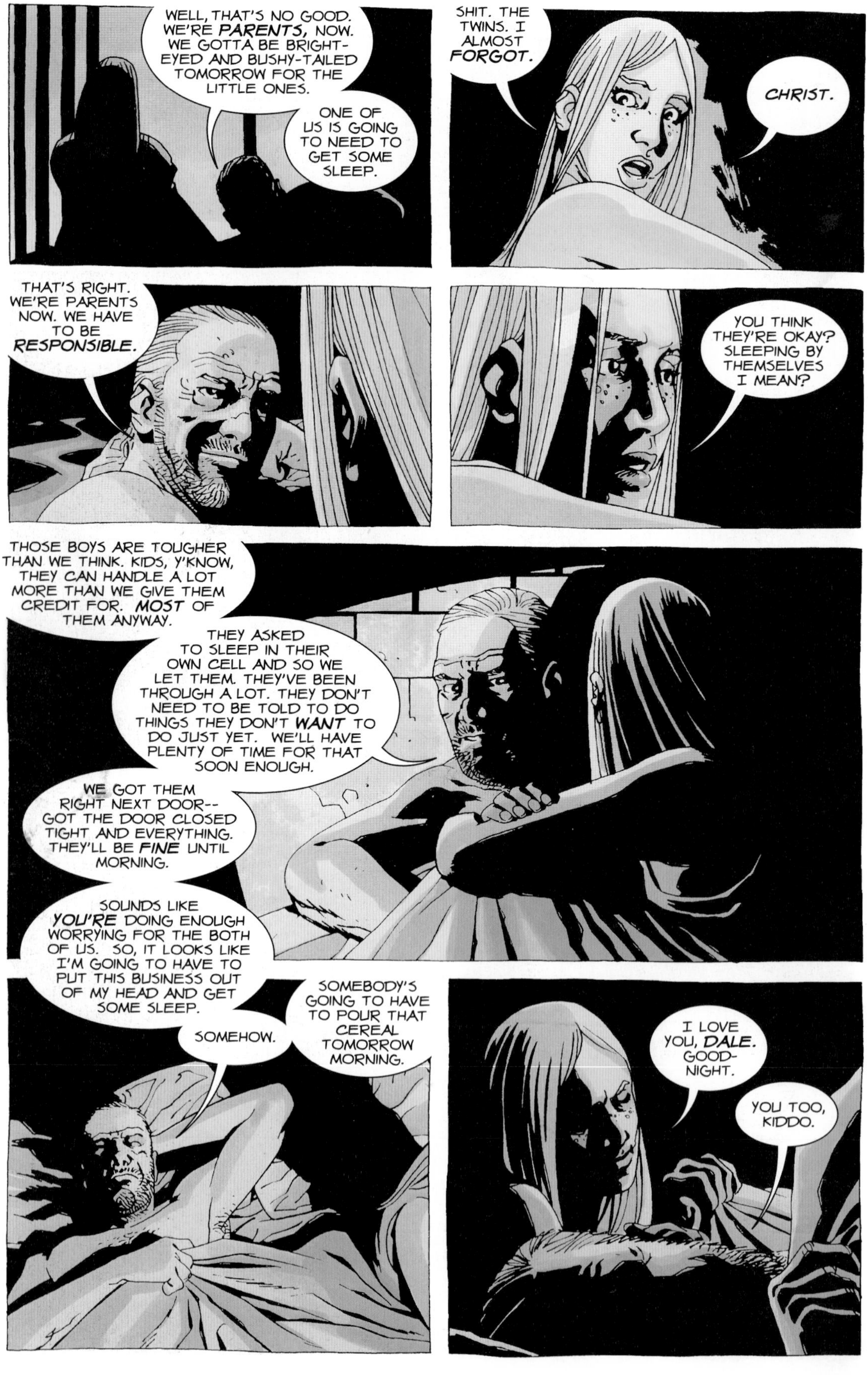
WELL, THAT'S NO GOOD. WE'RE PARENTS, NOW. WE GOTTA BE BRIGHT-EYED AND BUSHY-TAILED TOMORROW FOR THE LITTLE ONES.
ONE OF US IS GOING TO NEED TO GET SOME SLEEP.
SHIT. THE TWINS. I ALMOST FORGOT.
CHRIST.
THAT'S RIGHT. WE'RE PARENTS NOW. WE HAVE TO BE RESPONSIBLE.
YOU THINK THEY'RE OKAY? SLEEPING BY THEMSELVES I MEAN?
THOSE BOYS ARE TOUGHER THAN WE THINK. KIDS, Y'KNOW, THEY CAN HANDLE A LOT MORE THAN WE GIVE THEM CREDIT FOR. MOST OF THEM ANYWAY.
THEY ASKED TO SLEEP IN THEIR OWN CELL AND SO WE LET THEM. THEY'VE BEEN THROUGH A LOT. THEY DON'T NEED TO BE TOLD TO DO THINGS THEY DON'T WANT TO DO JUST YET. WE'LL HAVE PLENTY OF TIME FOR THAT SOON ENOUGH.
WE GOT THEM RIGHT NEXT DOOR-- GOT THE DOOR CLOSED TIGHT AND EVERYTHING. THEY'LL BE FINE UNTIL MORNING.
SOUNDS LIKE YOU'RE DOING ENOUGH WORRYING FOR THE BOTH OF US. SO, IT LOOKS LIKE I'M GOING TO HAVE TO PUT THIS BUSINESS OUT OF MY HEAD AND GET SOME SLEEP.
SOMEHOW.
SOMEBODY'S GOING TO HAVE TO POUR THAT CEREAL TOMORROW MORNING.
I LOVE YOU, DALE. GOOD-NIGHT.
YOU TOO, KIDDO.

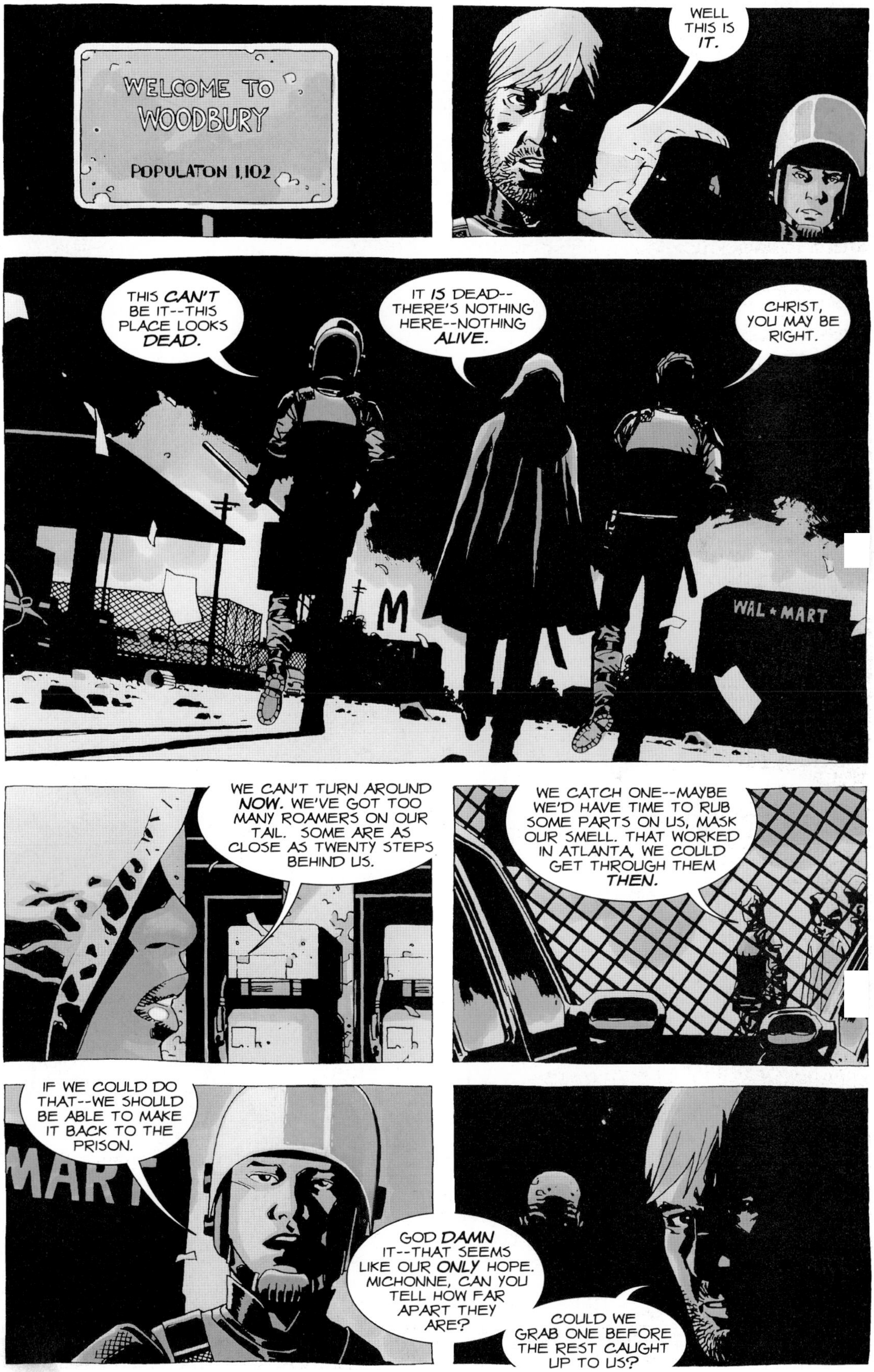

WELCOME TO WOODBURY
POPULATON 1,102
WELL THIS IS IT.
THIS CAN'T BE IT--THIS PLACE LOOKS DEAD.
IT IS DEAD--THERE'S NOTHING HERE--NOTHING ALIVE.
CHRIST, YOU MAY BE RIGHT.
WAL★MART
WE CAN'T TURN AROUND NOW. WE'VE GOT TOO MANY ROAMERS ON OUR TAIL. SOME ARE AS CLOSE AS TWENTY STEPS BEHIND US.
WE CATCH ONE--MAYBE WE'D HAVE TIME TO RUB SOME PARTS ON US, MASK OUR SMELL. THAT WORKED IN ATLANTA, WE COULD GET THROUGH THEM THEN.
IF WE COULD DO THAT--WE SHOULD BE ABLE TO MAKE IT BACK TO THE PRISON.
GOD DAMN IT--THAT SEEMS LIKE OUR ONLY HOPE. MICHONNE, CAN YOU TELL HOW FAR APART THEY ARE?
COULD WE GRAB ONE BEFORE THE REST CAUGHT UP TO US?

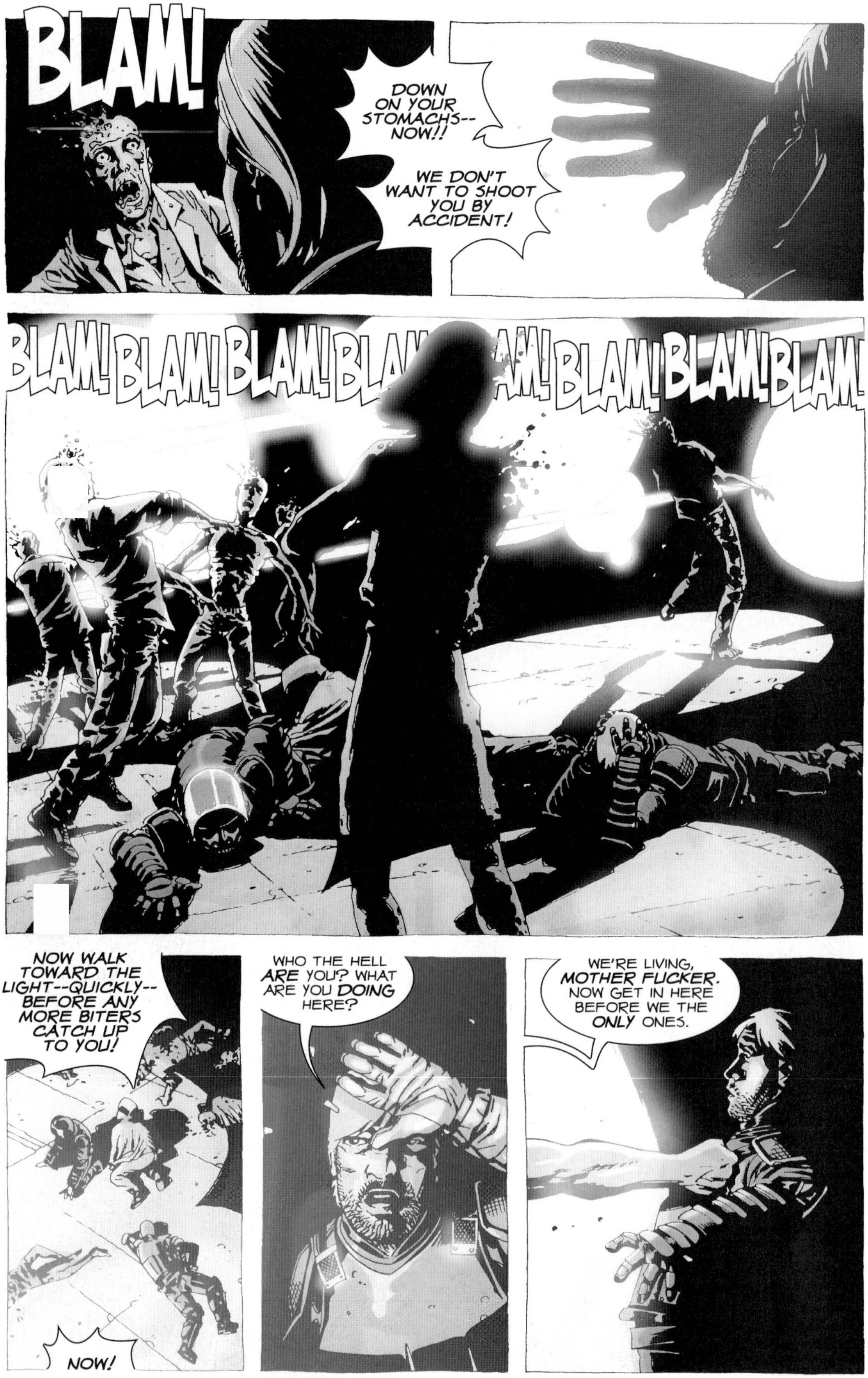
BLAM!
DOWN ON YOUR STOMACHS-- NOW!!
WE DON'T WANT TO SHOOT YOU BY ACCIDENT!
BLAM! BLAM! BLAM! BLAM! BLAM! BLAM! BLAM!
NOW WALK TOWARD THE LIGHT--QUICKLY-- BEFORE ANY MORE BITERS CATCH UP TO YOU!
NOW!
WHO THE HELL ARE YOU? WHAT ARE YOU DOING HERE?
WE'RE LIVING, MOTHER FUCKER. NOW GET IN HERE BEFORE WE THE ONLY ONES.

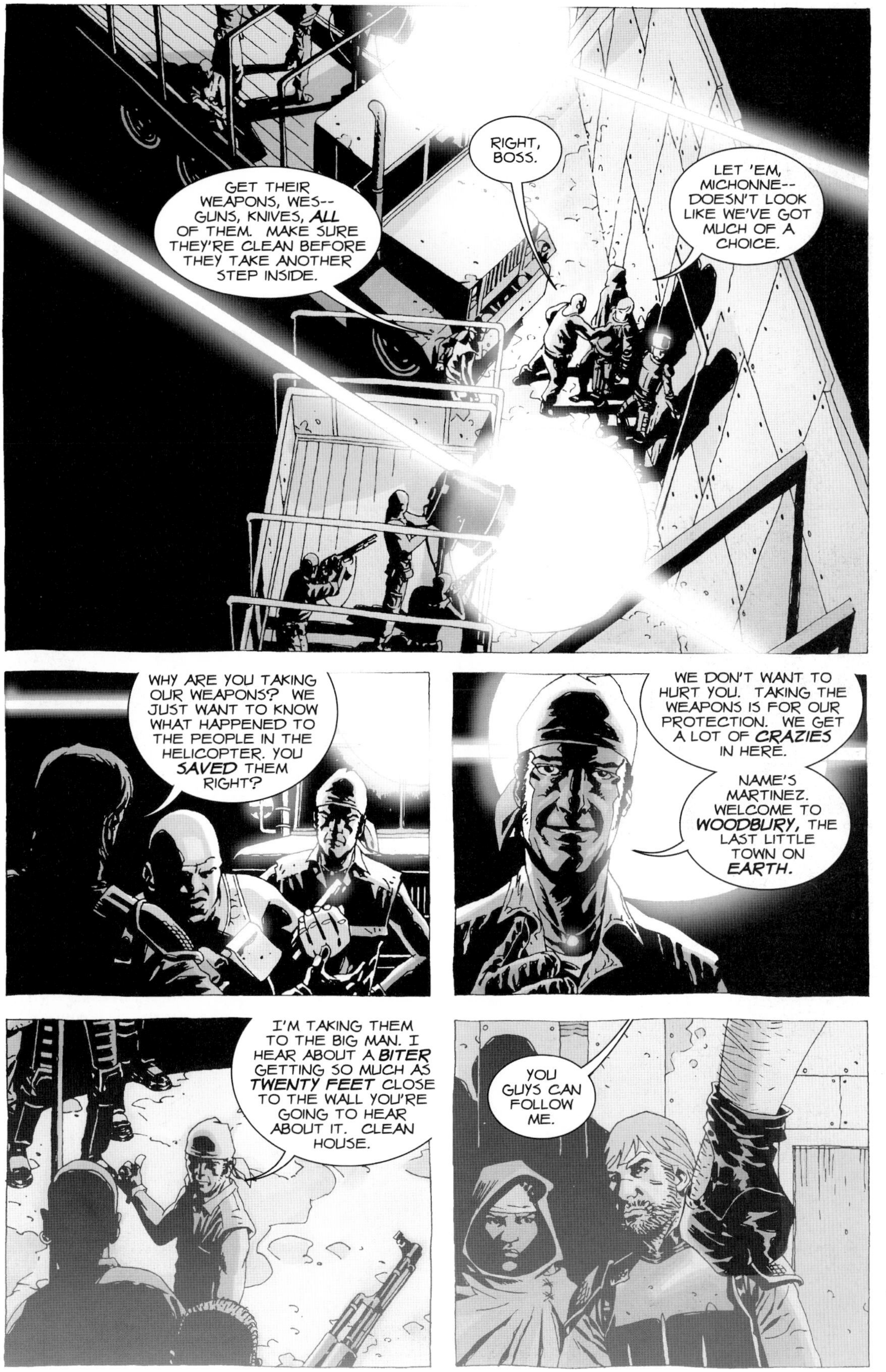
GET THEIR WEAPONS, WES-- GUNS, KNIVES, ALL OF THEM. MAKE SURE THEY'RE CLEAN BEFORE THEY TAKE ANOTHER STEP INSIDE.
RIGHT, BOSS.
LET 'EM, MICHONNE-- DOESN'T LOOK LIKE WE'VE GOT MUCH OF A CHOICE.
WHY ARE YOU TAKING OUR WEAPONS? WE JUST WANT TO KNOW WHAT HAPPENED TO THE PEOPLE IN THE HELICOPTER. YOU SAVED THEM RIGHT?
WE DON'T WANT TO HURT YOU. TAKING THE WEAPONS IS FOR OUR PROTECTION. WE GET A LOT OF CRAZIES IN HERE.
NAME'S MARTINEZ. WELCOME TO WOODBURY, THE LAST LITTLE TOWN ON EARTH.
I'M TAKING THEM TO THE BIG MAN. I HEAR ABOUT A BITER GETTING SO MUCH AS TWENTY FEET CLOSE TO THE WALL YOU'RE GOING TO HEAR ABOUT IT. CLEAN HOUSE.
YOU GUYS CAN FOLLOW ME.

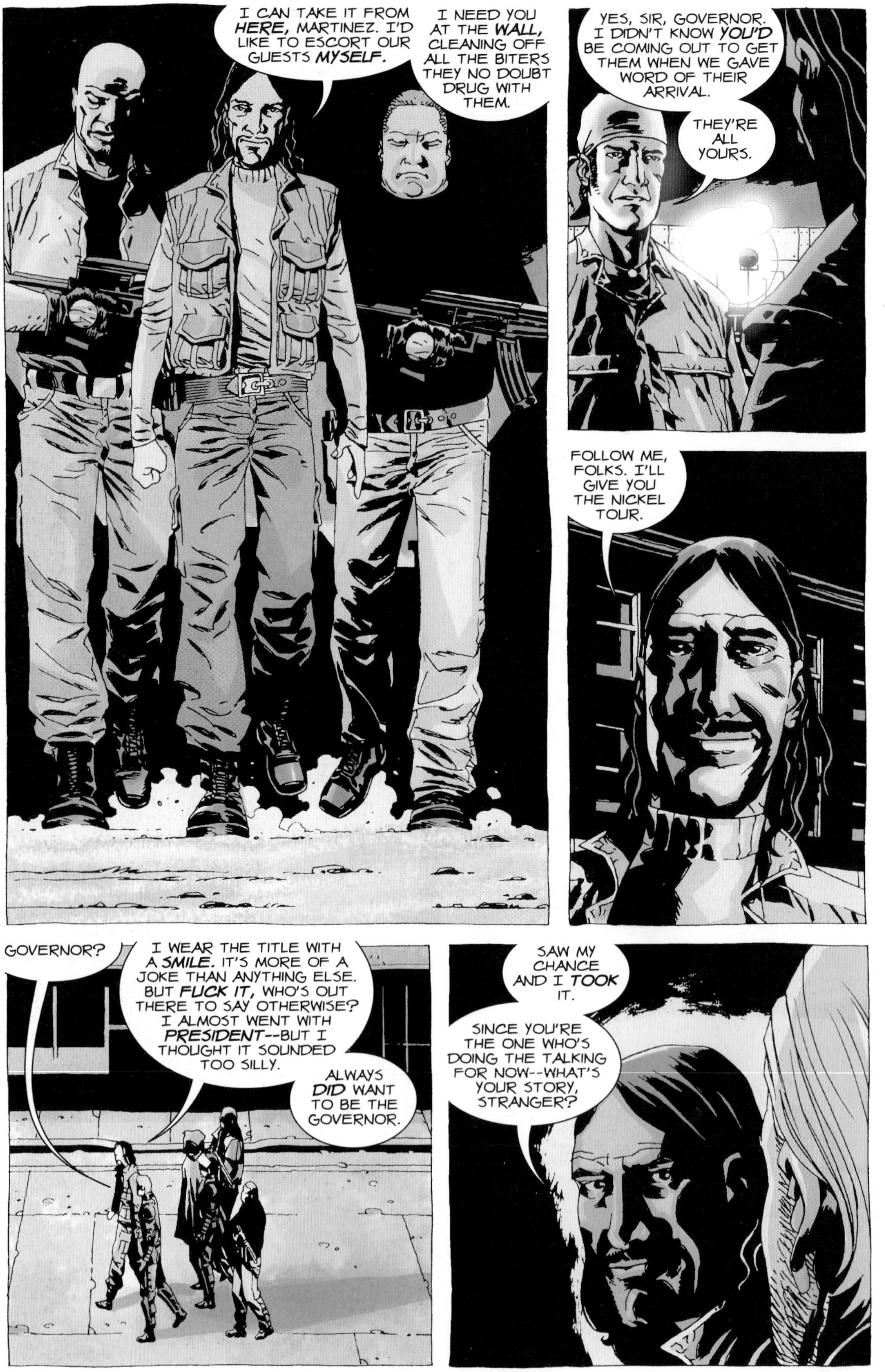
I CAN TAKE IT FROM HERE, MARTINEZ. I'D LIKE TO ESCORT OUR GUESTS MYSELF.
I NEED YOU AT THE WALL, CLEANING OFF ALL THE BITERS THEY NO DOUBT DRUG WITH THEM.
YES, SIR, GOVERNOR. I DIDN'T KNOW YOU'D BE COMING OUT TO GET THEM WHEN WE GAVE WORD OF THEIR ARRIVAL.
THEY'RE ALL YOURS.
FOLLOW ME, FOLKS. I'LL GIVE YOU THE NICKEL TOUR.
GOVERNOR?
I WEAR THE TITLE WITH A SMILE. IT'S MORE OF A JOKE THAN ANYTHING ELSE. BUT FUCK IT, WHO'S OUT THERE TO SAY OTHERWISE? I ALMOST WENT WITH PRESIDENT--BUT I THOUGHT IT SOUNDED TOO SILLY.
ALWAYS DID WANT TO BE THE GOVERNOR.
SAW MY CHANCE AND I TOOK IT.
SINCE YOU'RE THE ONE WHO'S DOING THE TALKING FOR NOW--WHAT'S YOUR STORY, STRANGER?

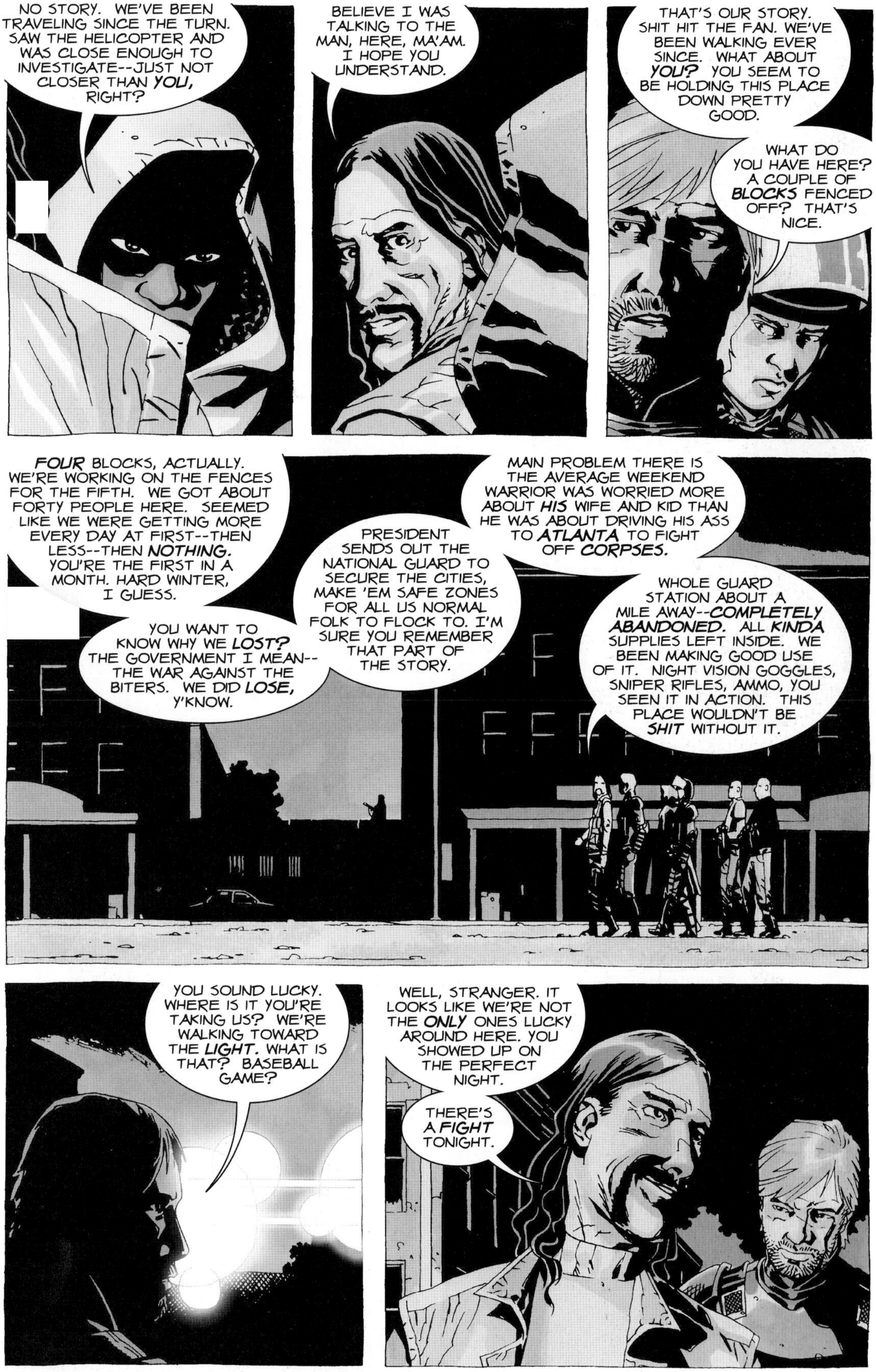
NO STORY. WE'VE BEEN TRAVELING SINCE THE TURN. SAW THE HELICOPTER AND WAS CLOSE ENOUGH TO INVESTIGATE--JUST NOT CLOSER THAN YOU, RIGHT?
BELIEVE I WAS TALKING TO THE MAN, HERE, MA'AM. I HOPE YOU UNDERSTAND.
THAT'S OUR STORY. SHIT HIT THE FAN. WE'VE BEEN WALKING EVER SINCE. WHAT ABOUT YOU? YOU SEEM TO BE HOLDING THIS PLACE DOWN PRETTY GOOD.
WHAT DO YOU HAVE HERE? A COUPLE OF BLOCKS FENCED OFF? THAT'S NICE.
FOUR BLOCKS, ACTUALLY. WE'RE WORKING ON THE FENCES FOR THE FIFTH. WE GOT ABOUT FORTY PEOPLE HERE. SEEMED LIKE WE WERE GETTING MORE EVERY DAY AT FIRST--THEN LESS--THEN NOTHING. YOU'RE THE FIRST IN A MONTH. HARD WINTER, I GUESS.
YOU WANT TO KNOW WHY WE LOST? THE GOVERNMENT I MEAN-- THE WAR AGAINST THE BITERS. WE DID LOSE, Y'KNOW.
PRESIDENT SENDS OUT THE NATIONAL GUARD TO SECURE THE CITIES, MAKE 'EM SAFE ZONES FOR ALL US NORMAL FOLK TO FLOCK TO. I'M SURE YOU REMEMBER THAT PART OF THE STORY.
MAIN PROBLEM THERE IS THE AVERAGE WEEKEND WARRIOR WAS WORRIED MORE ABOUT HIS WIFE AND KID THAN HE WAS ABOUT DRIVING HIS ASS TO ATLANTA TO FIGHT OFF CORPSES.
WHOLE GUARD STATION ABOUT A MILE AWAY--COMPLETELY ABANDONED. ALL KINDA SUPPLIES LEFT INSIDE. WE BEEN MAKING GOOD USE OF IT. NIGHT VISION GOGGLES, SNIPER RIFLES, AMMO, YOU SEEN IT IN ACTION. THIS PLACE WOULDN'T BE SHIT WITHOUT IT.
YOU SOUND LUCKY. WHERE IS IT YOU'RE TAKING US? WE'RE WALKING TOWARD THE LIGHT. WHAT IS THAT? BASEBALL GAME?
WELL, STRANGER. IT LOOKS LIKE WE'RE NOT THE ONLY ONES LUCKY AROUND HERE. YOU SHOWED UP ON THE PERFECT NIGHT.
THERE'S A FIGHT TONIGHT.

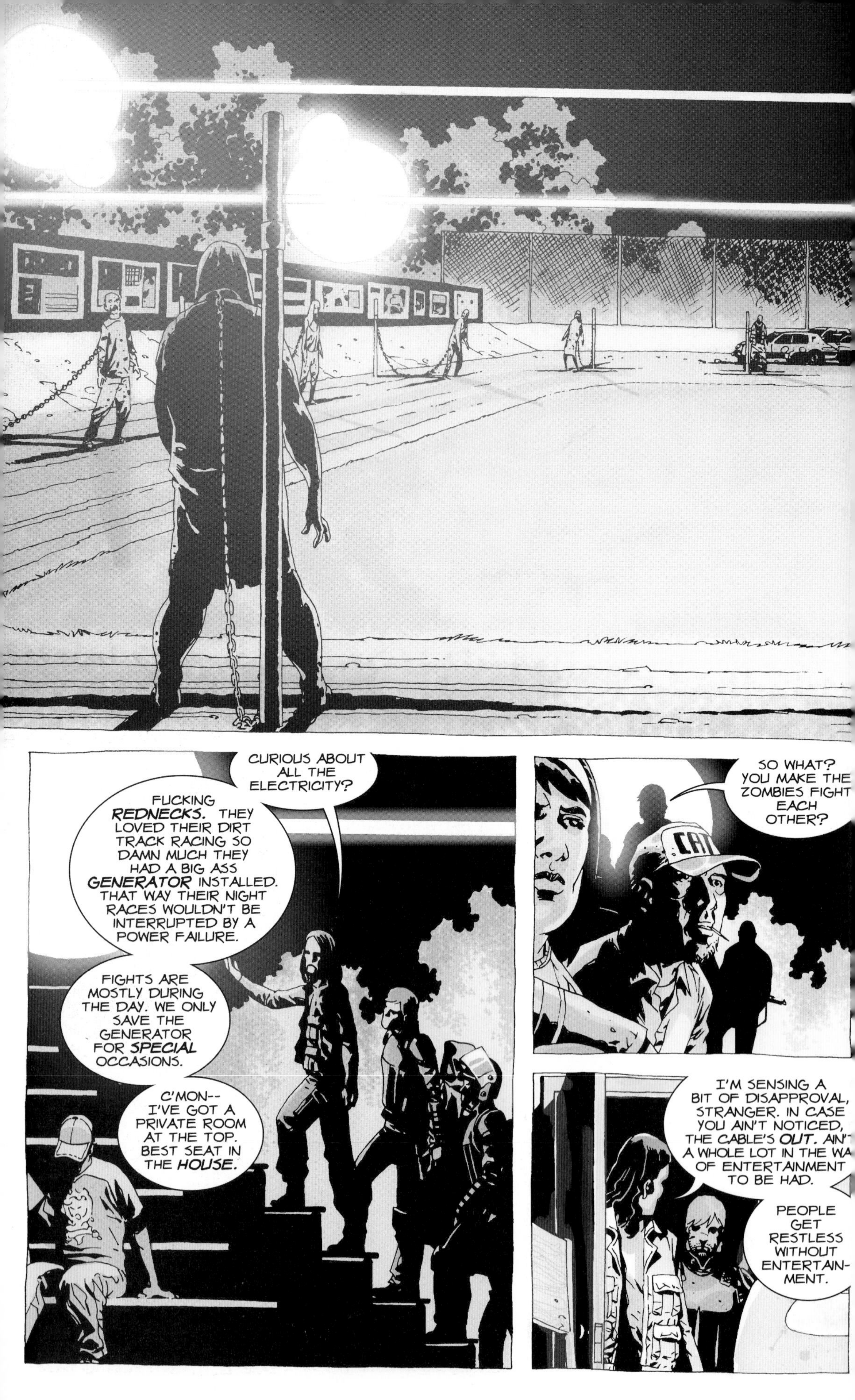
CURIOUS ABOUT ALL THE ELECTRICITY?
FUCKING REDNECKS. THEY LOVED THEIR DIRT TRACK RACING SO DAMN MUCH THEY HAD A BIG ASS GENERATOR INSTALLED. THAT WAY THEIR NIGHT RACES WOULDN'T BE INTERRUPTED BY A POWER FAILURE.
FIGHTS ARE MOSTLY DURING THE DAY. WE ONLY SAVE THE GENERATOR FOR SPECIAL OCCASIONS.
C'MON-- I'VE GOT A PRIVATE ROOM AT THE TOP. BEST SEAT IN THE HOUSE.
SO WHAT? YOU MAKE THE ZOMBIES FIGHT EACH OTHER?
CAT
I'M SENSING A BIT OF DISAPPROVAL, STRANGER. IN CASE YOU AIN'T NOTICED, THE CABLE'S OUT. AIN' A WHOLE LOT IN THE WA OF ENTERTAINMENT TO BE HAD.
PEOPLE GET RESTLESS WITHOUT ENTERTAIN-MENT.

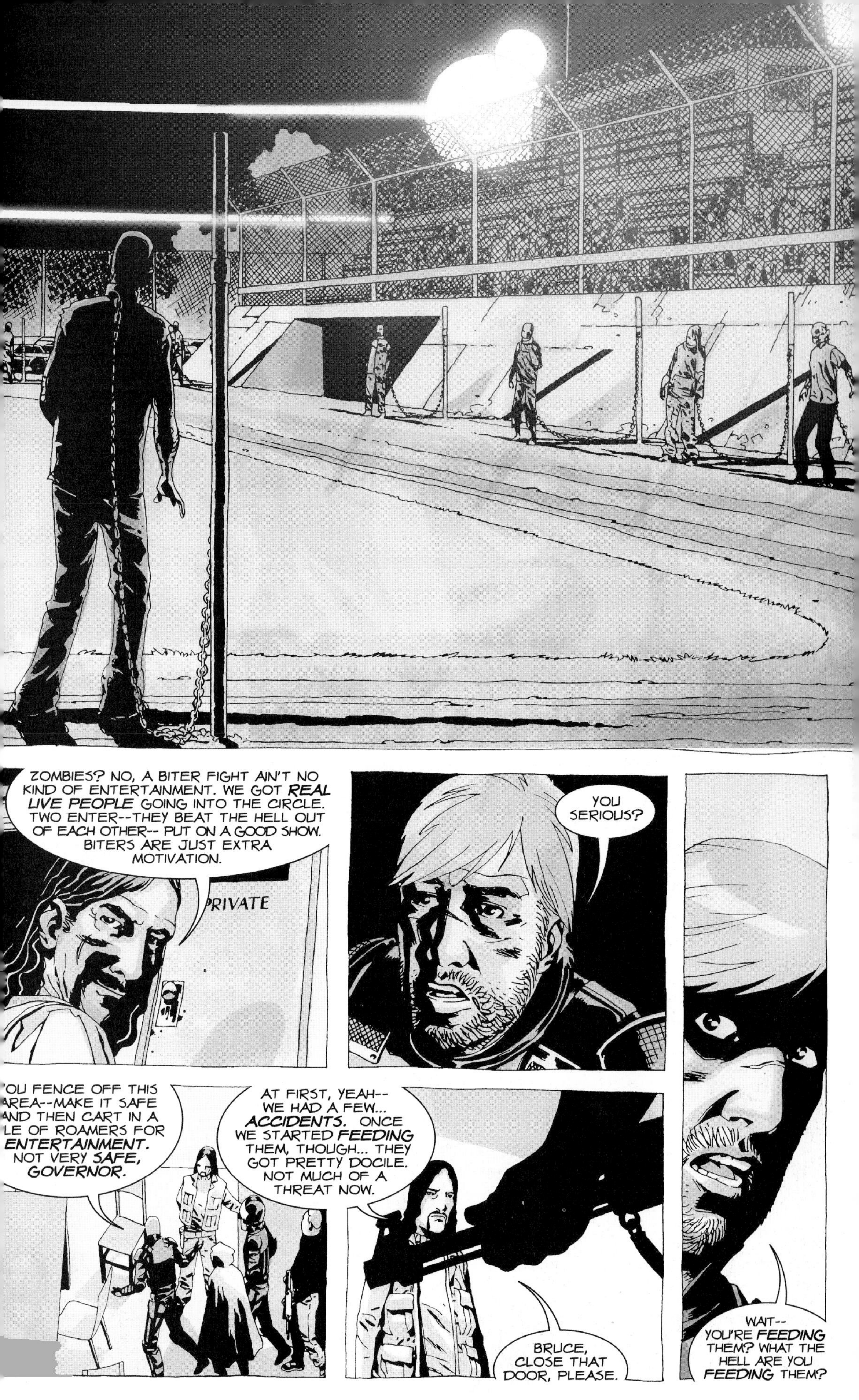
PRIVATE
ZOMBIES? NO, A BITER FIGHT AIN'T NO KIND OF ENTERTAINMENT. WE GOT REAL LIVE PEOPLE GOING INTO THE CIRCLE. TWO ENTER--THEY BEAT THE HELL OUT OF EACH OTHER-- PUT ON A GOOD SHOW. BITERS ARE JUST EXTRA MOTIVATION.
YOU SERIOUS?
OU FENCE OFF THIS AREA--MAKE IT SAFE AND THEN CART IN A LE OF ROAMERS FOR ENTERTAINMENT. NOT VERY SAFE, GOVERNOR.
AT FIRST, YEAH-- WE HAD A FEW... ACCIDENTS. ONCE WE STARTED FEEDING THEM, THOUGH... THEY GOT PRETTY DOCILE. NOT MUCH OF A THREAT NOW.
BRUCE, CLOSE THAT DOOR, PLEASE.
WAIT-- YOU'RE FEEDING THEM? WHAT THE HELL ARE YOU FEEDING THEM?

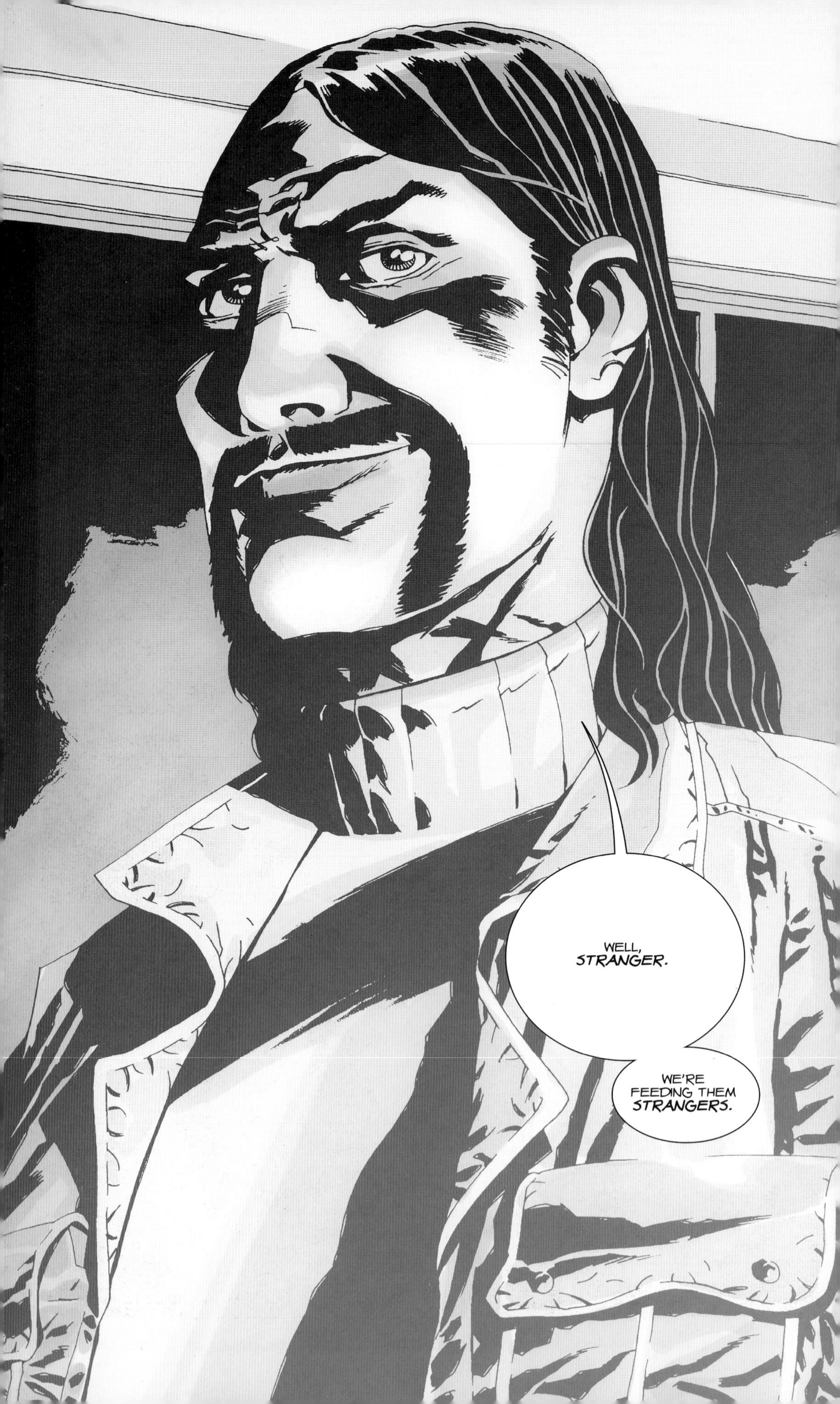
WELL, STRANGER.
WE'RE FEEDING THEM STRANGERS.

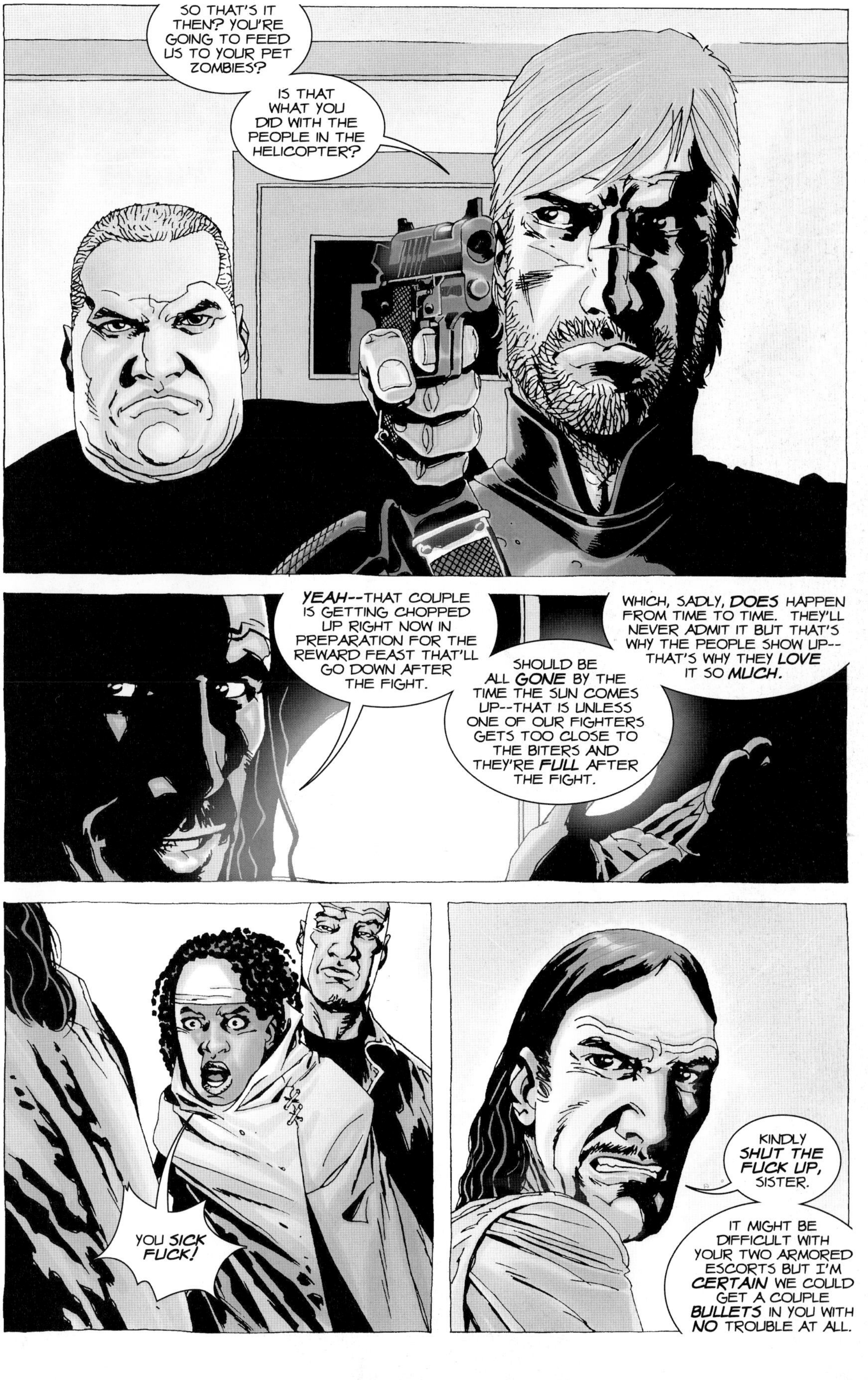
SO THAT'S IT THEN? YOU'RE GOING TO FEED US TO YOUR PET ZOMBIES?
IS THAT WHAT YOU DID WITH THE PEOPLE IN THE HELICOPTER?
YEAH--THAT COUPLE IS GETTING CHOPPED UP RIGHT NOW IN PREPARATION FOR THE REWARD FEAST THAT'LL GO DOWN AFTER THE FIGHT.
SHOULD BE ALL GONE BY THE TIME THE SUN COMES UP--THAT IS UNLESS ONE OF OUR FIGHTERS GETS TOO CLOSE TO THE BITERS AND THEY'RE FULL AFTER THE FIGHT.
WHICH, SADLY, DOES HAPPEN FROM TIME TO TIME. THEY'LL NEVER ADMIT IT BUT THAT'S WHY THE PEOPLE SHOW UP--THAT'S WHY THEY LOVE IT SO MUCH.
YOU SICK FUCK!
KINDLY SHUT THE FUCK UP, SISTER.
IT MIGHT BE DIFFICULT WITH YOUR TWO ARMORED ESCORTS BUT I'M CERTAIN WE COULD GET A COUPLE BULLETS IN YOU WITH NO TROUBLE AT ALL.

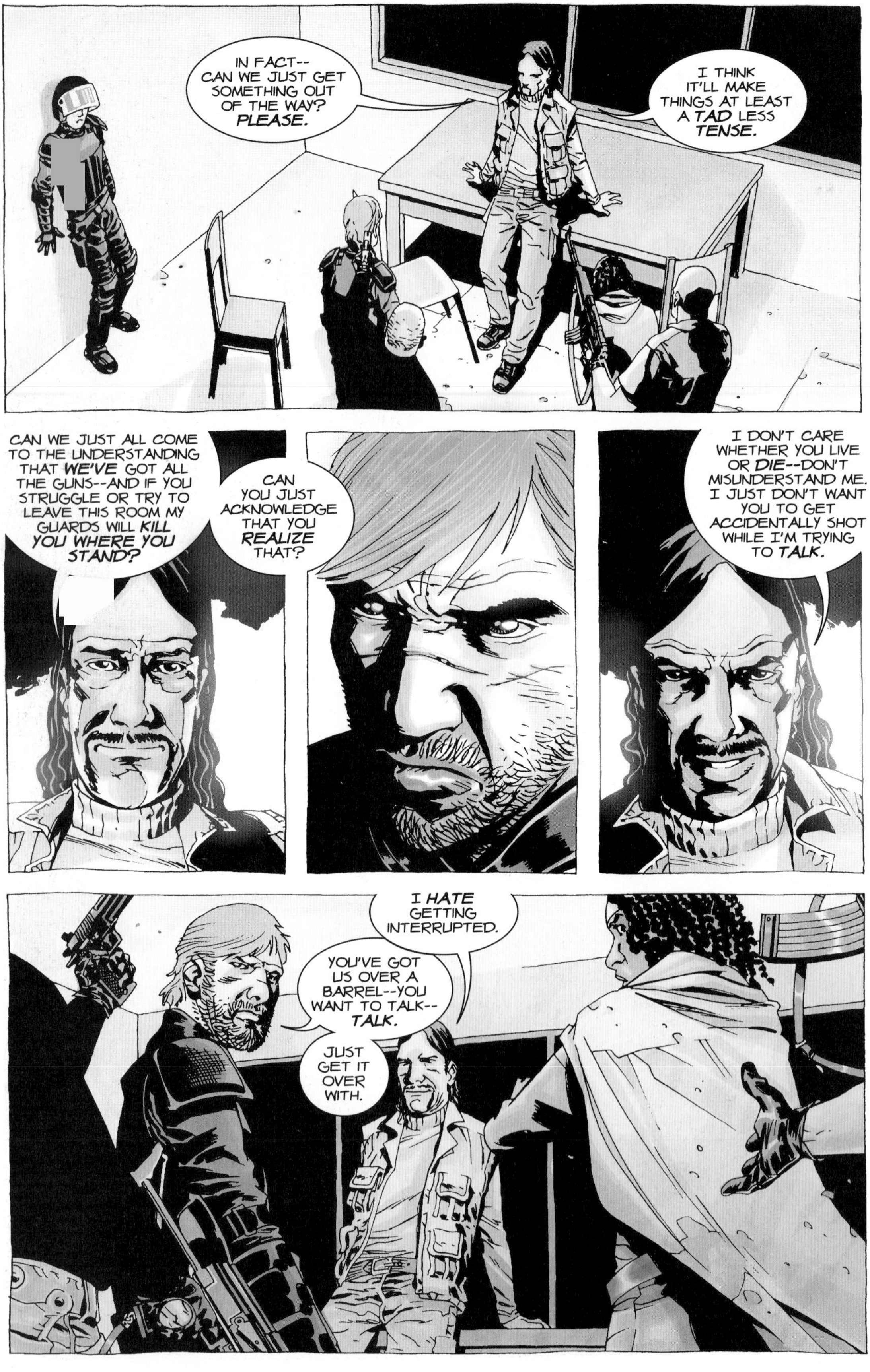
IN FACT-- CAN WE JUST GET SOMETHING OUT OF THE WAY? PLEASE.
I THINK IT'LL MAKE THINGS AT LEAST A TAD LESS TENSE.
CAN WE JUST ALL COME TO THE UNDERSTANDING THAT WE'VE GOT ALL THE GUNS--AND IF YOU STRUGGLE OR TRY TO LEAVE THIS ROOM MY GUARDS WILL KILL YOU WHERE YOU STAND?
CAN YOU JUST ACKNOWLEDGE THAT YOU REALIZE THAT?
I DON'T CARE WHETHER YOU LIVE OR DIE--DON'T MISUNDERSTAND ME. I JUST DON'T WANT YOU TO GET ACCIDENTALLY SHOT WHILE I'M TRYING TO TALK.
I HATE GETTING INTERRUPTED.
YOU'VE GOT US OVER A BARREL--YOU WANT TO TALK-- TALK.
JUST GET IT OVER WITH.

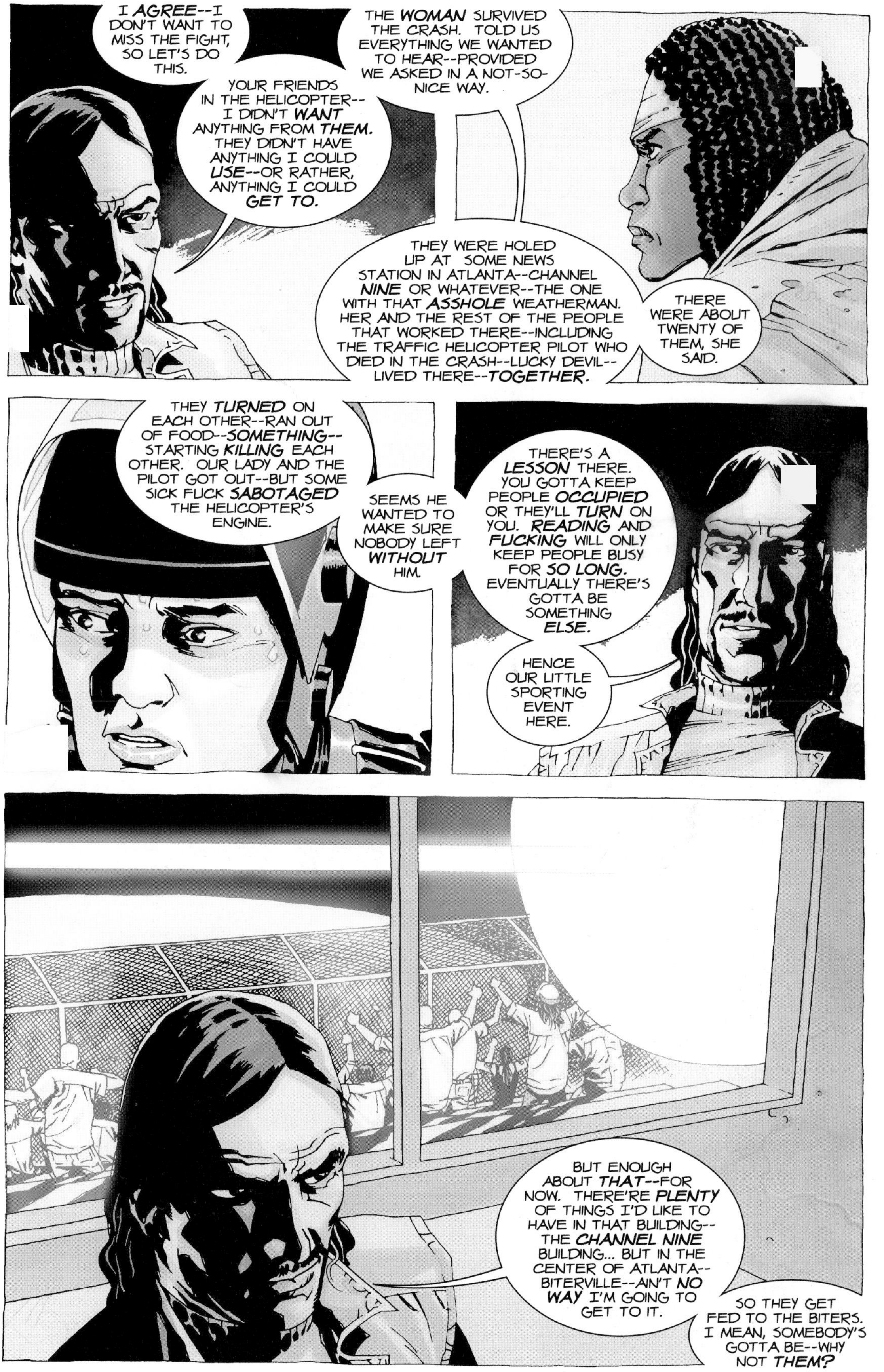
I AGREE--I DON'T WANT TO MISS THE FIGHT, SO LET'S DO THIS.
YOUR FRIENDS IN THE HELICOPTER--I DIDN'T WANT ANYTHING FROM THEM. THEY DIDN'T HAVE ANYTHING I COULD USE--OR RATHER, ANYTHING I COULD GET TO.
THE WOMAN SURVIVED THE CRASH. TOLD US EVERYTHING WE WANTED TO HEAR--PROVIDED WE ASKED IN A NOT-SO-NICE WAY.
THEY WERE HOLED UP AT SOME NEWS STATION IN ATLANTA--CHANNEL NINE OR WHATEVER--THE ONE WITH THAT ASSHOLE WEATHERMAN. HER AND THE REST OF THE PEOPLE THAT WORKED THERE--INCLUDING THE TRAFFIC HELICOPTER PILOT WHO DIED IN THE CRASH--LUCKY DEVIL--LIVED THERE--TOGETHER.
THERE WERE ABOUT TWENTY OF THEM, SHE SAID.
THEY TURNED ON EACH OTHER--RAN OUT OF FOOD--SOMETHING--STARTING KILLING EACH OTHER. OUR LADY AND THE PILOT GOT OUT--BUT SOME SICK FUCK SABOTAGED THE HELICOPTER'S ENGINE.
SEEMS HE WANTED TO MAKE SURE NOBODY LEFT WITHOUT HIM.
THERE'S A LESSON THERE. YOU GOTTA KEEP PEOPLE OCCUPIED OR THEY'LL TURN ON YOU. READING AND FUCKING WILL ONLY KEEP PEOPLE BUSY FOR SO LONG. EVENTUALLY THERE'S GOTTA BE SOMETHING ELSE.
HENCE OUR LITTLE SPORTING EVENT HERE.
BUT ENOUGH ABOUT THAT--FOR NOW. THERE'RE PLENTY OF THINGS I'D LIKE TO HAVE IN THAT BUILDING--THE CHANNEL NINE BUILDING... BUT IN THE CENTER OF ATLANTA--BITERVILLE--AIN'T NO WAY I'M GOING TO GET TO IT.
SO THEY GET FED TO THE BITERS. I MEAN, SOMEBODY'S GOTTA BE--WHY NOT THEM?

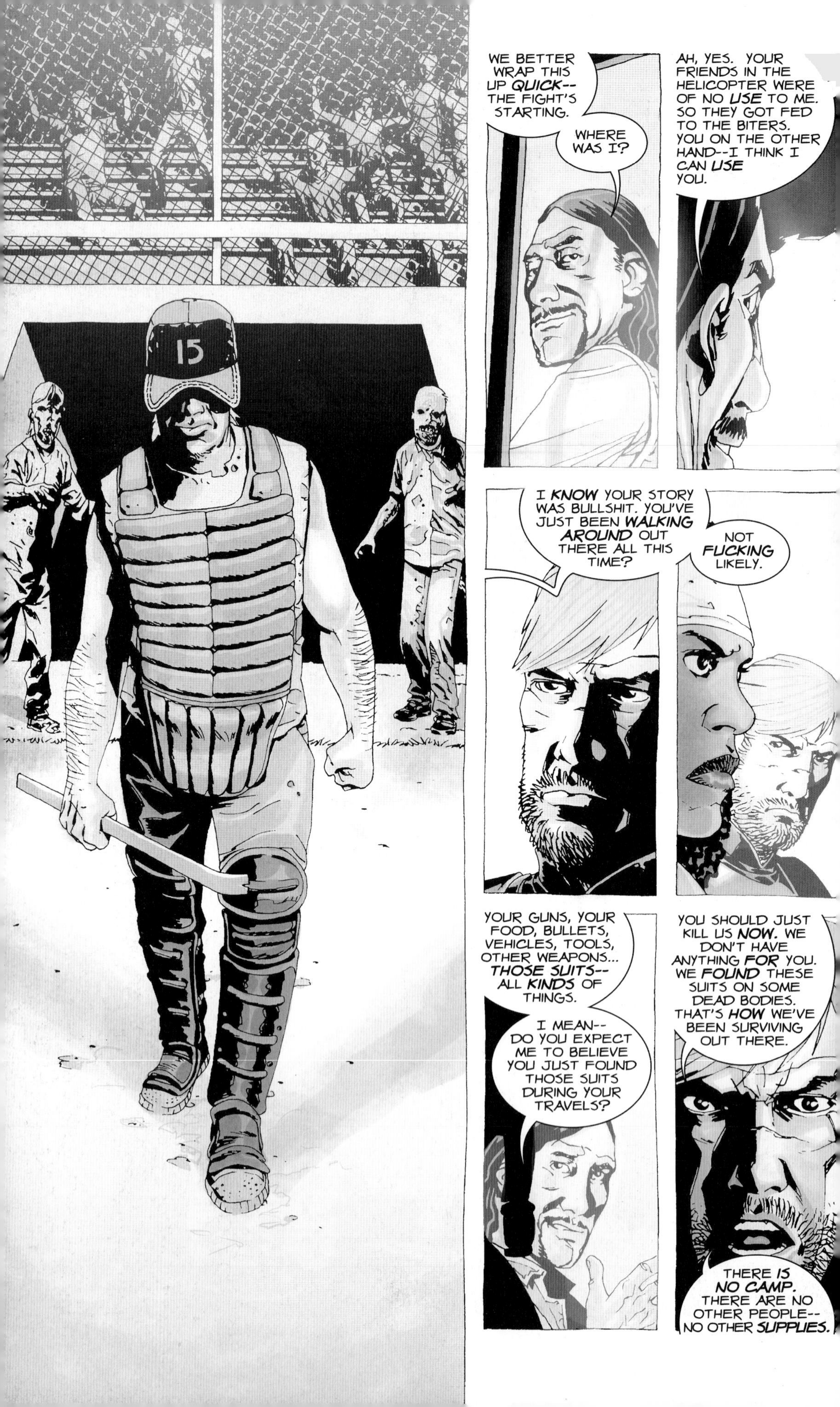

15
WE BETTER WRAP THIS UP QUICK-- THE FIGHT'S STARTING.
WHERE WAS I?
AH, YES. YOUR FRIENDS IN THE HELICOPTER WERE OF NO USE TO ME. SO THEY GOT FED TO THE BITERS. YOU ON THE OTHER HAND--I THINK I CAN USE YOU.
I KNOW YOUR STORY WAS BULLSHIT. YOU'VE JUST BEEN WALKING AROUND OUT THERE ALL THIS TIME?
NOT FUCKING LIKELY.
YOUR GUNS, YOUR FOOD, BULLETS, VEHICLES, TOOLS, OTHER WEAPONS... THOSE SUITS-- ALL KINDS OF THINGS.
I MEAN-- DO YOU EXPECT ME TO BELIEVE YOU JUST FOUND THOSE SUITS DURING YOUR TRAVELS?
YOU SHOULD JUST KILL US NOW. WE DON'T HAVE ANYTHING FOR YOU. WE FOUND THESE SUITS ON SOME DEAD BODIES. THAT'S HOW WE'VE BEEN SURVIVING OUT THERE.
THERE IS NO CAMP. THERE ARE NO OTHER PEOPLE-- NO OTHER SUPPLIES.

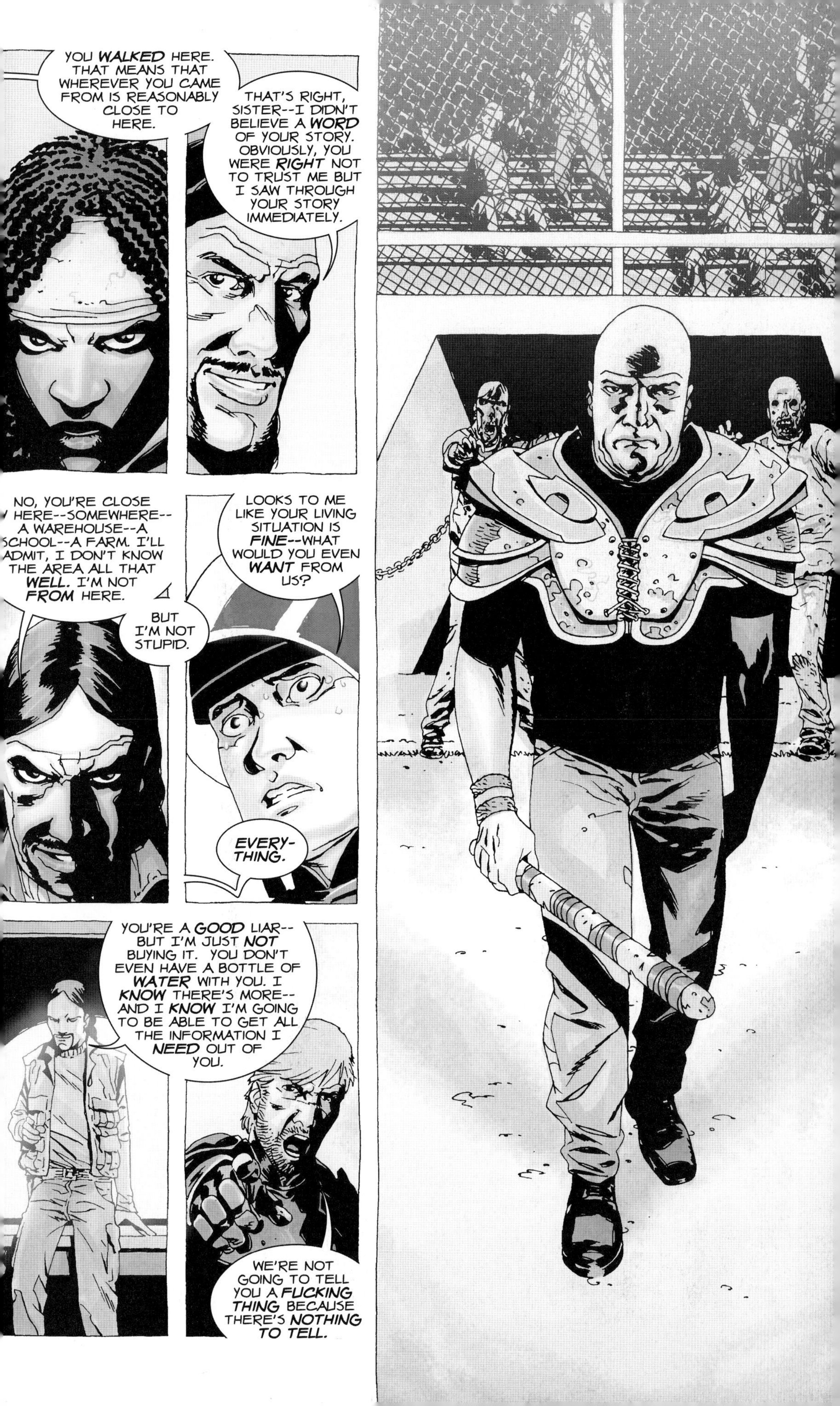

YOU WALKED HERE. THAT MEANS THAT WHEREVER YOU CAME FROM IS REASONABLY CLOSE TO HERE.
THAT'S RIGHT, SISTER--I DIDN'T BELIEVE A WORD OF YOUR STORY. OBVIOUSLY, YOU WERE RIGHT NOT TO TRUST ME BUT I SAW THROUGH YOUR STORY IMMEDIATELY.
NO, YOU'RE CLOSE HERE--SOMEWHERE--A WAREHOUSE--A SCHOOL--A FARM. I'LL ADMIT, I DON'T KNOW THE AREA ALL THAT WELL. I'M NOT FROM HERE.
BUT I'M NOT STUPID.
LOOKS TO ME LIKE YOUR LIVING SITUATION IS FINE--WHAT WOULD YOU EVEN WANT FROM US?
EVERY-THING.
YOU'RE A GOOD LIAR--BUT I'M JUST NOT BUYING IT. YOU DON'T EVEN HAVE A BOTTLE OF WATER WITH YOU. I KNOW THERE'S MORE--AND I KNOW I'M GOING TO BE ABLE TO GET ALL THE INFORMATION I NEED OUT OF YOU.
WE'RE NOT GOING TO TELL YOU A FUCKING THING BECAUSE THERE'S NOTHING TO TELL.

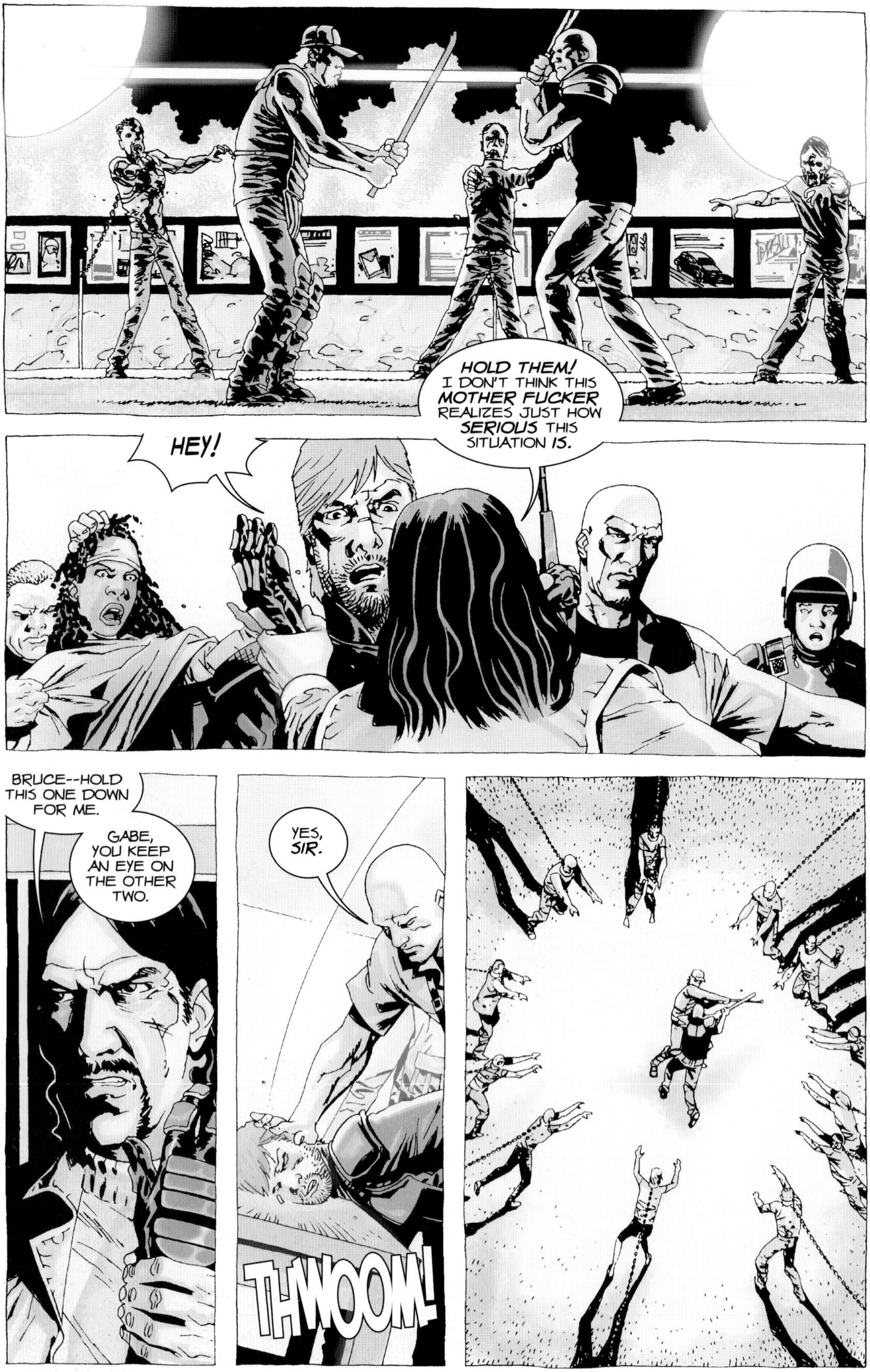

HOLD THEM! I DON'T THINK THIS MOTHER FUCKER REALIZES JUST HOW SERIOUS THIS SITUATION IS.
HEY!
BRUCE--HOLD THIS ONE DOWN FOR ME.
GABE, YOU KEEP AN EYE ON THE OTHER TWO.
YES, SIR.
THWOOM!

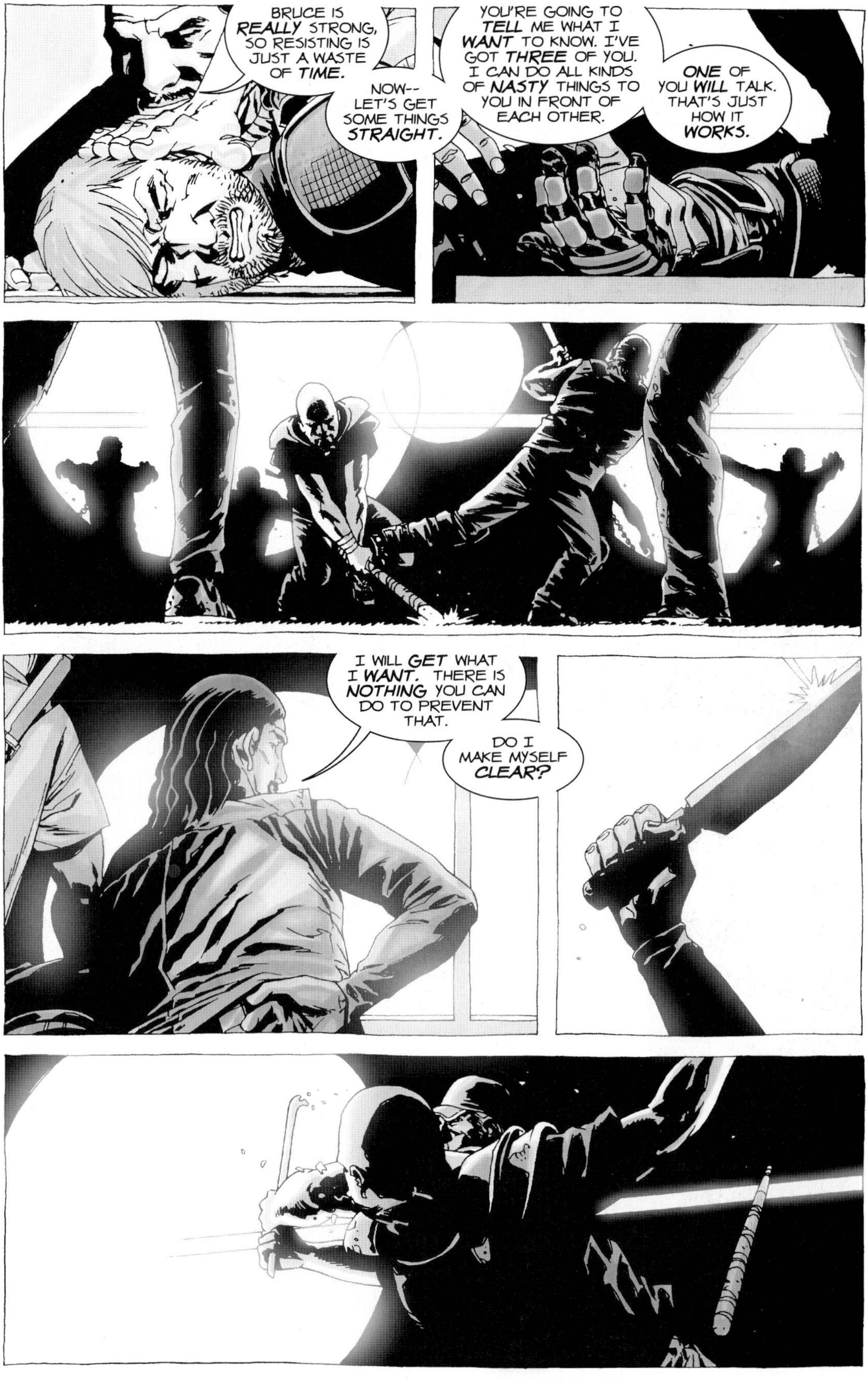
BRUCE IS REALLY STRONG, SO RESISTING IS JUST A WASTE OF TIME.
NOW-- LET'S GET SOME THINGS STRAIGHT.
YOU'RE GOING TO TELL ME WHAT I WANT TO KNOW. I'VE GOT THREE OF YOU. I CAN DO ALL KINDS OF NASTY THINGS TO YOU IN FRONT OF EACH OTHER.
ONE OF YOU WILL TALK. THAT'S JUST HOW IT WORKS.
I WILL GET WHAT I WANT. THERE IS NOTHING YOU CAN DO TO PREVENT THAT.
DO I MAKE MYSELF CLEAR?

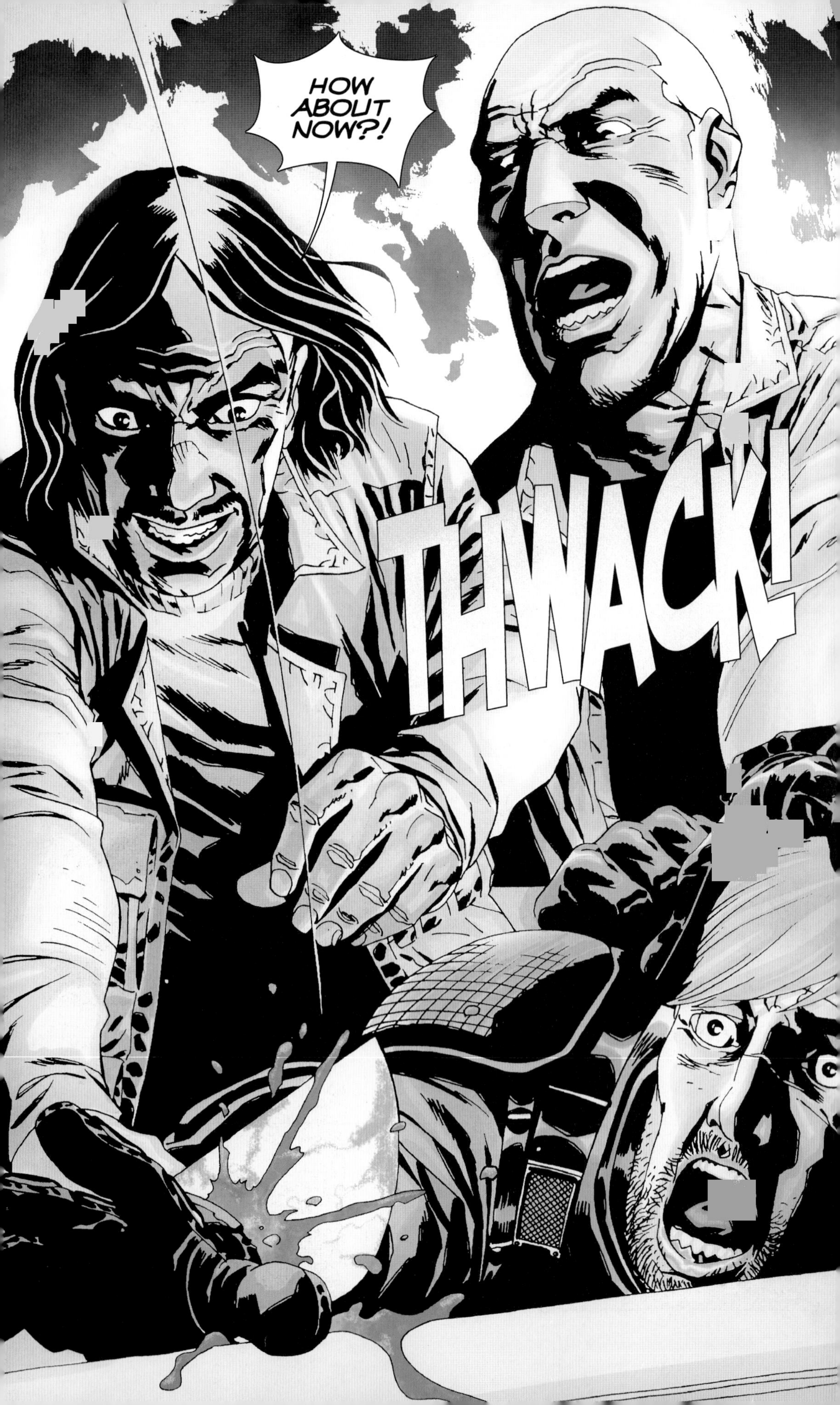
HOW ABOUT NOW?!
THWACK!

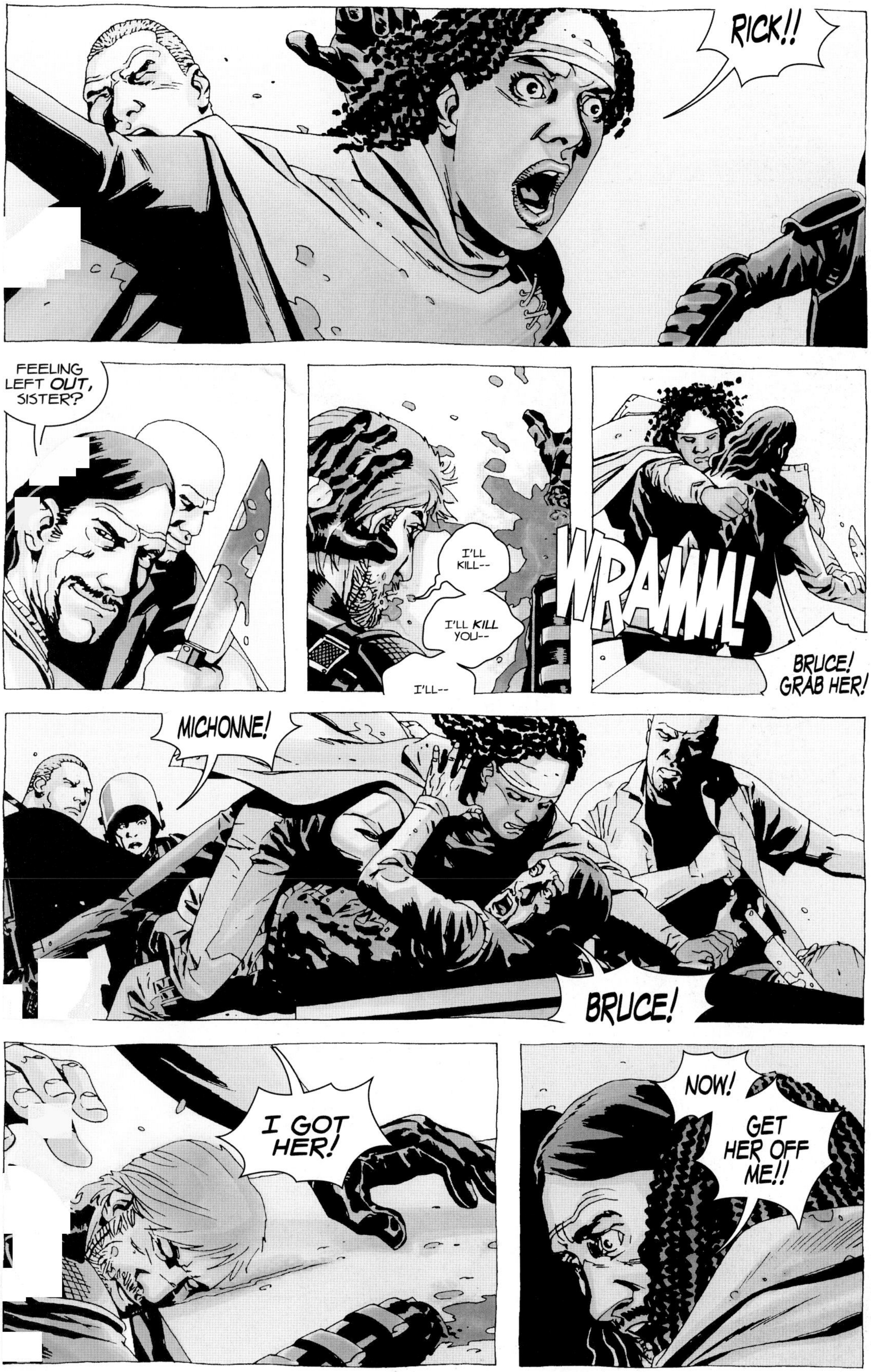
RICK!!
FEELING LEFT OUT, SISTER?
I'LL KILL--
I'LL KILL YOU--
I'LL--
WRAMM!
BRUCE! GRAB HER!
MICHONNE!
BRUCE!
I GOT HER!
NOW!
GET HER OFF ME!!

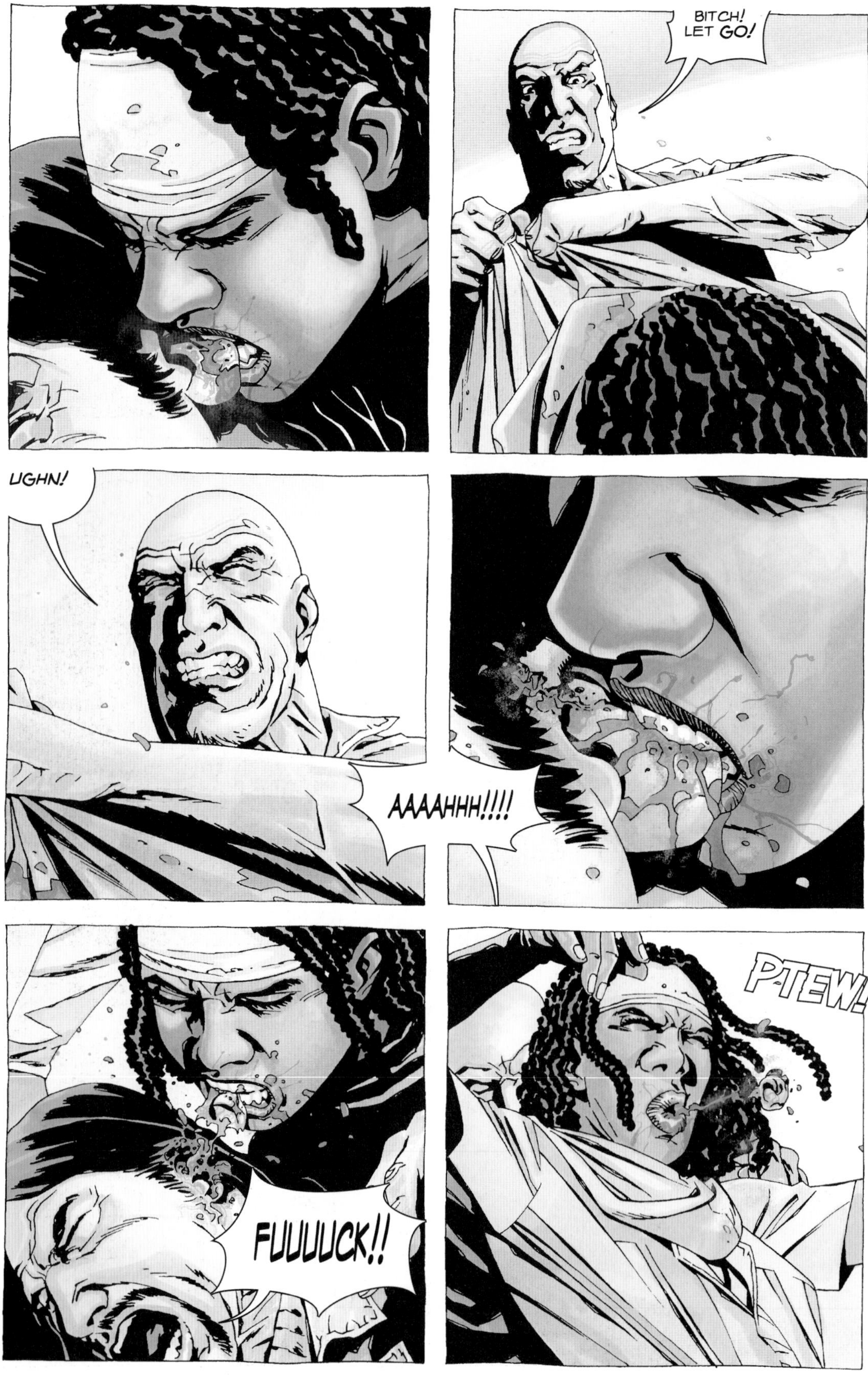
BITCH! LET GO!
UGHN!
AAAAHHH!!!!
FUUUUCK!!
PTEW!

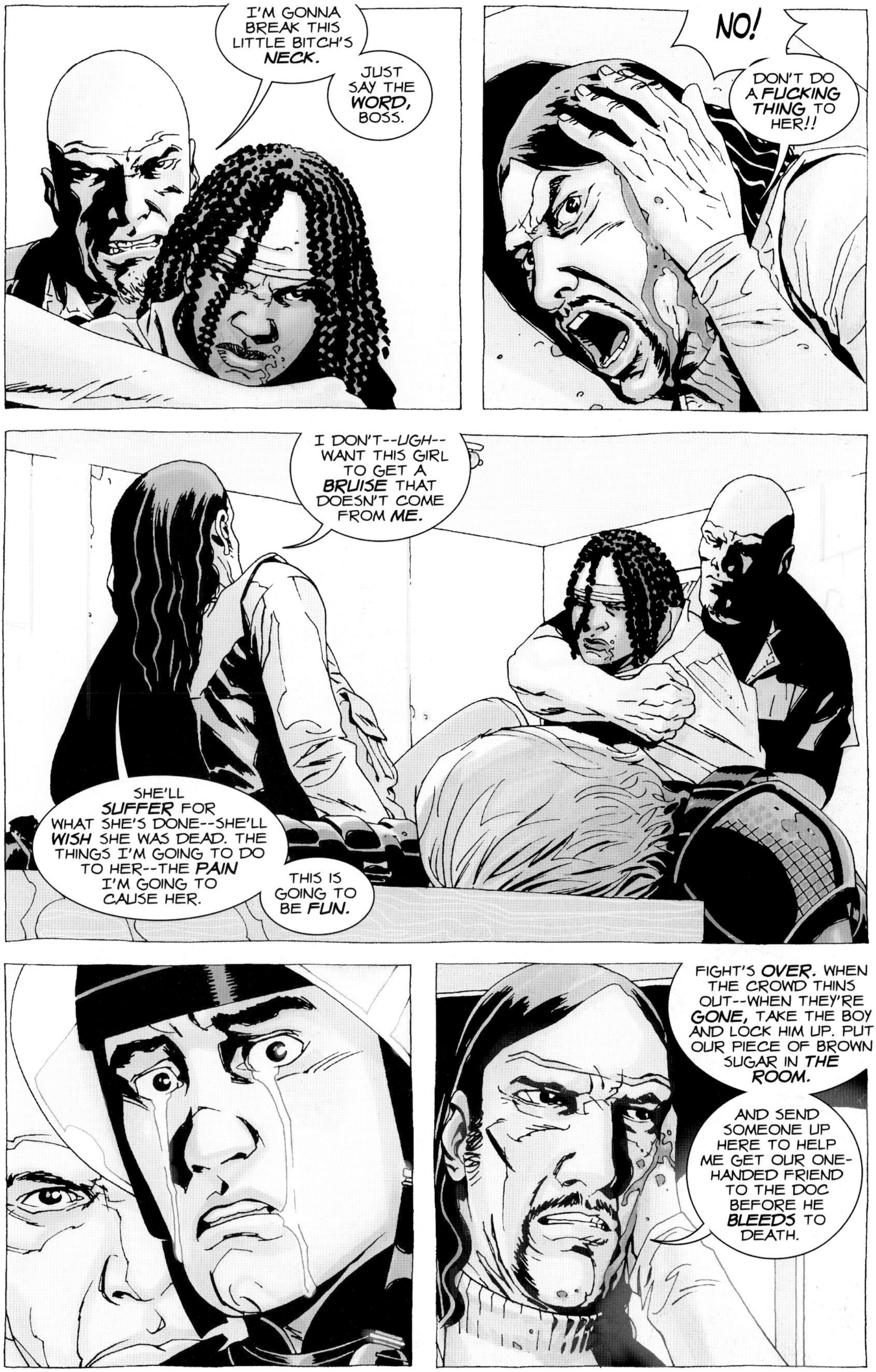
I'M GONNA BREAK THIS LITTLE BITCH'S NECK.
JUST SAY THE WORD, BOSS.
NO!
DON'T DO A FUCKING THING TO HER!!
I DON'T--UGH--WANT THIS GIRL TO GET A BRUISE THAT DOESN'T COME FROM ME.
SHE'LL SUFFER FOR WHAT SHE'S DONE--SHE'LL WISH SHE WAS DEAD. THE THINGS I'M GOING TO DO TO HER--THE PAIN I'M GOING TO CAUSE HER.
THIS IS GOING TO BE FUN.
FIGHT'S OVER. WHEN THE CROWD THINS OUT--WHEN THEY'RE GONE, TAKE THE BOY AND LOCK HIM UP. PUT OUR PIECE OF BROWN SUGAR IN THE ROOM.
AND SEND SOMEONE UP HERE TO HELP ME GET OUR ONE-HANDED FRIEND TO THE DOC BEFORE HE BLEEDS TO DEATH.

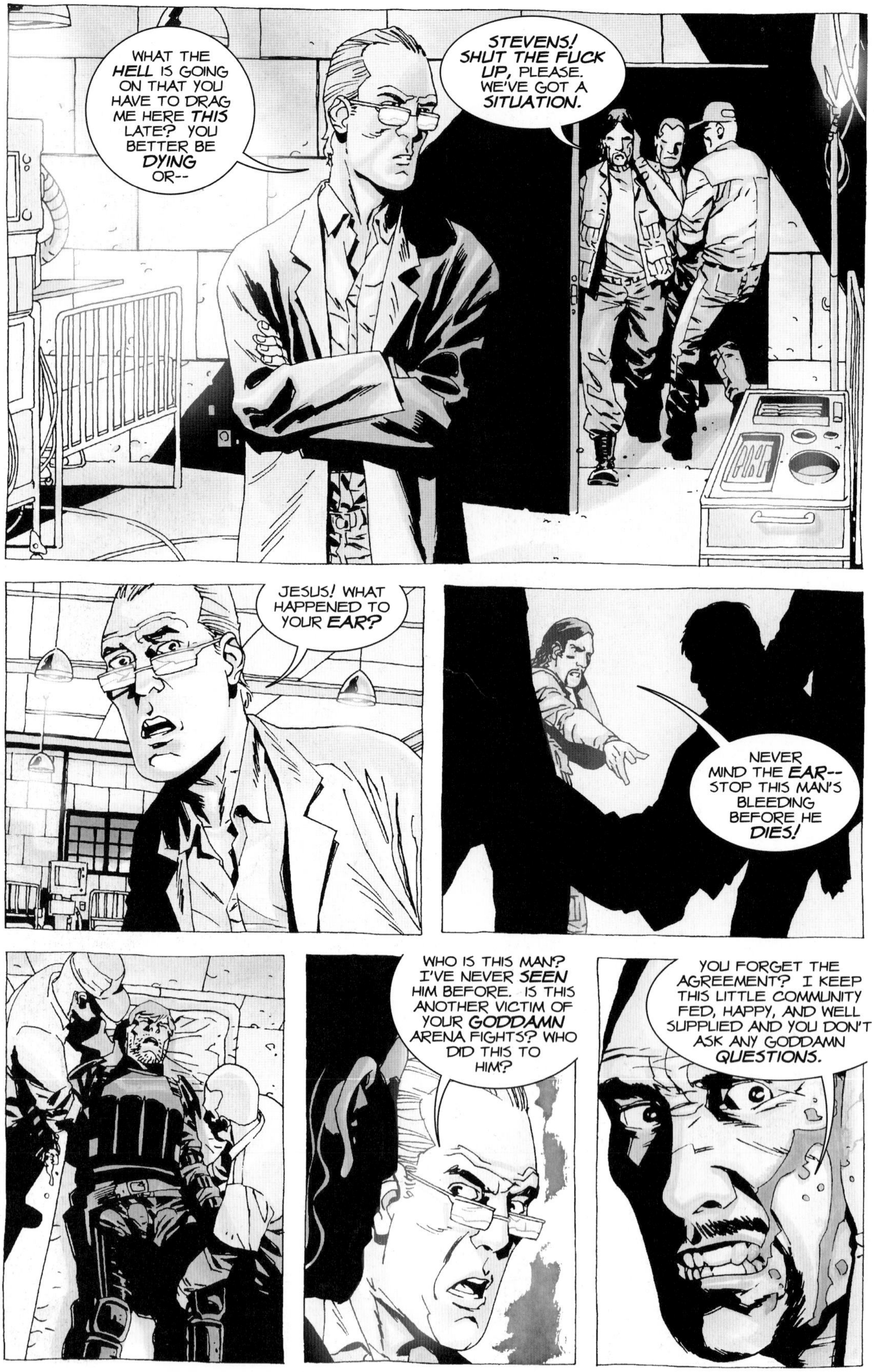
WHAT THE HELL IS GOING ON THAT YOU HAVE TO DRAG ME HERE THIS LATE? YOU BETTER BE DYING OR--
STEVENS! SHUT THE FUCK UP, PLEASE. WE'VE GOT A SITUATION.
JESUS! WHAT HAPPENED TO YOUR EAR?
NEVER MIND THE EAR-- STOP THIS MAN'S BLEEDING BEFORE HE DIES!
WHO IS THIS MAN? I'VE NEVER SEEN HIM BEFORE. IS THIS ANOTHER VICTIM OF YOUR GODDAMN ARENA FIGHTS? WHO DID THIS TO HIM?
YOU FORGET THE AGREEMENT? I KEEP THIS LITTLE COMMUNITY FED, HAPPY, AND WELL SUPPLIED AND YOU DON'T ASK ANY GODDAMN QUESTIONS.

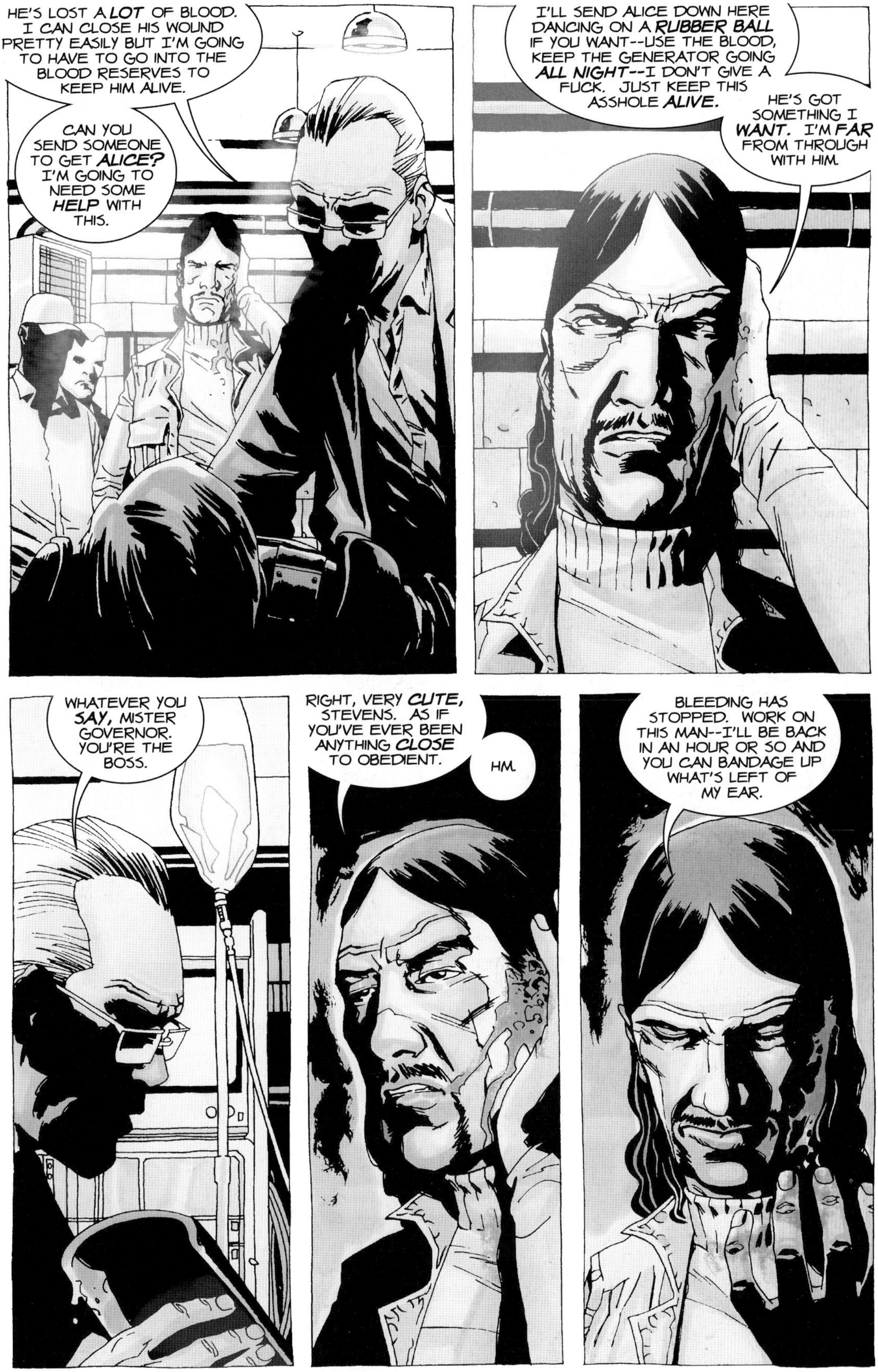
HE'S LOST A LOT OF BLOOD. I CAN CLOSE HIS WOUND PRETTY EASILY BUT I'M GOING TO HAVE TO GO INTO THE BLOOD RESERVES TO KEEP HIM ALIVE.
CAN YOU SEND SOMEONE TO GET ALICE? I'M GOING TO NEED SOME HELP WITH THIS.
I'LL SEND ALICE DOWN HERE DANCING ON A RUBBER BALL IF YOU WANT--USE THE BLOOD, KEEP THE GENERATOR GOING ALL NIGHT--I DON'T GIVE A FUCK. JUST KEEP THIS ASSHOLE ALIVE.
HE'S GOT SOMETHING I WANT. I'M FAR FROM THROUGH WITH HIM.
WHATEVER YOU SAY, MISTER GOVERNOR. YOU'RE THE BOSS.
RIGHT, VERY CUTE, STEVENS. AS IF YOU'VE EVER BEEN ANYTHING CLOSE TO OBEDIENT.
HM.
BLEEDING HAS STOPPED. WORK ON THIS MAN--I'LL BE BACK IN AN HOUR OR SO AND YOU CAN BANDAGE UP WHAT'S LEFT OF MY EAR.

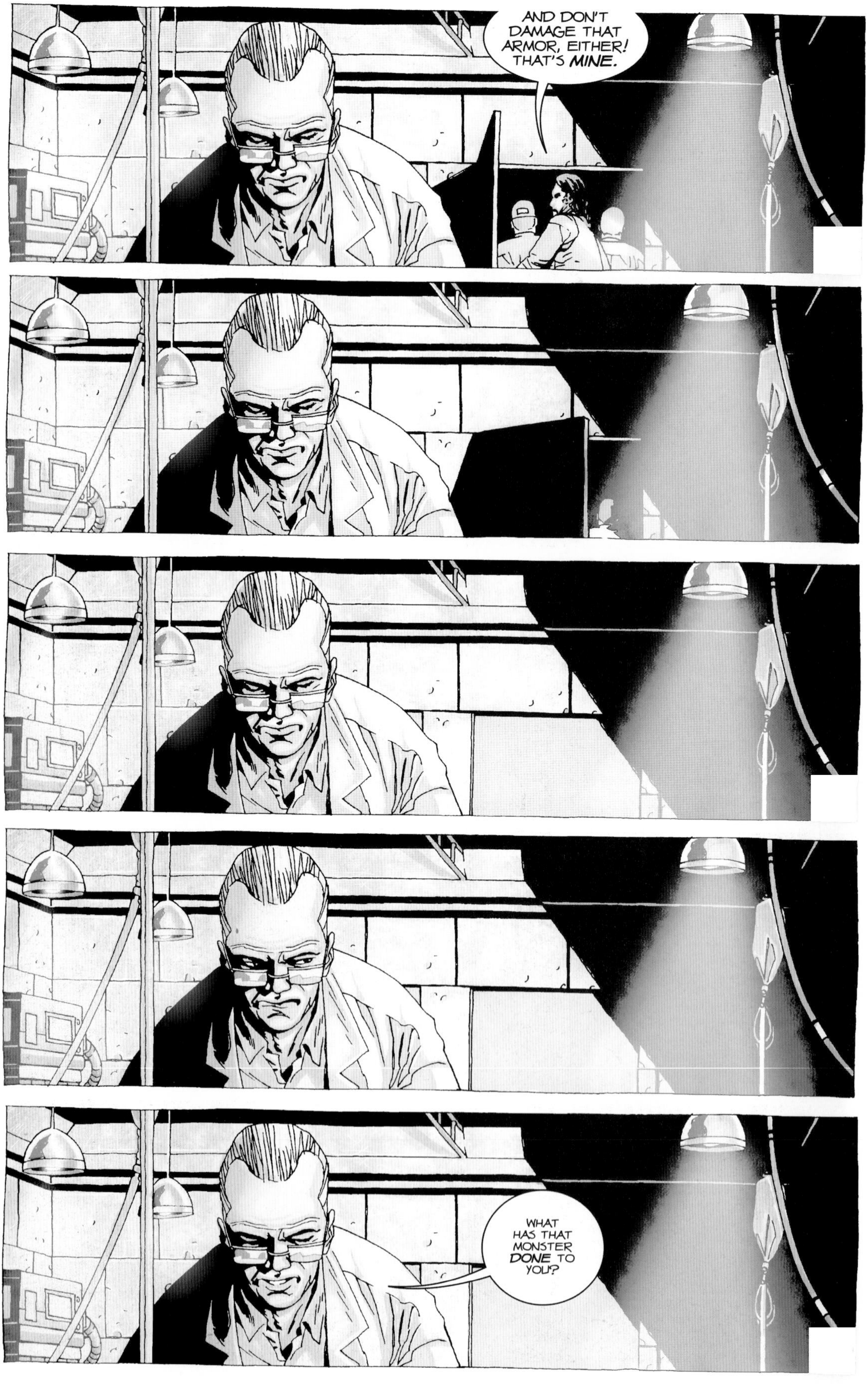
AND DON'T DAMAGE THAT ARMOR, EITHER! THAT'S MINE.
WHAT HAS THAT MONSTER DONE TO YOU!?

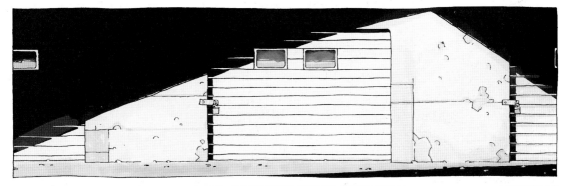

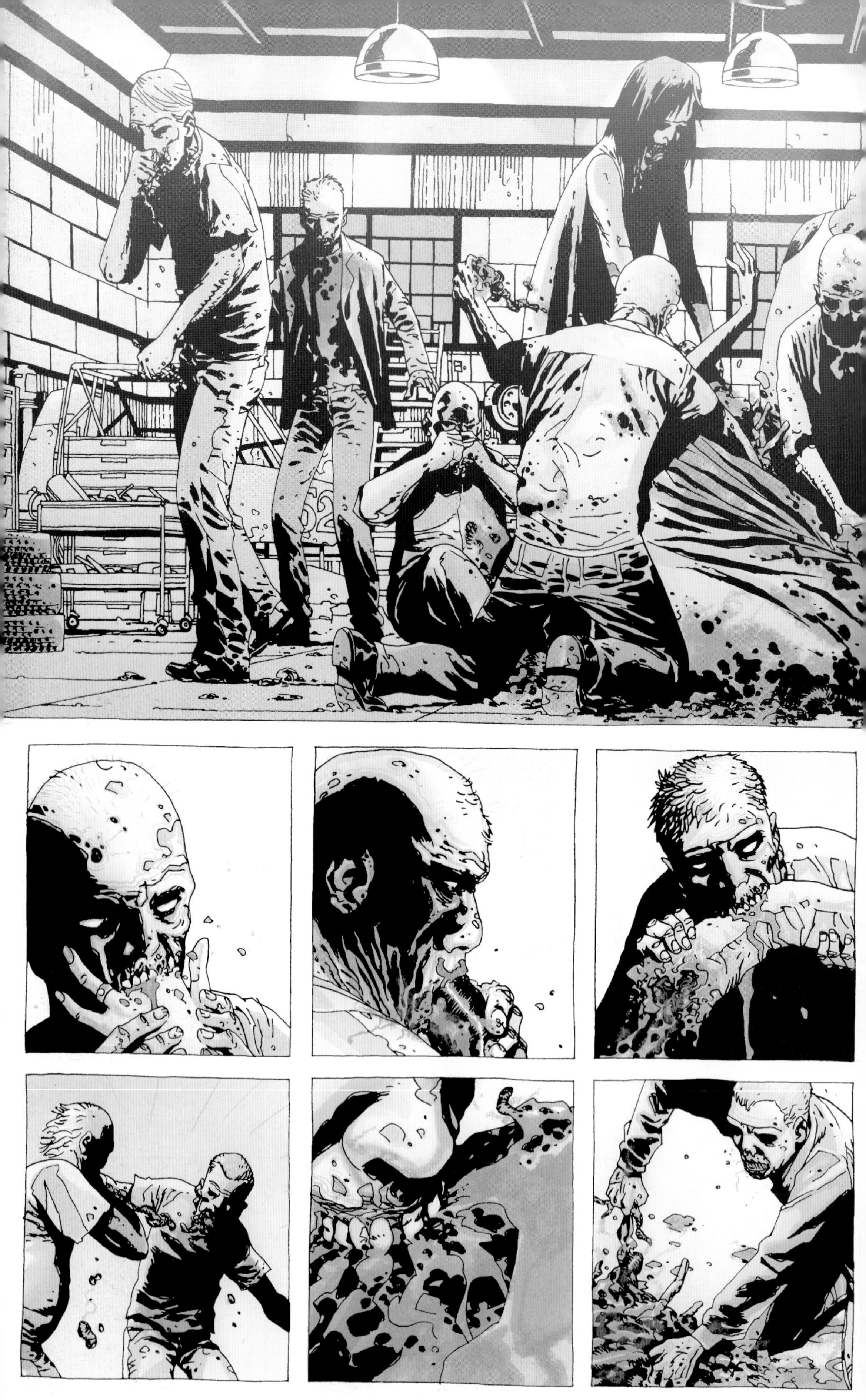

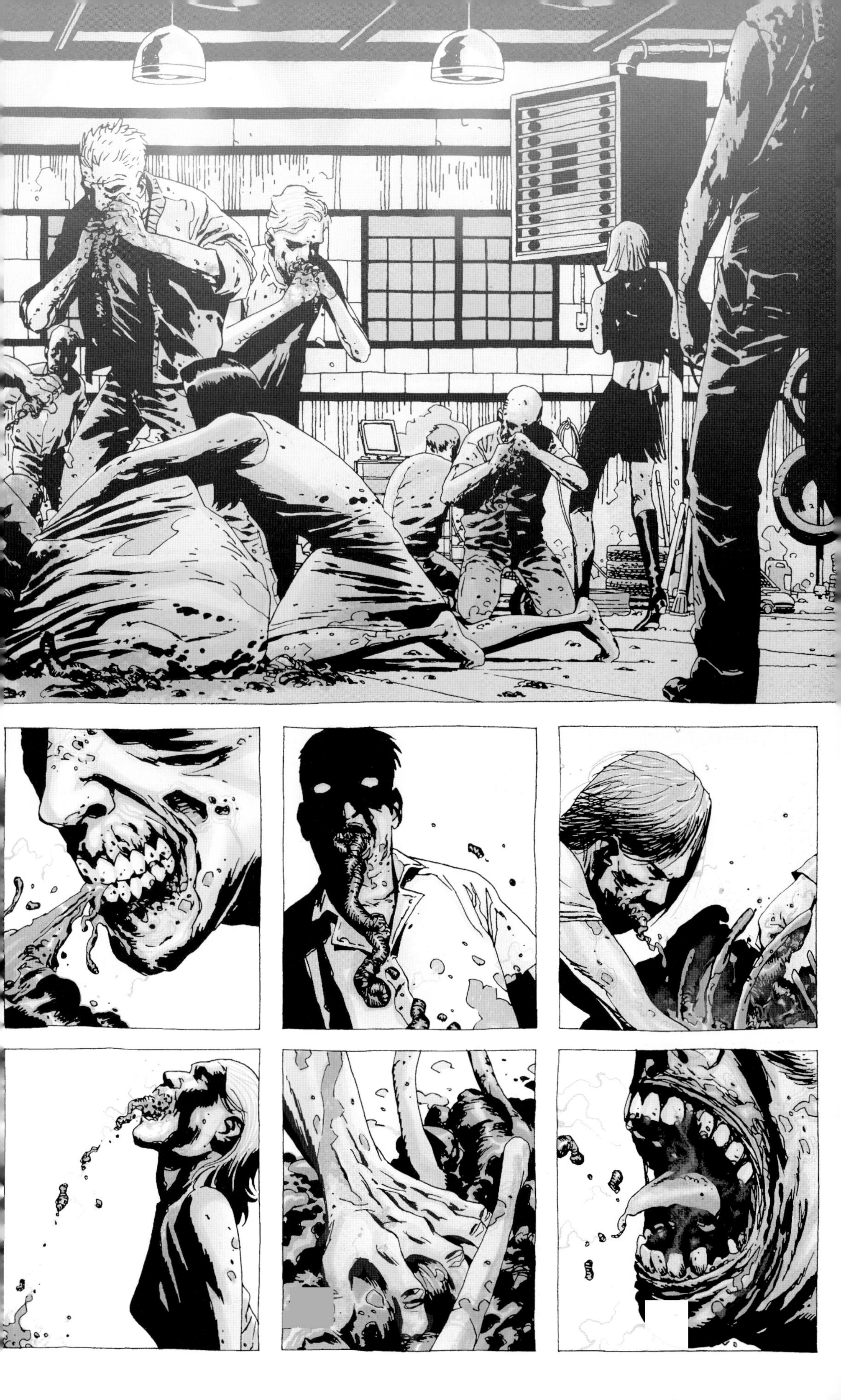

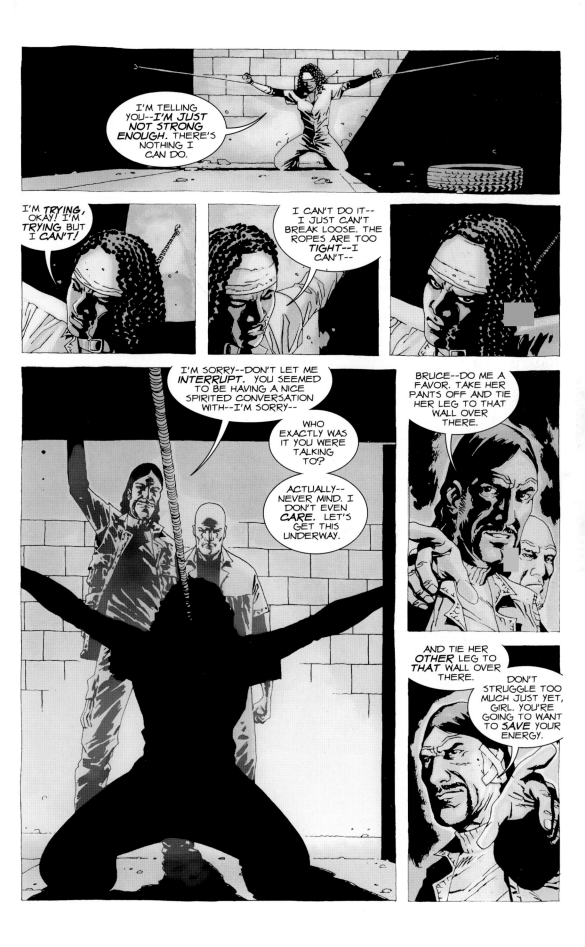

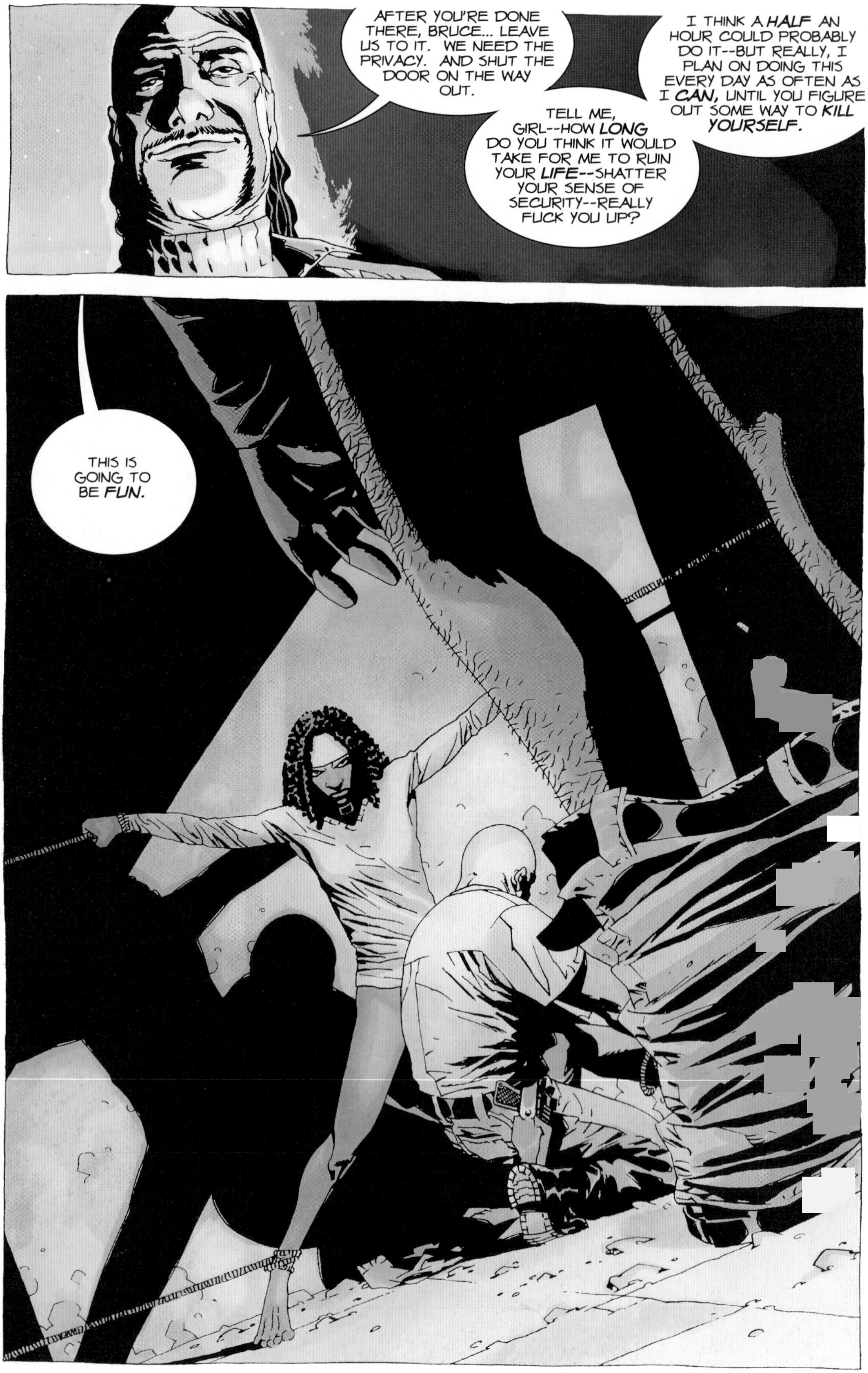

AFTER YOU'RE DONE THERE, BRUCE... LEAVE US TO IT. WE NEED THE PRIVACY. AND SHUT THE DOOR ON THE WAY OUT.
TELL ME, GIRL--HOW LONG DO YOU THINK IT WOULD TAKE FOR ME TO RUIN YOUR LIFE--SHATTER YOUR SENSE OF SECURITY--REALLY FUCK YOU UP?
I THINK A HALF AN HOUR COULD PROBABLY DO IT--BUT REALLY, I PLAN ON DOING THIS EVERY DAY AS OFTEN AS I CAN, UNTIL YOU FIGURE OUT SOME WAY TO KILL YOURSELF.
THIS IS GOING TO BE FUN.

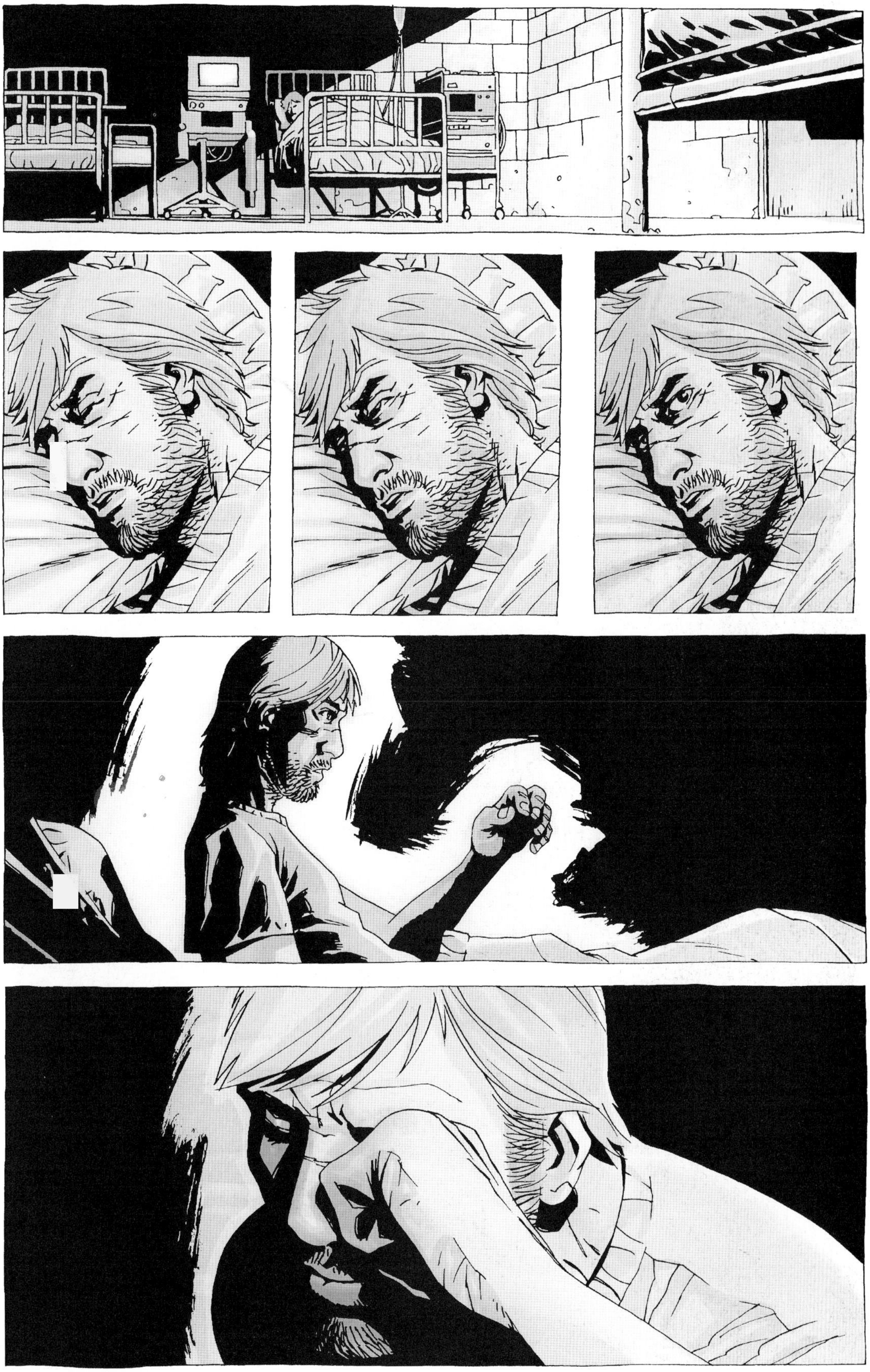

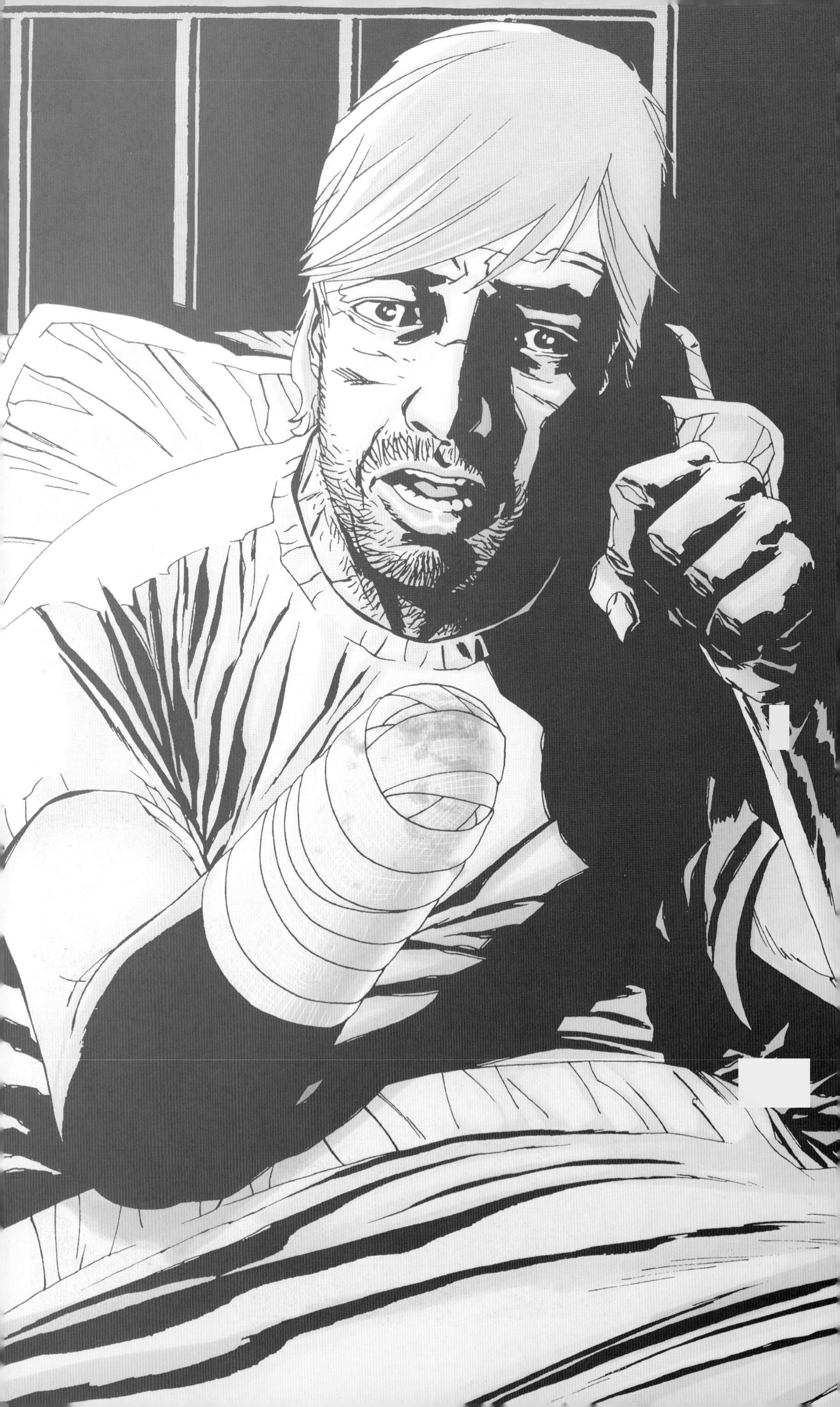

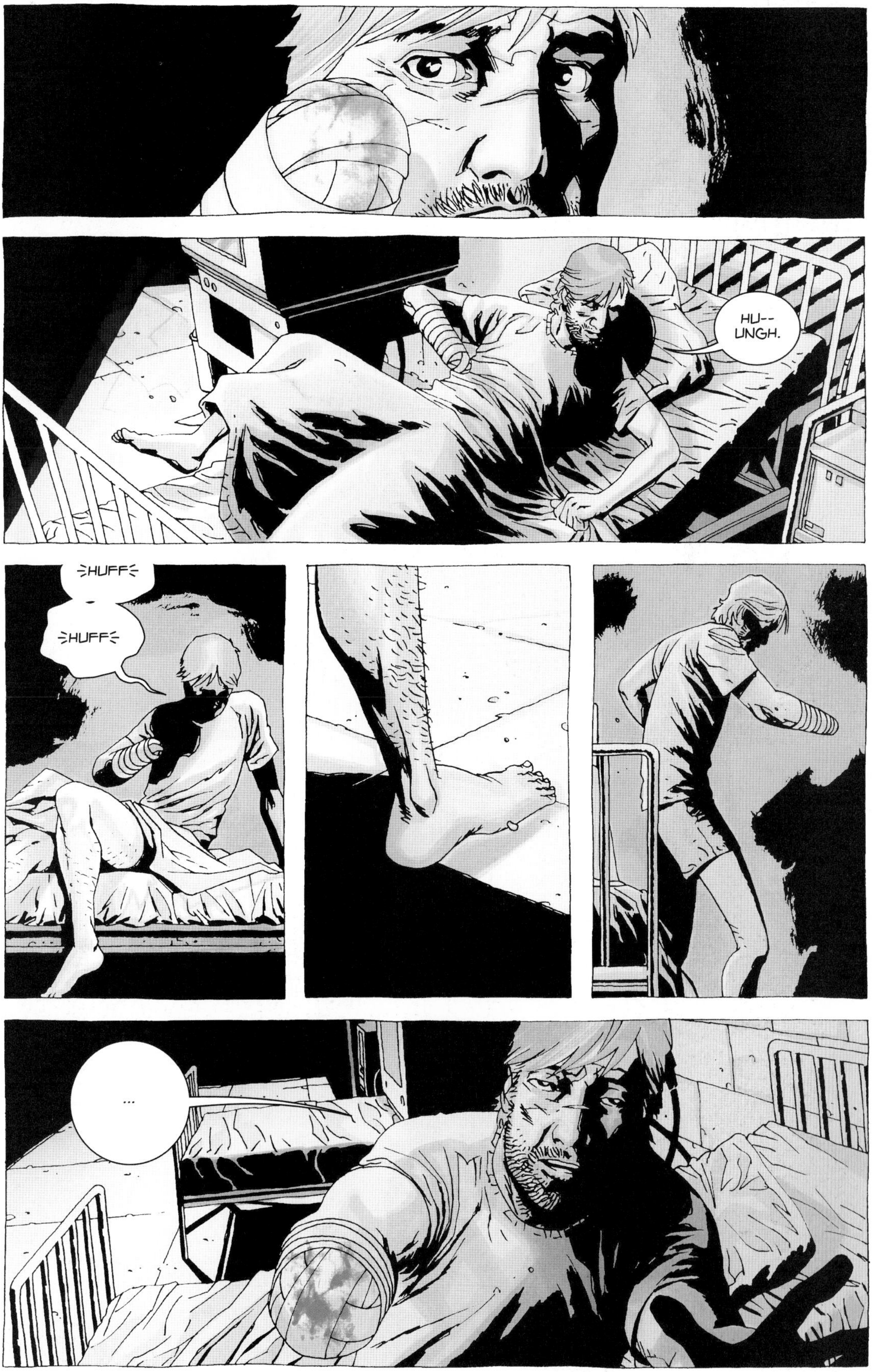
HU--
UNGH.
HUFF
HUFF
...

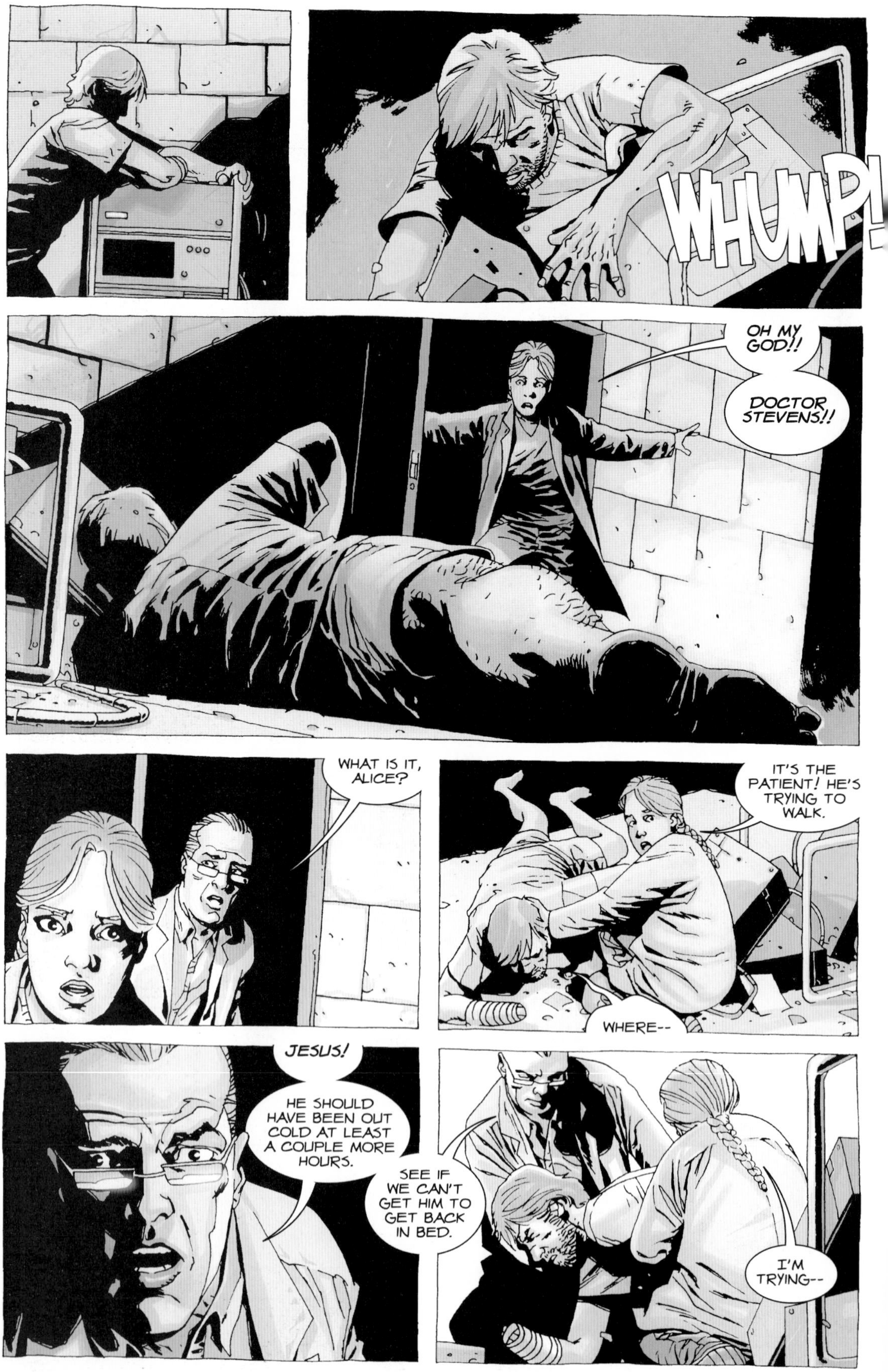
WHUMP!
OH MY GOD!!
DOCTOR STEVENS!!
WHAT IS IT, ALICE?
IT'S THE PATIENT! HE'S TRYING TO WALK.
WHERE--
JESUS!
HE SHOULD HAVE BEEN OUT COLD AT LEAST A COUPLE MORE HOURS.
SEE IF WE CAN'T GET HIM TO GET BACK IN BED.
I'M TRYING--

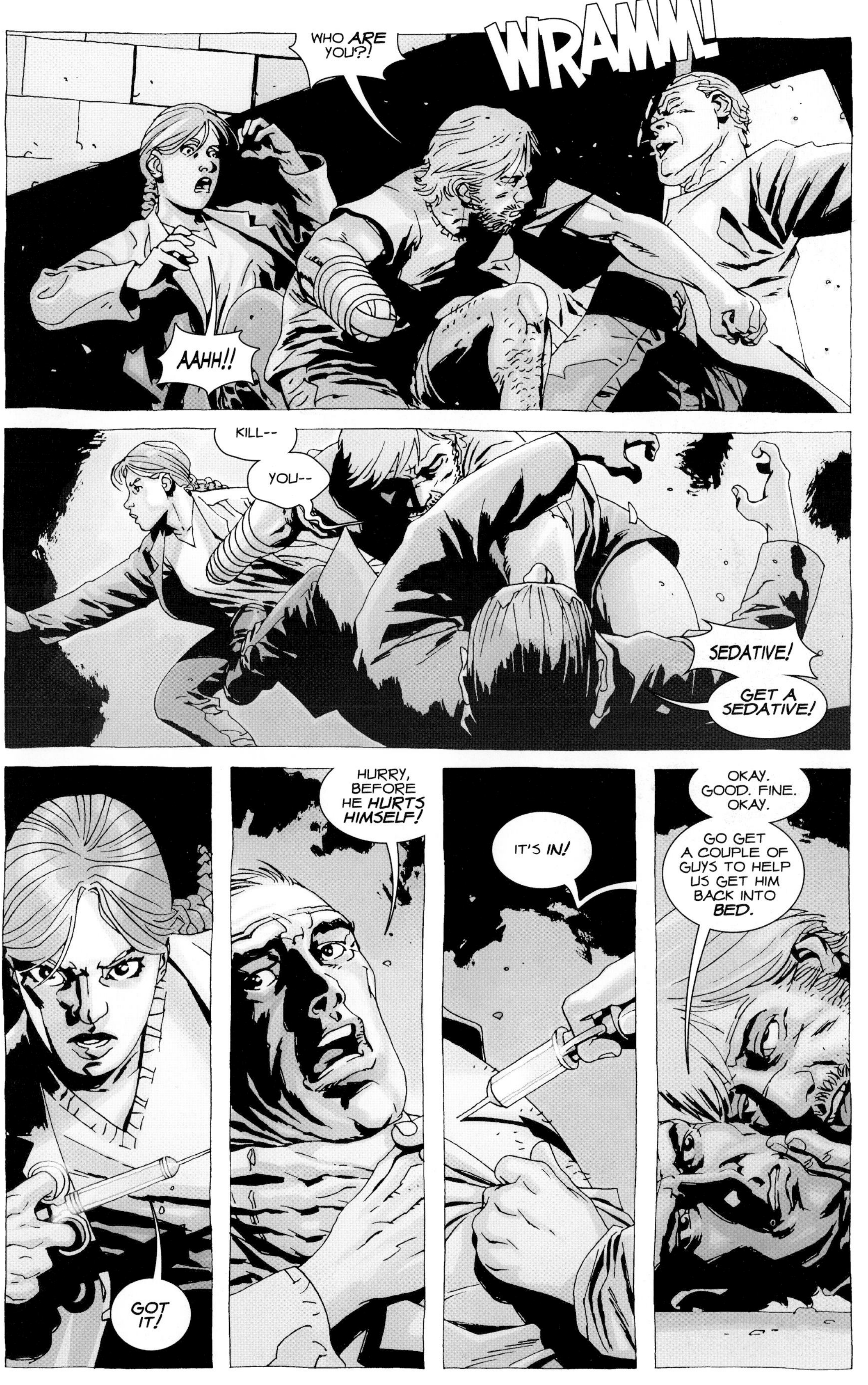
WHO ARE YOU?!
WRAMM!
AAHH!!
KILL--
YOU--
SEDATIVE!
GET A SEDATIVE!
GOT IT!
HURRY, BEFORE HE HURTS HIMSELF!
IT'S IN!
OKAY. GOOD. FINE. OKAY.
GO GET A COUPLE OF GUYS TO HELP US GET HIM BACK INTO BED.

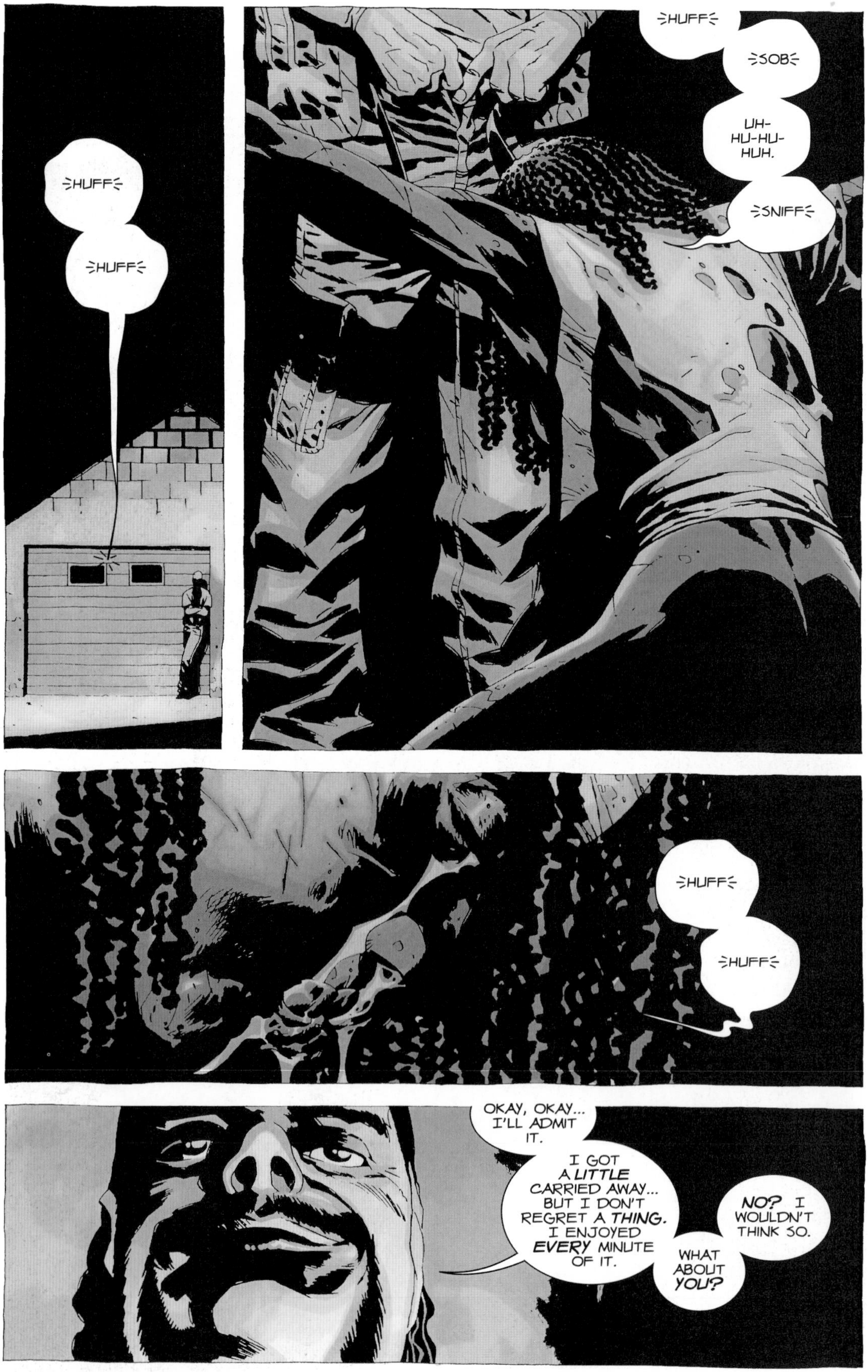

HUFF
HUFF
HUFF
SOB
UH-HU-HU-HUH.
SNIFF
HUFF
HUFF
OKAY, OKAY... I'LL ADMIT IT.
I GOT A LITTLE CARRIED AWAY... BUT I DON'T REGRET A THING. I ENJOYED EVERY MINUTE OF IT.
WHAT ABOUT YOU?
NO? I WOULDN'T THINK SO.

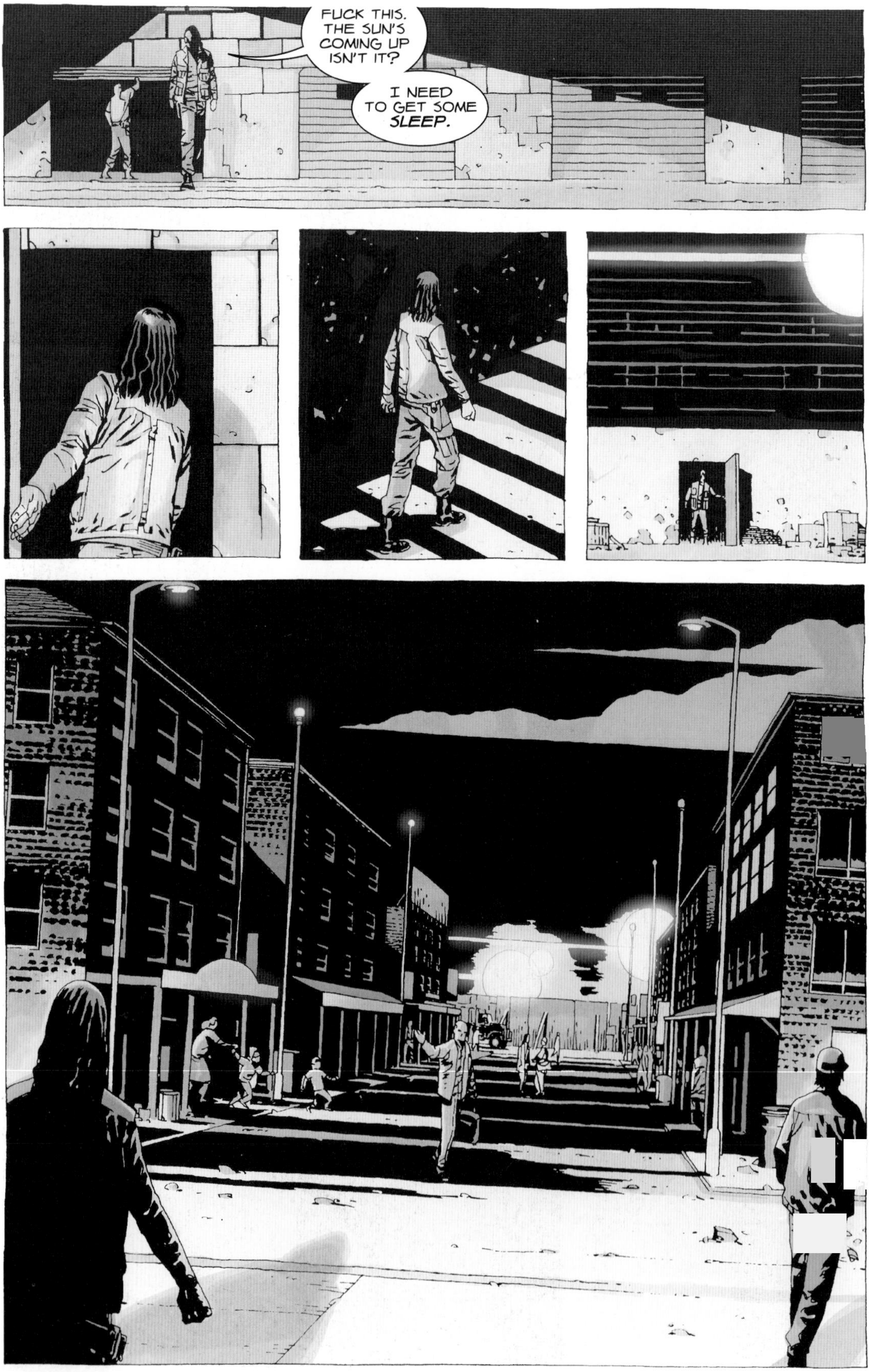
FUCK THIS. THE SUN'S COMING UP ISN'T IT?
I NEED TO GET SOME SLEEP.

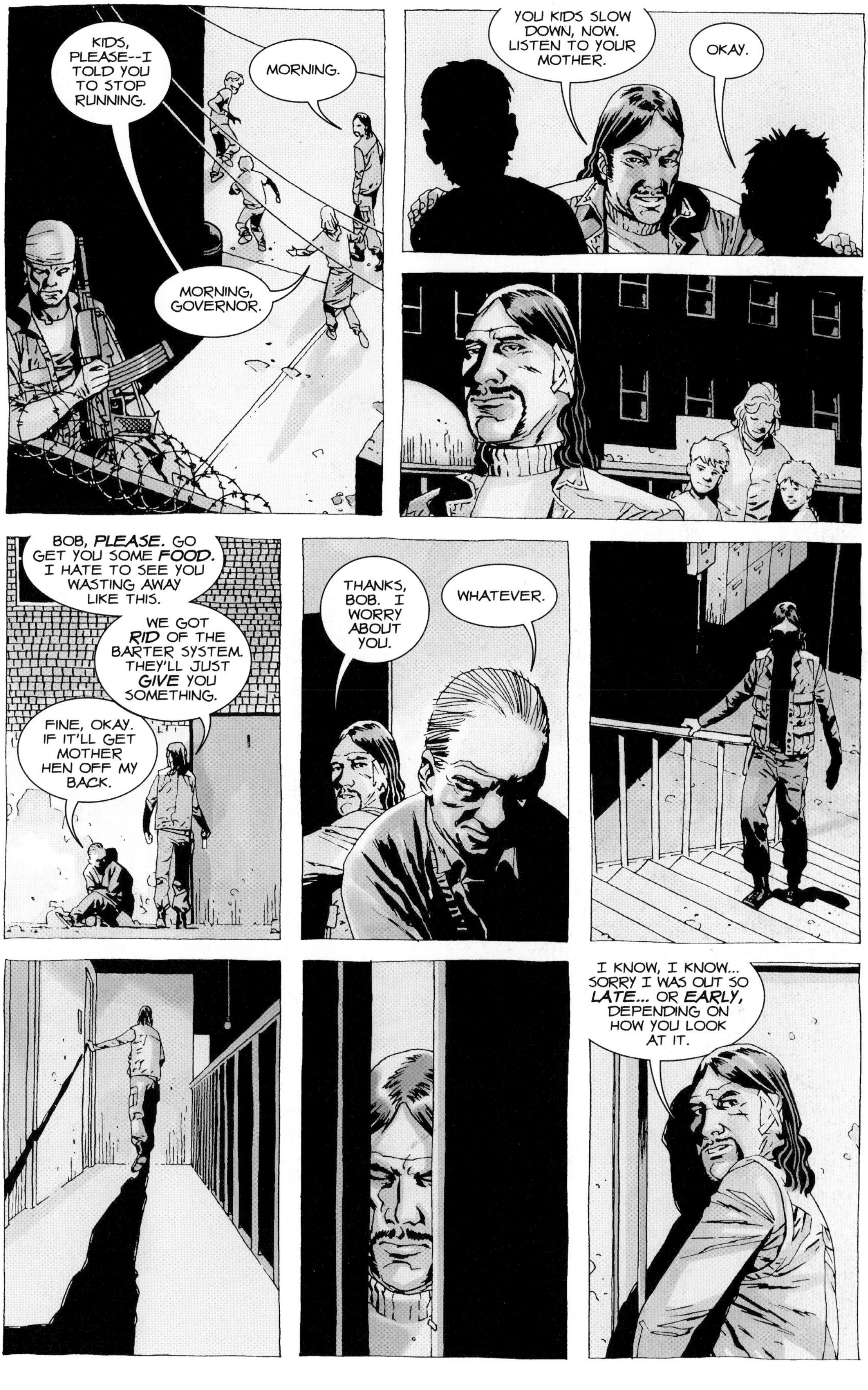
KIDS, PLEASE--I TOLD YOU TO STOP RUNNING.
MORNING.
MORNING, GOVERNOR.
YOU KIDS SLOW DOWN, NOW. LISTEN TO YOUR MOTHER.
OKAY.
BOB, PLEASE. GO GET YOU SOME FOOD. I HATE TO SEE YOU WASTING AWAY LIKE THIS.
WE GOT RID OF THE BARTER SYSTEM. THEY'LL JUST GIVE YOU SOMETHING.
FINE, OKAY. IF IT'LL GET MOTHER HEN OFF MY BACK.
THANKS, BOB. I WORRY ABOUT YOU.
WHATEVER.
I KNOW, I KNOW... SORRY I WAS OUT SO LATE... OR EARLY, DEPENDING ON HOW YOU LOOK AT IT.

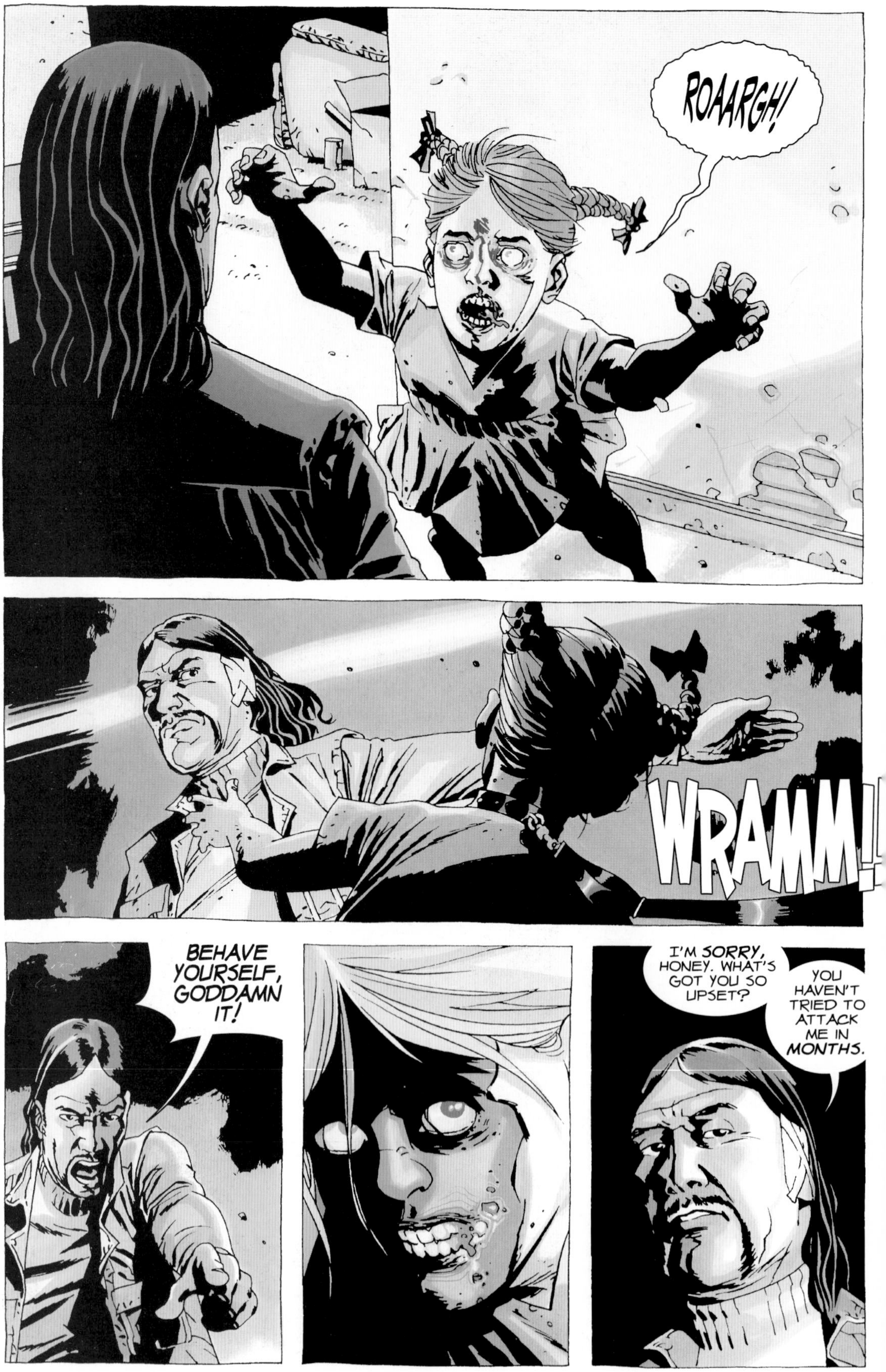
ROAARGH!
WRAMM!!
BEHAVE YOURSELF, GODDAMN IT!
I'M SORRY, HONEY. WHAT'S GOT YOU SO UPSET?
YOU HAVEN'T TRIED TO ATTACK ME IN MONTHS.

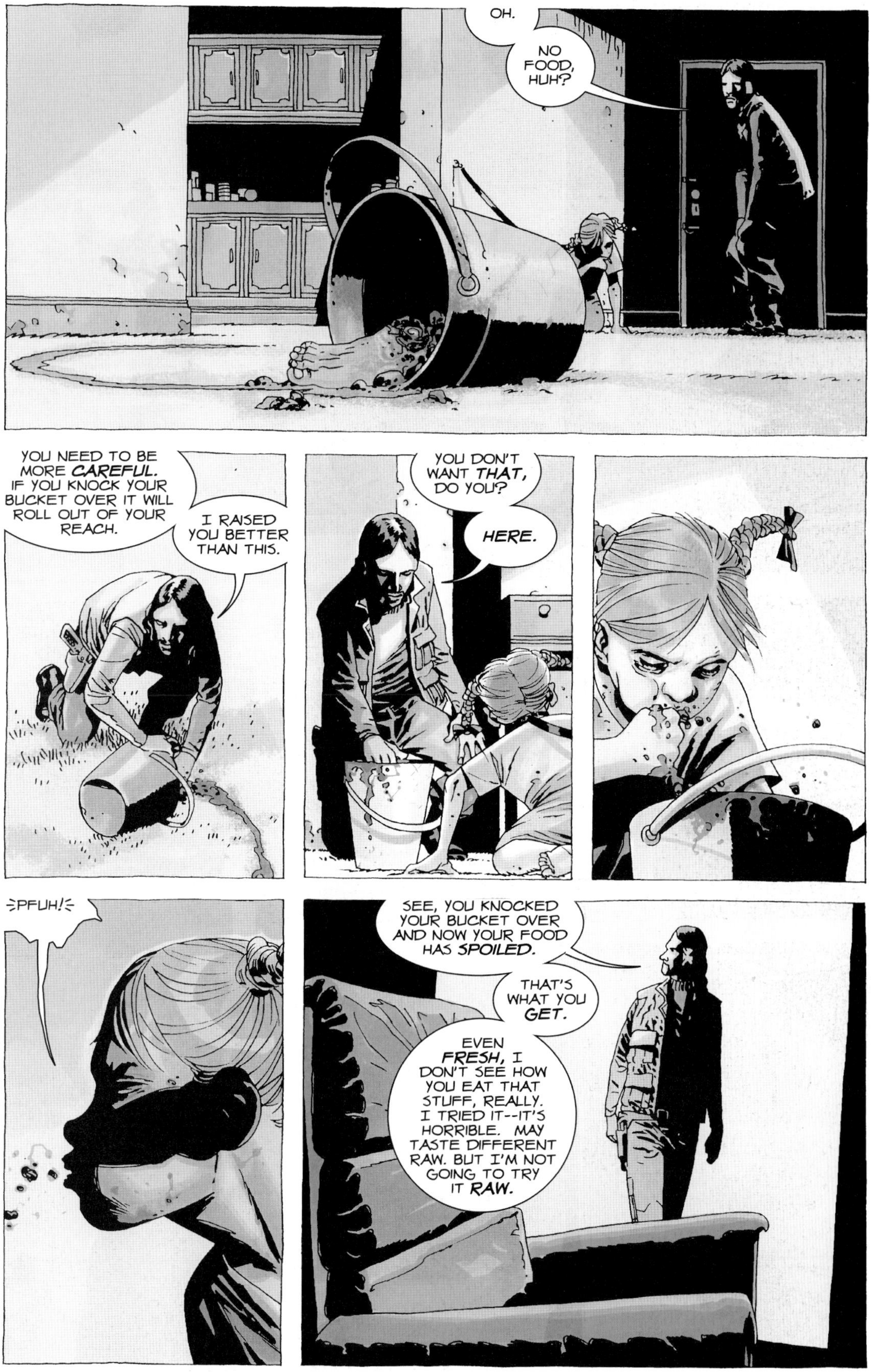
OH.
NO FOOD, HUH?
YOU NEED TO BE MORE CAREFUL. IF YOU KNOCK YOUR BUCKET OVER IT WILL ROLL OUT OF YOUR REACH.
I RAISED YOU BETTER THAN THIS.
YOU DON'T WANT THAT, DO YOU?
HERE.
PFUH!
SEE, YOU KNOCKED YOUR BUCKET OVER AND NOW YOUR FOOD HAS SPOILED.
THAT'S WHAT YOU GET.
EVEN FRESH, I DON'T SEE HOW YOU EAT THAT STUFF, REALLY. I TRIED IT--IT'S HORRIBLE. MAY TASTE DIFFERENT RAW. BUT I'M NOT GOING TO TRY IT RAW.

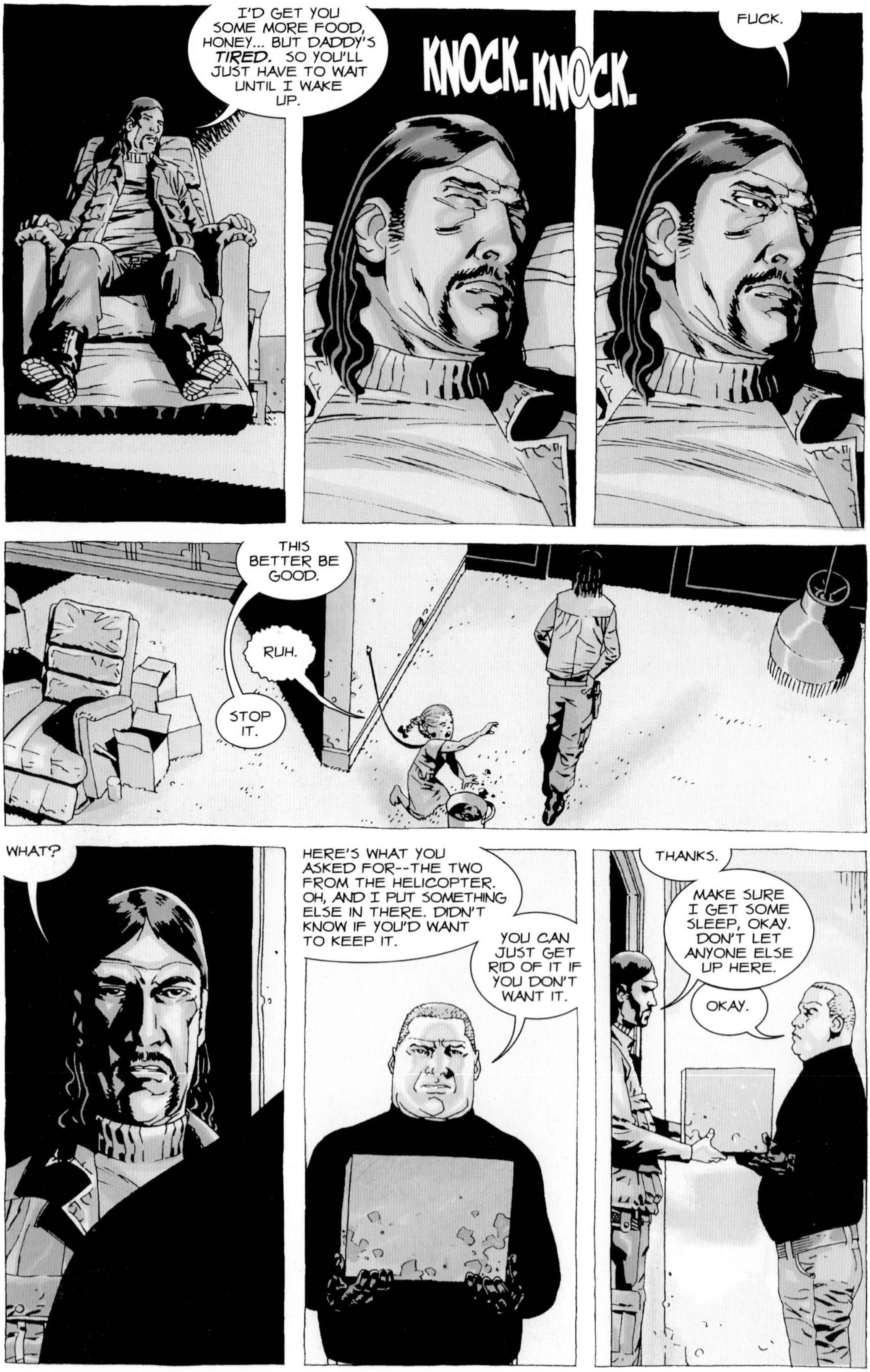
I'D GET YOU SOME MORE FOOD, HONEY... BUT DADDY'S *TIRED.* SO YOU'LL JUST HAVE TO WAIT UNTIL I WAKE UP.
KNOCK. KNOCK.
FUCK.
THIS BETTER BE GOOD.
RUH.
STOP IT.
WHAT?
HERE'S WHAT YOU ASKED FOR--THE TWO FROM THE HELICOPTER. OH, AND I PUT SOMETHING ELSE IN THERE. DIDN'T KNOW IF YOU'D WANT TO KEEP IT.
YOU CAN JUST GET RID OF IT IF YOU DON'T WANT IT.
THANKS.
MAKE SURE I GET SOME SLEEP, OKAY. DON'T LET ANYONE ELSE UP HERE.
OKAY.

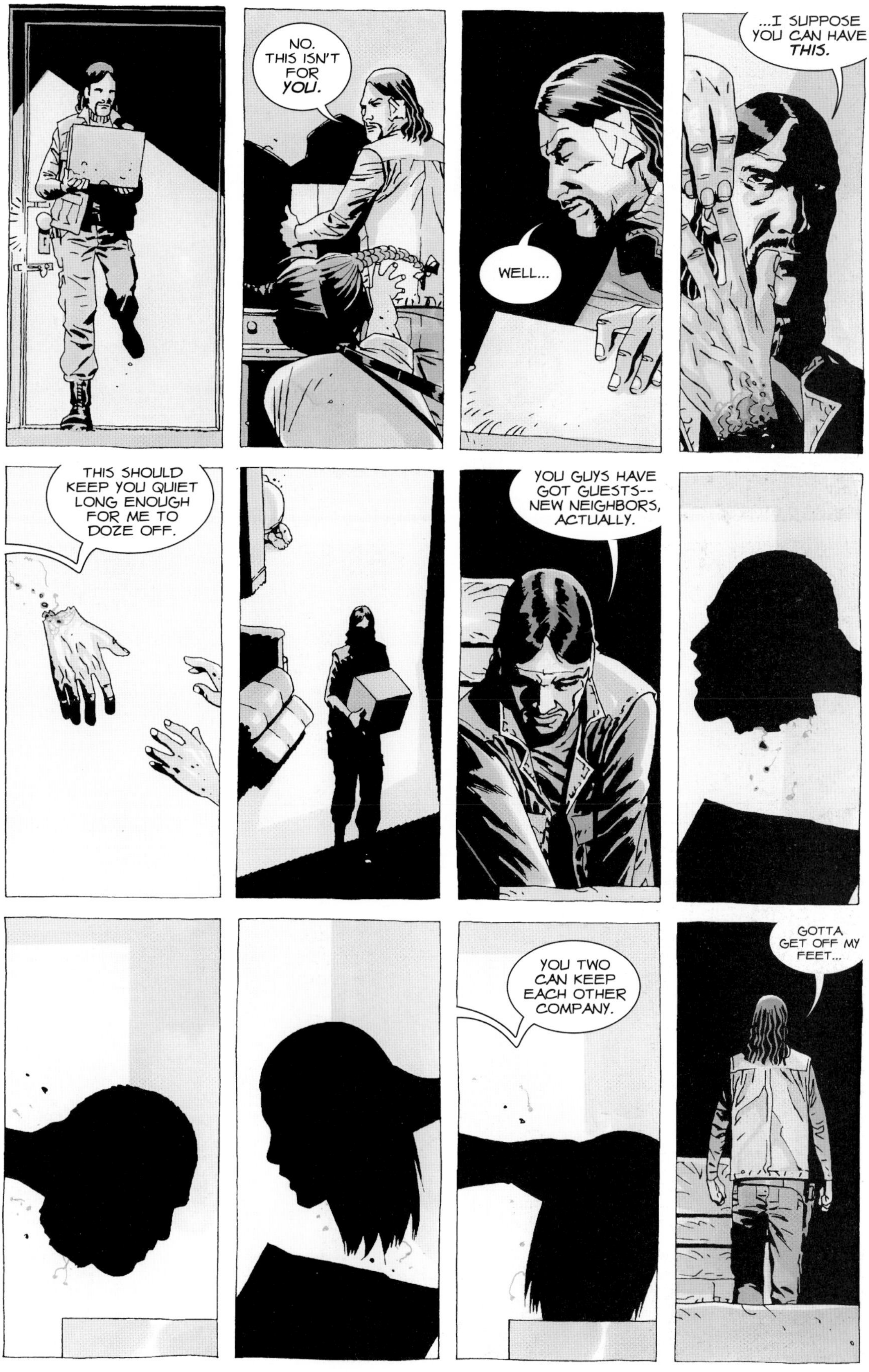
NO. THIS ISN'T FOR *YOU.*
WELL...
...I SUPPOSE YOU CAN HAVE *THIS.*
THIS SHOULD KEEP YOU QUIET LONG ENOUGH FOR ME TO DOZE OFF.
YOU GUYS HAVE GOT GUESTS-- NEW NEIGHBORS, ACTUALLY.
YOU TWO CAN KEEP EACH OTHER COMPANY.
GOTTA GET OFF MY FEET...

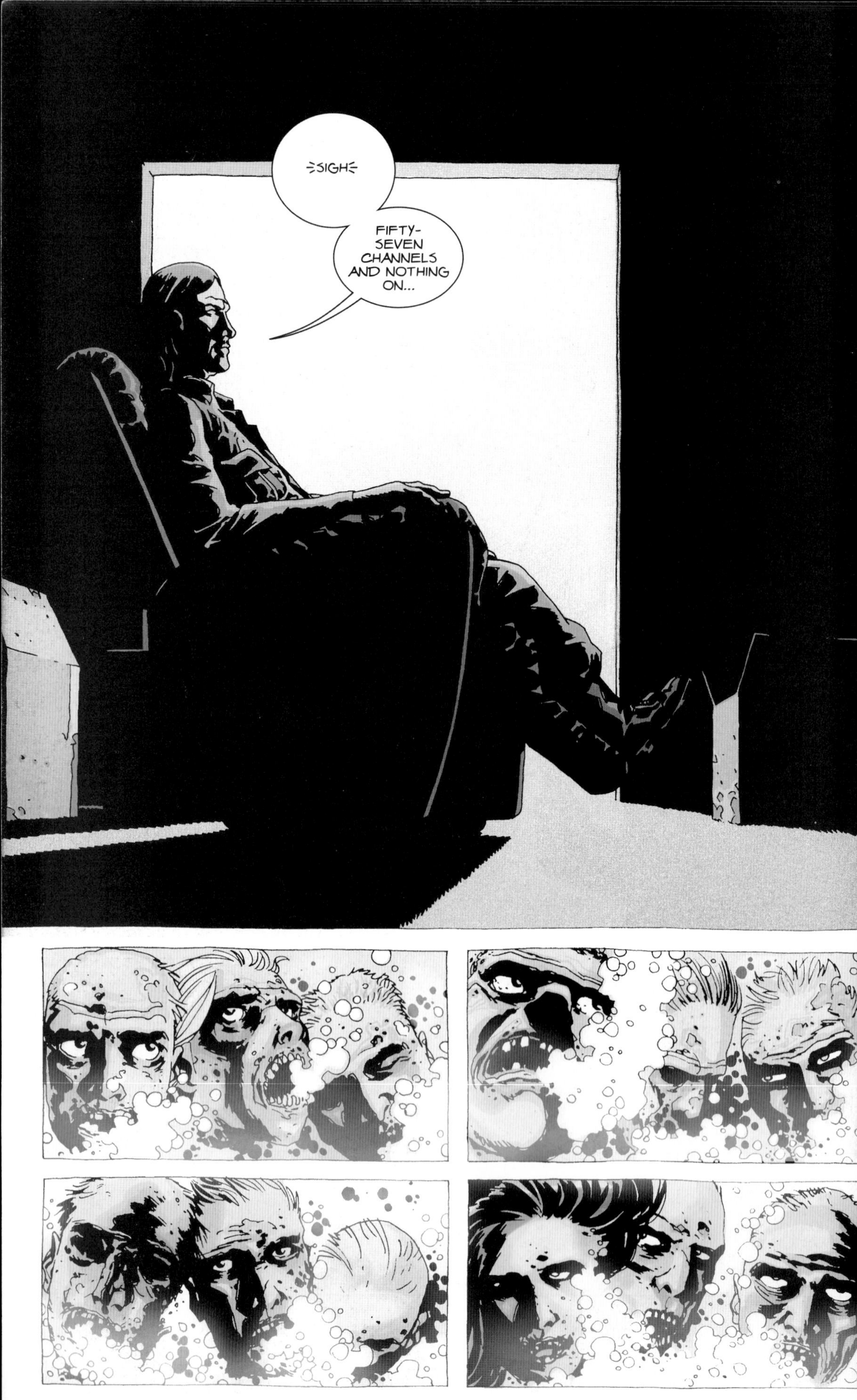

=SIGH=
FIFTY-SEVEN CHANNELS AND NOTHING ON...

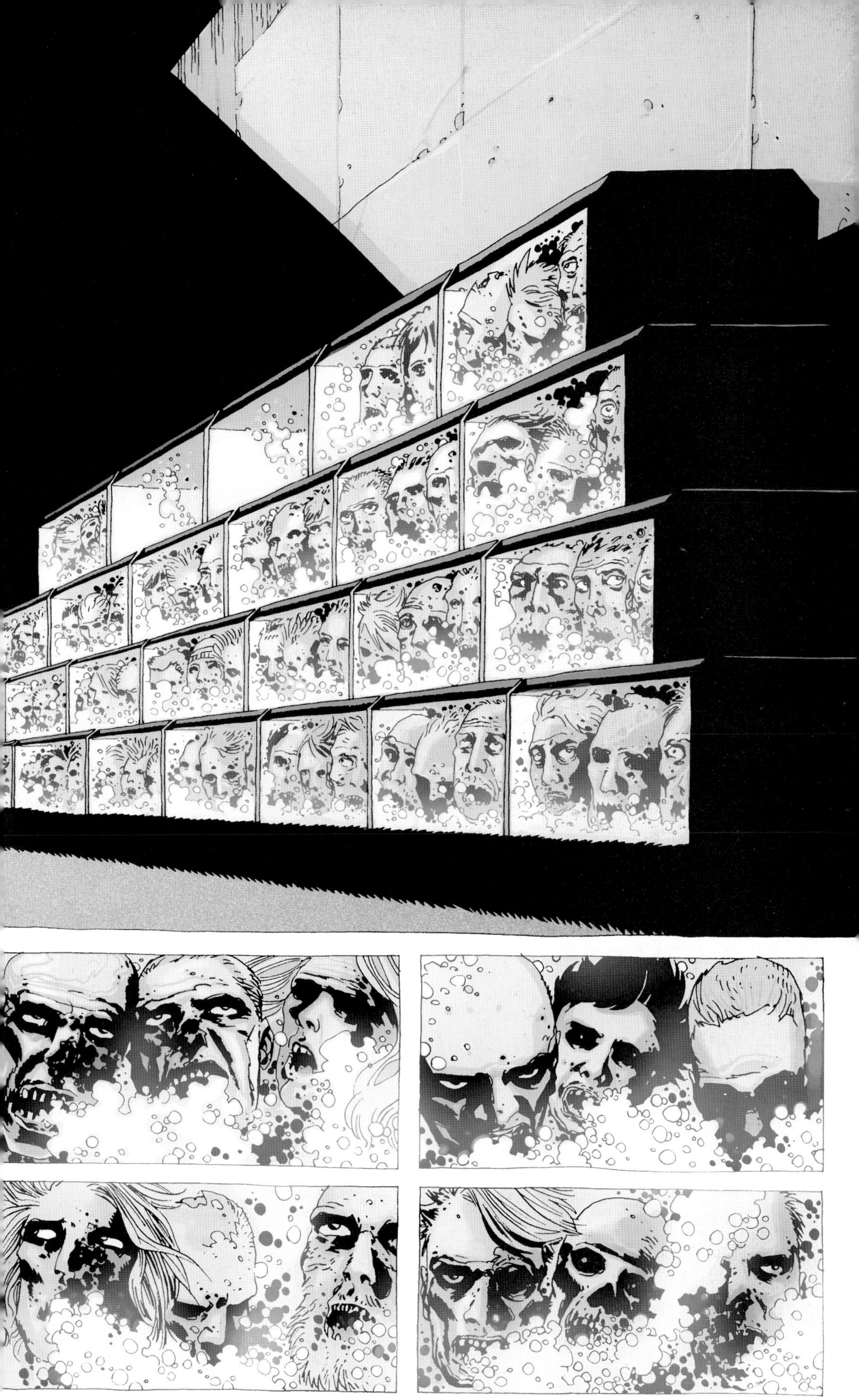

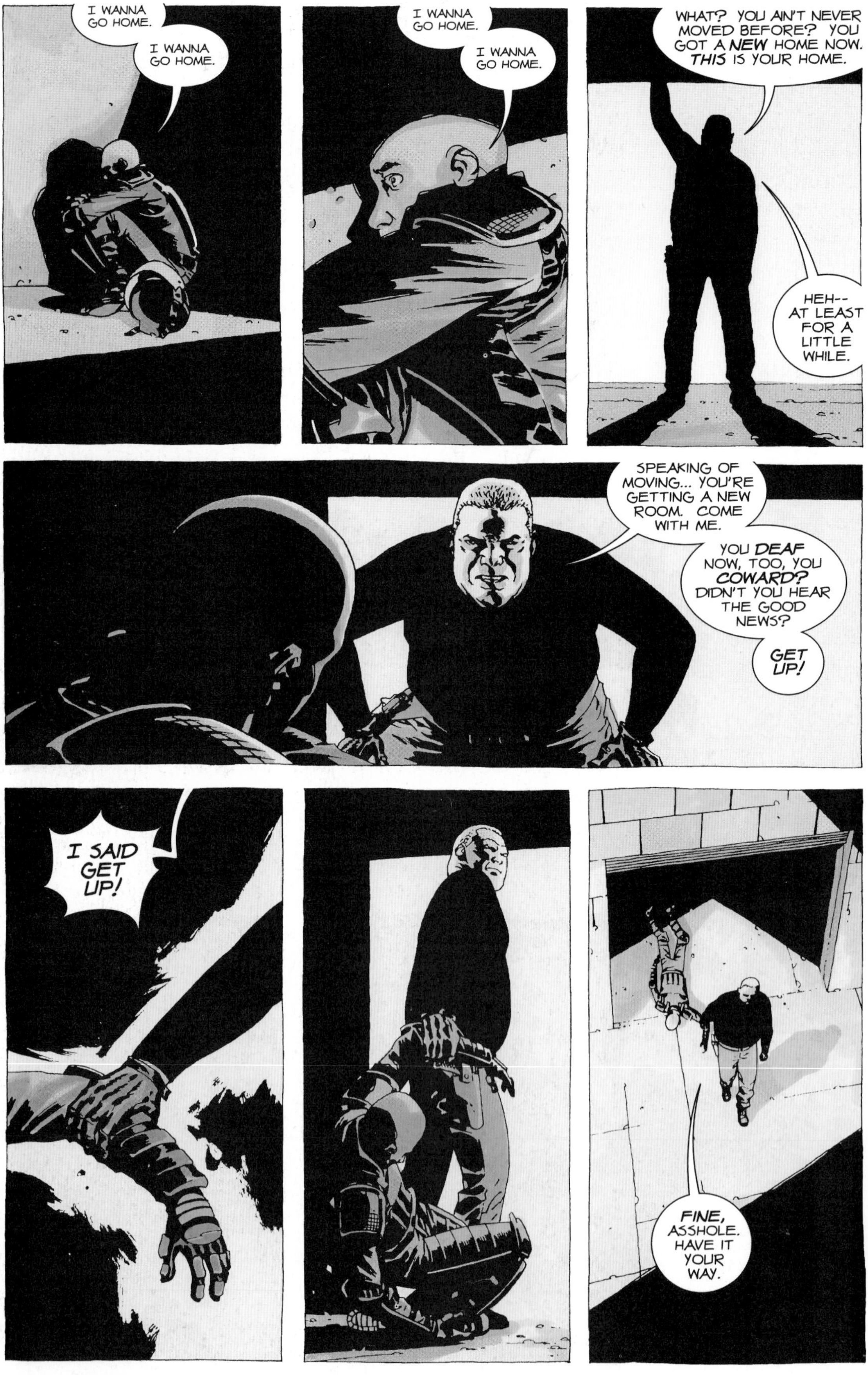

I WANNA GO HOME.
I WANNA GO HOME.
I WANNA GO HOME.
I WANNA GO HOME.
WHAT? YOU AIN'T NEVER MOVED BEFORE? YOU GOT A NEW HOME NOW. THIS IS YOUR HOME.
HEH-- AT LEAST FOR A LITTLE WHILE.
SPEAKING OF MOVING... YOU'RE GETTING A NEW ROOM. COME WITH ME.
YOU DEAF NOW, TOO, YOU COWARD? DIDN'T YOU HEAR THE GOOD NEWS?
GET UP!
I SAID GET UP!
FINE, ASSHOLE. HAVE IT YOUR WAY.

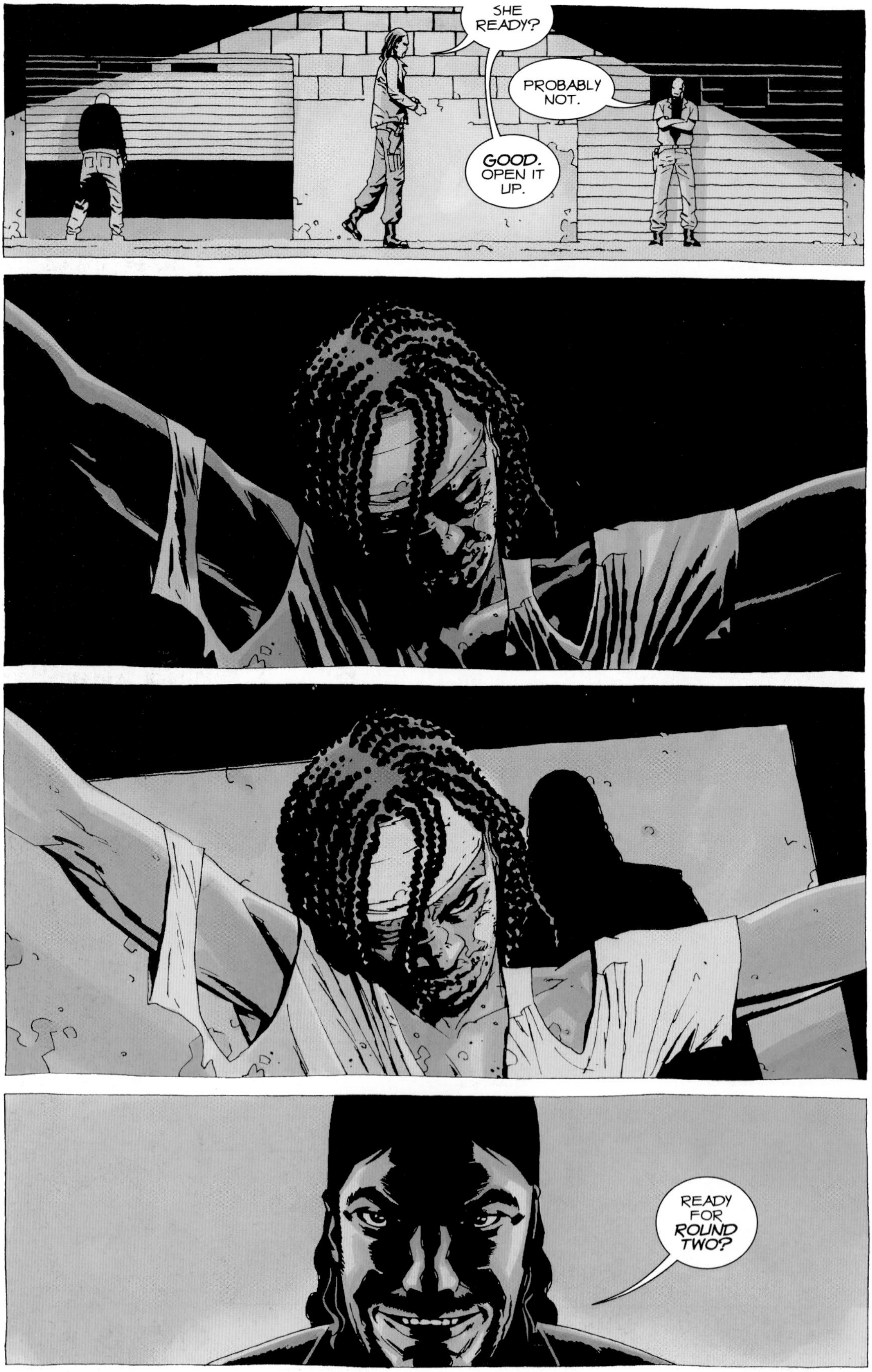
SHE READY?
PROBABLY NOT.
GOOD. OPEN IT UP.
READY FOR ROUND TWO?

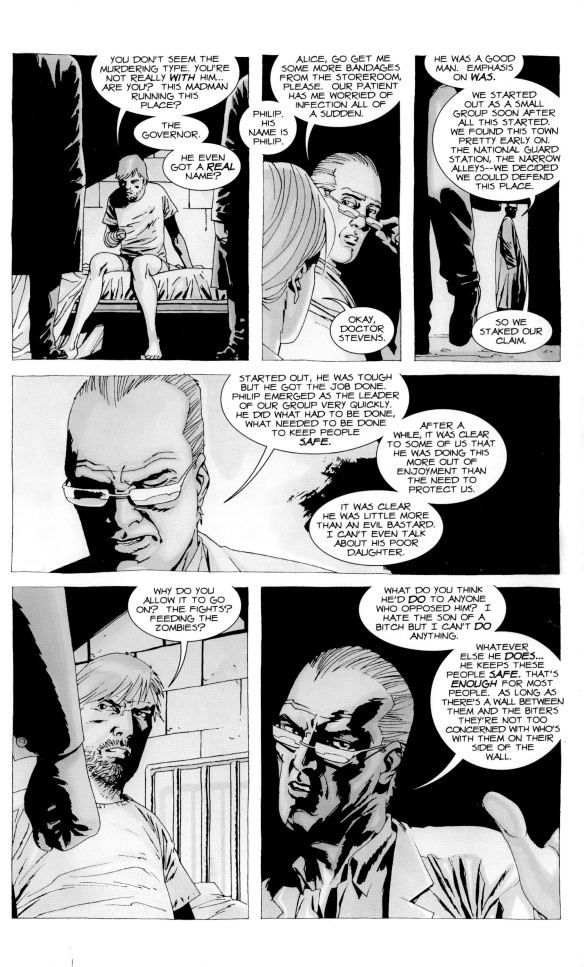

WELL SAID, DOCTOR. WELL SAID.

WHAT DO *YOU* WANT?

YOU SAID TO COME IN TODAY. YOU WANTED TO CHANGE MY BANDAGE.

BRUCE, POINT A GUN AT LEFTY OVER THERE.

SIT DOWN. I'LL MAKE IT QUICK. I'M SURE YOU HAVE IMPORTANT THINGS TO DO.

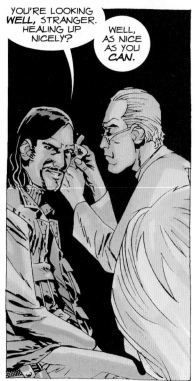

YOU'RE LOOKING *WELL*, STRANGER. HEALING UP NICELY?

WELL, AS NICE AS YOU *CAN*.

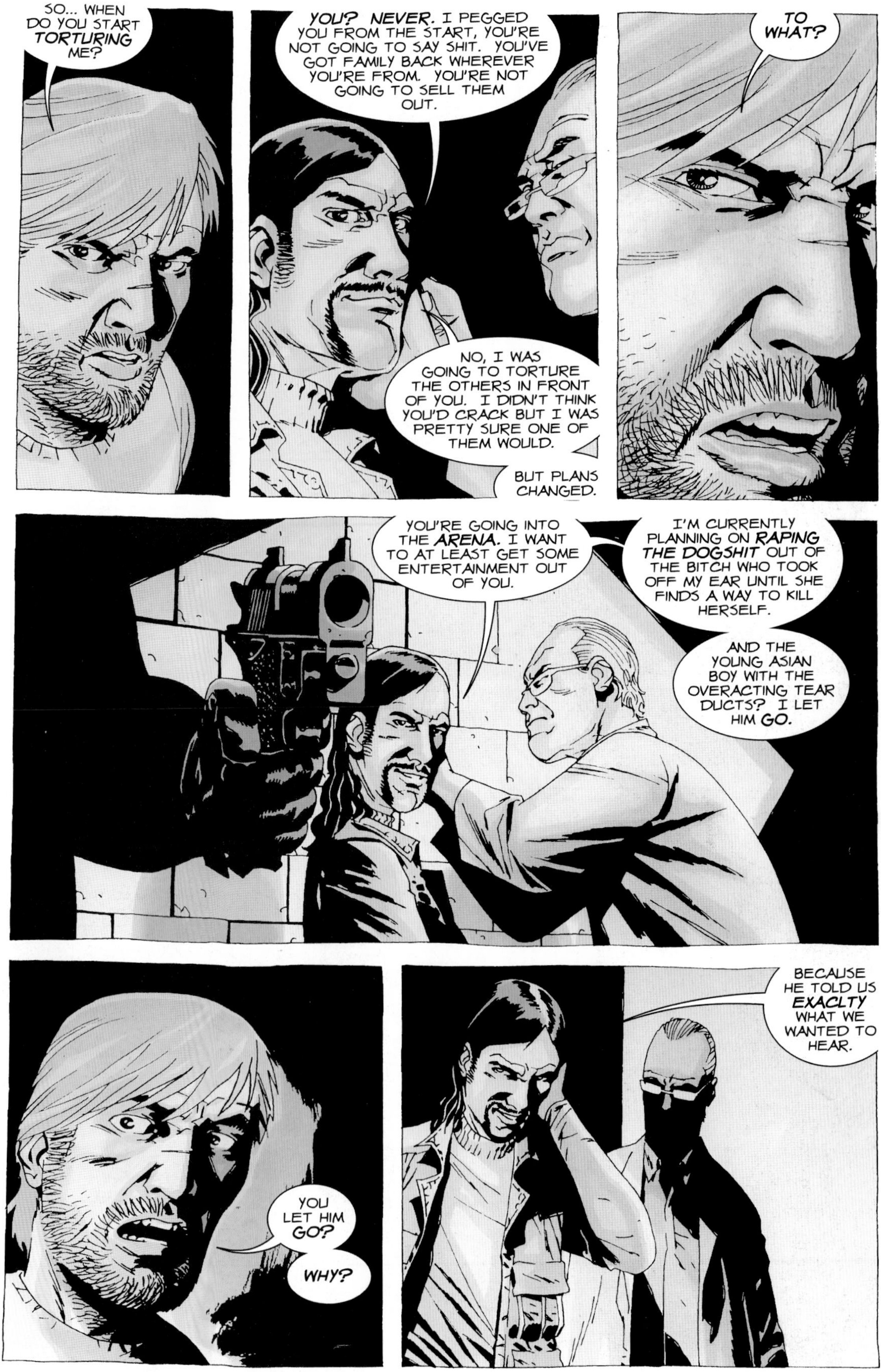

SO... WHEN DO YOU START TORTURING ME?
YOU? NEVER. I PEGGED YOU FROM THE START, YOU'RE NOT GOING TO SAY SHIT. YOU'VE GOT FAMILY BACK WHEREVER YOU'RE FROM. YOU'RE NOT GOING TO SELL THEM OUT.
NO, I WAS GOING TO TORTURE THE OTHERS IN FRONT OF YOU. I DIDN'T THINK YOU'D CRACK BUT I WAS PRETTY SURE ONE OF THEM WOULD.
BUT PLANS CHANGED.
TO WHAT?
YOU'RE GOING INTO THE ARENA. I WANT TO AT LEAST GET SOME ENTERTAINMENT OUT OF YOU.
I'M CURRENTLY PLANNING ON RAPING THE DOGSHIT OUT OF THE BITCH WHO TOOK OFF MY EAR UNTIL SHE FINDS A WAY TO KILL HERSELF.
AND THE YOUNG ASIAN BOY WITH THE OVERACTING TEAR DUCTS? I LET HIM GO.
YOU LET HIM GO?
WHY?
BECAUSE HE TOLD US EXACLTY WHAT WE WANTED TO HEAR.

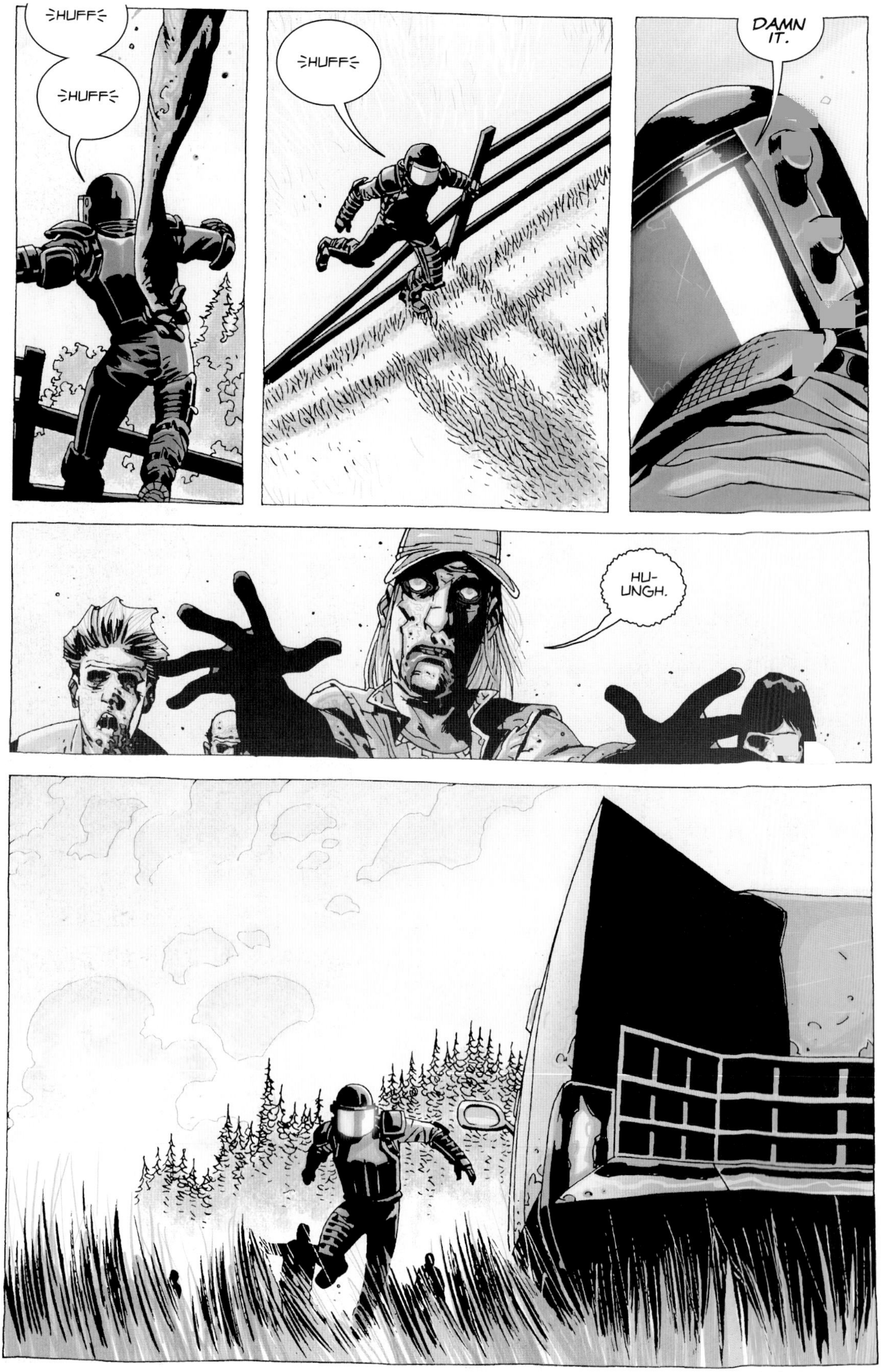

HUFF
HUFF
HUFF
DAMN IT.
HU-UNGH.

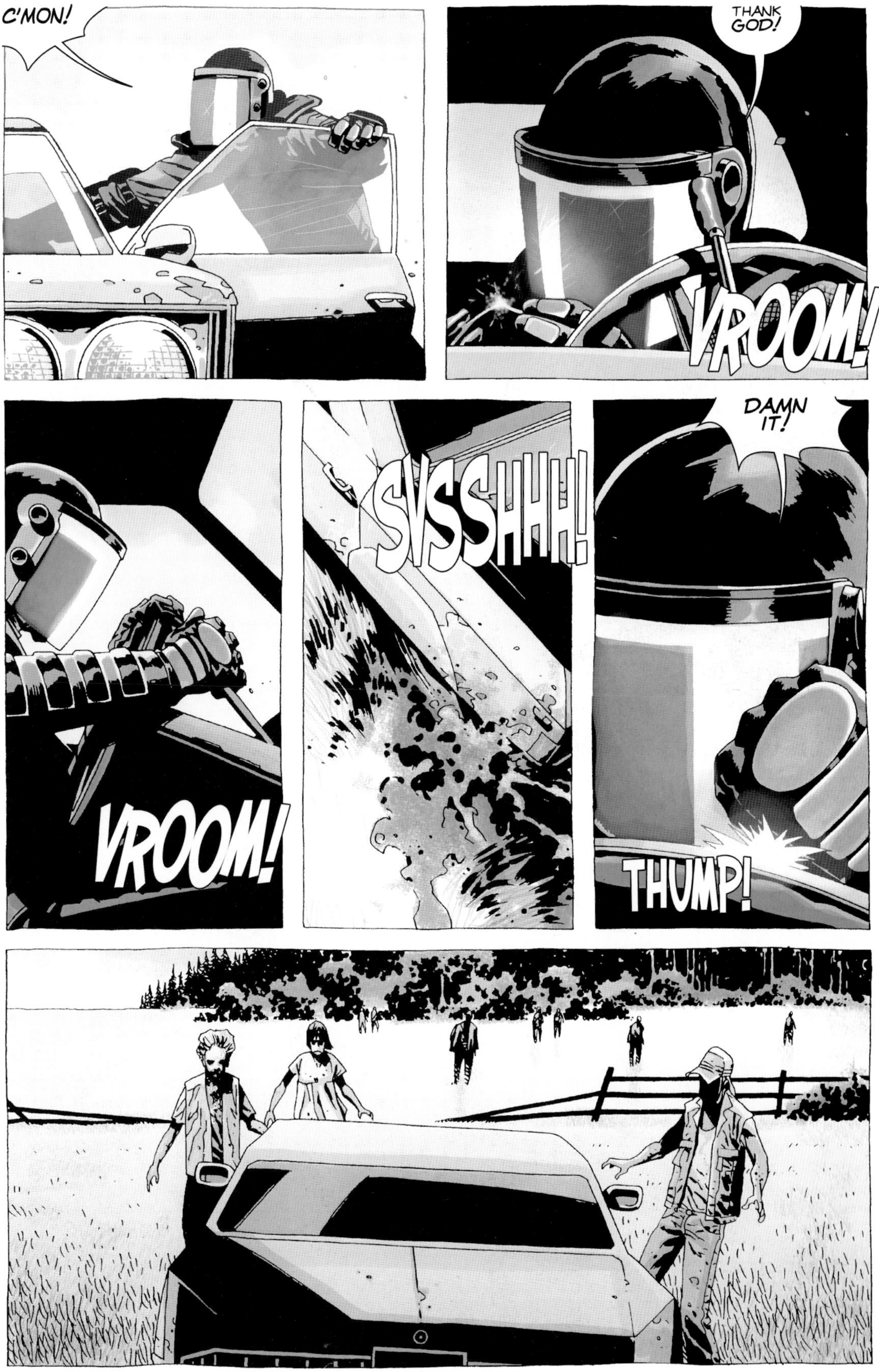
C'MON!
THANK GOD!
VROOM!
VROOM!
SVSSHHH!
DAMN IT!
THUMP!

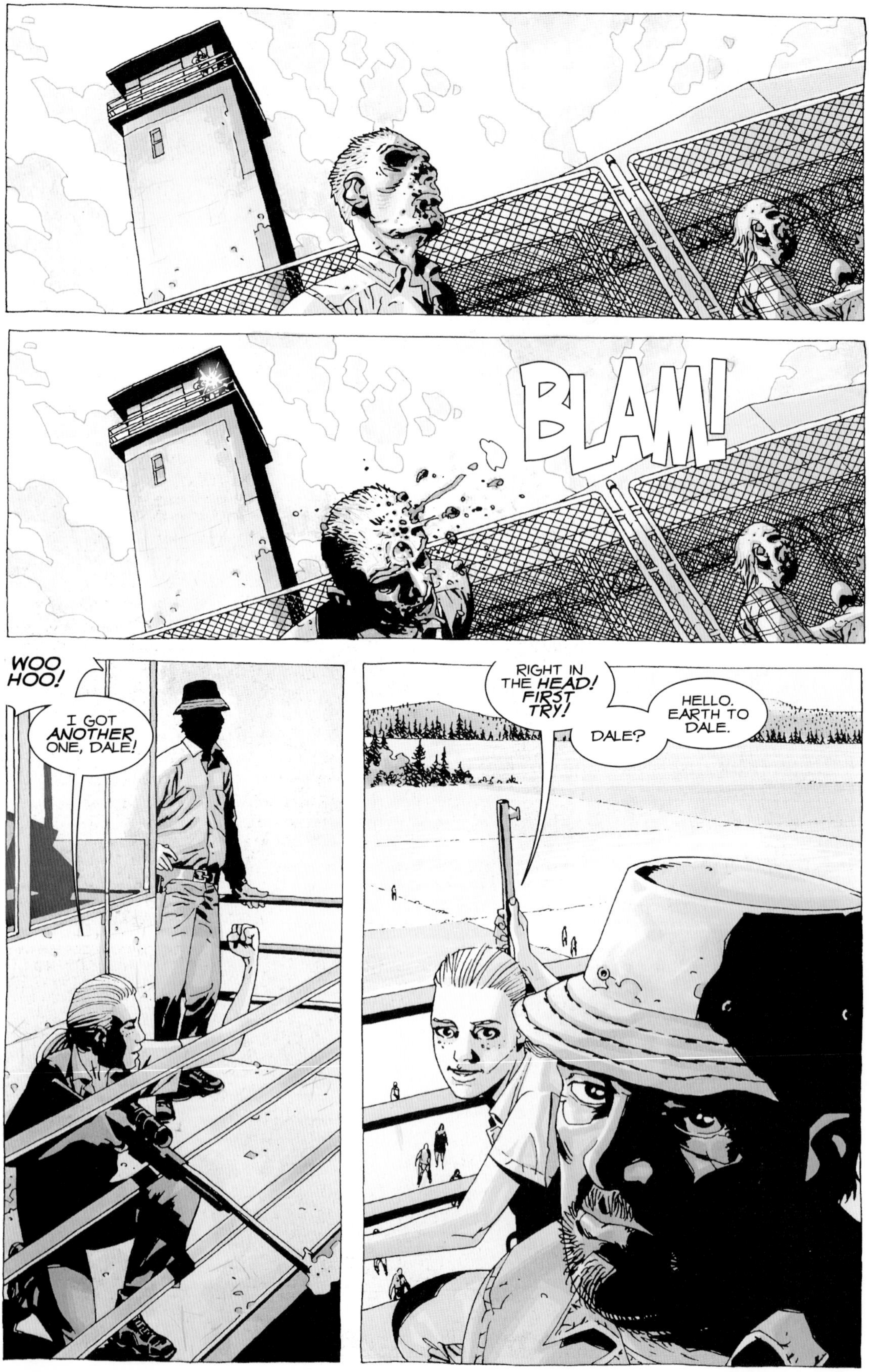
BLAM!
WOO HOO!
I GOT ANOTHER ONE, DALE!
RIGHT IN THE HEAD! FIRST TRY!
DALE?
HELLO. EARTH TO DALE.

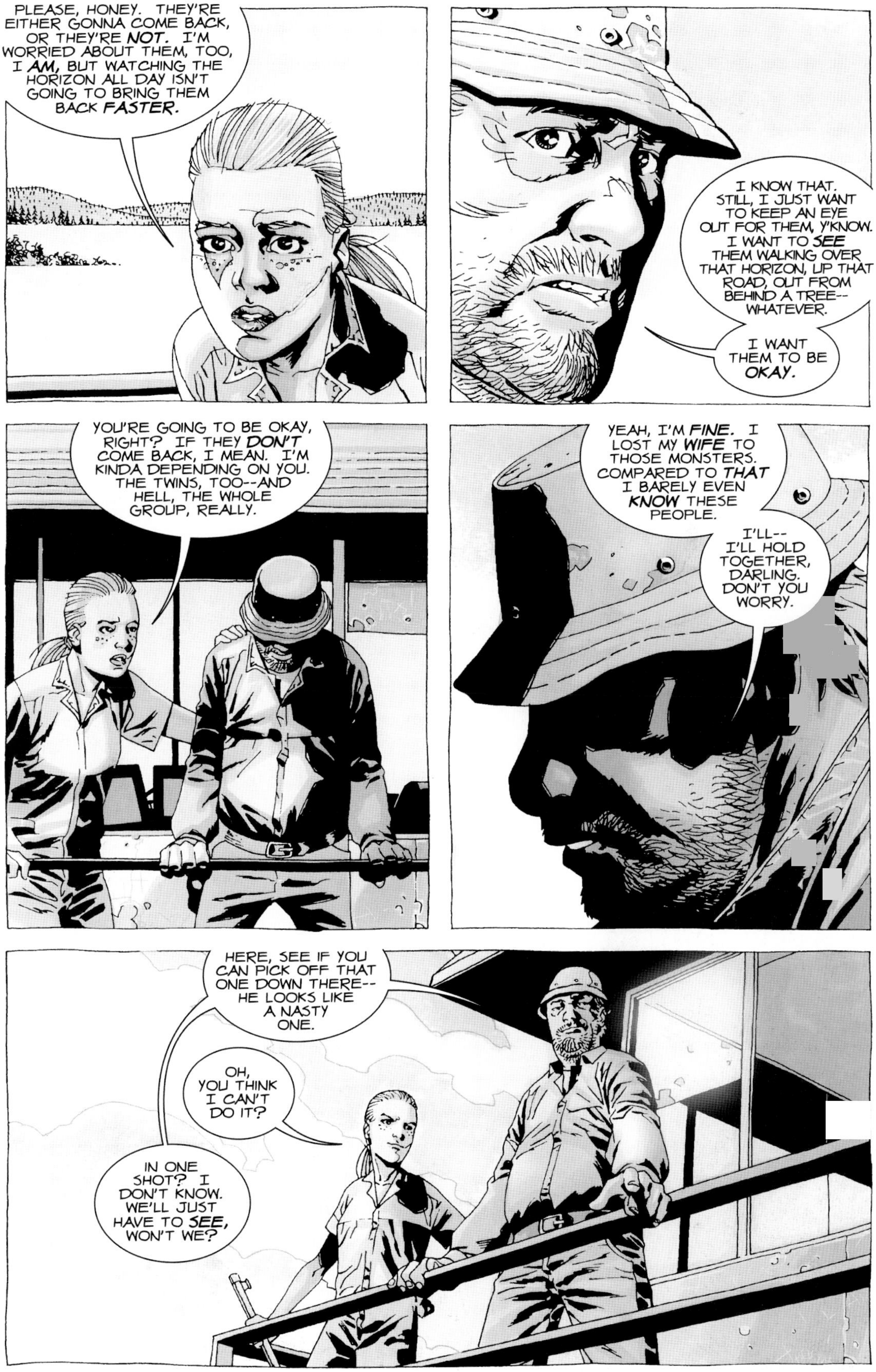
PLEASE, HONEY. THEY'RE EITHER GONNA COME BACK, OR THEY'RE NOT. I'M WORRIED ABOUT THEM, TOO, I AM, BUT WATCHING THE HORIZON ALL DAY ISN'T GOING TO BRING THEM BACK FASTER.
I KNOW THAT. STILL, I JUST WANT TO KEEP AN EYE OUT FOR THEM, Y'KNOW. I WANT TO SEE THEM WALKING OVER THAT HORIZON, UP THAT ROAD, OUT FROM BEHIND A TREE--WHATEVER.
I WANT THEM TO BE OKAY.
YOU'RE GOING TO BE OKAY, RIGHT? IF THEY DON'T COME BACK, I MEAN. I'M KINDA DEPENDING ON YOU. THE TWINS, TOO--AND HELL, THE WHOLE GROUP, REALLY.
YEAH, I'M FINE. I LOST MY WIFE TO THOSE MONSTERS. COMPARED TO THAT I BARELY EVEN KNOW THESE PEOPLE.
I'LL-- I'LL HOLD TOGETHER, DARLING. DON'T YOU WORRY.
HERE, SEE IF YOU CAN PICK OFF THAT ONE DOWN THERE-- HE LOOKS LIKE A NASTY ONE.
OH, YOU THINK I CAN'T DO IT?
IN ONE SHOT? I DON'T KNOW. WE'LL JUST HAVE TO SEE, WON'T WE?

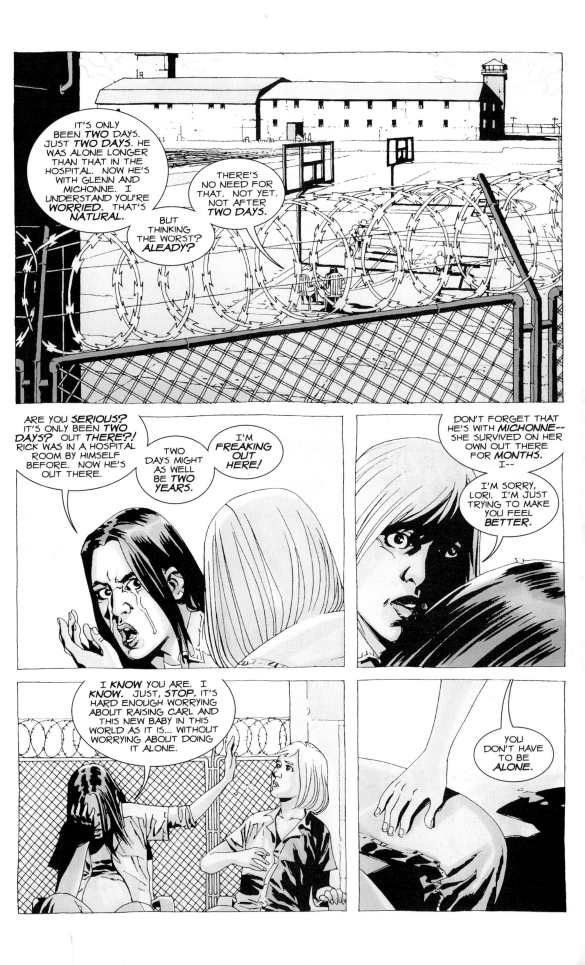

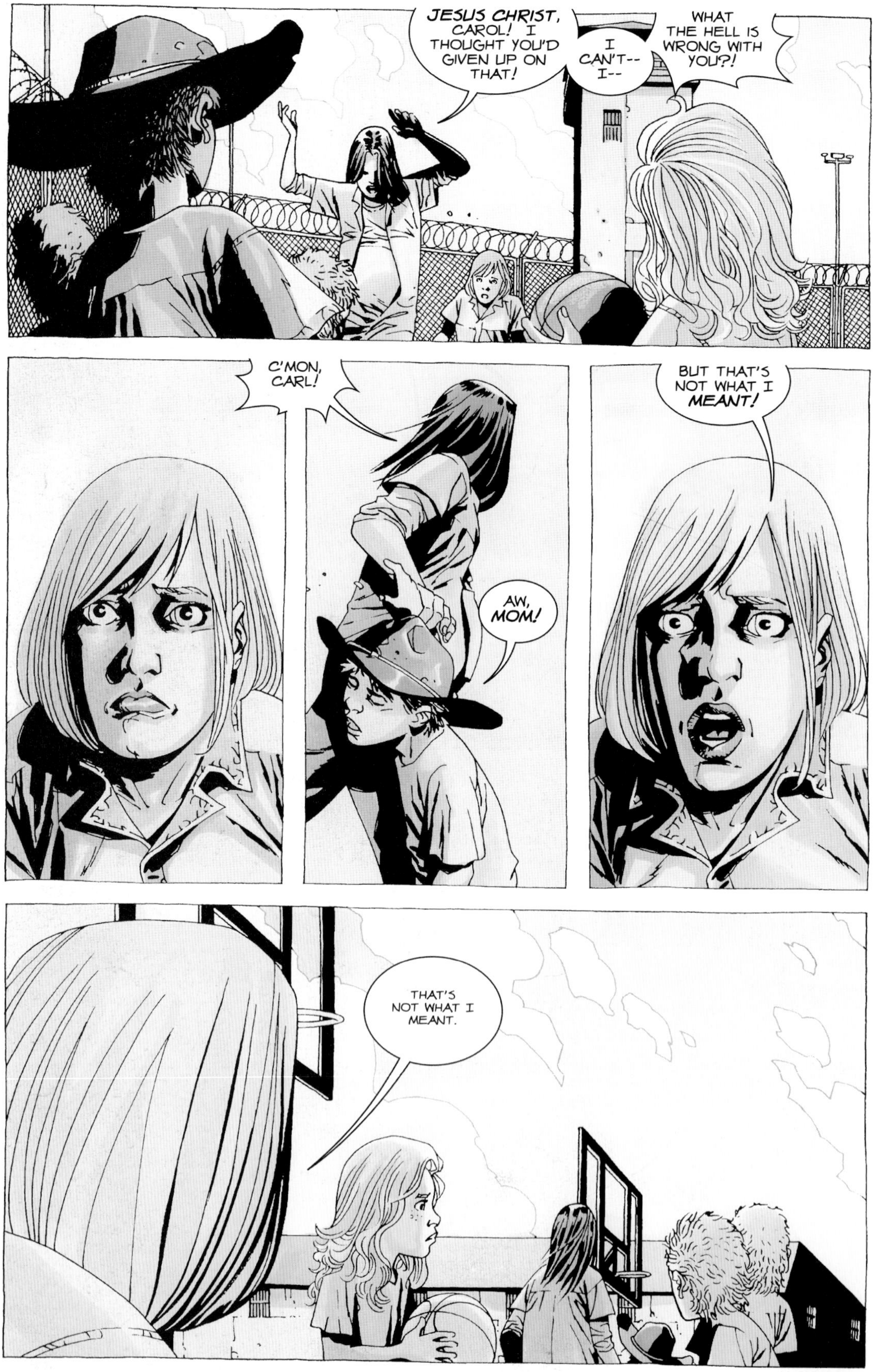
JESUS CHRIST, CAROL! I THOUGHT YOU'D GIVEN UP ON THAT!
I CAN'T-- I--
WHAT THE HELL IS WRONG WITH YOU?!
C'MON, CARL!
AW, MOM!
BUT THAT'S NOT WHAT I MEANT!
THAT'S NOT WHAT I MEANT.

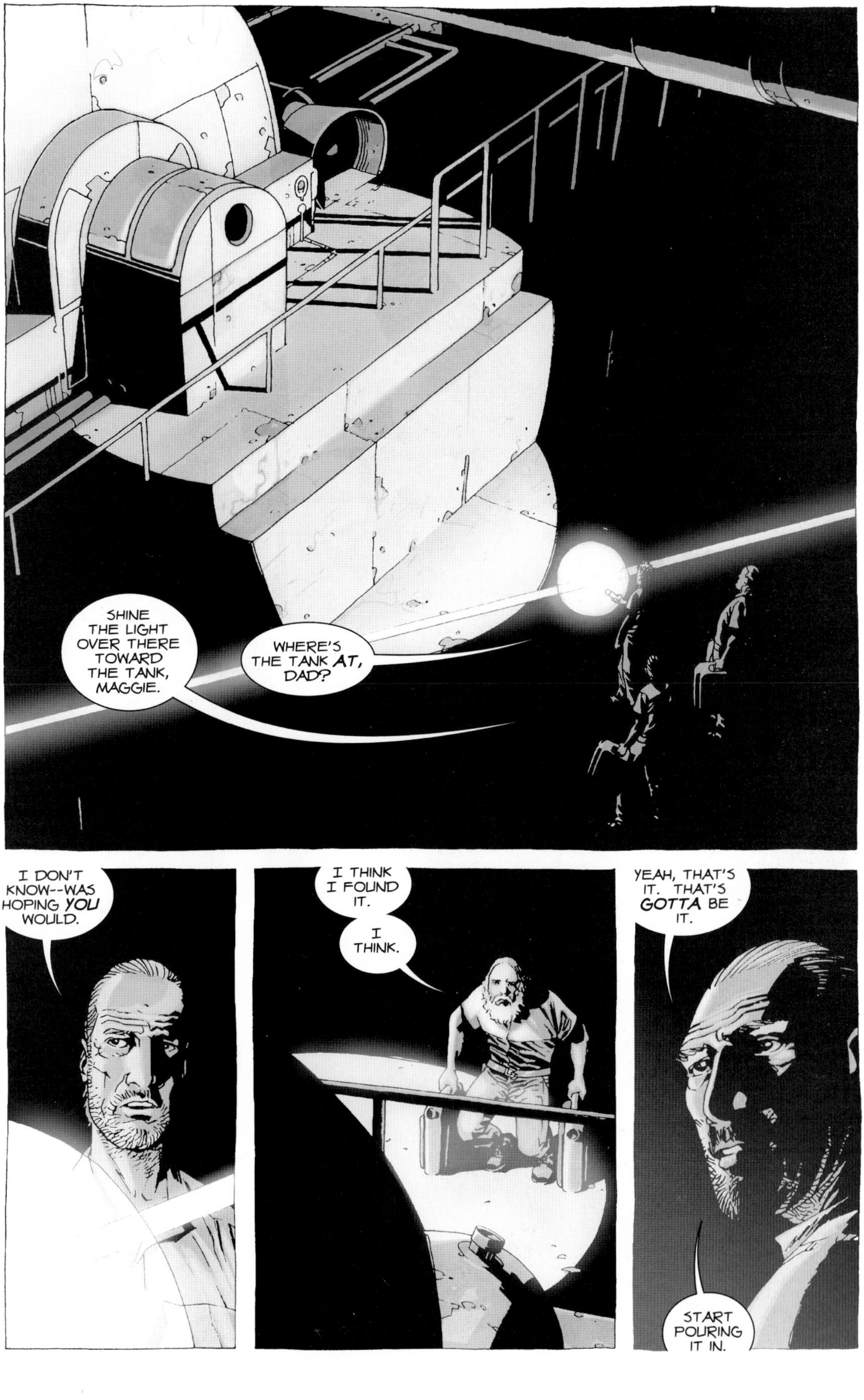

SHINE THE LIGHT OVER THERE TOWARD THE TANK, MAGGIE.
WHERE'S THE TANK *AT*, DAD?
I DON'T KNOW--WAS HOPING *YOU* WOULD.
I THINK I FOUND IT.
I THINK.
YEAH, THAT'S IT. THAT'S *GOTTA* BE IT.
START POURING IT IN.

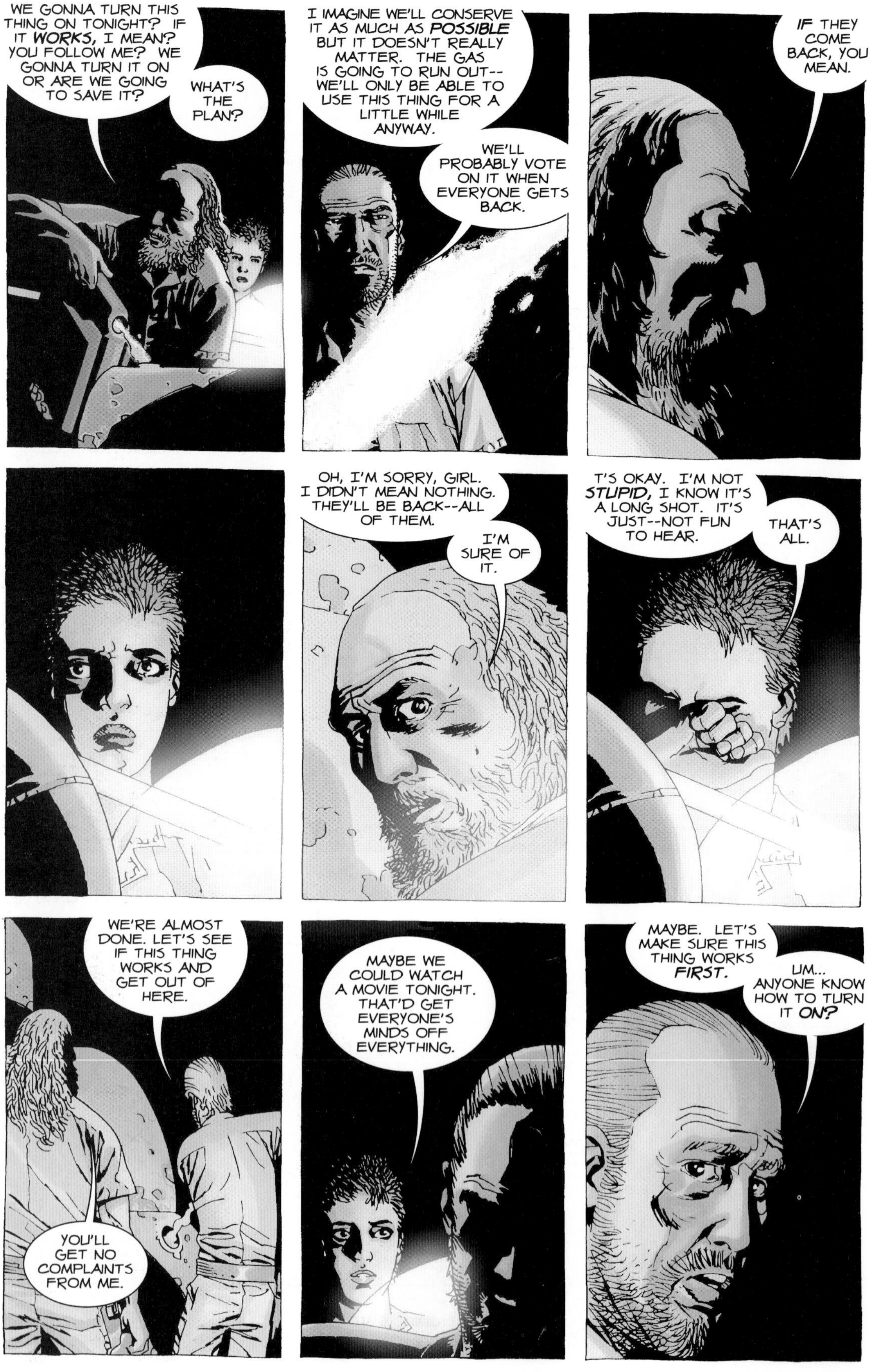
WE GONNA TURN THIS THING ON TONIGHT? IF IT WORKS, I MEAN? YOU FOLLOW ME? WE GONNA TURN IT ON OR ARE WE GOING TO SAVE IT?
WHAT'S THE PLAN?
I IMAGINE WE'LL CONSERVE IT AS MUCH AS POSSIBLE BUT IT DOESN'T REALLY MATTER. THE GAS IS GOING TO RUN OUT-- WE'LL ONLY BE ABLE TO USE THIS THING FOR A LITTLE WHILE ANYWAY.
WE'LL PROBABLY VOTE ON IT WHEN EVERYONE GETS BACK.
IF THEY COME BACK, YOU MEAN.
OH, I'M SORRY, GIRL. I DIDN'T MEAN NOTHING. THEY'LL BE BACK--ALL OF THEM.
I'M SURE OF IT.
T'S OKAY. I'M NOT STUPID, I KNOW IT'S A LONG SHOT. IT'S JUST--NOT FUN TO HEAR.
THAT'S ALL.
WE'RE ALMOST DONE. LET'S SEE IF THIS THING WORKS AND GET OUT OF HERE.
YOU'LL GET NO COMPLAINTS FROM ME.
MAYBE WE COULD WATCH A MOVIE TONIGHT. THAT'D GET EVERYONE'S MINDS OFF EVERYTHING.
MAYBE. LET'S MAKE SURE THIS THING WORKS FIRST.
UM... ANYONE KNOW HOW TO TURN IT ON?

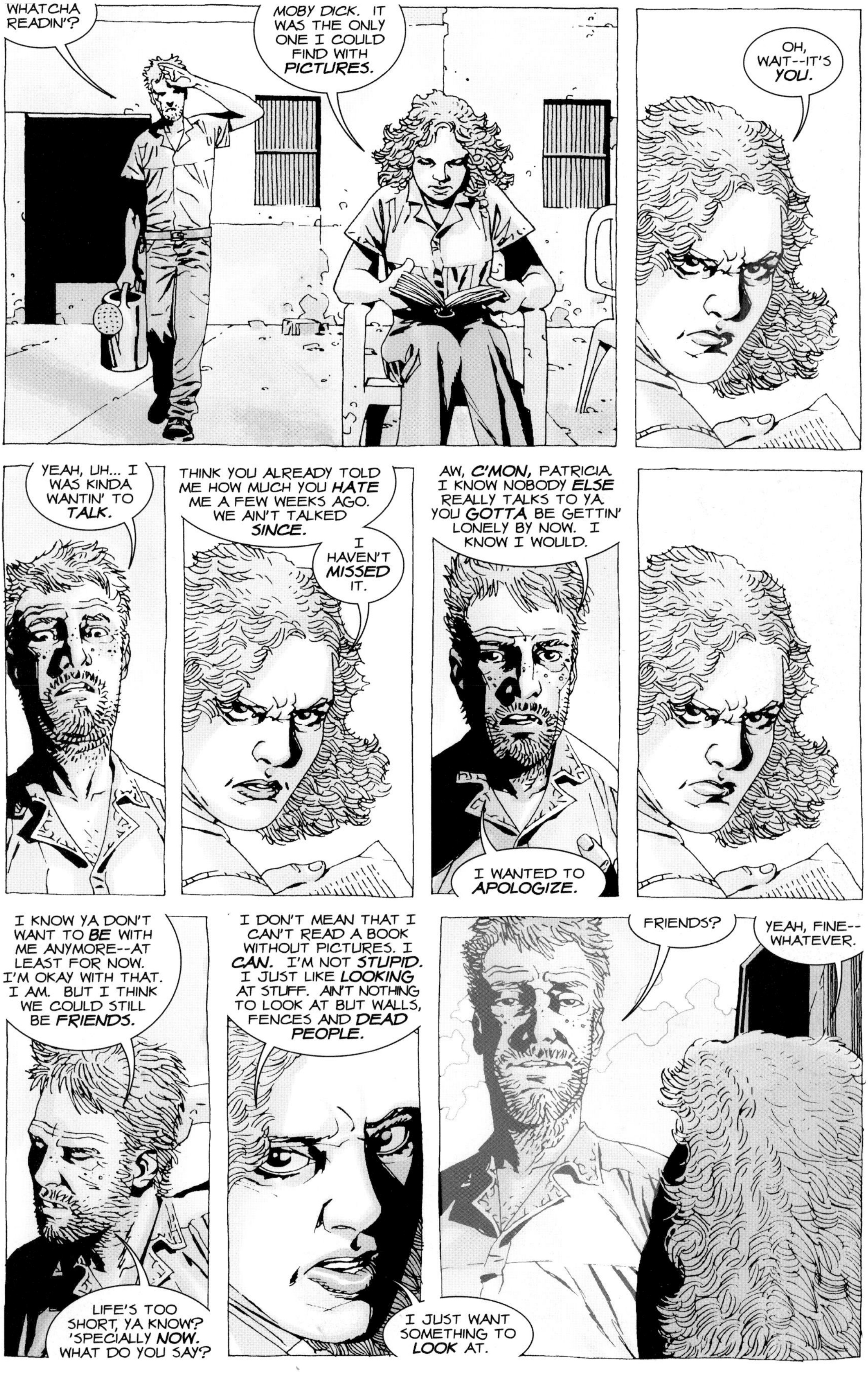

WHATCHA READIN'?
MOBY DICK. IT WAS THE ONLY ONE I COULD FIND WITH PICTURES.
OH, WAIT--IT'S YOU.
YEAH, UH... I WAS KINDA WANTIN' TO TALK.
THINK YOU ALREADY TOLD ME HOW MUCH YOU HATE ME A FEW WEEKS AGO. WE AIN'T TALKED SINCE.
I HAVEN'T MISSED IT.
AW, C'MON, PATRICIA. I KNOW NOBODY ELSE REALLY TALKS TO YA. YOU GOTTA BE GETTIN' LONELY BY NOW. I KNOW I WOULD.
I WANTED TO APOLOGIZE.
I KNOW YA DON'T WANT TO BE WITH ME ANYMORE--AT LEAST FOR NOW. I'M OKAY WITH THAT. I AM. BUT I THINK WE COULD STILL BE FRIENDS.
LIFE'S TOO SHORT, YA KNOW? 'SPECIALLY NOW. WHAT DO YOU SAY?
I DON'T MEAN THAT I CAN'T READ A BOOK WITHOUT PICTURES. I CAN. I'M NOT STUPID. I JUST LIKE LOOKING AT STUFF. AIN'T NOTHING TO LOOK AT BUT WALLS, FENCES AND DEAD PEOPLE.
I JUST WANT SOMETHING TO LOOK AT.
FRIENDS?
YEAH, FINE--WHATEVER.

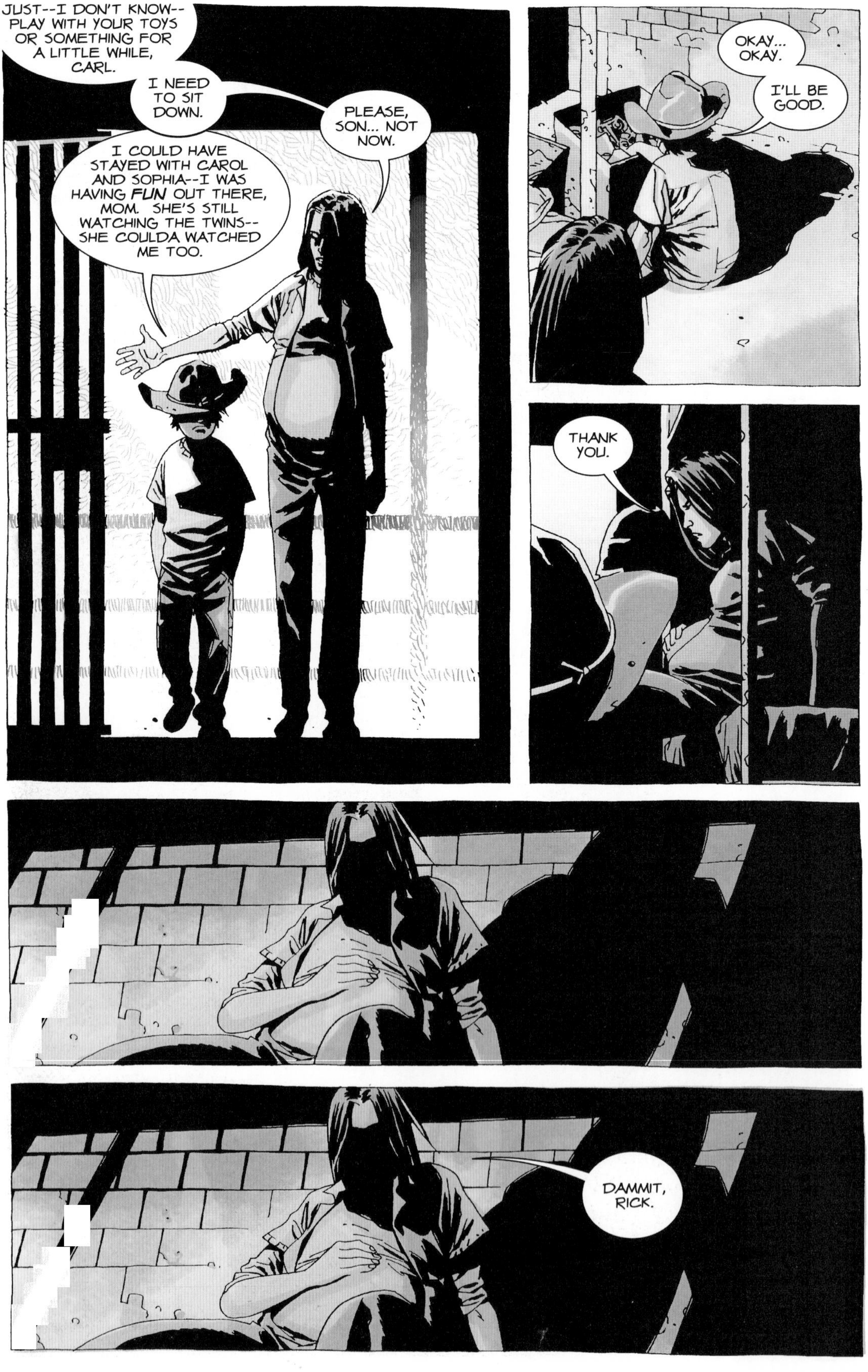
JUST--I DON'T KNOW-- PLAY WITH YOUR TOYS OR SOMETHING FOR A LITTLE WHILE, CARL.
I NEED TO SIT DOWN.
I COULD HAVE STAYED WITH CAROL AND SOPHIA--I WAS HAVING FUN OUT THERE, MOM. SHE'S STILL WATCHING THE TWINS-- SHE COULDA WATCHED ME TOO.
PLEASE, SON... NOT NOW.
OKAY... OKAY.
I'LL BE GOOD.
THANK YOU.
DAMMIT, RICK.

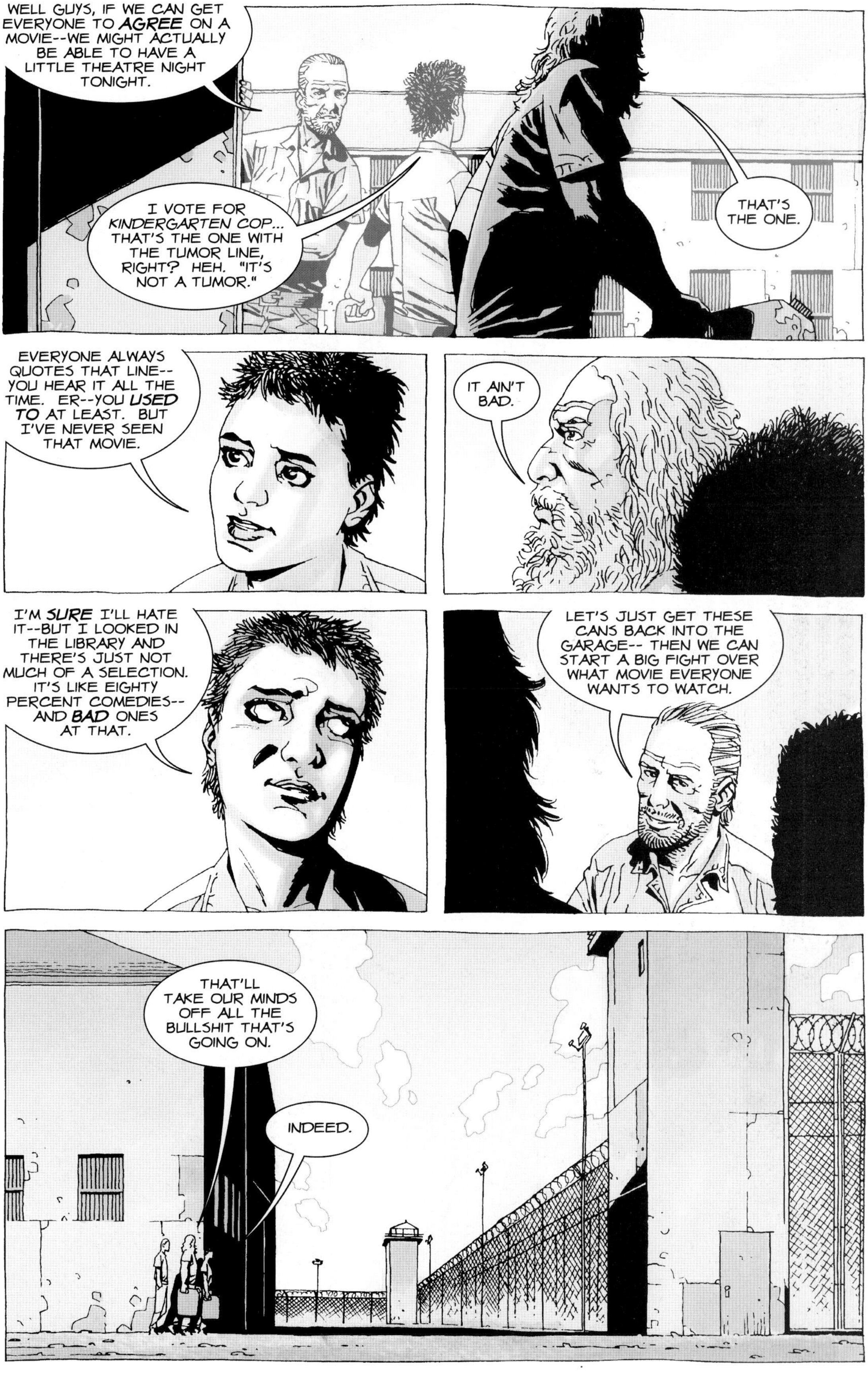
WELL GUYS, IF WE CAN GET EVERYONE TO AGREE ON A MOVIE--WE MIGHT ACTUALLY BE ABLE TO HAVE A LITTLE THEATRE NIGHT TONIGHT.
I VOTE FOR KINDERGARTEN COP... THAT'S THE ONE WITH THE TUMOR LINE, RIGHT? HEH. "IT'S NOT A TUMOR."
THAT'S THE ONE.
EVERYONE ALWAYS QUOTES THAT LINE-- YOU HEAR IT ALL THE TIME. ER--YOU USED TO AT LEAST. BUT I'VE NEVER SEEN THAT MOVIE.
IT AIN'T BAD.
I'M SURE I'LL HATE IT--BUT I LOOKED IN THE LIBRARY AND THERE'S JUST NOT MUCH OF A SELECTION. IT'S LIKE EIGHTY PERCENT COMEDIES-- AND BAD ONES AT THAT.
LET'S JUST GET THESE CANS BACK INTO THE GARAGE-- THEN WE CAN START A BIG FIGHT OVER WHAT MOVIE EVERYONE WANTS TO WATCH.
THAT'LL TAKE OUR MINDS OFF ALL THE BULLSHIT THAT'S GOING ON.
INDEED.

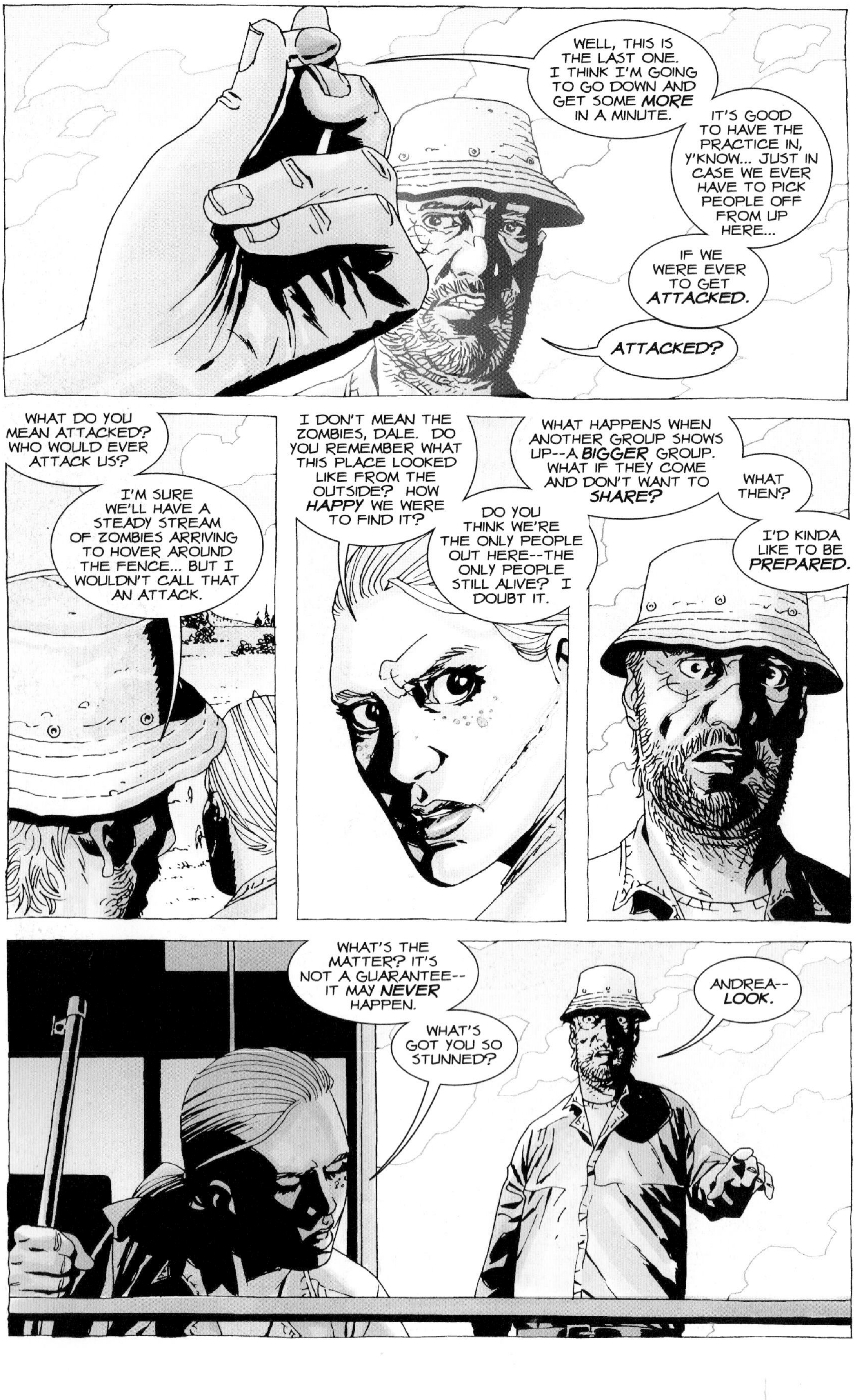
WELL, THIS IS THE LAST ONE. I THINK I'M GOING TO GO DOWN AND GET SOME *MORE* IN A MINUTE.
IT'S GOOD TO HAVE THE PRACTICE IN, Y'KNOW... JUST IN CASE WE EVER HAVE TO PICK PEOPLE OFF FROM UP HERE...
IF WE WERE EVER TO GET *ATTACKED.*
ATTACKED?
WHAT DO YOU MEAN ATTACKED? WHO WOULD EVER ATTACK US?
I'M SURE WE'LL HAVE A STEADY STREAM OF ZOMBIES ARRIVING TO HOVER AROUND THE FENCE... BUT I WOULDN'T CALL THAT AN ATTACK.
I DON'T MEAN THE ZOMBIES, DALE. DO YOU REMEMBER WHAT THIS PLACE LOOKED LIKE FROM THE OUTSIDE? HOW *HAPPY* WE WERE TO FIND IT?
DO YOU THINK WE'RE THE ONLY PEOPLE OUT HERE--THE ONLY PEOPLE STILL ALIVE? I DOUBT IT.
WHAT HAPPENS WHEN ANOTHER GROUP SHOWS UP--A *BIGGER* GROUP. WHAT IF THEY COME AND DON'T WANT TO *SHARE?*
WHAT THEN?
I'D KINDA LIKE TO BE *PREPARED.*
WHAT'S THE MATTER? IT'S NOT A GUARANTEE-- IT MAY *NEVER* HAPPEN.
WHAT'S GOT YOU SO STUNNED?
ANDREA-- *LOOK.*

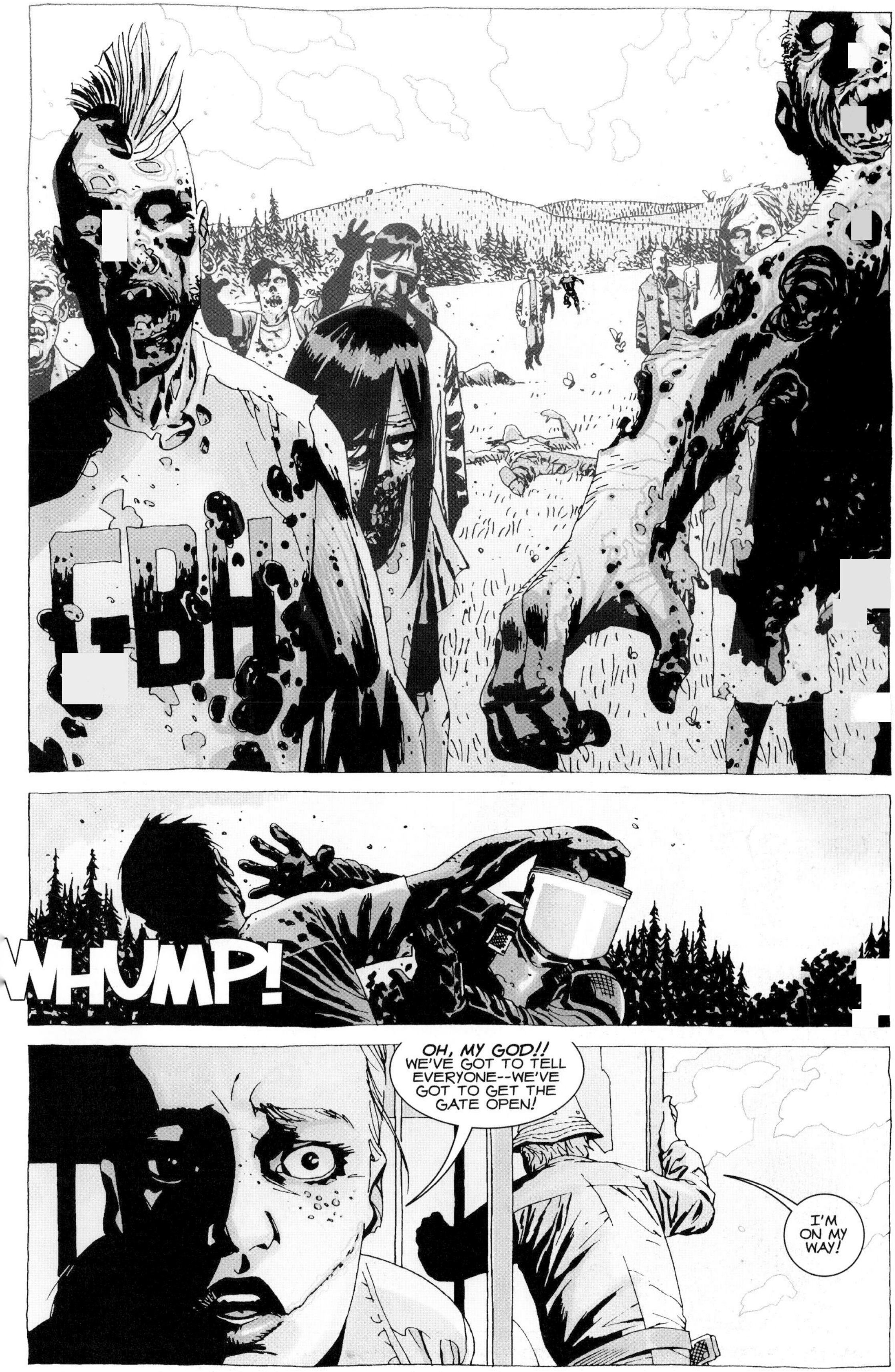
GBH
WHUMP!
OH, MY GOD!! WE'VE GOT TO TELL EVERYONE--WE'VE GOT TO GET THE GATE OPEN!
I'M ON MY WAY!

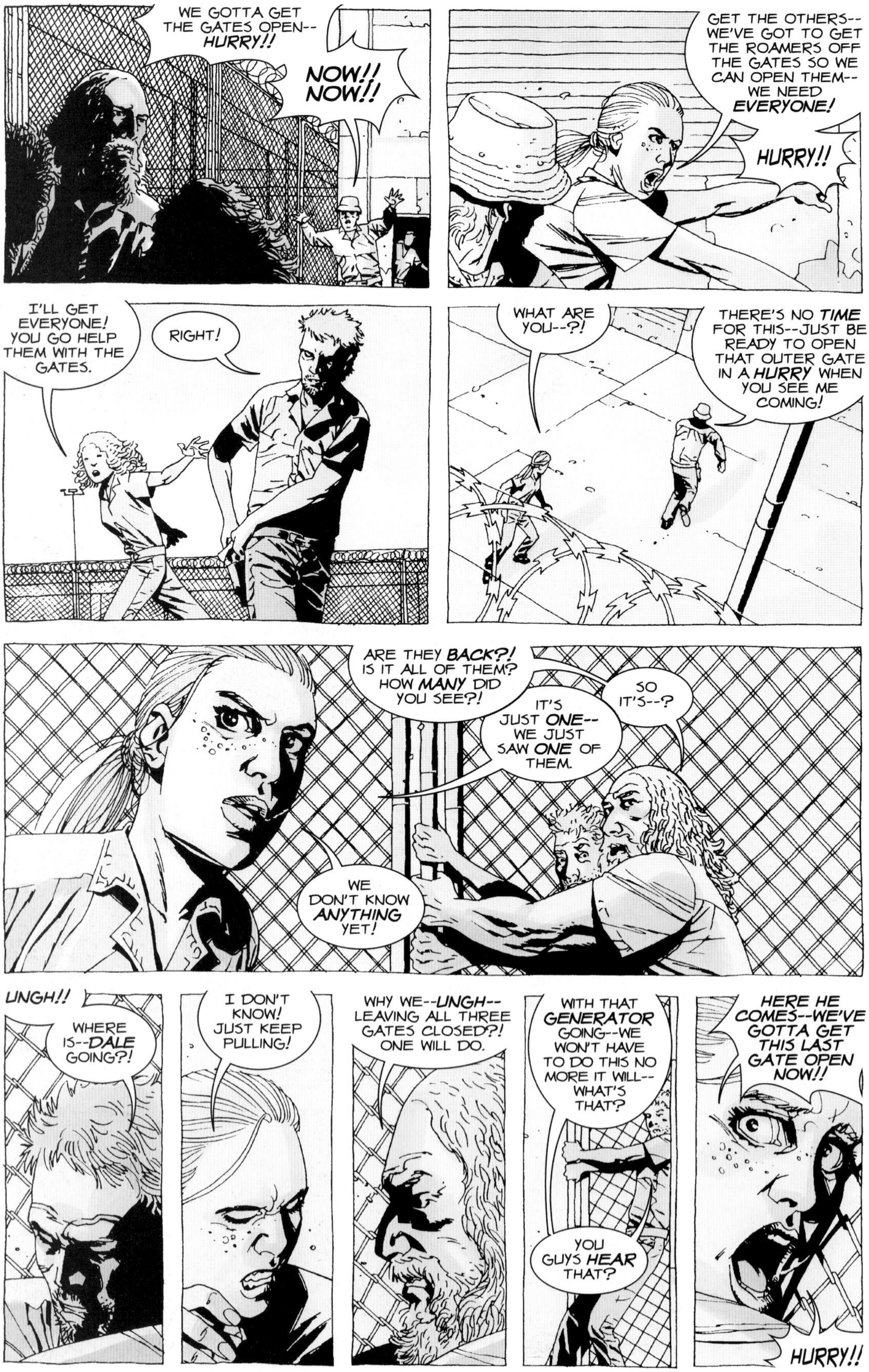
WE GOTTA GET THE GATES OPEN-- HURRY!!
NOW!! NOW!!
GET THE OTHERS-- WE'VE GOT TO GET THE ROAMERS OFF THE GATES SO WE CAN OPEN THEM-- WE NEED EVERYONE!
HURRY!!
I'LL GET EVERYONE! YOU GO HELP THEM WITH THE GATES.
RIGHT!
WHAT ARE YOU--?!
THERE'S NO TIME FOR THIS--JUST BE READY TO OPEN THAT OUTER GATE IN A HURRY WHEN YOU SEE ME COMING!
ARE THEY BACK?! IS IT ALL OF THEM? HOW MANY DID YOU SEE?!
SO IT'S--?
IT'S JUST ONE-- WE JUST SAW ONE OF THEM.
WE DON'T KNOW ANYTHING YET!
UNGH!!
WHERE IS--DALE GOING?!
I DON'T KNOW! JUST KEEP PULLING!
WHY WE--UNGH-- LEAVING ALL THREE GATES CLOSED?! ONE WILL DO.
WITH THAT GENERATOR GOING--WE WON'T HAVE TO DO THIS NO MORE IT WILL-- WHAT'S THAT?
YOU GUYS HEAR THAT?
HERE HE COMES--WE'VE GOTTA GET THIS LAST GATE OPEN NOW!!
HURRY!!

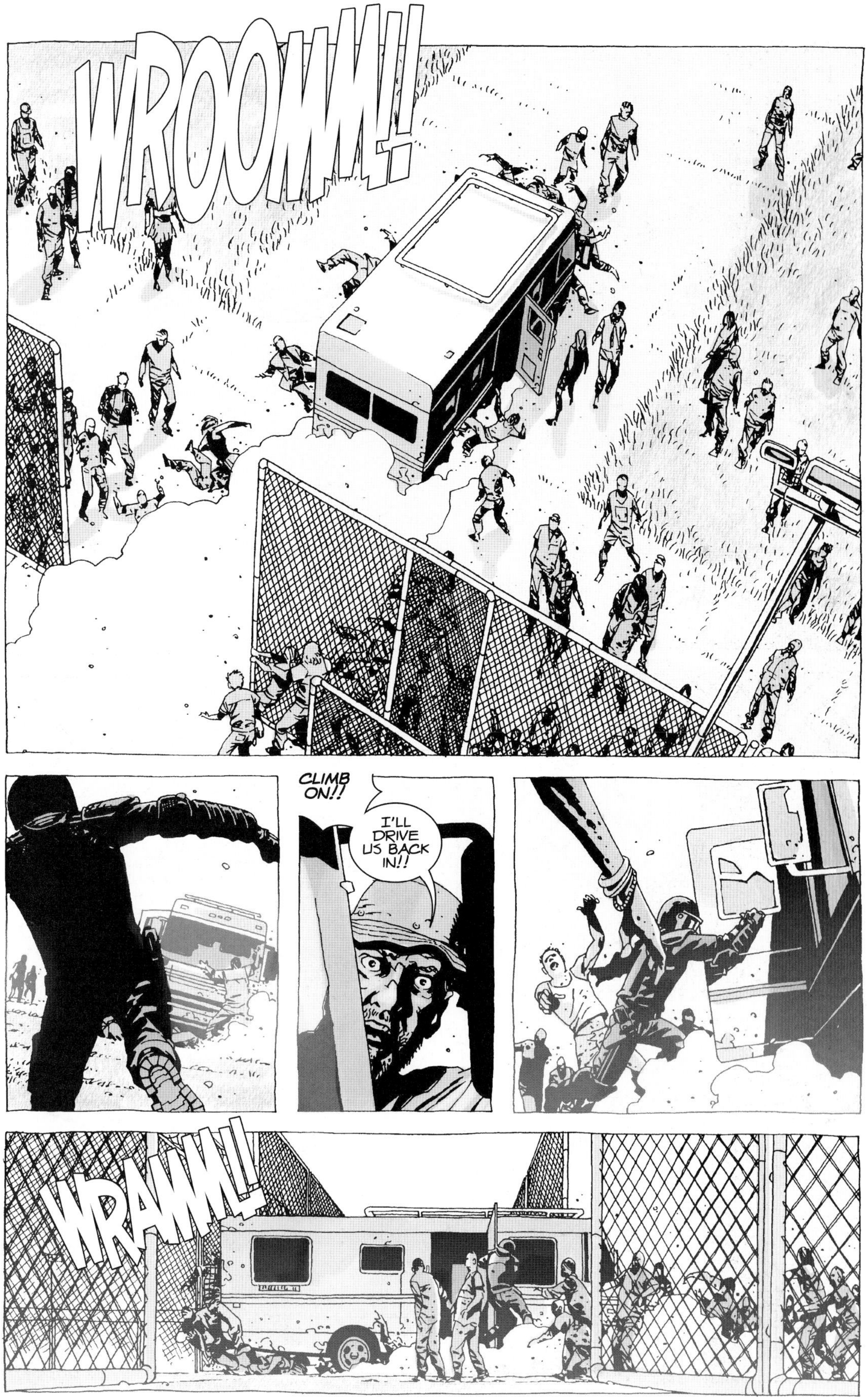
WROOMM!!
CLIMB ON!!
I'LL DRIVE US BACK IN!!
WRAMM!!

TO BE CONTINUED...

MORE GREAT BOOKS FROM ROBERT KIRKMAN & IMAGE COMICS!

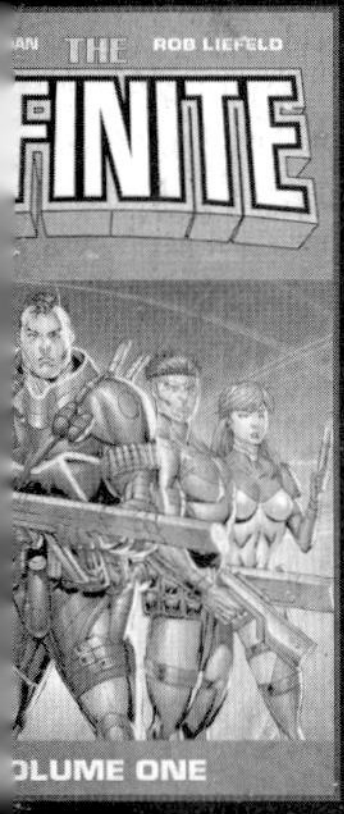
ROB LIEFELD
FINITE
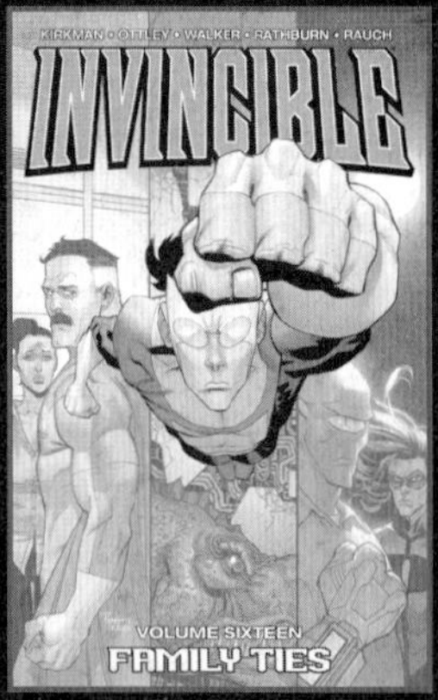
KIRKMAN • OTTLEY • WALKER • RATHBURN • RAUCH
INVINCIBLE
VOLUME SIXTEEN
FAMILY TIES
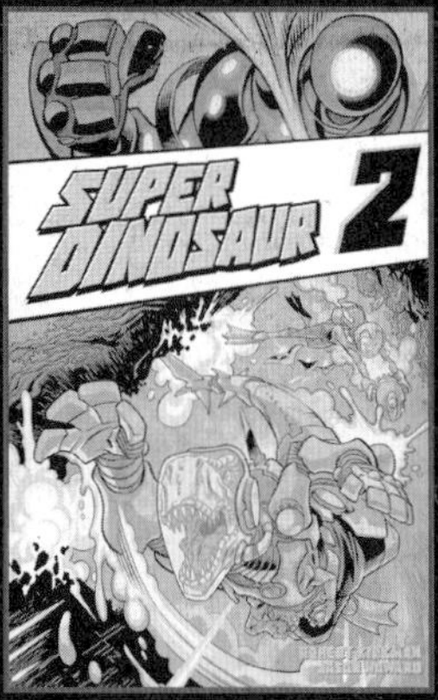
SUPER DINOSAUR 2
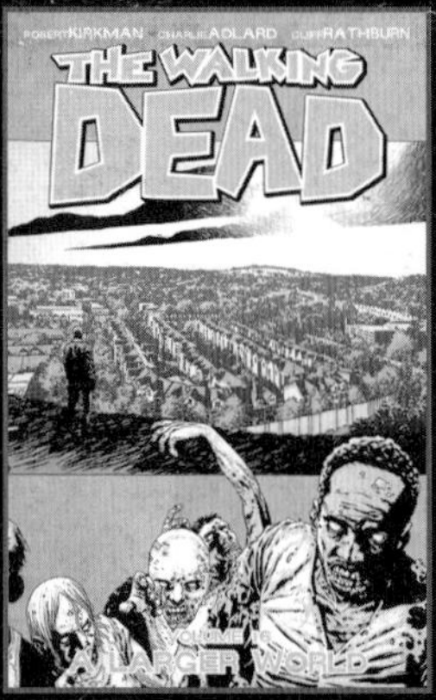
ROBERT KIRKMAN CHARLIE ADLARD CLIFF RATHBURN
THE WALKING DEAD
A LARGER WORLD
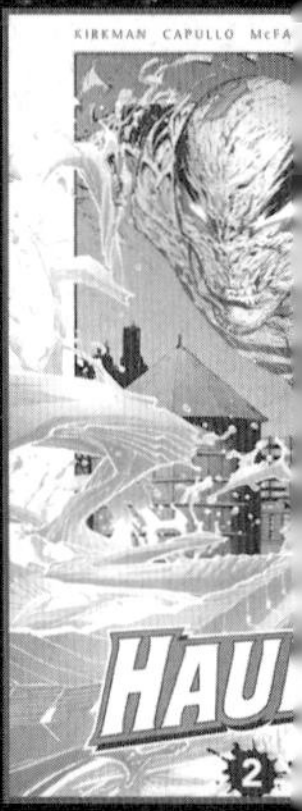
KIRKMAN CAPULLO
2

THE ASTOUNDING WOLF-MAN

VOL. 1 TP
ISBN: 978-1-58240-862-0
$14.99
VOL. 2 TP
ISBN: 978-1-60706-007-9
$14.99
VOL. 3 TP
ISBN: 978-1-60706-111-3
$16.99
VOL. 4 TP
ISBN: 978-1-60706-249-3
$16.99

BATTLE POPE

VOL. 1: GENESIS TP
ISBN: 978-1-58240-572-8
$14.99
VOL. 2: MAYHEM TP
ISBN: 978-1-58240-529-2
$12.99
VOL. 3: PILLOW TALK TP
ISBN: 978-1-58240-677-0
$12.99
VOL. 4: WRATH OF GOD TP
ISBN: 978-1-58240-751-7
$9.99

BRIT

VOL. 1: OLD SOLDIER TP
ISBN: 978-1-58240-678-7
$14.99
VOL. 2: AWOL
ISBN: 978-1-58240-864-4
$14.99
VOL. 3: FUBAR
ISBN: 978-1-60706-061-1
$16.99

CAPES

VOL. 1: PUNCHING THE CLOCK TP
ISBN: 978-1-58240-756-2
$17.99

HAUNT

VOL. 1 TP
ISBN: 978-1-60706-154-0
$9.99
VOL. 2 TP
ISBN: 978-1-60706-229-5
$16.99

THE INFINITE

VOL. 1 TP
ISBN: 978-1-60706-475-6
$9.99

INVINCIBLE

VOL. 1: FAMILY MATTERS TP
ISBN: 978-1-58240-711-1
$12.99
VOL. 2: EIGHT IS ENOUGH TP
ISBN: 978-1-58240-347-2
$12.99
VOL. 3: PERFECT STRANGERS TP
ISBN: 978-1-58240-793-7
$12.99
VOL. 4: HEAD OF THE CLASS TP
ISBN: 978-1-58240-440-2
$14.95
VOL. 5: THE FACTS OF LIFE TP
ISBN: 978-1-58240-554-4
$14.99
VOL. 6: A DIFFERENT WORLD TP
ISBN: 978-1-58240-579-7
$14.99
VOL. 7: THREE'S COMPANY TP
ISBN: 978-1-58240-656-5
$14.99
VOL. 8: MY FAVORITE MARTIAN TP
ISBN: 978-1-58240-683-1
$14.99
VOL. 9: OUT OF THIS WORLD TP
ISBN: 978-1-58240-827-9
$14.99
VOL. 10: WHO'S THE BOSS TP
ISBN: 978-1-60706-013-0
$16.99
VOL. 11: HAPPY DAYS TP
ISBN: 978-1-60706-062-8
$16.99
VOL. 12: STILL STANDING TP
ISBN: 978-1-60706-166-3
$16.99
VOL. 13: GROWING PAINS TP
ISBN: 978-1-60706-251-6
$16.99
VOL. 14: THE VILTRUMITE WAR TP
ISBN: 978-1-60706-367-4
$19.99
VOL. 15: GET SMART TP
ISBN: 978-1-60706-498-5
$16.99
VOL. 16: FAMILY TIES TP
ISBN: 978-1-60706-579-1
$16.99
ULTIMATE COLLECTION, VOL. 1 HC
ISBN 978-1-58240-500-1
$34.95
ULTIMATE COLLECTION, VOL. 2 HC
ISBN: 978-1-58240-594-0
$34.99
ULTIMATE COLLECTION, VOL. 3 HC
ISBN: 978-1-58240-763-0
$34.99
ULTIMATE COLLECTION, VOL. 4 HC
ISBN: 978-1-58240-989-4
$34.99
ULTIMATE COLLECTION, VOL. 5 HC
ISBN: 978-1-60706-116-8
$34.99
ULTIMATE COLLECTION, VOL. 6 HC
ISBN: 978-1-60706-360-5
$34.99
ULTIMATE COLLECTION, VOL. 7 HC
ISBN: 978-1-60706-509-8
$39.99
THE OFFICIAL HANDBOOK OF THE INVINCIBLE UNIVERSE TP
ISBN: 978-1-58240-831-6
$12.99
INVINCIBLE PRESENTS, VOL. 1: ATOM EVE & REX SPLODE TP
ISBN: 978-1-60706-255-4
$14.99
THE COMPLETE INVINCIBLE LIBRARY, VOL. 2 HC
ISBN: 978-1-60706-112-0
$125.00
THE COMPLETE INVINCIBLE LIBRARY, VOL. 3 HC
ISBN: 978-1-60706-421-3
$125.00
INVINCIBLE COMPENDIUM VOL. 1
ISBN: 978-1-60706-411-4
$64.99

THE WALKING DEAD

VOL. 1: DAYS GONE BYE TP
ISBN: 978-1-58240-672-5
$9.99
VOL. 2: MILES BEHIND US TP
ISBN: 978-1-58240-775-3
$14.99
VOL. 3: SAFETY BEHIND BARS TP
ISBN: 978-1-58240-805-7
$14.99
VOL. 4: THE HEART'S DESIRE TP
ISBN: 978-1-58240-530-8
$14.99
VOL. 5: THE BEST DEFENSE TP
ISBN: 978-1-58240-612-1
$14.99
VOL. 6: THIS SORROWFUL LIFE TP
ISBN: 978-1-58240-684-8
$14.99
VOL. 7: THE CALM BEFORE TP
ISBN: 978-1-58240-828-6
$14.99
VOL. 8: MADE TO SUFFER TP
ISBN: 978-1-58240-883-5
$14.99
VOL. 9: HERE WE REMAIN TP
ISBN: 978-1-60706-022-2
$14.99
VOL. 10: WHAT WE BECOME TP
ISBN: 978-1-60706-075-8
$14.99
VOL. 11: FEAR THE HUNTERS TP
ISBN: 978-1-60706-181-6
$14.99
VOL. 12: LIFE AMONG THEM TP
ISBN: 978-1-60706-254-7
$14.99
VOL. 13: TOO FAR GONE TP
ISBN: 978-1-60706-329-2
$14.99
VOL. 14: NO WAY OUT TP
ISBN: 978-1-60706-392-6
$14.99
VOL. 15: WE FIND OURSELVES TP
ISBN: 978-1-60706-392-6
$14.99
BOOK ONE HC
ISBN: 978-1-58240-619-0
$34.99
BOOK TWO HC
ISBN: 978-1-58240-698-5
$34.99
BOOK THREE HC
ISBN: 978-1-58240-825-5
$34.99
BOOK FOUR HC
ISBN: 978-1-60706-000-0
$34.99
BOOK FIVE HC
ISBN: 978-1-60706-171-7
$34.99
BOOK SIX HC
ISBN: 978-1-60706-327-8
$34.99
BOOK SEVEN HC
ISBN: 978-1-60706-439-8
$34.99
DELUXE HARDCOVER, VOL. 1
ISBN: 978-1-58240-619-0
$100.00
DELUXE HARDCOVER, VOL. 2
ISBN: 978-1-60706-029-7
$100.00
DELUXE HARDCOVER, VOL. 3
ISBN: 978-1-60706-330-8
$100.00
THE WALKING DEAD: THE COVERS, VOL. 1 HC
ISBN: 978-1-60706-002-4
$24.99
THE WALKING DEAD SURVIVORS' GUIDE
ISBN: 978-1-60706-458-9
$12.99

REAPER

GRAPHIC NOVEL
ISBN: 978-1-58240-354-2
$6.95

SUPER DINOSAUR

VOL. 1
ISBN: 978-1-60706-420-6
$9.99
VOL. 2
ISBN: 978-1-60706-568-5
$12.99
DELUXE COLORING BOOK
ISBN: 978-1-60706-481-7
$4.99

SUPERPATRIOT

AMERICA'S FIGHTING FORCE
ISBN: 978-1-58240-355-1
$14.99

TALES OF THE REALM

HARDCOVER
ISBN: 978-1-58240-426-0
$34.95
TRADE PAPERBACK
ISBN: 978-1-58240-394-6
$14.95

TECH JACKET

VOL. 1: THE BOY FROM EARTH TP
ISBN: 978-1-58240-771-5
$14.99

TO FIND YOUR NEAREST COMIC BOOK STORE, CALL: 1-888-COMIC-BOOK